HOMEGROWN MUSE

Sally Boyington

Wordsmith Pages

Homegrown Muse © 2012, 2024 Sally Bennett Boyington

All rights reserved. No part of this book may be reproduced in any form or by any electronic or mechanical means, including information storage and retrieval systems, without written permission from the author, except in the case of a reviewer, who may quote brief passages in a review.

Please purchase only authorized electronic or print editions and do not participate in or encourage the electronic piracy of copyrighted material. Your support of the author's rights is appreciated.

This is a work of fiction. Names, characters, places, and incidents either are the product of the author's imagination or are used fictitiously, and any resemblance to actual persons, living or dead, is entirely coincidental.

Originally published under the name Sally Bennett

ISBN: 978-1-951303-08-2 second paperback edition

Published by Wordsmith Pages
www.wordsmithpages.com

To my family, who set me on the right path,
and to Matt, for inspiring me to pursue my dream

Other Books by This Author

Swallowing the Sun
(#1 of Tales of the Watermasters)

Rainbow Knife
(#2 of Tales of the Watermasters)

Deep Roots in a Dry Place:
An Illustrated Poetic Natural History of Sonoran Desert Plants
(conversations with ChatGPT and image-generating AIs)

Coming Soon
Bitter Wind
(#3 of Tales of the Watermasters)

For links to purchase books and read samples go to
www.wordsmithpages.com

Readers' Praise for Homegrown Muse

"A wonderful, well-written book that had me captivated from the start."
Bonnie Lamer, author of the Witch Fairy Series

"An entertaining read."
Amazon reviewer Cheryl M-M

"A lovely read."
Barbara Silkstone, author of the Mister Darcy Series of Comedic Mysteries

HOMEGROWN MUSE

One

LYSISTRATA SMITH SHUT OFF THE ENGINE and reached for the door handle out of habit. She paused, hand in midair. Then she leaned the other direction and tilted the rearview mirror for a quick look at herself.

Her lips burned and felt swollen from the chiltepine mole sauce she'd made to spice up some leftover chicken. She wanted to be sure the lingering effects of her pre-event snacking didn't show on her face. The last thing she wanted was for the tony people at this reception to think somebody had smacked her in the mouth.

She already had enough strikes against her.

She wasn't rich, powerful, or beautiful. She figured she would be about as welcome as a weed in a flowerbed.

But when she'd received the unexpected invitation to the opening for the Highline Resort a few days earlier, the timing was too perfect to pass up. This might be her only chance to speak with Tank Turnbull informally, for as a land developer, he traveled in rather different social circles from her.

She wanted to make him see reason on his latest venture. Too bad she had no idea what to say.

Lyssa focused on the mirror. Her hazel eyes skimmed past their own reflection and came to rest on her mouth. Her lip color was a deeper rose hue than normal, but she supposed the other guests would believe she was simply wearing lipstick.

She opened the door and slid off the bench seat. Her low heels dimpled the fresh blacktop as she stepped down. She placed a hand on the grainy, faded paint of the pickup's top to catch her balance. Then, tempted to climb back into the truck and drive away, she drew in a deep, steadying breath.

This, finally, was her opportunity to make a difference, she reminded herself. If that meant rubbing elbows with people she never wanted to spend time with, at a black-tie reception for the opening of a project she'd had only a peripheral involvement with, so be it. She was not going to leave before having a chat with Turnbull.

Lyssa dropped her hand to her side and turned to take her first look at the Highline. What fronted the parking lot was an expanse of earth-toned stuccoed wall broken periodically by wrought-iron bars set within narrow, arched openings. At the far end, the upper stories of a massive, blocky building rose out of a screen of feathery-leaved young mesquite and paloverde trees.

Plastered walls swept up until they curved into a parapet and vanished. The lavenders and golds and pinks of a fading Phoenix sunset suffused the sky above the rounded crest; below, logs serving as decorative roof-beams jutted out of the plaster every few yards along the face, alternating with terracotta drainage tiles. Deep window slits under the log-ends slanted at an angle that would catch the morning sun of winter. Her architect father would approve, she thought.

She made sure her keys and the invitation were in the small envelope-purse clipped to a black ribbon that went around her waist. Then she had no more excuse for delay. Starting toward the broad, sweeping entrance, she discovered that her snug black dress forced her to shorten her usual stride, and having her heels sink into the ground with each step was disconcerting. As she drew near the few small groups of well-dressed strangers who lingered to chat among themselves or perhaps to wait for others of their party, she felt conspicuous.

The doors to what she assumed was the Grand Ballroom stood open, allowing light and music and laughter to spill out into the lingering late-summer heat. Inside, brilliantly hued gowns and glittering jewelry vied for supremacy with stark combinations of black and white.

A hundred Tank Turnbulls might be waiting, a hundred opportunities to exert a healthy, sane, and sensible influence on Phoenix development—and still it wasn't enough to make her step through those doors. She turned away and walked slowly along the landscaped path that intersected the broad approach from the left, inside the perimeter wall. This was where she felt comfortable. Outside and alone.

Flower-studded cliffroses and desert marigolds lined flagstone walkways that wound in and out of terraformed hillocks. She stepped out of the urban world of concrete, pavement, and expensive cars shimmering in the lingering heat, and into a cool oasis.

Several feet away, where they could be seen but not felt by the unwary pedestrian, were sharp-tipped agaves and ocotillos. The crooked branches of creosote bushes filled in the middle band of foliage wherever the slender trunks of trees had left a gap. Tall, armless saguaros marked the walkways branching off to the low-slung individual casitas that would soon house guests in what she was sure would be decadent comfort.

She expected nothing less from Dane Callicott, president and CEO of Callicott Properties, and the creative genius behind this, Phoenix's newest resort. The man who had asked her to come. Even his company wasn't tempting enough to make her want to go in just yet.

Lyssa strolled along the path, ever deeper into the grounds. The renewing scent of plants and earth, leavened by a slight tang of moisture in the air, became more distinct as she left the entrance behind. Although the native plants required little water, the overall effect was that of a lush, almost tropical exuberance. Brilliant landscaping, she thought in admiration.

An eddying breeze chilled her shoulders, shifting the cayenne-red curls that spilled from the black headband dug out of the back of her closet in honor of tonight's event. Lyssa wrapped her hands around her upper arms and continued onward.

She stepped on several dozen flagstones before she figured out what made them unusual. Despite the visual effect of spalling and layering that gave them the appearance of natural stone, the surface was flat and even. Either they were genuine and leveled with some sort of invisible coating, or they were artificial but made by a process she had never heard of.

Lyssa threw a quick look over her shoulder to reassure herself that she was alone and unobserved. Then she slipped off her shoes to feel the material underfoot. She'd never encountered anything quite like this, though the texture reminded her of vinyl flooring. Aware of how foolish she must look, she enjoyed the sensation of freedom only briefly before bending over to put on one shoe, then the other. The ankle bearing her weight wobbled as she uncoiled her second leg.

A strong hand closed around her elbow to steady her.

Lyssa gasped in surprise and pulled away.

"Careful," she heard from a masculine voice near her ear.

She turned her head to meet the amused eyes of Dane Callicott. Of course he would be the one to catch her gawking, barefoot, like a hillbilly farmgirl.

He let go and chivalrously extended an arm. "I wondered if you would come."

The sleeve of his pale jacket glimmered in the lowering evening light. Then she realized he meant for her to grab onto him. She barely resisted a derisive snort at the courtly gesture, so patriarchal that both of her mothers would have been mortally offended. She shifted to face him. "The Highline is beautiful, Dane. Just perfect."

His blue eyes flickered. Dane stared over her head at his creation. He passed a hand through blond hair that Lyssa had always thought made him look more like a California surfer-dude than a third-generation land baron. His gesture left the carefully styled hair rumpled. "You don't need to sound so surprised." He sounded displeased. "What did you expect?"

Lyssa crossed her arms and tapped the fingers of her right hand on her forearm. "I'm not surprised. I expected pretty much what I see here. After all, you told me right from the start what you were planning to do with the place."

Dane jammed his hands into the pockets of his cream-colored tuxedo pants. "Yes, well. Beauty doesn't really cut it in this business. The true test will be whether the rooms and conference center fill up with paying guests. Hard to imagine a worse time to bring this project online."

Lyssa told herself that whatever beast was on his back tonight, it was none of her business. Still, she didn't like to hear him talk about the Highline so crassly. "That's a bit of a change from when you first described your plans," she reminded him.

The memory was as clear to her as if the six years since that day of their first meeting had never elapsed. "You said you didn't want to build the average, everyday luxury palace, a place that could be set down in Vegas or Chicago as easily as here. You were going to combine the ancient and the modern, with a balance of private space and public, just as the Hohokam did a thousand years ago on this very spot. You were going to contrast indigenous architecture with the latest in 'green' technology to appeal to the niche market." She found herself tapping her foot on the smooth flagstone and stopped the nervous motion.

"That's how to measure your success, Dane. Against your intention, not balance sheets that don't exist yet. This place is exactly as you led me to expect."

One of his long-fingered hands came to rest below the top button of his jacket, rubbing back and forth as though his stomach was tied in knots. "Tell that to my investors."

"If money is so all-fired important, then what about the savings on operating costs from the situational architecture, solar-powered lights, low-maintenance and water-saving landscaping—" She punctuated her list with little stabs of her forefinger toward each of the elements in turn.

"Pocket change."

"Pocket change!" Lyssa reined in her surge of exasperation. Probably to Dane Callicott, a third-generation land baron, savings of a few thousand a month would seem like nothing more than that, she reflected. What she wouldn't do for it! "Surely every little bit counts."

Dane tossed her an unreadable look and dropped his hand from his midsection, gesturing toward the ballroom. She became aware of a whiskey-smooth trumpet phrase and a burst of loud conversation emanating from within.

"Well, thanks for the expert advice," he said. "Shall we go in, so you can see the rest of it? That way you can fawn over the inside, too."

"I'm enjoying the breeze, if not the company. Don't let me keep you from your guests." She turned on her heel, feeling her slightly sweat-dampened foot slide within the shoe. But she kept her ankle from twisting and began to put some ground between them.

To her surprise and irritation, he joined her. "The breeze is pleasant," he said.

She flashed him a look, but his high-wattage smile told her nothing of what he was thinking as they strolled in step.

After a few moments he asked, "What are you doing here, Lyssa?"

"Here?" She stopped on one of the flagstones and frowned up at him. He had sent her the invitation—or so she'd thought. It had come from his office.

He swung around to block her way.

"What, exactly, are you asking?" Lyssa was struck with a sudden and preposterous fear that he knew she was planning to confront Tank Turnbull. "I assumed I was here because I was invited."

"I meant 'here,' as in working for Clearview. Pandering to—what did you call us back then? Land sharks. Wasn't that the term you used?"

She felt heat rise in her cheeks and thanked the natural tawniness of her skin for hiding her tendency to blush. She had indeed mentioned something like that to him, in an elevator on the way up to the Callicott offices that very first day, before she knew who he was. He had the look of an outdoorsman, not a paper pusher.

"As for why you're here at this particular place and time," he continued before she could summon a response, "I could hardly forget what you did to get the Highline off the ground."

"So to speak," she finally managed to say.

He inclined his head. "No pun intended. You saved Callicott millions of dollars in environmental cleanup costs. If you hadn't suggested siting the resort farther south, the whole project would have had to be cancelled."

Lyssa bit her tongue. Not hard, just enough to keep from blurting out the first word that came to mind, which had to do with livestock and manure, on which she truly was an expert. "Why do you do that?" she asked.

"Do what?"

"Reduce everything to money."

"Not everything," he said grimly. "Just those things that have to produce."

"I would think," she began, "that you could take pleasure in having created something worthy of existing in its own right."

"Art for art's sake, you mean? No, I don't have that luxury."

"For crying out loud, Dane." She placed her hands on her hips. "With the kind of money you've got backing you, you can have any luxury you want." Lyssa couldn't help but think what she could do with one one-hundredth part of his fortune: save her parents' farm, to start with. Then use the rest to shake up the status quo. She cast him a sidelong look and caught him rubbing absently at his sternum. Either that was a habit she'd never before noticed or the man had a case of heartburn tonight. Probably caused by his foul mood, which was certainly doing nothing for her.

"You'd think so, wouldn't you?"

"And what do you think?" she challenged.

"I think—" He broke off. When he spoke again, it was in a very different voice, light and amused. "I think you're a constant surprise. When I first met you and heard you going on about stewardship of the earth, I had you pegged as a wild-eyed environmentalist. The last thing I expected to find was an advocate of compromise."

She caught her lower lip between her teeth. "I might have been a bit over the top in my younger days. Who isn't?" She struggled to match him for lightness as she declared, "I prefer to think of myself as a conservationist."

Then he turned solemn again. "What are you doing in this business, Lyssa? What have you done to your principles?"

"My principles are still solid."

"But you saved me—that is, Callicott Properties—from assuming the liability for those leaking underground gas tanks, even though it meant leaving the tanks where they were until some other sucker came along to buy that property. Why did you do that?"

She started along the serpentine path again. She didn't glance at him. Couldn't. "It wouldn't be fair to make you pay for cleaning up someone else's mess."

"That's how the process works. The ones responsible are long gone, so pick someone with deep pockets to solve the problem. It's expected."

"So sue me if I don't contribute to that part of it." Her face heated.

"You should have come to work for me. Then you'd have a more realistic view of how things are done."

"We've been through this before. You don't need full-time research staff at Callicott. I'd be twiddling my thumbs all day."

"You need to feel useful, is that it?"

The mockery in his voice slapped at her. "Useful isn't the point," she snapped back. "It's a matter of knowing that when I leave this earthly existence, I've had some positive effect. Like wilderness hiking: take only pictures, leave only footprints. I want my lingering footprints to be—I don't know. Sasquatch-like. Bigger than life." Nerves straining, she continued, "I want to leave behind something like the Highline. That's why it bothers me that you don't recognize how unique it is, how special, how important."

He stopped, facing away. "How different, you mean!"

Maybe that was what she meant. Lyssa swiped a hand over her chin. She knew all about being different. And she'd suffered plenty of bruised spirits from other people's perception that different was bad.

"Different is risky," he went on. "Callicott Properties can't afford to do risky. There isn't a person in there"—he swept his arm toward the ballroom, which was, thanks to the winding path, once more in front of them—"who thinks the Highline has a chance of surviving its first season."

"More likely they're afraid it will." Lyssa knew what she was saying wouldn't get through, but still she had to make the effort. She couldn't let Dane go on believing that the Highline Resort was a failure. "Change is frightening. When other developers see there's a market for this kind of—"

He snorted. "The kind of people in there *are* the market, and they wouldn't stay at the Highline if you paid them."

"Oh, come on." She didn't have much patience for his whining: Dane Callicott, the golden boy of Phoenix development, resigning his dream to a bunch of narrow-minded bean counters? "Maybe the old guard is resistant to the idea, but you know, or you should, that they're simply terrified!"

"Of what?" He turned and stared at her, mouth compressed into a narrow, disbelieving line.

"That you're right. That they're wrong. That their comfortable, predictable world is destined to change. All they can see is this lifetime, this one tiny slice of the universe. If they can, they'll scare you off of the future. Instead you can demand the right to claim it. Embrace it. Make it your own."

"You know," he muttered, "sometimes it's like you're speaking in tongues."

Lyssa made one last try. "Open your heart to the future, seek the truth down deep in your soul, and the understanding will come. You're a visionary, Dane Callicott. Don't let anyone take that away from you."

"Right. You're overlooking one thing. People who have visions tend to be burned at the stake."

"I'll grant you, men like Tank Turnbull aren't going to accept a revolution easily. But even the worst of the die-hards will eventually have to admit that it's time to look at what you've done with the Highline. They can't keep building in unspoiled areas forever without paying a steep price. They'll come around. They'll be forced to."

Lights shining from above and from below warred with each other to make his face appear haggard and strained. The music of trumpet and drums woven into a jazz rhythm cut faintly through the stillness.

"Eventually, maybe." Dane punched his hands into his pockets. "I can't afford to wait. Your perspective is fine in the abstract, but I have fifty-some employees depending on me, a board of directors to answer to, and my mother, who has her own ideas of what a Callicott Properties project is supposed to look like. The Highline isn't going to satisfy any of them."

"Moneywise, you mean." Her voice took on an edge.

He stared at her. "If I recall, you got paid for your work on the

Highline, and you didn't have to risk any of your own wealth for it. Those of us who have other people counting on us can't afford to abide by holier-than-thou principles."

His words cut all the more deeply because they were so ironically untrue. "You don't know anything about me, Dane Callicott. I think we'd better leave it at that."

Lyssa pushed past him and walked into the Grand Ballroom, chin up and stride deliberate. She bore her shaking hands stiffly at her sides.

How could he believe her so shallow as to be motivated by greed? She almost wished her father hadn't already put out the word among his architect friends that the Highline would be a bellwether project for sustainable development. She would like to hurt Dane Callicott where it counted—in his inflated bank account!

VIVIAN CALLICOTT WATCHED HER SON stride into the ballroom and pause, searching the crowd with his eyes. She frowned. Her gaze then settled on the redhead in a black dress who had stalked through the doors ahead of him. Dane and Lyssa Smith both looked thunderous. Fortunately he turned away with a scowl and did not follow the girl once he made sure she was there.

Vivian smoothed out her frown to prevent it from settling into wrinkles. She found herself stroking her pearl necklace and moved her hand back to her side.

Miss Smith wore no jewelry that Vivian could see. The square bodice of the outdated dress emphasized the width of the young woman's shoulders. She was too everything, Vivian concluded. Too much golden skin, marking too much time in the sun. Too much hair, of too bright a color and falling in outrageous curls too extreme to be anything but natural. Too little dress, showing too much bare leg.

Vivian recalled the guest list very clearly. Miss Smith's name had not appeared on it. Extricating herself politely from the small group within which she stood, she went in search of Dane's assistant.

Upon discovering the petite platinum blonde presiding over the buffet tables, Vivian reflected that the contrast between the two young women could not be greater. There was nothing excessive about Claudia Montgomery. Except, perhaps, her ambition. Claudia's desire to become Mrs. Dane Callicott had not escaped Vivian's notice.

With a practiced smile, she said, "Lovely reception, Miss Montgomery. You are to be congratulated."

"Thank you." After one sidelong glance at Vivian, the near-colorless eyes under carefully drawn brows shifted back toward Dane. "It came together well enough. I'm sorry you had to be bothered with the invitation list, but Dane insisted."

Vivian stared at Claudia until the younger woman's gaze met hers. "Fortunately it could never be a bother for me to refresh my contacts with old friends and business partners." She let the assertion stand for a few heartbeats as she inclined her head and smiled in acknowledgment when a passing couple greeted her. "Tell me, Miss Montgomery, do you have any idea what Lyssa Smith is doing here?"

"No. Dane—" Claudia caught herself, evidently remembering the formality that Vivian insisted on retaining within the Callicott hierarchy. She glanced away. "That is, Mr. Callicott had me add her to the invitation list."

"Then she does have an invitation." Vivian felt a twinge of disappointment mixed, to her surprise, with hurt. Dane had always allowed her to be the final arbiter of who attended these official events. It was her way of maintaining an involvement in the business without, she hoped, making him feel as though she was interfering with his decisions. She set aside the emotion and pursued the important point. "Why would that be?"

With a lift of her chin Claudia explained, "Apparently he wanted Miss Smith to attend the opening because *she* gave him the inspiration for the resort."

"Indeed?" Vivian's brows raised in mild inquiry. Behind them her mind raced. So Lyssa Smith, a junior employee of a business only marginally associated with Callicott Properties, had been the one to encourage Dane to throw away Callicott money on this venture.

As if the exterior was not unusual enough, the interior was even more disconcerting, filled with contrasting colors and peculiar patterns, from the geometrical shapes in the carpet to the primitive designs of the fired clay and custom-finished metal fixtures scattered throughout the rooms. Designs taken from artifacts and rock art, she recalled him explaining to someone tonight.

Given Dane's history, his mother had assumed that he'd conceived of the resort on his own, as one last creative fling. When she attributed any part of the blame to someone else, it fell on his executive vice-president, Alex Garcia, who held what she considered a dangerous amount of influence over her son. Still, Alex was an employee, loyal to the company and with some outstanding abilities, when given the opportunity to exhibit them. For an outsider to have affected one of Dane's projects was not to be borne. She set her jaw.

"What are you going to do about Lyssa Smith?"

The interruption annoyed Vivian, but she would not show it. "There is nothing to do. She happens to be one of our guests this evening, no more and no less."

The stormy eyes narrowed. "If you wish," Claudia offered with a casual air, as though the answer made no difference to her, "I could keep an eye on her."

Vivian reflected, not for the first time, that she loathed Claudia Montgomery. "A charming offer, but unnecessary. I have my ways of learning all that I need to know." She inclined her head by way of saying she was done with this conversation, then walked away.

A glance toward where she had last seen Lyssa Smith told Vivian that she should not have wasted time with Claudia. Red faced and choleric, Thomas Turnbull stood with his back toward one of the decorative piers, confronted by the very woman who was at the forefront of Vivian's concerns.

Her hand rose to her breast to cover the quickened thudding of her heart. She had not felt so indignant since . . . Indeed, she could not remember ever having felt such an explosion of outrage in all her life. Telling herself to be calm, that a soothing mien would alleviate the situation better than emotions, Vivian started toward that side of the room, determined not to allow the reception to be ruined with an unseemly display. Unfortunately, people had already started to stare, and to nudge each other and whisper.

Thomas's voice could be heard from fifty feet away. "You've seen these cactuses, have you? And I suppose you're a trained botanist, able to tell one little cactus species from another?"

"Actually—"

"You've got proof that they're where you say they are?"

"What sort of proof would it take to convince you it's at least worth doing a survey? The soil maps are right for their growth. You have my word that they exist. Don't you think you should at least have it checked out? Or do you prefer to be told what you want to hear on an EA—"

"That's the most ridiculous goddamned thing I've ever heard!" Thomas bellowed.

Vivian winced, wishing she had worn something other than wide slacks and a long, slitted tunic, which wrapped around her legs and slowed her pace through the avid-eyed crowd.

"I never bought a favorable environmental report in my life!"

Thomas spat out the denial as Vivian drew to a halt beside the squared-off pair. "And you can't prove any of this. Vivian! What's going on, when a man can't even come to a party without getting harassed by some jumped-up little—" He cleared his throat and stared fixedly into space, as if all of a sudden he had become aware that "little" was not a word that could apply to a female whose chest was on a level with his eyes.

"Surely Miss Smith did not mean to offend, Thomas." She flashed the girl a glare meant to intimidate.

"I really didn't say—"

Thomas interrupted. "She came up yammering to me about what's none of her damn business."

"Endangered species are my business as much as his. It should be a matter of concern for all of us. Not that I accused him—"

"And she asked when I was going to be turning my eyes toward green architecture, like this monstrosity. As though the Highline would ever have been approved by the board in your husband's day!"

"Well." Vivian took Thomas's gnarled hand and patted it, hoping to lower his blood pressure before he exploded. With a stab of regret she remembered having talked around the dissenting board members, including this old friend, to gain their approval for Dane's pet project. At the time, she could see only the necessity for transferring Stewart Callicott's authority to his son. "I'm sure she doesn't know the whole story. You do some fine projects, Thomas. Time-tested success is something to be proud of."

Some of the color faded from his face and neck.

Redheaded temper apparently in full force, the girl set her hands on her hips and cast Vivian a withering look. "He and his kind can't keep buying up land in the foothills and encouraging sprawl. If the price of gas and commuting time don't kill prospective residents' interest, the lack of water will. Not to mention risking endangered species—"

Vivian stood her ground. "My dear, you apparently forget that I am one of his kind. So is everyone here tonight." *Except you.*

But the girl ignored the unspoken implication. "I would think you, of all people, could appreciate the way the Highline turned out. This is your son's shining moment. Or should be. No matter what some hidebound board of directors thinks."

"Why, Miss Smith!" Vivian dropped Thomas's hand and grasped the mouthy woman's bare arm with a fierceness that startled even herself. "We should get to know one another better. You have such a unique outlook on other people's business." With the troublemaker in hand, she marched off, heading for an alcove near the service area and trusting that no one would have the nerve to follow, much less attempt to overhear. Everyone but this uncouth creature understood the unspoken rules quite well.

Miss Smith snatched her arm away before they reached the alcove. Nevertheless she followed along obediently enough, although the first words out of her mouth showed that she had not been cowed. "I can't believe Dane's own mother would take sides against him."

"He is *Mr.* Callicott to you," Vivian corrected.

"Oh, please. What century are you living in?" Temper-darkened eyes narrowed on her. "Wait, you called me by name earlier, when you frogstepped me over here. I don't recall having met you before. How did you know who I am?"

"I make it a point to know everyone Callicott does business with. Might I ask what excuse you have for accusing Mr. Turnbull of unethical conduct?"

Miss Smith crossed her arms. "A warning, not an accusation. Although if he isn't careful, he will step over that line. When he does, do you really want to be so closely associated with him?"

"One professional woman to another, I would let you in on a few home truths. First, Callicott Properties will never do another project like the Highline Resort."

"Why not?"

"Why not? Haven't you heard what people are saying?"

"Of course I have. The Highline is different. That's not a failing on its part, but a strength." The girl stood even taller, if such a thing was possible. Muscles rippled in her shoulders as she unfolded her arms and gestured around the ballroom. "This place is special, and once word gets out in the larger community, people will be eager for the chance to come and see it. I would think you could at least pretend to stand by Dane in this."

"How dare you!"

Vivian felt the blood wash into her face. She remembered how painful it had been to relinquish her role at Callicott so Dane could become established, the way she'd helped him build up the company he had inherited, her encouragement to throw all of his energy into becoming the pragmatist she always knew he could be instead of the artist he fancied himself as.

"That wasn't fair of me, was it?" Miss Smith's expression eased, and her stance relaxed. "I'm sorry. It's just that it seems like everyone here is deliberately blind to the potential—"

"I am not interested in your opinion." Vivian choked off the overwhelming desire to slap those taut young cheeks. As guests nearby turned to see what had caused her to raise her voice, she hissed, "I am telling you to stay away from my son!"

The obtuse girl had the nerve to look confused.

"This is my company, and I won't have it ruined at the whim of someone who is too ignorant and naive to know a disaster when she sees one! You may think it wise to take credit for this awful place now, but you'll learn soon enough that you have made a serious mistake."

The younger woman narrowed her eyes. "I would like to take credit for the Highline, really I would, because I know it's going to have a long-lasting and revolutionary impact." She jabbed a finger at Vivian's heaving chest. "But this is Dane's baby, from footings to roof joists. You'd best admit that, unless you want to drive him away. What's more, you're underestimating his influence. The development world is conservative, yes, but it can't continue as it has been. Especially in these tough economic times. You're dealing with finite resources. Dane understands that." The girl's focus seemed to turn inward. "He's got a wise soul. Deep, old, grounded. It just needs the corners knocked off."

Vivian growled. She was horrified to hear the sound come out of her throat. "Young lady, you have no idea who you are dealing with!"

She spun on her heel and stalked off.

In a blind, throbbing rage she made her way to the nearest ladies' room. A brief inspection showed it to be mercifully empty. Vivian thanked heaven that Dane had not made the resort so exclusive that the restrooms had attendants.

The faucets were automatic, though, and when she tried to run water over her wrists to cool her blood, she was unable to position her forearms deeply enough. The water insisted on splashing over her hands and on her tunic. To add insult to injury, it was preheated.

Furious at herself, at Lyssa Smith, at Dane, at Thomas, at the entire roomful of guests, she pulled down one paper towel, and another, and another, until she wound up with too many to hold in both hands. Practically sobbing with the force of her frustration, she divided them into four groups and folded each stack into a small neat pad. Then she plunged them into the sink and allowed the lukewarm water to run off her hands—flashing over her diamond wedding band and dotting her muted rose-gold bracelets with beaded-up droplets—and onto the towels.

The exercise helped. She laid the soaked pads on the polished marble vanity top to let them cool.

Vivian Callicott studied herself in the mirror, from the top of her golden-tinted pageboy haircut to her stubborn chin, taking in the shapely face kept youthful by sound genes, regular visits to her dermatologist, the occasional discreet tuck, and a measure of imperturbability that she wore like her shaping undergarments.

She could almost accept changing outwardly as time caught up with her. She could not deal with losing her edge, as evidenced by the fact that a confrontation with a woman half her age had sent her fleeing for cover.

With the chilled towels she bathed the insides of her wrists, where her pulse still beat with an intensity and rapidity that frightened her. She told herself that nothing in tonight's events constituted a disaster.

Dane had to have realized his mistake now, after hearing from his investors, both those who had sunk capital into the Highline and those who might be tapped for future projects. He had to understand, just as she did, that the reputation of Callicott Properties was at stake.

And he would never repeat his mistake—of that, she was almost positive. Unless someone managed to convince him otherwise. Someone capable of making both Dane and Vivian lose their composure. Someone capable of standing up to someone of Thomas Turnbull's stature and criticizing him for his long success. Someone capable of making a rational argument and then sweeping off onto some convoluted, nonsensical, insane philosophical diatribe.

Vivian balled up the wet towels and tossed them in the round, brass-encircled opening in the vanity top. Then she placed her hands on the marble and leaned toward the mirror.

When she spoke, she directed her words not to the woman in the mirror but to the man who had left her a widow when the Highline was not yet even a stray thought in his son's mind. "I swear, Stewart, I will do whatever is required to keep the company strong. I may have given our son too much latitude in the past, but no more. I will make sure the next generation receives your legacy, no matter what."

She received no answer—but then, she had expected none. She was not a woman given to idle fancy, and she knew her husband had been silenced forever. It was just that speaking to him made her feel not quite so alone.

Two

AS MRS. CALLICOTT STALKED OFF, the remnants of Lyssa's anger subsided. She wasn't exactly being Little Miss Mary Sunshine tonight, she reflected.

Shaking off the regret, she followed her hostess. People eyed her with catlike glints of superiority. To avoid the disparaging gazes, she made a show of taking in her surroundings. She was soon captivated by the way in which the muted southwestern tones of turquoise and terracotta accent pieces blended with the bronze and copper fixtures and the brighter hues of the carpeting and walls, all complementing one another in color and form with an understated elegance that could come only from custom design and hand-wrought artisanry—which translated into great expense in both time and money.

Lyssa considered that the latter was probably all that Vivian Callicott could see when she looked around the Highline. But why Mrs. Callicott should have chosen to take out her frustration on Lyssa remained a mystery: it wasn't as though Lyssa could be any threat to either Dane or the company.

Then again, looking back on the past few minutes, Lyssa knew she sounded ridiculous. *Dane needs a few of his corners knocked off?* How could she have said such a stupid thing?

She felt like a fool. Not so much for losing her temper and those completely unnecessary arguments, but for lapsing into the philoso-babble she'd spent years trying to root out of her lexicon. She had let Dane push all her buttons and had been woefully off-balance for her encounter with Tank Turnbull, not to mention being so rude to Dane's mother.

But none of that was the worst experience of the night. That honor belonged to the lingering doubt that Dane had planted in her mind: *had* she compromised her principles over the years?

A sudden craving for fresh air struck her. Lyssa needed to clear her lungs of the cloying perfume and new-construction smells that hung in the air. The heavy, ornately carved Mexican-style doors, wide open to nightfall and freedom, stood only a few yards away.

The fine hairs on the back of her neck stirred as she walked toward them. She suppressed a shiver and lengthened her stride.

She was only halfway to safety when a woman about her own age intercepted her. Given the hostile atmosphere around her, Lyssa at first distrusted the smile being aimed her way. The stranger—a few inches shorter than Lyssa despite balancing gracefully on three-inch heels—had sleek golden-brown hair and wore a gown so tastefully, exquisitely, unquestionably expensive that Lyssa knew it would never wind up in a thrift store as her dress had done. The garment was a statement of class, high waisted and fitted perfectly to the toned body underneath. Lyssa figured the color was taupe, or ecru, or some such hue that only professionals knew the word for.

The woman smiled sympathetically. "Was it worse to have Tank escape, or to be steamrollered by Vivian Callicott?"

"I beg your pardon?" Lyssa blinked, not sure she had heard right.

"She is something, isn't she? Hard to stand against when she gets an idea in her head."

Something flickered through the cabbage-green eyes—sadness, maybe, Lyssa thought. But it vanished as quickly as it had appeared, leaving nothing but intelligence and good humor. The woman laughed. She extended a delicate hand that felt soft and velvety against Lyssa's calluses when their palms met.

"You sound like you know her well," Lyssa answered warily.

"Pretty well. My family and Dane's have been . . . connected for years. Julia Nolin."

"Lyssa Smith." Reclaiming her hand, Lyssa measured her companion. Julia had exactly the sort of innate elegance that suited Dane's world. Lyssa felt an unreasonable jolt of envy.

"I saw you come in with Dane. More or less."

"Let's say, less rather than more. He wasn't particularly happy with me at that moment."

Julia laughed. "Oh, Dane has an artist's temperament." She cocked her head to one side. "I wanted to meet you tonight. I've heard so much about you."

Lyssa first wondered, *From whom?* Hard on the heels of that thought was the hope that at least some of it had been positive. "It was very nice meeting you, Julia, but I'm afraid I have to be going." She smiled politely and shifted her weight.

Eyes widening, Julia reached out and laid her fingers on Lyssa's arm as though that feather-light touch would be enough to stay her. To Lyssa's surprise, it was.

"You can't think to leave so soon—you've barely arrived. Dane wouldn't want you to go without saying a proper goodbye."

"Oh, I rather imagine he would."

Julia grinned. "He'll get over his mood pretty quickly. Or are you referring to that little spat with Tank?" She waved her hand negligently. "That lecherous old goat could stand to hear the truth a little more often. He's gotten away with his crap for too long as it is."

Both shocked and amused by the forthright language, Lyssa glanced around to see if anyone was listening. The curious, condemning onlookers seemed to have faded away. "I didn't accuse Mr. Turnbull of anything, you know," she said quietly. She hadn't expected such an over-the-top reaction. The report summary that had prompted her to seek him out had seemed innocuous. Then again, she reflected, since it hadn't been intended for her eyes, she had skimmed through it rather quickly. The file had been lying open on her boss's desk; upon reading the name on the label, she had been unable to resist a look. It was exactly the sort of project that her employer had once sworn Clearview Engineering and Consulting didn't do.

"No need to explain it to me. I enjoyed seeing Tank put on the spot for once." Julia studied Lyssa with a cheerfully uplifted brow. "So you work for Clearview. I never would have guessed. How do you like being among all those left-brainers?"

Lyssa had to laugh. "Oh, I don't know. I don't have to spend much time in the office."

"Let me guess. It's all cubicles, right? Not a door in the whole place." Julia shook her head in mock commiseration. "And all their pencils lined up just so."

"That's it exactly!" Lyssa chuckled. "I suppose you've seen your share of offices like that."

"Oh, honey, I *live* in an office like that!"

The admission and the warmth in Julia's voice combined to set Lyssa at ease. She decided her escape could wait a few minutes. A person would have to be a complete fool to turn her back on a prospective friend.

"I'm a mortgage broker," Julia explained, naming her employer almost as an afterthought.

Lyssa filed the information away. When the Jacobson land came up for sale, she would need someone like Julia Nolin on her side. She nodded sympathetically as Julia launched into a description of the satisfaction she took in enabling people to buy their dream homes. "How's business right now?"

Julia shook her head. "The slump hit Phoenix hard. Hasn't come back yet."

She felt someone approaching behind her. Quickly she turned her head, half expecting to find Dane.

Julia broke off her narrative and extended both hands to the man who came striding up. "You know Alex Garcia, don't you?" she asked Lyssa.

His black tuxedo swallowed the color of Julia's dress and left it looking washed-out and pale. Her face, though, blossomed into a radiance that more than made up for his effect on what she wore. Lyssa wondered whether Julia had any idea how revealing her expressions were. Not like the stony-faced man who joined them.

"We've met," Lyssa ventured, sticking out her hand, "although you probably don't remember—"

"Lyssa Smith, from Clearview."

Her fingers vanished within his, swallowed up in a grip a shade too firm for comfort.

"I'm impressed." Returning the pressure, Lyssa tossed Dane's executive vice-president a cool smile and took back her hand.

"I have a good memory for names and faces."

Julia smirked at him. "Just not for pairing up the two correctly. But Lyssa is pretty memorable, I have to admit." To Lyssa she said, "Alex is the one who sang your praises to me."

"Oh?" So some of it must actually have been good, she thought. She wouldn't have expected it. She'd only met the man a few times.

Dane joined them, then, as if critical mass had been reached. He nodded at Alex, then draped his arm around Julia's shoulders and gave her a quick squeeze. "Alex, Julia." He glanced at Lyssa.

His expression seemed off, weirdly vague, as though he was less *there* than usual. But the others didn't seem to notice.

"Lyssa." He nodded to her. "I see you've all met."

Daringly she answered, "I've met all kinds of interesting people tonight."

"Good, good, glad you're enjoying yourself."

Obviously he hadn't been listening.

"So have I, actually." He directed the words to Alex.

Lyssa, feeling awkward and unwelcome, shifted to make her escape, but before she could say a polite goodbye, Dane grasped her bare arm above the elbow. Butterflies took wing in her stomach, along with a wish that the man would stop grabbing at her. He didn't look at her—simply prevented her from leaving, unless she wanted to enact another minidrama for the audience.

He continued, "A prospective investor from back east has heard about the Highline. He sent one of our local politicos to check us out."

Lyssa thought of her earlier petty wish that she hadn't talked to Cal about the resort. She was pretty certain that that talk was what brought about this news of Dane's.

"And?" Alex prompted.

"He's too ill to come out here, so he invited me to New York to present any ideas I might have for another project like the Highline." Dane grimaced. "As though there could ever be one," he added quietly.

"Oh, Dane, that's wonderful!" Julia exclaimed.

Alex's heavy eyebrows drew together. He pursed his lips. "Are you going to take him up on the invitation?"

"Of course he's going," Julia declared. She bumped Alex teasingly with her shoulder. "It's New York!"

Dane shrugged. After a moment he said, "There's not much point, is there?" He sighed and with his free hand absently rubbed his forehead. "We don't really have anything on tap."

Alex's frown of concentration deepened.

"Dane. Hello!" Julia drawled. "Have you ever thought of using that gorgeous head of yours for something other than hanging your hair on? It's a trip to New York! A vacation. Now, I know that you—unlike Alex—don't take time for yourself, but how can you even think of not going?"

Alex came out of his brown study enough to direct a hard look at Julia.

"There's the thought of explaining my reasons to my mother," Dane confessed. "Not to mention justifying to a stranger why he should feel confident in placing several million dollars' worth of trust in me before the numbers for the Highline start to come in."

Placing her hands on her hips, Julia faced him, a David to his Goliath. "I never thought I'd say this to you, but you're too modest."

Dane sighed again. He glanced at Lyssa, then away. "Because I'm willing to let the marketplace be the judge?"

"That's a part of it, yes." Julia poked him in the chest with a well-manicured finger. "Life is not all about money, Dane."

The idea must sound different coming from Julia, Lyssa thought, for Dane listened intently.

"It's obvious that this is all yours!" Julia went on. "Only you could have managed to get a project of this magnitude from concept to completion in ten years—"

"Seven," he murmured.

"—quite amazing, really. Only you could have taken an established neighborhood and convinced everyone—everyone, Dane—" with a dramatic toss of her head "—that they should be delighted to sell their homes and move into a trailer park—"

"Prefabricated houses, and it's a lovely community," he corrected.

Alex's face went still. Lyssa was fascinated by the light that sparked within his coal-black eyes. She listened with only half an ear to the words skipping back and forth between Dane and Julia.

"There. You see?" Julia asked. "After you snowed them with that crooner's voice and batted your baby blues at them, those poor, lonely, gray-haired widows never stood a chance. On top of everything else, you convinced them it was their idea all along!"

"Julia! You of all people should understand why those homeowners agreed to be relocated. They could all see the neighborhood dying around them. I merely offered an alternative."

"And convinced the dim-witted powers-that-be that it was a part of their regional plan all along. It's marvelous, the way you get your own way in everything—"

Dane's fingers dug into Lyssa's arm. "Not everything," he said, oblivious to her gasp of protest.

Busy trying to pry herself free, she nearly missed Julia's waspish reply. "If you're still thinking about that, I've told you time and again, all you have to do is take it up again."

"I think you should go," Alex weighed in.

Dane and Julia stared at him.

Lyssa knew from her architect father's dinner-table conversation that eco-investing had become legitimate, funded by people who had a vast enough fortune that they could afford to put their money where their principles were. She held her breath, waiting to see what Alex Garcia would suggest. He'd always impressed Lyssa with his sharp mind for business. If he saw the possibilities in setting up the Highline Resort as an example of green architecture and establishing Callicott

Properties on the national scene at the same time, surely he would be able to convince both Dane and Vivian Callicott that this was a course worth pursuing.

Alex's gaze flickered toward Lyssa. She figured he didn't want to talk Callicott business in front of her. She tried to move away again, but with a warning squeeze Dane held her in place.

"You should go to New York," Alex repeated.

"Why?" Dane asked. "What would I hope to accomplish? Even if we had a project to talk about, Alex, we can't afford to take the risk."

"There's that Tucson resort Mike's been talking to you about. In an older community—'with character,' I think he put it. A long history as a guest ranch. It sounds interesting."

Lyssa recognized the unfurling of curiosity and tried to stamp it out. The last thing she needed was to become emotionally invested in another Callicott project.

"That's—" Dane seemed at a loss for words. He rubbed his forehead again. "We'll talk about it later," he finally said.

Alex nodded. "Give it some thought over the weekend."

"Come on," Dane told Lyssa. "Let's get something to eat." He hardly gave her a chance to say goodbye to Julia before hauling her away, his hand still clamped on her arm like a vise.

"I was on my way out." Lyssa craned her neck to see the doors receding in the distance as he escorted her deeper into the ballroom.

"Surely you can spare me a few minutes?" Dane's expression was strained. "I haven't had a chance to eat since noon, and it takes a lot of fuel to keep this body going." He rubbed his stomach with his free hand and grimaced.

She dug in her heels. "You can't just drag me off because you feel like it. Whatever you have to say to me, say it here and get it over with." She suspected he intended to make it clear that she was never to harass his mother or guests in the future. Not that that would be a problem; if he would just let her go, she would never have to see any of them again.

Except maybe Julia, and that would be her own business, not Callicott's.

Halted by her resistance, he looked at her, then at his hand gripping her arm. Only then did he seem to come back from whatever mental state he had been in. He took in their immediate surroundings with a bemused glance.

They stood next to the champagne fountain. "Want some champagne?" Without waiting for her answer he grabbed up a long, delicate flute and began to fill it from the flowing stream.

Lyssa had never tried champagne. She figured—the way her luck was going tonight—she was likely to choke on the bubbles or spew out her first mouthful in dislike. She'd never been conditioned to any commercial alcohol, only the fruit wines, hard cider, and homebrew that her parents made.

"No, thanks," she said, holding up her hand in refusal. "I'd better not. I'm driving."

"Go ahead. It's nonalcoholic."

She studied his too-innocent air. "It is not."

Dane shrugged, unrepentant. "I hate to drink alone." He offered the flute again. "Just take a few sips. Have some food first. If you load up on protein, the alcohol won't affect you as much."

"You have absolutely no shame, you know that?" Lyssa struggled against the laughter welling up in her throat. "You'll say anything to get your own way."

"Now you sound like Julia. It's actually very rare that I get my own way." He shrugged one shoulder and set the flute down next to its empty companions.

"Do you expect me to believe that?"

"It would be nice if you would."

Beyond him Lyssa saw a flutter of icy blue fabric heralding Claudia's exquisitely timed appearance. She was a little surprised, when she considered the matter, that Dane's assistant had taken so long to come to his rescue.

"Lyssa, I'm so glad I found you," Claudia said in her husky voice, imbuing every word with sincerity. "Mr. Levitt was looking for you earlier."

Dane released Lyssa and strolled over to the buffet table, draped with a heavy linen coral-colored tablecloth several shades darker than the wall behind it. He began loading up two plates without asking her preferences—or even if she was hungry.

Rarely got his own way, my fanny! she thought.

"Mr. Levitt," Claudia prompted, her blond head practically vibrating with outrage at being ignored. "Don't you think you should see what he wanted?"

"Not particularly. I'm not here as his employee tonight." Lyssa smiled blandly at her. The opportunity to yank Claudia's chain outweighed Lyssa's desire to take advantage of the out the other woman was offering. "I'm Dane's guest."

Dane returned with two heaping plates. His eyes went back and forth between the mounds of food as if he'd just become aware of what he was doing. "Ah, here." He shoved his burden at Claudia. Her dainty hands, flashing with several pale sparkling stones, came up to accept the laden plates. "Great reception, Claudia. You've done well."

He walked away without another word to either woman.

Absently, for she found herself more concerned with Dane's odd behavior than being polite to Claudia, Lyssa suggested, "You really should find someplace to put those." She indicated the sagging plates with a gesture but studied Dane.

"Mr. Levitt *is* looking for you, you know," Claudia told her with malicious satisfaction.

Lyssa didn't doubt it. She watched as Dane reached out to touch one of the plaster-relief pillars that she assumed held the retractable walls that would make the grand ballroom a flexible space for meetings and conferences. His gait was awkward, as if his shoes pinched.

Lyssa knew about shoes pinching, for hers were killing her toes.

But that sort of physical discomfort didn't explain his abrupt departure. Both times, she realized. First from Julia and Alex, and now from her and Claudia. Lyssa frowned.

Claudia evidently wasn't finished with her attempt to put Lyssa off-balance. "He didn't seem pleased that you called Mr. Turnbull a criminal."

It took Lyssa a moment to realize that the other woman was still referring to Simon Levitt, not Dane. "Tell me, Claudia, didn't anyone listen to what I actually said to Turnbull? I'm a little tired of being misunderstood."

"I don't think there's any misunderstanding. Mrs. Callicott and I know what you're after."

Lyssa studied Claudia for a minute. She tapped the nearest plate. "You might want to put those down."

"What?"

"You're dripping." The glaze on the stuffed grape leaves—which were quite possibly from her parents' farm, like most of the produce weighing down the buffet table—was about to ooze onto the terribly expensive-looking gown.

Claudia gasped and sought an open spot on the nearby serving tables. With the blonde distracted, Lyssa walked toward the back of the room, following Dane's course.

Worry for him overcame common sense. Darned if she was going to leave before making sure he was all right.

Beyond the last pillar was a set of double doors she assumed led to the kitchens of the new "Anton's at the Highline" restaurant. She looked through the porthole windows in the doors but saw no one in the featureless service hall. When she turned around, she jumped and choked back a shriek.

Dane slumped against the pillar, gasping for breath. She rushed across the small space that separated them and put a hand on his shoulder. "Dane?" She shook him lightly when he didn't respond. "Dane? Are you all right?"

HE SAGGED AGAINST the nearest upright surface, clenching his teeth and trying to breathe past the pain that radiated from his breastbone. Panting shallowly, he fought for each burst of air.

She sounded impatient. Weren't women supposed to become soft and mushy and nurturing when one was in trouble?

She'd burrowed under his arm and was pressing him against something hard.

"'M fine."

"Okay, that was a stupid question. I'll have someone call an ambulance." She started to pull away.

"No!" he choked out. The stylized, larger-than-life ocotillo carved in relief on the curvature of the pier was digging into his back. He could feel every one of the whiplike sharp-tipped branches against his tensed muscles, through his shirt and the jacket of his tuxedo. The awareness was good. It meant his chest wasn't hurting so much now, if he could notice other, more minor, discomforts.

"Look, I don't know what's happening, but you're obviously in trouble."

Dane turned his head and saw the chalk-white line of his sleeve lying across an expanse of skin, an ebon dress, and curls of Venetian red. He recalled Goethe's color system: red had the highest energy. It suited her. "No, I'm fine." He inhaled cautiously. Her hair smelled like apple spice cake, very earthy and domestic. Not what he had expected. But then, Lyssa never was.

"You're clutching your chest."

"Am I?" He looked down to see that his hand was wrapped around the tucked front of his thin champagne-colored silk shirt. "So I am. It's nothing. Muscle spasms." The intermittent attacks had bothered him through his last year of college, during his father's final illness, and even after he had taken over Callicott Properties, but he hadn't experienced one for almost a decade. Until now. The stabbing pain began to ease.

Lyssa was eyeing him in appalled fascination. Flecks of gold in her irises softened the olive tone of the outer ring, which shaded into terre verte near the pupil in a complex palette of colors. If only he'd been a painter, he could have worked for days to capture that image.

"Uh-huh. Muscle spasms."

"That's right." He forced his hand down and tried to surreptitiously square his shoulders and open up his chest, but a quick jolt had him hunching again and breathing with caution.

"Is that anything like the 'heart palpitations' from the days before EEGs?"

Heart palpitations sounded like they belonged with little old ladies in long dresses, Dane thought. "No. It's perfectly harmless."

Warily she asked, "Is this a normal guy thing, this denial of pain or illness?"

"Normal guy?" He couldn't help but smile at the way she worded it. His chest loosened a little more. "Does that mean you don't think I'm normal, or that you don't know a lot of normal guys?"

He got no answer.

"Shouldn't you lie down or something? The kitchen is right through there." She nodded toward the nearby serving doors. "Maybe they have a place—"

"No, it's better like this."

As he straightened, she pulled away, leaving behind the echo of her warmth and strength. Dane rubbed his chest, which still had a slight catch above his sternum.

Her eyes followed the movement of his hand. "Sorry if I bothered you," she said abruptly, "but I've never been around anybody sick before."

"I'm not *sick*, exactly." He didn't want to appear weak in Lyssa's eyes. Bad enough that he let her witness his disgruntlement over his guests' opinion of the Highline. *Let her witness it?* Hell, she'd borne the brunt of it. And it wasn't fair of him—she, at least, had seemed sincere in her admiration, if not very creative. By way of distraction he asked, "You've never been around *anybody* sick?"

Lyssa shrugged. Bared by the square neckline of her dress, the muscles in her shoulders bunched and shifted under her skin. He could not recall ever before having seen her in a dress, much less noticing that she had legs. Long, toned, tanned legs with no sheen of stockings. Nothing but bare skin. A lot of it. He felt another surge, this time well below his chest and having nothing to do with pain.

She stirred, bringing his gaze, if not his scattered thoughts, back to her well-proportioned face. "My family—we've had the good fortune to be a remarkably healthy lot."

"In all the years we've known each other, this is the first time you've mentioned your family," he pointed out.

"You're sure you're all right?"

"I'm fine. Why are you trying to change the subject? You've met my mother. You know all my family secrets."

"Hardly," she informed him dryly. "I don't even know whether to believe you that you're not dying of a heart attack."

Did she know that was how his father had died? he wondered. That was why he didn't want to make a big deal out of it. His mother would worry.

Her half smile faded. "If you'll excuse me, I think it's past time for me to go home. I've made a fool of myself enough tonight."

"Don't go." Dane took a step forward. He didn't want her to leave yet. He vaguely remembered having dragged her by the arm through the ballroom. But then, he was pretty sure, he had left her talking to Claudia at the buffet tables. He wasn't quite sure how she had come to be with him behind the pillar. Still, there she was, and apparently by choice.

"Look, what I said earlier. About your principles." Seeing her head snap up, with fire in those eyes, he rushed on. "I know you have to do something to make a living. And you're working within the same system I am. Didn't I hear you have a promotion pending?" Then he faltered. Her hand went up to play with her bright, glowing hair. He forgot what he was about to say.

"Come on. I'm hungry." Brushing away the curl she was toying with, he claimed her hand and went to lead her back toward the buffet.

She resisted. "Would you let go of me? I don't want anything to eat. I have to leave."

"You're going to turn into a pumpkin if you're not out of here by midnight? Or—I know! You're a vegetarian," he speculated, giving a snap of his fingers. "Opposed to the waste of energy and clearing of rain forests for the sake of meat production. Concerned with the fate of free-ranging dolphins. Can't eat anything with a face."

Her glower intensified. She yanked herself free. "I hate it when people deny their animal nature," she said in an apparent non sequitur. "Vegetarianism is for cows, not predators. We've had millions of years of biological conditioning to operate at the highest trophic level."

He cocked his brow at the technical explanation.

"The top of the food chain," she clarified.

He suppressed a grin, enjoying her underestimation of his intelligence. "Are you willing to put your money where your mouth is? If you won't let me feed you from this spread," he gestured toward the tables, "at least agree to go out for a steak with me next week."

"What?"

"You don't need to sound so shocked." Dane thought quickly. "Don't think of it as a date. More of a business meeting. A chance to help me lay out a strategy for this New York investor. I saw your face when Alex suggested the Tucson project. You were intrigued—admit it." He pointed a finger at her and waggled it back and forth.

The corners of her mouth twitched, but she didn't quite smile. "I don't think dinner would be a good idea."

On that note she left.

He rounded the pillar to watch her go. The crowd split before her and stared after her before breaking into whispers. Evidently everyone had heard of the business with her and Tank. And his mother.

Only after Lyssa had passed through the carved wooden doors did he realize that he had neither apologized nor coaxed her to let him buy his way out of his predicament with dinner. "Damn it," he said under his breath.

Three

LYSSA SAT IN HER BOXY GRAY CUBICLE. Her laptop, on the workstation in front of her, hummed and chirped as it cycled on.

She'd spent the weekend at her parents' farm, helping with the unending round of chores as usual, but her mind had been in turmoil. Between worrying about Dane's health, fretting about his comments on her principles, and imagining herself out of a job over what she had said to Tank Turnbull, she nearly hoed down a healthy stand of young New Zealand spinach before her mother Paris stopped her. Her exasperated parents found more mindless tasks for her to do, and so the days passed. Here it was Monday already.

Although trying to concentrate on the notes she had taken Friday afternoon, she could not get her mind right. With a shake of her head, Lyssa admitted she couldn't stop thinking about Dane Callicott. She'd spent a large part of the past two days reliving the sight of him white-faced and shaking, clutching at his chest and leaning against the decorative pier as if it would keep him from falling down dead on the floor.

She shut her eyes in a vain attempt to stifle her imagination. He said his chest pains were nothing more than muscle spasms, but he couldn't have been truly aware of half of what he was saying that night. Her hand went out to the telephone. She halted the motion, impatient with this urge to involve herself in Dane's personal life.

Both hands lifted to tangle in the mass of curls that fell over her shoulder, as if keeping them occupied would prevent her from making the call. She had no right to meddle.

But his mother—who had both the right and the responsibility to look out for Dane—didn't seem to be paying attention. Lyssa was still angry that Vivian Callicott seemed more concerned with her company's reputation than her son's pride, not to mention his health.

Reminding herself—again—that it was none of her business, Lyssa stared blindly at her computer screen. Everybody knew it was a mistake to try to rescue people who weren't a part of your inner circle of intimates.

Dane had already demonstrated that fact of life, by turning on her when she tried to restore his faith in the Highline.

Maybe it was just that she didn't understand those who breathed the rarefied air of money. She did sort of blame Dane for everything that had gone wrong that night.

Had she been trying to prove something to him? Or herself? She'd allowed her frustration with him to goad her into speaking with Turnbull, but she still didn't believe that she'd said anything out of line. Certainly she hadn't revealed any privileged information: not the location of the planned subdivision, the name of the pristine foothills that were to be graded and have parts lopped off, the species of rare cactus that would be in jeopardy. She hadn't completely lost her head Friday night.

But intentions didn't always translate into results, as Dane had informed her. Simon Levitt, for example, might see the whole series of incidents at the reception in an entirely different light.

Lyssa pulled her hands out of her hair, angry with herself for allowing her worry to fester.

She was a good employee. She'd given the company several years of loyal and conscientious service. What's more, Simon had known from the beginning that Lyssa had strong feelings about humankind's responsibility for the environment. Agreeing wholeheartedly with the necessity for taking the long view, he had promised that Lyssa would not find herself in a moral dilemma if she agreed to come and work for him. And then the recession struck.

So here Monday morning was at last, only to find her sitting at her desk—in a cubicle exactly like the ones she and Julia had laughed about—wondering if she would still have a job this afternoon because the grand poo-bahs of the development world couldn't grasp the fact that places like the Highline were what they all needed to produce if they wanted their companies to survive the changing times.

The telephone rang. Lyssa flinched. She stared at the jangling noisebox as if it were a snake poised to strike. This was it—she thought, glancing at the clock on her toolbar at the bottom of the screen—the call from Simon.

Another ring broke the silence. Lyssa stretched out her hand and lifted the receiver. "Hello," she said through a dry, tight throat. An instant later, she realized she'd forgotten the formulaic phrasing: *Hello. Clearview Engineering. This is Lyssa.* Simon would undoubtedly tot up this transgression on her scorecard, too.

"Lyssa?" The smooth, even voice wasn't Simon's. "Lyssa, it's Dane Callicott."

"I know. I mean, I recognized you. Your voice." She rolled her eyes at the ceiling.

"Why are you calling?" she prompted at the same time he said, "I'm calling because I feel so lousy about the way your evening ended." He laughed. "Having your host keel over on you like that—anyway, it must have been quite a shock. I thought you might have been a little worried."

Lyssa couldn't think whether it would be more dangerous to confirm or deny that she had stewed over his condition all weekend. "*Are* you all right?" she finally asked.

"Oh, sure, sure. Like I told you, it's just muscle spasms."

Something in the way he said it made her decide never to mention the subject again. "Good. That's fine, then." She waited to find out what he was really calling about.

After his next few pleasantries failed to draw more than a polite rejoinder from her, Dane's well-modulated voice started to take on an edge. "I'm sure you're busy," he said. "Maybe you could make some time to talk over dinner this week."

"Why?" This was why she didn't date, she thought. A handsome, wealthy, charming man was asking her to spare him a few hours of attention, and she felt as wary of him as if he were a patch of poison ivy.

There was a scientific and rational explanation for her wariness, she told herself. Men were a foreign species: *Homo sapiens testosteronus.* She'd never indulged in the mating rituals that occurred all around her in college, and after. It had never been the right time, or her focus lay elsewhere, or she was waiting for the heart of her soul, as her Papa Ari would say.

And face it, Dane Callicott was not good practice material.

"Why? Lyssa, it's just dinner." He sounded exasperated.

To him it might be just dinner, but to her it seemed like ground she shouldn't cross. "I don't think—"

"Oh, come on, Lyssa," he persisted. "What can it hurt? One evening out of your life. Say you're free on Wednesday."

"No, I don't want—"

He spoke right over her protest. "We can keep the time flexible. Right after work, later in the evening, whichever is most convenient for you."

"I really can't talk now. I'm at work," she reminded him.

"Give me your home number, then, and I'll call you tonight." Dane sounded irritated.

Lyssa closed her eyes and gathered her resolve. "No, I—"

He cut her off. "Listen. If you're thinking this is a come-on, get past it."

Her eyes snapped open.

"You remember that Tucson project Alex mentioned as a possibility for that New York investor?"

"Yes, I remember." Her voice was curt, but she couldn't help it. A come-on! What a graceless expression. And what on earth was she supposed to think when he kept badgering her to go out with him?

"I'd like to have your input on it."

Lyssa kicked herself mentally for feeling the satisfaction that rose in her at the implied compliment. That was just the sort of mood Dane was good at creating.

"Tell me you're free to come to dinner on Wednesday with my friends from Tucson," Dane coaxed. "They'll fill us in on the details."

Us. Lyssa wondered how stupid she was to let that one short word tempt her. This wasn't a date he was proposing. Not a come-on. It was business. What's more, it was Callicott business, and that meant Dane was up to something. But he might be up to something positive, something that would result in another project like the Highline. Something that would restore Lyssa's faltering sense that she was in the right place, doing the right thing. Something that would make sure she still had a job next week.

A muffled rap on the entrance to her cubicle made her start. She glanced over her left shoulder and saw Barbara Pierce in the opening.

Barb wore a severe pantsuit, in a bittersweet-chocolate brown today. Lyssa also noted a barely suppressed excitement in her manner. She wondered if Barb had heard about Tank.

Lyssa leaned back in her chair, adopting as casual a pose as she could manage. Her palm went damp on the handset of the phone.

She'd lost track of what Dane was saying until she heard, "Seven o'clock it is, then."

"Yes. Fine," she murmured, eyeing Barb warily. Then it hit, what he had said, and she'd absentmindedly agreed to. She sat bolt upright again. "No—wait! Dane!"

"I'll pick you up, if you give me your address," Dane offered.

Barb listened avidly. Her eyes glittered.

"I'll have to call you with that information," Lyssa muttered.

After a few more comments back and forth, with Lyssa guarding her tongue, Dane hung up. She put down the phone and stared at Barb, wondering how much her supervisor had heard. Or guessed.

"You know," Barb began, "since Simon is already upset with your unprofessional conduct, this isn't a real good time to take a personal call during business hours."

Lyssa felt like saying it wasn't Simon who cared, that the restriction on calls was one of Barb's more annoying rules, along with forbidding the posting of personal items like photographs and artwork in the cubicles. Instead, locking her hands upon each other to keep them from playing with her hair, she clamped her mouth shut. The sooner Barb went away, the sooner Lyssa could call Dane back and straighten him out.

"I assume that was Mr. Callicott?" Barb went on smugly. "Unless you know something I don't"—her tone implied that that would occur when Yuma froze over—"we're not working on anything for Callicott at the present time. He called to chew you out for making a scene at his party the other night, didn't he?"

There were at least two aspects of this situation to be grateful for, Lyssa told herself. First, Barb wasn't at the reception to watch Lyssa's encounters with Tank Turnbull and Vivian Callicott in person; and second, she evidently hadn't picked up on the fact that Lyssa had agreed to a date, of sorts, with Dane Callicott.

Not that that was the important message to take away. Barb was the one who would be writing the environmental impact assessment that would either bring Tank Turnbull one step closer to his apparent goal of paving over the entire desert, or put up at least a momentary roadblock in his way. Since Lyssa's initial hope of making the old developer think about the ramifications of his plan had failed abysmally, it was time to work on the other end of the equation.

Barb put one hand on her hip and the other on the worktable in front of Lyssa. She leaned in, too close. "As of today, you are officially off the Turnbull project."

"I didn't think I was ever officially on it." Lyssa forced her fingers to separate, then picked up a pen and twiddled with it to keep her hands occupied. "If I recall, you asked me to do you a favor and check out the ownership transactions, since I was going to the records office anyway. It saved you the trip, I think you said."

She refrained from mentioning her suspicion that Barb didn't know how to search for land history information. Outside of Simon's hearing, Barb generally scoffed at the necessity for that sort of froufrou nonsense; an ambitious female in the male-dominated field of engineering, she demanded hard facts. Lyssa had a few of those to lay the groundwork. "Do you want to see what I found?"

"By all means, let's have it." Barb's smile was cold and reptilian, not reaching her eyes.

Lyssa reached for the keyboard, where the dialog box was waiting for her input. "Do you mind?" She stared meaningfully over her shoulder at Barb. She hadn't logged on yet, and she had a thing about letting someone else watch when she entered her password.

Barb shrugged and straightened, turning toward the opening of the cubicle.

Lyssa felt silly as she pressed the sequence of keys. Every employee's password was on file in Simon's office, and Barb—as Simon's second in command—had a key to those locked files. If she really wanted to access Lyssa's computer, she could.

After one glance at the half-sheet of names and dates that Lyssa brought up and printed out, Barb looked sharply at her. "This is all you have?"

"I imagine that's why Simon didn't put me on the EA team to start with," Lyssa said dryly. "This property hasn't changed hands very often, and its purpose not at all. It's been minimally productive grazing land as far back as records were kept."

"But still." Barb shook her head. Her mouth compressed into a thin white line. "No mining? No DOT survey reports?" She eyed Lyssa with suspicion, as though certain that the younger woman knew more than she was admitting.

"I didn't get that far. I just stopped at the county recorder's office." She took a deep breath and plunged ahead, hoping she'd done Barb enough of a favor to earn a brief truce—surely her boss would remember that they were on the same side. "I do know something about that part of the Valley, though. This land Turnbull has optioned, it's right in the middle of a small range of an endangered species of pineapple cactus."

Barb purred, "I heard that you made some wild accusations like that. You know that for a fact, do you? You've surveyed this land yourself, with your precious botany degree?"

"It's not whether *I've* done a visual survey, is it? It's whether *you're* planning to make sure one gets done before you turn in a favorable report to Tank Turnbull."

Barb's skin went pale across her nose, throwing her nostrils into stark relief. She glared at Lyssa. "Are you accusing me of something?"

"You know your job and the responsibilities that go with it. At this point, there's no blame to lay," she said carefully, picking her way through the verbal minefield that yawned before her. "But Turnbull is a desperate man. He'll cause the company nothing but trouble, Barb."

"I'm sure you think so, after the weekend. Turnbull and Callicott and the rest of them are what keeps your paycheck coming, and don't you forget it." The color returned to Barb's face, and her expression turned sly. "You know, if Simon buys Valley Archaeology, there's bound to be somebody in that bunch who can do your job. And without letting her mouth run away with her."

Lyssa tried not to react to the threat. She'd made no protest when Simon had offered to promote her to a supervisory position if and when he acquired the small contract archaeology firm. In fact, it had seemed like a great opportunity. The more she earned in the next few years, the closer she would be to rescuing her parents from the precarious position in which they'd unwittingly placed themselves.

Barb allowed herself a triumphant grin. "Poor Lyssa. I had so hoped your curiosity would get the better of you and tempt you into reading the Turnbull file if I gave you the opportunity. I never dreamed it would turn out so well, though." She laughed. "I thought you'd go to Simon with some feeble protest about Turnbull's plans. To have gone straight to the man himself, now, that shows an initiative I never would have expected of you."

Barb dropped her hand onto Lyssa's shoulder.

"But you made it too easy," Barb complained. "I'll give you one more chance to figure out your place around here. If you're smart, you'll forget all about this little cactus and its mythical range. Or I won't be responsible for what happens to you. You will." She spun on her neat brown leather heel and left the cubicle.

Lyssa's hands were shaking, so she folded them together in her lap. Barb had set her up. That file had been deliberately left out for her to find and read.

Barb wasn't ignorant of the existence of the pineapple cactus on Turnbull's land—she was being paid off. That explained why Tank Turnbull had reacted so violently at the reception. He *had* bought a positive report and undoubtedly had expected to get away with it.

But who could Lyssa go to with her suspicions, if Barb was in Turnbull's camp? Simon? Hardly, if he was as upset with her as Claudia and Barb had suggested. The fact that Simon hadn't called her into his office yet and told her to pack up her things and get out did not mean she could do no wrong in his eyes. She was an employee, paid to do exactly what her employer told her to do, paid with the blood money that came through the destructive hands of clients like Tank Turnbull. It would be Lyssa's word against Barb's that the results of the Clearview investigation were predetermined.

All that Lyssa had for hard evidence were the soil maps in the special collections room at the university library, and they merely showed the potential range of the cactus. Unless she went out there herself, on private property, and identified the cactus plants in place, and—what then? Took pictures? How could she prove where she was, when one rock-strewn desert floor looked much the same as another?

She thumped her forehead into her hands. She'd put her job, her promotion, her family's livelihood on the line for a patch of tiny cactuses that the majority of the ignoramuses who moved into Tank's subdivision would walk right past and never see—that is, if any of the plants survived the perils of construction.

She might have guessed that Barb would never allow Lyssa to be promoted out from under her thumb. But how could she have predicted what lengths her boss would go to, to ruin Lyssa's credibility—and maybe, ultimately, get her fired?

What good were scruples against an enemy who had none?

Then again, she asked herself, did she really mind the thought of getting fired over this? If Simon was changing the rules on her and Clearview was becoming an unsuitable place to work, if she would have to overlook principles and ethics and even the law to keep her job, then the money she was putting toward her family's future was tainted anyway.

There were other jobs. And in two days she was to have dinner with a man who made a habit of offering her one.

Lyssa decided not to call Dane after all to cancel their un-date. There were worse situations than sitting down to a meal with a man who claimed to owe you and was in the enviable position of being able to help you out of a jam.

Maybe it was someone else's turn to rescue her, for a change.

Four

DANE ENDED the telephone connection, satisfied at having overcome Lyssa's objections. The fact that she had objections, though, nagged at him.

He slipped off the headset, disengaging the cord when it caught on the collar point of his shirt, a meandering line breaking up the quiet pinstriping of Vandyke brown against ivory. He slouched against the leather of his chair and stretched out his long legs, angling them off to one side of the massive walnut desk drifted with papers. His attention was caught by the contrast of the yellow ochre hue of his slacks against the dark, heavily grained wood. The crease broke at his knees, creating an interesting shadow effect in the early-morning light that streamed in through the window at his right side.

Then he recalled himself. Regardless of Julia's opinion, he was no artist anymore, to be distracted by lines and colors. He clasped his hands behind his head and leaned back to review the brief conversation he just had with the unpredictable Lyssa Smith.

He'd called her intending to apologize and seal the peace offering with dinner, but before he could think of a graceful way to introduce the words "I'm sorry," she made it plain that he would have to practically blackmail her into having dinner. He'd left a great deal unsaid between them.

First was his apology for taking out his disappointment on her. She had said the Highline was beautiful, and that irritated him at the time. Unlike most of the others who told him the same thing Friday night, though, Lyssa meant every word. From her the compliment was not shallow and unperceptive, a polite lie uttered simply because it was expected. She had seen beyond the architect's design to Dane's intention. She had remembered his dream.

Plus, she recognized the environmental aspects, which no one else had done. Then again, he mused, she should. Many of the ideas for energy and water conservation had come from her. So he owed her for that, too.

The invitation to the reception was intended as a reward for her part in shaping his vision of the Highline, but it hadn't worked out that way. Dane was pretty sure Lyssa was in trouble with Simon because of that flap with Turnbull. Her stiffness on the phone might have even been because Simon was in her office at that very minute, reprimanding her for her ill-considered remarks.

All she had to do, he reminded himself, was tell her employer she was going out to dinner with Dane Callicott, and all would be forgiven. He wasn't being egotistical in assuming there would be some benefit to her for agreeing to see him outside of a business setting.

Still, he almost reached for the telephone headset again. He didn't think it would be an abuse of his long-standing friendship with Simon Levitt to ask that she be cut some slack. Dane kept his hands interlaced behind his head, though, squelching the temptation to interfere. Lyssa was too good an employee for Simon to come down hard on her for this one little dust-up. And it wouldn't hurt her to squirm a little.

Dane unlocked his hands and sat up. A faint burning sensation started in his gut. He rubbed at it, hoping it was merely indigestion and not something more insidious, something that wouldn't go away with antacids. Something uncomfortably like guilt.

He'd accused Lyssa of turning her back on her principles. Ironic, that, since her steadfast defense of principles was what had set Tank Turnbull off. No matter what Dane had said at the reception, he knew Lyssa Smith was the last person in their business who would sell out for money.

Dane considered digging in the desk drawer for the antacids he kept there, but he decided the chalky tablets wouldn't give him any relief this time. No matter how he tried to rationalize having manipulated Lyssa into having dinner with him, he couldn't get around the fact that he'd done it only partly because she could be a strong ally at Callicott Properties. She could help him and Alex drag the company into the twenty-first century despite holdouts like his mother.

And as a side benefit, having her around—seeing her socially once or twice—would be a jab at his mother, who had spent much of the weekend railing about Lyssa Smith. As for why Dane was so tempted by that prospect, he supposed it came down to Vivian's persistence in pressing him about when he and Julia were going to get serious. She'd started on that refrain right after he and Gail broke up. After ten years of it, Dane had had enough. His mother's dislike of Lyssa gave him the perfect opportunity to throw a red herring her way.

Besides, he felt alive with Lyssa. She was never quite what he expected—and his life over the past decade had turned into a slough of predictability. He was about ready to drown in others' expectations of him.

Even his social life had become tedious. He could sketch the outlines of every scene in advance.

Take this week, for example. Mike and Gail would come up from Tucson on Wednesday as planned, since they'd had to miss the Highline reception because they had something to do with one of their kids. The three of them would normally catch a ball game in the afternoon, talk some business, and then go out to dinner, all pretending that things were the same as they had been in college. The specific colors of the picture might be different, some of the nuances of angle and intensity might vary, but the overall effect was always the same.

Only this time, Dane was resolved, the business negotiations would include Alex, and the dinnertime conversation would include Lyssa, and Dane would prove that he had not put his life on hold just because his fiancée had betrayed him and married his best friend when his back was turned.

"HE'S WAITING FOR YOU, Mrs. Callicott. You can go right in."

Vivian stared at Claudia Montgomery until the younger woman looked up. Their eyes clashed, blue against icy gray.

Claudia fancied herself a conduit for power at Callicott Properties, controlling the flow of information and the execution of crucial tasks. She packaged herself to give that impression, too: expensive clothing, hairstyle, makeup, and presence. But still her cotton-candy-pink suit was from a department store and the rest of the package too deliberate to impress a woman who had seen such ploys many times over the years.

Vivian curled her lips in a humorless smile. Her own tailored suit-dress, a subtle maroon with gray pinstripes, was one of a kind. It had never been hung on a rack to be pawed through by up-and-comers. Her shoes, simple pumps a shade lighter than the dress, were custom fit. Her nails were carefully trimmed and buffed to a natural shine. Her hair was the exact color it had been on her wedding day. If she had acquired a few more wrinkles since then, she could console herself with the knowledge that she wore her experience on her face. Unlike women her age who believed the lies and promises of cosmetic surgeons, she knew she bore no resemblance to a walking death's-head. The work she had undergone was invisible to the eye, merely enhancing her bone structure and maturity.

Miss Montgomery wilted under that smile and the silence.

Satisfied, Vivian finally said, "I'll just do that." She may have acquired some interesting tidbits of information from Dane's assistant a half hour earlier, but that did not by any means put the two of them on an equal footing. For thirty-five years Vivian had freely come and gone, without needing permission, in the office Dane was currently using.

She pressed down on the curved brass latch and went in. There was Dane, slouched in his chair, the only thing he had changed in the office during his tenure as head of Callicott Properties. His mode of dress was as tasteful as her own, she saw at a glance, with a tasteful off-white pinstriped shirt and yellowish slacks, neatly creased even though his posture was atrocious.

Her eyes went to the picture of her husband that hung behind Dane's desk. She felt the familiar pang of sorrow that had diminished over the past ten years but had not vanished entirely. She liked this photograph better than the formal painted portrait that hung in the reception area of Callicott Properties; it showed Stewart's more human side, with the barest hint of a smile and a few crow's-feet around his eyes.

When she looked at her son, who had gotten to his feet and was grinning at her, she had an urge to tell him how like his father he was. A young, strong, healthy version of Stewart Callicott. Not that appearance was any guarantee of health. She would never have imagined losing her husband so soon after his fiftieth birthday. But time kept ticking away; that was the one guarantee in life.

She wasted no time on greetings but went straight to her purpose. "A new investor, Dane? Really, do you think it wise?"

He did not ask how she had found out. Nor did he seem surprised that she had. His grin didn't fade one whit. He simply looked at her out of sapphire-blue eyes identical to her own and said, "Wise? Probably not."

What was she to reply to that? Dane was going to be difficult, she realized. She mustered her argument. "You have a whole world of loyal, dependable associates and allies from here to the West Coast. What on earth can you be thinking, to simply drop them and go all the way to New York for someone we have never heard of?"

"In the first place—"

Vivian fortified herself against the amusement she heard in his voice.

"—the phone lines run all the way to the Atlantic now, so broadening our horizons a little doesn't mean I have to leave here and go to the big city. In the second place, those loyal, dependable allies aren't likely to be interested in sinking their capital into the same kind of projects Gaspar Adams specializes in."

The name sounded foreign, sophisticated, and very east-of-the-Mississippi to Vivian. She felt the situation slip a notch from her grasp. "Rightly so, I would say," she asserted. "Callicott investors do not appreciate taking chances with their money. You know what they think of the Highline, Dane." Now she was almost pleading, Vivian realized. She stiffened her spine and went on, "Callicott Properties has a reputation to uphold. Throwing that away on resorts and community redevelopment is unacceptable. Especially these days."

"I agree totally," he said in his smooth way.

"With which part?"

"I don't plan to ruin Callicott—either financially or reputationally. Is that a word, by the way? Reputationally. I may have to look that up."

"Dane Haldemar Callicott, you did not answer my question."

"What was it again?" He smiled blandly and kept his gaze steady on her face.

"Do you plan to go back to what Callicott is known for doing successfully, or are you expecting to use this Adams to support another unproven project like the Highline? You must admit I have reason to ask. I want to know why you are all of a sudden looking for money outside of our normal pool of investment capital." Vivian took a step closer and put her hand on his arm. "This worries me, Dane. The Highline will take a long time to recover from."

Dane looked at her hand but didn't pull away. "Are you so certain it's going to fail? Keep in mind, its distinctiveness is what drew Adams' attention in the first place." He held up a hand to stop her ready retort. "Don't worry, I'm not going to try for a repeat of the Highline Resort. It's a one-off."

Vivian wished she could believe him. She knew he would never lie to her outright, but with his ability to mince words he would have made a good lawyer. She eyed him. "Just what *do* you have as a prospect for this New Yorker?"

Mother's intuition pays off again, she thought triumphantly, as he flicked a quick look at the papers scattered across his desk. Vivian scanned the typewritten letters and document files, looking for an unfamiliar name, something out of the ordinary. She supposed later that was why her eyes passed twice over the little pad that Dane kept at his elbow for doodling on while he was on the telephone.

When she recognized the woman's face she had to remind herself to breathe. "Oh, Dane," she muttered unhappily under her breath. It was a sketch of Gail O'Neill. No more than half a dozen scratched lines from a pen, but enough to show the outward appearance of his ex-fiancée, if not the inward character. Dane had never seen Gail's true character.

She half reached for the paper but stopped herself. She had no need for a closer look. "You are not involving yourself with that woman again, are you? Tell me you have more sense than that."

He grinned, surprising her. "It's not what you're thinking." He looked fondly down at the pad that lay in the midst of the chaos on his father's desk.

But he was lying to her—or himself. It was exactly what Vivian was thinking. She was absolutely certain of that.

She knew her son better than to imagine he would have an affair with a married woman, no matter how much he believed himself in love with her. Gail O'Neill was in real estate, and her husband was in construction, and the two of them had been trying for years to entice Dane into working on a project with them.

Vivian was at first amazed that Claudia had not warned her, but a moment's reflection told her Claudia was undoubtedly ignorant about Gail. That was good. Dane's young, ambitious pursuer did not know her designated prey as well as she thought, after all.

"Dane," Vivian said.

He lifted his head, but his gaze did not quite meet hers.

"You cannot use some outsider's money to build Gail O'Neill whatever dream she is offering you in Tucson. I will not have it."

His eyes widened and locked with hers. He sank into his chair, forgetting that she was still standing. "It's not like that. It's a feasible project."

She began to pace upon the carpet in front of his desk, from door to window and back again. Her mind was putting together the rest of the pieces. She halted and faced him. "Another resort. How could you, Dane?"

Warily he replied, "Not an unproved one this time. This place has a lot of history behind it."

"A resort and redevelopment, then," she said in disgust. She watched as her beloved son, so much like his father in appearance but not at all in nature, rubbed his forehead as though the conversation was giving him a headache.

Pacing again, she reminded him, "Callicott did not make its reputation by putting up pretty buildings that serve no purpose beyond temporarily housing tourists." Anything based on the tourist industry was too risky, with the economy not yet in recovery. She stopped and swung around, then planted both hands on the desk. "Your grandfather saw that the potential lay in commercial and industrial properties. How can you justify another resort project without first seeing how the Highline does financially?"

"I'm asking you to have a little faith. I know Tank and his cohorts haven't held back their criticisms." His eyes did not drop from hers even when she narrowed hers in warning upon hearing that hateful nickname. "The old way of doing business may have worked for my grandfather and my father, but it can't continue indefinitely. For one thing, they're not making any more land."

"This is no laughing matter," she said in response to the old joke.

"Of course not. It never is, with you." He rose to his feet and bent toward her until they were nearly nose to nose. "Everything has to be 'What would your father have done?' Why didn't you remarry and move on with your life instead of making the company the be-all and end-all of your existence?"

Vivian slapped him. As he reared back in shock, she pressed both hands to her cheeks. Heat erupted along her nerve endings, and then she went cold. She extended a hand beseechingly. "I'm sorry, Dane. I'm sorry. I didn't mean to . . ."

"No, it was—" Dane shrugged, but one shoulder, on the side she had struck, lifted higher, as if to belatedly protect him from the blow. "I shouldn't have said that. I just think you would be happier if you had something besides Callicott Properties to worry about."

"There's you," she ventured.

The look he threw her made her feel even more frozen inside. She had hit her son, she thought. How could she have done such a thing? It was the provocation of knowing that he wanted to involve East Coast money in her company. "I don't want to argue."

He managed a smile. His lips were thin and the expression failed to warm his blue eyes, but it was meant to be reassuring. She latched onto that thought.

"Of course not. Neither do I," he said.

Vivian forced herself back to the real issue. "This resort. It is in Tucson, I assume?"

His smile vanished. He nodded.

"That makes it a two-hour drive, at least. Who do you think is going to manage things up here while you spend your time dealing with the inevitable problems there?"

"Alex. He doesn't have enough to do anyway."

Vivian flinched. If Dane ever found out she and Claudia made sure the Garcia boy had plenty of free time on his hands, she would never hear the end of it. She turned away, staring blindly out the window. "Well, certainly he is capable enough," she allowed, inserting enough doubt in her voice to imply the opposite, "but he is not the one people call when they need something done."

"They ought to."

She looked sharply back over her shoulder. Dane had propped one hip against his desk.

He continued, "Alex is much better with all this business stuff than I am, you know. I think it comes to him naturally, and then of course he has the MBA to back it up. Besides, he likes it."

Vivian was taken back by the wistfulness in her son's voice as he talked of his friend. It was not envy, although he was undoubtedly right in believing that Alex Garcia had an innate talent, which seemed to be missing from Dane's Callicott genes. The thought occurred to her that seeing how the Garcia boy liked what he did was what made Dane sound almost sad. She turned to face her son, willing him to look at her. "That may be, but we cannot all do what we want."

"I know." Dane twisted the heel of one shoe on the carpet and eyed the toe with practiced disinterest.

"Dane . . ." She trailed off, uncertain of what she could tell him. She decided there was nothing she could say, so she focused on the main point. "This thing with the O'Neills, I won't have it. You are not going to a stranger for capital, and you are not doing another resort, and you are not getting yourself tied up in another community redevelopment mess, and you are not giving any more authority to that Mexican boy." She found herself talking faster and louder, and still he ignored her until the end, when she pushed as far as she dared.

He glared at her. "Don't be racist, Mother."

"You know I am nothing of the sort. But no one will accept a Garcia in this town. I cannot allow him that much control over my company."

"I thought it was my company!" he exploded. "You dragged me into it ten years ago and shoved it down my throat and made me take it over. If you think I've done such a piss-poor job of it, why don't you just do it yourself!"

"There is no need to be crude." Vivian did sympathize with him, though she didn't know how to tell him so, without encouraging him to think things could be different. "I think you have done a marvelous job of it. Overall, that is," she added carefully. "For myself, I even like the Highline well enough. It is—" She cast around for a diplomatic way to phrase her opinion. "It's unusual, and I can see where it would catch some people's attention. But easterners have no understanding of how business is done out here, Dane." She moved closer and laid her hand on his arm. "You already know who you can trust." She squeezed gently.

As he glanced at the pad beside him on the desk, she knew she would not have to remind him of Gail's betrayal. He reached up a hand to toy with one of the buttons on his subtly striped shirt but made no other response.

"The board of directors is behind you," she told him, dropping her voice to a gentle murmur. "Your investors will come around soon enough. You certainly know I will support you, one hundred percent. All you have to do is go back to what Callicott is good at."

"You really think that's all?" He twisted at the button. "Didn't you pay attention to anything Lyssa said to Tank the other night?"

At the mention of the girl's name, Vivian tensed. She had briefly forgotten that particular thorn in her side. "Miss Smith has nothing to say that I find to be of any significance," she declared. She found herself digging her fingers into Dane's shirtsleeve and pulled her hand away.

"You should. The world has changed, and Callicott Properties has to change, too. Maybe the Highline was a mistake. Maybe it's too much, too soon. But strip malls and industrial parks are a thing of the past."

Vivian crossed her arms and stared back at her son. "That is not what I am advocating, and you know it. There are other ways of— well, anyway, I would not expect Lyssa Smith, of all people, to advise you to throw away your own history. Callicott has traditions. Change merely for the sake of change—"

He interrupted her savagely. "Is that what you think I'm doing?"

"I have no idea what you are doing, Dane. You never tell me anything. You leave me to find it out on my own. After the fact."

The telephone rang, ending their standoff.

"I have to get this," he said. "It's probably a call from New York. Adams was going to check his schedule and get back to me to set up a conference call."

"Then you *are* going through with it? Over my protest?"

"I was hoping for your support." He walked around the desk and seated himself, picking up the headset telephone that Claudia Montgomery had recently convinced him to use. "Callicott."

The high-tech device enhanced his executive look. Vivian supposed that was a large part of its appeal as far as Claudia was concerned. Dane was oblivious to nuances like that. Nor was he interested in the modern technological tools of business generally. His computer monitor sat on a small table behind him, under his father's picture, screen saver running because Claudia had turned the machine on for him and he had undoubtedly not touched it since. Vivian knew more about computers and conference calls and e-mail than her son, who had the nerve to lecture her about keeping up with change in how business was done.

She supposed he liked the fancy telephone, or at least used it, because it left both his hands free. She watched Dane fumble through the papers to find a pen. As he talked, he absentmindedly pulled the notepad closer and started to mark over Gail's face. She wondered if he even noticed.

I was hoping for your support, he had said. Vivian's heart started beating again, replacing her temporary numbness almost painfully, like the pins and needles that rushed into fingers and forearm after a bump to one's funny-bone. That was exactly what she had experienced, she thought—just a bump.

And yet Vivian felt the throbbing of blood in her head, in her fingertips, all the way to her toes in her special-order pumps. *I'm doing this for you!* she wanted to scream. Whether he believed it or not, Dane was more important to her than the company. But she also knew that Dane *was* the company. What threatened the one would ruin the other.

How could he not understand that?

Vivian loved her son, but by no means did she think he was perfect. Growing up, he used to lapse into daydreams and fanciful musings from which he would emerge with stories or pictures that made no sense to her or Stewart. Although he had eventually outgrown that foolishness, still there were parts of his nature that his mother could not comprehend.

She left his office with as little ceremony as she had entered.

She could do nothing about Gaspar Adams or the Tucson resort project right away; to change Dane's mind about either one of those problems would require time, information, and a great deal of focused attention from her. Alex Garcia was another complication. The company would need him if she couldn't shift Dane away from his plans. As for Gail, Vivian had been trying to oust her from Dane's life for a decade, but the woman was like one of those creatures in a horror movie that would not stay dead.

About all Vivian could think to do right now was get rid of Lyssa Smith. The Tucson project sounded as if it would require a thorough land-history report. Getting rid of Dane's preferred researcher would force a brief delay, at least. Besides, the girl was a dangerous influence on Dane.

And she had upset Thomas at the reception.

Thomas Turnbull had been Vivian's first suitor, before Stewart had come into her life and swept her off her feet with his tall good looks and determined courtship. He had remained a faithful friend, an undemanding companion in the lonely years since her husband's death. Vivian felt a loyalty toward him that she would never admit. She might have turned down Thomas's proposals throughout her long widowhood, but still she did not like to see him hurt.

She wanted to tell Dane that the reason she could not remarry had nothing to do with the company and everything to do with the fact that no one could ever replace Stewart in her heart—but that was none of his damned business.

"Mrs. Callicott?"

"What is it now!" Vivian whirled on Claudia Montgomery.

"N-nothing. I just wondered if you were feeling all right. You look a little flushed."

Vivian surveyed her, from the top of her platinum chignon to the swell of carefully bought assets at the edge of a lacy camisole. She bit back a vicious urge to say, *Well, dearie, you look a little pale.* "It must be from the surprise of learning that Dane is charging into this next endeavor as a favor to his ex-fiancée."

Claudia blanched. The only color left on her face was from the delicate sweep of rouge, as artificial as her breasts and eyebrows.

"You could have warned me he's been talking to the O'Neills,"

Vivian continued, twisting the verbal knife. "But maybe you were unaware of their relationship. It has been a few years since his last go-round with her." Without waiting for Claudia's reaction, she returned to her own office just down the hall.

Vivian walked over to her long, sleek Art Deco desk and sat down. She reached out to turn on her monitor, then typed in her password. While her desktop loaded, she pulled her fine gold-trimmed half-glasses from the center drawer and put them on. She composed the first part of the letter in her head.

> *Due to Lyssa Smith's tendency toward indiscretion, I must insist that she be removed from access to all information concerning Callicott Properties, Inc. Nor, from this date forward, will Callicott accept any reports or opinions bearing her name or for which she performed research or had any involvement whatsoever.*

That might not be enough to get the girl fired, though it would certainly make Simon Levitt question the wisdom of keeping her in his employ. Vivian supposed Dane would be furious. But by the time the truth came out, it would be too late for him to salvage any kind of business relationship with Lyssa Smith—and certainly would put paid to any personal relationship Miss Smith might have been hoping for. If the girl had half as much backbone as she had indicated by standing up to Thomas at the reception, she would not readily forgive being made a pawn in this game between mother and son.

Vivian adjusted the glasses upon her nose, tilted her head back until the screen was in focus, and began the process of getting rid of the simplest problem among the many that currently plagued her.

Five

LYSSA HAD BARELY ENTERED her tiny studio apartment and closed the door behind her when she heard three sharp raps on the battered weirdwood. She hesitated, then sighed. So much for taking the next few hours to prepare for her job interview cum dinner date with Dane. After carefully draping her new dress across the sagging couch cushions, she went to see what Paulina wanted.

She opened the door and, as she had expected, found her neighbor there, cane uplifted to knock again. "How do you do that?" she demanded in mild exasperation. "I just came in ten seconds ago."

Paulina blinked hazy dark eyes behind her thick trifocals. "It's a gift." She lowered the cane. "You're home early."

Lyssa mentally crossed her fingers, hoping to be able to get back to her vital preparations if she got rid of Paulina quickly and without admitting she had plans for the evening. "I had some errands to run," she said airily. "Today was my usual day in the Gov-Docs archives, so I was just up the street."

"You're in luck. Ball game's still on."

"Oh." Lyssa had forgotten the Diamondbacks were scheduled to play. She liked baseball and enjoyed sharing the games with Paulina—not that watching was as much fun as playing, for a former softball catcher. "Sure, why not? But only for a few minutes."

"Oh? Got a hot date tonight?" Paulina chuckled.

"Very funny. Ha-ha." Lyssa figured she had to give some reason; her neighbor would latch her gums into the subject and not let go. "I do have to go out later. A business meeting."

"Business! Girl, when are you going to tell those stiffs you work for to go piss up a rope? Come on, the commercials must be about over by now."

Lyssa stepped out, closed her door, and followed Paulina into the apartment across the hall.

The frail woman threw a glance at the television and saw that the ads were still running. "Damn. New pitcher," she explained. She hobbled to the refrigerator, with Lyssa close behind, and took a carton of chocolate cherry Bordeaux ice cream from the freezer. Paulina handed it to her with a wink. "A little something to take the edge off."

Together they said, "Always eat dessert first."

Paulina nodded. "Particularly when you have a business meeting. Lord knows there's never anything edible at those." She led the way past the coffee table to the couch.

As she sat, Lyssa ignored the question in her friend's voice. "I imagine you're right." She filled her mouth with her favorite ice cream.

The opposing team's new pitcher threw a slider that went wide of the plate. Paulina gave a satisfied snort and asked, keeping her eyes glued to the screen, "So, what did they do to you today?"

"Nothing." Lyssa frowned. She tucked her feet under her on the couch and waved her ice-cream spoon toward Paulina. "That's what's so strange. I know Simon must be upset about that thing with Turnbull, but he hasn't said anything about it. We just talked about my upcoming promotion." Lyssa almost wondered whether Dane had called and put a bug in Simon's ear. But would he do that for her, unasked?

"You say he doesn't like to be put on the spot. The wuss."

"Barb is positively gloating, though. That's always a bad sign."

But Paulina was done listening. "Yeah! Attaboy!"

The Diamondbacks had a man on first, though Lyssa couldn't have said who it was or how he had gotten there. Lyssa thought she probably should just leave. She didn't have the mental energy to devote to fun.

Her neighbor looked away from the TV and lifted her chin to bring Lyssa into focus. Her eyes glinted behind the heavy lenses. "I told you last year to quit that job. They're always on you for something. It's like you're not supposed to have a personal life." She shook her head, and the flesh under her chin wobbled. "Not that you do anyway. When's the last time you went on a date? I worry about you sometimes, girl."

Lyssa cast the gray-haired woman a suspicious glance.

"Well?" Paulina asked. "We're talking here."

"You're talking nonsense, is what you're talking. I want to vent about my job, which stinks, and you get off on the subject of my personal life."

"Yeah, but ain't that what bothers you about Clearview? That they won't allow you to have any opinions of your own, particularly when that means calling a spade an effing shovel?"

"Why do I tell you these things?" she asked rhetorically. "You have a memory like an elephant. Watch the game." She pointed her spoon at the television.

"Because I'm a nosy, meddlesome old woman." Paulina laughed. "And because you have a tendency toward rescuing those in need." She glanced around the room, hung with the overflow of plants Lyssa acquired from the college students who came and went every few years in adjacent apartments. "Plants, animals, people. You know I'd be lonely if you didn't take pity on me."

Lyssa hunched her shoulders. She had never told Paulina about her plans for the future. This seemed to her as good a time as any to prepare the old dear for the idea that Lyssa could not stand to live in town forever. "About that—" she began.

"Did you see that hit?"

"No, I missed it. Paulina, I need to tell you—"

"Double to right field! Whoo-ee. Two runs on that one." Paulina pumped her free hand with the remote in a victory salute as the second runner beat the throw to the plate. Then she refocused on Lyssa. "Sorry, what were you saying?"

Lyssa blinked and gazed at the images flickering across the screen. "Two runs scored on a double? I didn't know they even had another guy on base." She shook her head. Now the pitching coach was striding toward the mound. Lyssa wondered why she pretended to watch the game. She hadn't even checked the score. "You know, I really ought to go. I need to—"

Then she sat bolt upright on the couch, squashing the small ice cream carton in one hand as she grabbed, too late, for the remote that Paulina held. "Whoa!" she exclaimed. "Did you see that?"

She'd spotted a familiar face as the camera panned across the spectators in the ballpark. It was Dane, laughing, with a dark-haired woman seated beside him.

Paulina held it out of her reach. "No sound. I'm too old to spend my last few years listening to a bunch of numb-nuts spouting statistics."

"I wasn't going to turn it up. I just—" But the scene had long since vanished, and the remote wouldn't have done her any good anyway. Lamely she concluded, "I know that guy."

"What guy?"

"He was sitting in the stands. Behind the plate. The camera just went past him, and—" Lyssa slumped back against the overstuffed couch cushions. "Never mind."

Paulina looked appalled. "Let me get this straight. You know a guy who could have taken you to BOB tonight? With seats behind the plate? And you're sitting here with me eating ice cream? What is wrong with you, girl!"

"There's nothing wrong with me," Lyssa muttered. "It's not Bank One Ballpark anymore. They keep changing the names. You can keep all the stats in your head, but you can't remember what they call the field?"

Paulina jabbed the remote at her. "Think about it. Those are big-bucks seats. Postseason, at that!"

"It's a business write-off, I'm sure."

"Better and better. So, what's this guy's name?"

"That was Dane Callicott."

"Leave it to you." Paulina rolled her eyes, magnified behind the split lenses. "You find a guy who likes baseball and has both money and the good sense to write off his amusements as business expenses, and what do you do? You spoil his party. Way to tick off the man, Lyssa."

"I did no such thing, and he is not ticked at me. In fact, he's—" She caught herself before admitting he'd badgered her into going out with him. "He's the one who arranged tonight's . . . meeting. Not to yell at me, either. To talk about a job."

"Really? What do you want another job for? Marry this guy and get yourself set for life before Barb Pearce fires your ass."

Lyssa choked on her ice cream. She dropped the spoon and carton on the coffee table as she coughed. When she regained her breath, she demanded, "Where did that come from?"

"What?" Paulina gazed placidly back at her. "The thing about Barb? You told me yourself, she gave you a warning."

"It's not her decision."

"You say the big boss won't sneeze without her permission."

"I don't—" Lyssa stopped, not liking to even think about Simon's increasing reliance on Barb Pearce. "I'm a darn good employee. I do my job, I do it well, and I do it on time with a minimum of fuss."

"Yes, but . . ."

"But what?"

"You struck at a powerful man's pride, and you did it in public. I've got three grown sons, Lyssa. I know what men do when they're in that kind of mood, the big babies." She put one of her cold, gnarled hands on Lyssa's. "If you're not careful, you'll find yourself without any job."

"At least you'd never have to listen to me bitch about Clearview again."

"You wouldn't need a job if you had a rich husband to take care of you."

"That's crazy! Where would you get the idea that I'm looking to get married? Much less that I would consider marrying for money!"

"It's as easy to love a rich man as a poor one, they say," Paulina advised with a knowing look. "Especially for someone as fixated on money as you are."

"Someone as . . . what?" Lyssa burst out in disbelief. "Did you say I'm fixated on money?"

"That's right. Not that I'd blame you for looking out for yourself for a change, not after all these years of living like a pauper."

Lyssa clasped her hands together in her lap to keep from tearing out fistfuls of hair. "I am fiscally conservative."

Paulina snorted. "Dearie, you're so tight, you squeak. With an education like yours, you must be making damn good money. Not that anybody would ever guess, to look at the way you live. You drive a broken-down wreck, you dress like a bag lady, and you live in a dump like this!"

"You live in a dump like this!" Lyssa retaliated.

"That's right." Paulina fixed her with a pointed look. "Because neither of the lazy-ass bums I married had any ambition. I don't know what you do with your paycheck, but you need to either see somebody about your problem or marry into money."

"My problem?" Lyssa squeaked. She gathered herself together, determined to get out of there before she flamed up and said something that neither of them would ever forgive—or forget. "Gee, look at the time," she said, without so much as a glance at her watch. "I have to go. Let me know tomorrow how the game ends."

In a moment she was out the door and halfway to the security of her own place. Paulina had ruined everything, she fumed as she flung open her door and strode in.

She was not mercenary, and she had no problem with money, other than the fact that she still didn't have quite enough. She'd been scrimping and saving ever since college, but not for herself. No, it was to make sure her parents' neighbor could never exercise his legal right to sell their water rights out from under them. She had to have enough cash to buy out Don Jacobson, enough to convince the man—who, unlike her, was genuinely tight with his money—that he would be better off selling to her than trying to put the squeeze on her parents. And then she had to have enough to establish her mail-order herb business right there on Jacobson's property; that dream had kept her going through all these years of being a country girl transplanted into the big city.

She came to a halt at the couch and stared down at the teal-blue silky material laid out against the coarse tweed of the cushions. A city-girl's dress. Intended to look expensive and stylish—even though it had cost her hardly anything. This dress, only the second one she'd owned in her life, had come not from a thrift store but off the clearance rack at a resale boutique.

If Lyssa wore it tonight, would it make her as false and shallow as Paulina evidently thought her? Her elderly neighbor had planted an insidious seed, Lyssa realized.

How could she wear the pretty dress without wondering whether she bought it to be attractive for Dane, rather than as job-hunting clothes? How could she prepare to see him as a prospective employer rather than a prospective mate and plan out what to say and how to react? And how could she meet this woman—who must be one of his "friends" from Tucson—knowing how shocked she had been to see him with someone else?

Someone else, she scoffed, which implied that Lyssa was *a* someone to him, which was not something he'd ever hinted at. "Blast!" she exclaimed into the silence of her cramped apartment. How was she supposed to face Dane with all these thoughts running around like mice feet in her brain?

DANE LEANED against the door of his beloved Boxster S and watched as Mike and Gail walked away. Mike's left arm hung loosely around his wife's waist as they made their way through the parking lot toward their own vehicle. They would go back to the hotel together, change clothes together—get naked together—and together meet Dane and Lyssa at Anton's in a little while.

Noticing a tightness in his chest, Dane tried to breathe deeply through it. The upper buttons of his shirt strained uncomfortably in their hand-tailored holes. He wished he'd worn a polo shirt, as Alex had. Something to give him some breathing room.

He asked, "So, what do you think?"

Alex was the only one he trusted to tell him whether the Spirit Ranch property in Tucson might be a suitable prospect or, as his mother seemed to think, a disaster worse than the Highline. As he waited for the answer, he found himself rubbing his fingers over his stomach even though it wasn't churning at the moment. He shoved his hands in his pocket to keep them still.

"I don't know." Alex shrugged, a restless, uneven movement of his shoulders in the Prussian-blue knit shirt. "The photos helped some, but I don't have a good sense of what needs to be done. Are we talking restoration, renovation, or razing the buildings and starting over?" His face took on the look of a granite block, solid and immovable. "I wish Gail had let Mike talk more about the specifics. I'd like to know what he thinks needs to be done."

Dane didn't like the implied criticism. "The thing is, she knows the market."

"Is that the thing, Dane?" Alex smirked but didn't renew their old argument about Dane's ex. "She knows some aspects of the local real estate market down in Tucson, I'll grant you that. But as far as picturing how you might be able to turn that tumbledown mess into a nationally known destination spot—like it was in its prime—no. Not Gail. I think you're the only one who has that kind of imagination."

"I see."

"No, you don't. I don't know how to advise you, Dane, about the Spirit Ranch project, except—be careful how deep you get into this one until you've had a chance to check out the land history, the title, any constraints the city might place on the use of the property . . . You know the drill."

Dane felt the pressure in his midsection rise, and his head began to throb. Not badly, just a warning, he thought. "You think I have some reason to be suspicious of Gail and Mike? Be careful, Alex."

Alex shook his head. "Loyalty to old friends is a good thing. It speaks well of you. Just don't let it blind you to the business end. Gail is a salesman. She knows how to present properties in the best light. Mike, now, he's more like me. Somebody has to be practical. But not you. You're the dreamer."

Dane didn't feel like much of a dreamer anymore. Even after seeing the photos he didn't have a sense of what the Spirit Ranch might look like when it was done.

With the Highline, the end result had been clear in his mind from the beginning—at least, he corrected himself, as soon as Lyssa had suggested siting the resort along the Highline Canal. The canal had been in place in one form or another for a thousand years, which led him at the outset to think about the connections with history, with the ancient Hohokam culture that thrived in the desert so long ago.

Briefly he considered focusing on the historical aspects of the Spirit Ranch for his inspiration. That notion naturally made him think of Lyssa. She could make it all come alive in his mind: what the flavor of the place had been; who had visited and why; how the Spirit Ranch managed to retain its appeal to wealthy easterners for several decades after most dude ranches in the region vanished.

His headache intensified. After the lecture from his mother, he'd decided to limit Lyssa's association with this project. Tempting though the idea of jarring his mother had seemed in theory, in practice he lacked the stomach for it. Dane couldn't align himself too closely with Lyssa. To his mother, she had become the enemy, emblematic of every change that threatened Callicott Properties.

He realized, on meeting Alex's expectant gaze, that he'd lost the thread of the conversation. "I'll think about it," he said.

It must have been an adequate response, because Alex nodded in acceptance. "Don't let Gail talk you into anything definite at dinner tonight."

"I'm not planning to talk business after all," Dane admitted. They had dealt with most of the important aspects already, during the game. If Lyssa wasn't going to be deeply involved, there was no need to bring up the subject over dinner. "This is more a social visit than a pitch. It will be Gail's—and Mike's—first look at the Highline, since they had to miss the reception."

"Right. So you're taking them to Anton's? That was a good move, Dane, to talk Anton into starting a second location at the Highline."

"I thought so." And had been proud of himself for it: if anything made the Highline last out the first year or two, it would be the fine dining experience offered by one of the most temperamental head chefs in the city. "Do you want to come? Bring a date, and we'll make an evening of it."

"Some other time."

"Sure. Another time." Dane didn't press. He supposed his friend had had enough of Gail for one day. The two of them had never gotten along.

Dane admitted to himself that Gail's attitude toward him pinched at him a little. She seemed to believe he would jump at the opportunity she was offering, even if it meant putting his family business on the line. If Mike, who had a more level head on his shoulders, had not been there to back her up, Dane might have considered how to gracefully refuse the prospect.

But he neither refused nor accepted. Nor, despite the impression Dane had given his mother, had he given Adams a definitive answer even to the simple question of whether he was willing to go to New York for a meeting. Something held him back from a commitment to either end, the project or the money. This next step seemed like a turning point, from which Dane might very well find it impossible to go back.

He said goodbye to Alex, got in the Boxster, started it up, and took some antacids and aspirin out of the glove compartment while he waited for the convertible top to fold back. The antacids at least were chewables. The aspirin tablets he washed down with the putridly warm bottled water that had sat in the center console all afternoon.

He glanced at the clock. He had time before dinner to plan his strategy. Now that he was closer to the moment of reckoning, he wondered if it was a bad idea to bring Lyssa and Gail together.

Maybe he could delicately suggest that Lyssa be more cautious than usual in what she said and how she said it. He rejected that notion right away. Lyssa's honesty and directness were among her best qualities. It wouldn't be right to start making her over just to make tonight's dinner more comfortable for himself. Besides, he didn't want to make her feel self-conscious about that incident with Tank. Bad enough that it had colored his mother's opinion of her and, as a result, had caused Dane to change his own plans.

She hadn't wanted this dinner with him in the first place. He had no business even thinking about dictating how she would act during it. But still, it was tempting.

Six

WHEN LYSSA WALKED into Anton's at the Highline that evening beside Dane, she felt windblown and tattered and overheated—and happy. She had not been prepared to be picked up in a fancy convertible, but she might have guessed Dane Callicott would have an extraordinary car. The brief drive had been fantastic, although the buffeting wind had kept conversation to a minimum.

Not that Lyssa had minded. She'd waited at the front of her apartment building to prevent him from coming in for her and getting an up-close look at the worn linoleum and peeled, faded paint and cracked concrete. She remembered sliding into the tan, milkweed-soft leather passenger's seat, smoothing the black dress toward her knees, and turning to greet him.

He, of course, was polished and suave in dark olive slacks and a billowing gray green shirt. His gaze was drawn to the building, and his mouth set in a disapproving line. Then he looked at her. He smiled, a boyish, coaxing, I-always-get-my-way kind of smile. "This place looks like hell."

She'd expected something like that. "Great car."

He shook his head. "Okay, you don't want to talk about your family or where you live. I can take a hint." He started the car and slipped it into gear.

She had never ridden in anything like his dark green machine: smooth, fast, absolutely solid, and noisy from the resistance of the air and the country music blaring on the radio. At the stoplights he talked a little about the O'Neills, the people they were going to meet, but he said nothing about the Tucson resort project.

The main building of the Highline was lit from ground level by soft salmon-colored lights that made the walls seem to glow. Dane had turned his sexy car over to a valet and ushered Lyssa into the restaurant. It was smaller and cozier but resembled the adjacent ballroom in its contemporary southwestern colors and textures and furnishings.

As the hostess escorted them toward a table set for four, Lyssa saw an unfamiliar woman, not the fresh-faced, dimpled brunette she'd expected from the TV broadcast of the ball game. But a closer look proved that Gail O'Neill was, in fact, the same person, merely a plastic version in a purplish rose ruffly dress, with sophisticated makeup changing the contours of her face and her hair fluffed and styled.

Lyssa's hand crept to one of her own tangled curls. Her hair, held back from her face at the beginning of the trip by a black scrunchie, had worked free and now hung in Medusa-like masses.

Then she thought about the black linen slouchy jacket she'd tossed on over her dress, and her hand dropped to tug surreptitiously at the hem, which had a tendency to fall unevenly. Lyssa had thought the jacket would make her look more professional. She now regretted the decision, both because the extra covering added to the hectic color she felt in her cheeks and because she was certain she looked sloppy next to the carefully pressed and buffed brunette.

The couple stood to greet them. Mike O'Neill was wiry, his blunt-fingered hands and open, honest face weathered.

Dane shook the man's hand. "Mike! You had no trouble finding the place, I see." He hugged the tiny woman and kept one arm around her shoulders while he stepped back far enough to admire her. "Gail, you look wonderful." He pressed a kiss to her forehead.

Lyssa felt like a hulking crow next to a dainty little finch. She noted that Gail had a habit of dimpling up at Dane while he was looking at her but a disconcerting way of staring assessingly at Lyssa when his attention drifted elsewhere.

"So, what do you think of the Highline?" Dane asked of Mike at the same time Gail leaned toward Lyssa and said, "Lisa, is it?"

"Lyssa," she corrected. Gail's eyes—an odd light brown, almost yellow, she observed—bore into her.

"Of course. How unusual. But I'm sure you've heard that before."

Mike cleared his throat and said, "So, Dane, if we're not getting special treatment just because we're friends of yours, I'd say you have a gold mine here. The staff treated us like royalty when we checked in. It's got appeal, that's for sure. Think you can do the same kind of thing with the Spirit Ranch?"

"Let's not talk about that," Dane put in smoothly. "I've had enough of business this afternoon. Haven't you?" He gazed at Gail and smiled.

Lyssa set her back teeth. So much for her plan to appear professional and efficient and employable tonight, she thought. *"Come to dinner on Wednesday with my friends from Tucson,"* Dane had said. *"They'll fill us in on the details."* What was he doing?

"I agree entirely," said Gail. "How thoughtful of you." Her husband laughed, and she batted her eyes at him. "Don't let's talk business at all tonight. This afternoon was plenty for me."

"I might believe that if I didn't know you so well, love." Mike reached over to touch her hand.

Dane eyed them without expression.

Lyssa picked up the menu that lay in front of her and scanned it. When no one said anything she asked, "So was it talk of business or the game that was plenty for you, Gail?"

"The game?" the other woman asked, flicking a glance toward Dane.

The selection was much the same as at the original Anton's, Lyssa noted, and she decided on baked trout with her favorite chipotle cream sauce. "I saw you in the stands when the camera passed over the section behind the plate. You seemed to be enjoying yourself well enough." She put down the menu.

"I don't care much for baseball, as a rule." Gail dimpled at Dane. "But Dane insists on taking us out to the ball game, just like old times, whenever we come up during the season."

Despite her better judgment, driven by a deplorable sense of curiosity, Lyssa persisted. "For someone who doesn't care much for baseball, you seemed to be having a swell old time."

"Of course, if you were watching, you must be a fan." Gail's voice held a hint of disdain. "I've always considered baseball rather plebeian. And, of course, sports are so unfeminine."

Mike and Dane looked at each other with lifted brows.

"Then why do you go?" Lyssa asked.

Gail smiled. Her teeth were perfect. "Dane would be disappointed if we didn't. It's a tradition. He never played in college, but Mike did, and Dane and I always sat up in the stands together. Now, my son Kyle plays ball. He's just like his daddy."

Dane stirred in his heavy wooden chair.

Mike said, "Dane and Lyssa don't want to hear about Kyle, dear."

"But we're Dane's second family. Of course he's interested. Aren't you, Dane?"

"You know I am."

Lyssa decided that Dane was either a very good liar or a masochist. He had delivered that reassurance with every appearance of sincerity. "A second family. How interesting." Lyssa reached for one of the herb rolls that had appeared on the table from the hands of an unobtrusive server.

"Children complicate things sometimes," Gail offered. "Like last week. We weren't able to come up for the Highline reception, because the babysitter got sick and we had no one to leave the boys with. I'm sure you know how that is, Lyssa. Or maybe you don't. Do you have any children?"

"No."

"No? Really." Gail stared wide-eyed at her as if she had said she was a serial killer. "Married?"

Lyssa broke the roll in half with a vicious twist. "Do you mean now, or ever?"

Dane choked on his water.

"Well, I assume you're not married now," Gail said. "Have you ever been?"

"No."

"Why, I was barely out of college when I—" She broke off, staring at her husband, who had gone very still.

Dane's hand clenched, white-knuckled, on his glass.

The petite brunette made a quick recovery. "So, are you one of these women who put her career first? You'll make time for family later?"

Lyssa hesitated before saying, "In a manner of speaking." It was the reverse, of course. She had to take care of her family—meaning her parents—first, and then she could work on her career. And maybe, at some point, the rest of her life.

"So what is it you do for a living?"

"Dane didn't tell you? I'm a land-history researcher."

"Oh, you're that one."

Lyssa did her best to ignore both the disparaging tone and the bird-of-prey eyes turned on her. "In fact, he said you would fill me in on this Tucson resort—"

Dane interrupted. "We should take business off the table entirely tonight." To Lyssa he explained, "Gail has a tendency to be a workaholic. She's one of the most successful real-estate agents in

Tucson. I thought we might make this trip more of a vacation for her."

Noting that Gail wore a cat-that-ate-the-canary expression, Lyssa commented, "A vacation where you talk business at the ball game but don't want to discuss it at the dinner table."

All three stared at her.

Then Gail laughed. "I'm sure it has nothing to do with you, Lisa, if that's what you're worried about."

Dane glanced at Gail but said nothing.

Lyssa didn't bother to correct the deliberate mispronunciation. She was here partly to prove to Dane that she could be around his kind of people and not make a scene. Fortunately, the arrival of the waiter kept Lyssa from having to come up with a polite response.

Dane ordered for all four of them. His surprise when she spoke to the waiter to change her entrée gave her no little satisfaction.

"You don't like chicken?" Dane asked with a lift of his eyebrow after the waiter had left. "Anton prepares it with a delicious herbed garlic sauce."

"I know." Most of the herbs were ones that she had planted and tended. Lyssa shrugged. "I prefer the trout."

"You've been here before?"

"The original location," she said calmly, "but yes, Dane, I'm probably as familiar with the menu as you are." His startled disbelief stung.

Granted, Anton's was woefully expensive, but she could have afforded it on occasion even if she didn't have an in with Anton himself. Then she recalled the shabby exterior of her apartment and backtracked mentally. The notion of her being a regular at a four-star restaurant probably seemed as unlikely as the possibility of him loading manure on her parents' farm seemed to her.

Once the waiter left, the conversation got rolling again, mostly between Dane and Mike. Lyssa discovered that the two men had worked construction together during the summer in their last few years of high school; she pictured the experience as boot camp for a soft-muscled rich kid. Dane's laughing protests couldn't stop Mike from describing how much difficulty the young Callicott had in trying to master a hammer, let alone a plasterer's trowel, and how their first concrete floor cracked straight through and needed to be redone by an irate foreman and crew. After Mike shared half a dozen or so similar episodes and Dane retaliated with his own stories, Lyssa began to enjoy herself.

Then Gail, who had sat listening with a preoccupied smile—the woman always seemed to be smiling—leaned toward Lyssa. "We'll just take a few minutes to get better acquainted while the men are talking about the past. It's really too bad of them to go on and on. So, tell me, if it's not a secret—Wherever did you get that dress? Such classic lines. They just don't make styles like that any more."

Involuntarily Lyssa glanced at Dane. She was not quite sure why Gail wanted to play alpha bitch, but that was unmistakably the setup he'd gotten her into. "I've had it for a while."

"I suppose it's a favorite?"

It's an only, she might have replied. But that was no longer true. Lyssa had another dress now but had chosen not to wear it. "I suppose it is."

Gail leaned closer and dropped her voice. "You don't like me very much, do you?" She eyed Lyssa expectantly and seemed a little disappointed by the lack of a response. "That's all right. I understand. Still, if you don't mind a little advice—"

Lyssa did mind. She fiddled with the knife, wishing it were sharper. To take a page from Papa Ari's philosophy, she reminded herself, this encounter was no more than a brief tangential meeting of her outermost soul-circle with Gail's: soon over and best forgotten. Although if going to work for Dane meant she would have to deal with Gail on the Tucson resort, the whole plan seemed much less palatable. And what did Gail O'Neill mean, that she understood? Understood what?

"You might want to invest a little more in your appearance. Dane has very fine taste, and high expectations."

Their soups and her salad arrived, so Lyssa didn't have to think of a reply. She toyed with the crisp greens coated lightly with walnut oil and wondered whether any of the ingredients were plants she'd hoed or weeded over the weekend while at her parents' farm. She'd been distracted by the incident with Tank, she knew that, but she couldn't remember now exactly what she had accomplished while waiting for Monday to come, to make sure she still had a job at Clearview.

Lyssa set down her fork. "About this resort."

Dane glanced at her. A small furrow appeared between his brows.

"Oh, can't we put that off until after dessert? This is supposed to be my downtime," Gail interrupted. After the men assured her that would be fine, she looked at Lyssa and her eyes flared in triumph.

If this was how it would go, Lyssa thought discussing the resort project with the O'Neills was a bad idea after all. Through the meal, she drank iced tea while the others had microbrew, and she listened to them convivially dredging up one story after another from their shared past. Something hot and hateful rose in her throat as she realized that time and again Gail would steer the conversation away from any subject Lyssa could participate in.

Finally Dane ordered mango sorbet for all of them. She liked Anton's sorbet, particularly with the tangy ginger citrus sauce he drizzled over it to cut the sweetness of the mango, so she didn't protest Dane's patronizing action. And the chill might take away the heat of her resentment.

"Time to visit the little girl's room," Gail announced.

Lyssa wondered briefly why the three of them were gazing expectantly at her, but then she figured out that she was supposed to go along. She had never understood the purpose of pairing up to go to the restroom, and as with the other parts of female culture that she didn't comprehend, she had made a practice of avoiding it. Stifling a sigh, she rose and laid her napkin neatly on the pale coral tablecloth, covering that unfortunately blunt knife.

She did learn one thing from Gail. The bathroom was where women went to war.

Gail pulled an amazing arsenal out of her envelope-sized purse: she touched up her brows and her lids and her cheeks and her lips and then tweaked out a recalcitrant hair that marred the shape of her expensive coiffure. Lyssa had a lipstick, but after she applied the subtle lip-colored tint she had nothing more to do but stand in aggrieved fascination and watch Gail at work.

Gail posed her face several times in the mirror. "Finished already?"

"That's right."

"I'm going to be honest with you."

Lyssa figured that would be a first.

"If I thought you had a snowball's chance in hell of keeping Dane's interest, or gaining his mother's approval, I would see you gone so fast it would make your head spin."

"Oh?" Lyssa wondered if this was going to turn into a knock-down drag-out catfight. She had never seen one, much less been in one, but Gail was working herself into a frenzy.

"Fortunately, you're too pathetic to waste my time on," Gail sneered. "Wearing an old dress like that to Anton's—I wonder the maitre d' didn't make you eat in the kitchen."

He might have, Lyssa thought, if he'd recognized her. She always ate in the kitchen at Anton's original location.

But the other woman wasn't finished. "And your hair, looking like you'd just tumbled out of bed. Dane might take you as a lover for a while"—although the scorn in her voice implied that she doubted it—"but he's never going to marry an overdone slut like you!"

Lyssa balled her hands into fists and wished she could use them on that made-up face. One punch to the nose, and all that expensive war paint would go to waste, she thought nastily.

Then she reminded herself that the insults were just words. She deliberately eased open her fists and slowed her breathing. She knew from long experience that insults could be allowed to hurt only if they came from someone important in one's life. She hated and despised Gail, and the feeling was mutual; that had been evident all evening.

She considered denying any interest in Dane but knew her protestations would be useless. A woman would have to be deaf, blind, and a blithering idiot not to have a few fantasies about herself and Dane Callicott. Lyssa was none of those things. She had noticed his attributes. She just wasn't in the market for a man. She decided that attack would be a better strategy than denial.

"He didn't choose to marry you, either," she said coolly.

"But he did!" Gail's triumph boiled off her. "We were engaged—until I decided I'd rather have Mike."

And that proves that Gail is insane, Lyssa thought. She found herself pinned by those predatory yellow eyes. "Are you finished?"

"Is that all you have to say?" Gail looked incredulous.

"Yes."

"My God. You just wait until Vivian Callicott is finished with you." Gail turned around and stalked from the room.

Lyssa scrubbed her hands over and over. The shock gradually receded. She finally stared at her pinkened skin and thought of Lady Macbeth. No amount of soap and friction would wash away the truth: Dane had been engaged to that uber-bitch. Lyssa dried off with the soft paper towels—no gas-station-quality recycled materials here—and dropped them through the round hole in the marble vanity top.

Dane smiled at her as she walked back to the table. The conversation stalled midsentence. She took her seat and tried not to feel too self-conscious.

Then Gail said, "You know, Dane, we aren't being fair to Lisa. She's obviously trying to be straightforward about her interest in this project. We owe her the same."

Mike grimaced. "Gail—"

"I'm always straightforward," Dane replied with his usual easy manner, but Lyssa noticed that his right hand plucked at the placket of his shirt.

"It's just that—" Gail switched her attention to Lyssa. "We feel it would be advisable to use a local company for the preliminary report and survey. Someone from Tucson," she clarified.

The chill of betrayal overtook Lyssa. She folded her arms and struggled to remain calm. "We?" She shot an accusing glare at Dane.

He threw up his hands, palms out, in a gesture of denial. "Don't include me in this. I haven't even committed to the project yet."

Gail's eyes didn't waver from Lyssa's. "Not to put too fine a point on it, Lisa, but your violation of the confidentiality agreement between Clearview and Thomas Turnbull is . . . Well, let's just say it's been a topic of conversation. We don't want our privileged information getting out. Certainly not in public like that. I'm sure you can't blame us. It's just business."

Dane's brows had pulled together, and he was opening his mouth— to utter more lies, Lyssa supposed. "You told them about what happened with Tank?" she demanded, rounding on him. "Is this how you decided to get your revenge? By embarrassing me in front of your friends?"

"I didn't tell them any such thing. Because it isn't true. But then, I wouldn't have to, would I? With such a dramatic scene, rumors like that are all over the state by now, I expect!" He closed his eyes and pinched the bridge of his nose, then rubbed a hand across his chest. "Now be quiet," he ordered, "and let me sort this out with Gail."

Turning toward her, he asked gently, "Now, Gail, you didn't mean to imply that *I* told you Lyssa wasn't to be trusted, did you?"

"Of course not!" Mascara-enhanced eyelashes fluttered up toward the penciled-in brows, and her forehead creased slightly. "But I can't recall who it was that told me. It must have been someone else who was there that night . . ." She raised one forefinger to her mouth, curving it below her lower lip as if she had to think. "I'm sorry, Dane," she said after a moment. "I didn't realize Lisa would take it so personally. The way I heard the story, it came across as quite funny."

"Her name is Lyssa." For the first time all evening, Dane's voice wasn't smooth and soft when he spoke to Gail O'Neill.

"Yes, of course." Gail blinked. Then she reached out and covered Dane's hand with both of hers. "But I thought—"

He seemed oblivious to the gesture. His brows drew together over his nose, and he looked dangerously pissed as he glared at Lyssa. "You still don't believe me, do you?"

Lyssa was still considering how carefully calculated Gail's *we*'s and *us*'s had been. "I don't know, Dane. Don't press me for an answer just now, all right?" Restless and confused, she pushed her heavy tangles of hair back over her shoulder. She had known in the restroom that Gail was setting her up for something. Maybe Dane hadn't actually agreed to exclude her. Maybe for once he was the one being manipulated.

She glanced at Mike, who was staring fixedly at his wife, white lines rimming his nostrils and lips. She moved on to Gail, who had withdrawn her hands from Dane and seemed puzzled by her husband's attitude. *Seemed* being the operative word, Lyssa thought. Little wifey was used to playing these two off against each other.

Then Lyssa looked at Dane. He was drawing patterns in the condensation on the outside of his water glass. She ran her tongue over her teeth and broke the silence. "Let's just finish dessert and call it an evening."

After a few minutes of stilted conversation, she found herself locked into Dane's car again with nothing between her and the stars on this balmy moonless evening. Windblown curls slapped her face and her eyes stung from the force of the air rushing past, but there was no Gail jabbing at her with hard, spiteful, goading words.

It was a short drive, and Dane soon pulled into the drive of her apartment parking lot. He stopped the car, put it in park, cut the engine, and pulled the keys out of the switch, all without saying a word.

Did he expect to be invited in? She moistened her dry lips. "Thank you for—" *a lovely evening?* She bit her tongue to quell the semihysterical laughter that welled up inside her. "A nice dinner," she finished. "And for the ride home." She fumbled for the door handle, unable to find it in the dark.

"I'm not leaving you to walk up from the parking lot in the middle of the night." His hands tightened on the steering wheel when she started to protest. "Damn it, Lyssa, this isn't the best of neighborhoods. Humor me."

"Fine." She was suddenly and unbearably exhausted. Nothing about this evening had worked out the way she had planned; what was the point in keeping Dane from seeing every last detail of how she lived? She pressed her curls back, running her fingers through them as best she could, and caught him watching her.

Abruptly he slipped from the driver's seat and came around the front of the car to open Lyssa's door. He offered his hand to help her out. When she was standing in the angle between the car's frame and the door, he bent his head and brushed his mouth across hers. He drew back quickly as if he had felt the same jolt she had.

Static electricity, Lyssa told herself, pressing her tingling lips together.

Dane brought his warm hands up to her face and tilted it an angle that seemed to suit him. He kissed her again.

Seven

DANE LOCKED HIS MUSCLES against the urge to seize. He wanted to drag Lyssa closer, draw her vitality through his skin into his very bones, deepen the kiss into what it promised. But he schooled himself to patience. This was neither the place nor the time.

Gently he moved her out of the way and closed the car door. He turned her toward the apartment. With the merest hint of pressure between her gracefully curved shoulder blades he overcame her momentary resistance. "Don't worry, I'm not about to pounce," he said, as much to remind himself as to reassure her.

As they neared the two-story apartment building, he observed with a grimace that his initial impression had been, if anything, overly generous. The place was beyond dilapidated, of similar age and condition to the buildings he'd had to tear down to make way for the Highline. He supposed it had a history, and Lyssa probably could recite that for him chapter and verse, but if it were his, he would have it condemned, razed, and hauled away, right down to the last cracked slump-block and crumbling chunk of mortar.

Then he had no inclination to think about his surroundings, because Lyssa was climbing the stairs in front of him. The bottom of her shapeless jacket hung crookedly upon swaying hips encased in black, and the night breeze seemed a few degrees warmer. He hurried up the last few stairs to her side so his eyes wouldn't lead him into temptation. His hand slid under the loose jacket almost of its own volition and pressed against her lower back as he threw her a bland smile and forced his pace to slow. Frightening her off was not a part of his plan.

The moment they were inside her apartment, Lyssa asked, "You want something to drink?"

He realized those were the first words she had spoken since they had left the car. "Coffee would be nice."

"I only have tea." She paused. "Herbal."

Dane suppressed the desire to refuse her offer. The few herbal teas he had tried tasted like grass clippings and hay. Still, her politeness would buy him some time to poke around and get to know her better. "That'll be fine."

While she busied herself in the kitchen, opening cupboard doors and rattling about in what he considered a vast amount of effort for so little return, he shoved his hands in his pockets and assessed her private space. The apartment was smaller than he would have expected. It did nothing to contradict his opinion of the unprepossessing exterior of the building, which was by location and appearance nothing more than downscale student housing. While he didn't know exactly how generously Simon Levitt compensated the Clearview employees, Lyssa was a well-educated professional with an advanced degree. Dane knew that she should be able to afford something far better than the worn, threadbare, rickety furniture that looked as if it had been purchased at a fire sale in 1960, placed within these walls decades ago, and never moved since.

Yet the room didn't lack charm. It was filled with primary colors and an air of opulence that derived from the jungle-thick foliage hanging from the ceiling and rising from nearly every flat spot. Velvety deep-pile rugs, throws, and pillows covered the avocado-green shag carpet and distracted the eye from the shabby upholstery of the furniture. A rainbow of painted storage boxes broke up the straight lines of walls and floor. Mismatched books in a panoply of colors filled a pair of bookshelves framed by two doors.

At first Dane assumed that one led to her bedroom, but then his mind started making calculations. The entrance to the adjacent apartment was not far down the hallway in that direction. Was it possible that she slept in this room, maybe on that couch, which looked as if several litters of dogs could have been born on it sometime during its disreputable past?

Lyssa interrupted his speculation. "So, why didn't you warn me that you and Gail were . . ." Her hand went up into the rich cinnabar curls, and he wanted to follow it, bury himself in it. After a momentary hesitation she finished, "Were a couple."

What had she intended to say? he wondered. Lovers? The possibility pleased him. If Lyssa was jealous, that would explain her subdued attitude in Gail's company. Of course, so could Gail's atypical behavior.

He strolled over to the breakfast bar and leaned on it, watching her from under the shallow overhead cupboard while he chose his words. "You picked up on that, did you?"

"It would have been hard to miss," she said dryly.

"Given the situation, there was no reason to talk about what's long over."

"The situation. You mean the business dinner that wasn't?" Her voice dripped with irony.

Dane refused to feel guilty. He had his reasons. "Right."

She opened the refrigerator and took out a small jar of what looked like milk. When she loaded up a wooden applicator with honey he realized what she was about.

"I usually take mine naked." Her head shot up, and he kicked himself mentally. "I mean, plain. But however you usually make it will be fine." He straightened and walked around the breakfast bar into the kitchen area.

Lyssa renewed her deft adulteration of the stuff. When she was finished she held out a mug that to Dane, not wanting it at all, looked to be about the size of a barrel. "Try it before you decide whether you like it or not. The calcium in the milk acts as a calmative."

"Thank you." Because she was watching, he took a cautious sip of the stuff. He was pleasantly surprised. It was much better than he had expected: smooth, rich, layered with subtle flavors.

"Why did you really invite me?"

"To dinner?" Dane looked up from his perusal of the pale, fragrant milky liquid and assumed his most innocent smile. "Is it so hard for you to imagine that a man would simply enjoy your company and want to spend more time with you?"

"It's hard for me to imagine that you would do anything without an ulterior motive."

Perhaps it was how near she came to the truth that shook his determination to go slowly with her, he thought. Or maybe it was the scorn in her voice.

He set down his mug on the breakfast bar and reached for her. The possessive surge that came over him as his mouth met hers was a shock, and he ended the kiss, then felt the loss.

"Do I need to ask if this is okay?" He eased toward her, nibbling and teasing and stroking until he could feel her heart racing under his fingers as they traced their way down her neck. Before he knew it, he had the softness of her breasts filling his hands, felt the heat of her through her shirt, smelled the apple-pie-and-cinnamon scent of her.

She cried out and twisted away. "Stop! Stop it!"

Dane let her go without uttering a protest.

He hadn't been with a woman for a long time. Hadn't felt the urge, at least not in a way that deserved acting upon. Until tonight he'd been tempted to blame his general lack of interest on stress. Or maturity. Even Claudia's revealing clothes and flirtatious manner in the office produced nothing more than admiration for the sheer artistry of her performance.

Lyssa, though . . . She stirred more than his blood. She created a tsunami of feelings and wishes.

She wrapped her arms protectively around herself and backed away, circling the counter to place it as a barrier between them.

"Why should we stop?" he asked reasonably enough. "That was pretty spectacular, you must admit."

"Stop it!" She put up a hand to ward him off, but he met it with his own.

Forcing back the primitive impulse to toss her over his shoulder and take her to his cave, he instead let his large hand and her smaller one rest together, palm to palm. "This is a perfectly normal attraction between us, man to woman. Don't be afraid of it. I want you, and I'm pretty sure you want me."

She met his gaze unflinchingly. "I don't."

"Don't try to tell me you didn't want that kiss." Dane heard the sharpness in his voice and softened it. "You were going right over the edge with me."

She had felt good against him. More than good. Right. The plains and hollows of her back, the curves and dips of womanly softness, her skin so velvety, textured with fine, minute hairs that rose along with goosebumps and shivers at every stroke of his fingers.

"I liked where we started out, I'll admit that," she confessed in a shaky voice. "But you're moving too fast for me. I can't do this." She dropped her hand away from his.

Dane studied her. She didn't seem afraid now. Embarrassed and upset, maybe, but certainly not terrified, not like she had been for an instant. So what had caused her to pull away, when a kiss and a little petting made them both go up in flames? "Why not? We're both adults here. Free to do what we please. Or . . . I am, at least. I just assumed . . . Is there some guy in the background?"

"Guy?" She laughed, but the sound was tight and strained.

"Somebody's got a claim on you?"

"A claim? Did you really just say that? My fathers told me about guys like you—"

Okay, she had not one father but two. Stepfamilies were common enough these days. The thought of two irate fathers coming after him with shotguns did cross his mind, though. Just how far from normal were the guys that she knew?

"Are we back to the 'normal guy' thing? Because if we are, let me assure you, Lyssa, this is pretty normal."

"I know what's normal. I'm talking about what's wise." Her eyes stayed fixed on his, although color tinged her honey-toned cheeks. "I've never done this before."

"Done what? Kissed a man?"

"That wasn't a kiss. That was . . . I mean . . . the whole hands thing." She gestured at her front.

"Hands thing? You expect me to believe that you've gotten to be thirty-odd years old—"

She muttered something incomprehensible.

"—and no man has ever touched you like this before? I'm supposed to think you're some kind of virgin?"

"Is there more than one kind?"

"Is that what you're saying?"

"Yes!"

Dane's hands were shaking. "Just my luck. I wind up standing here with a hard-on caused by the oldest living virgin in Phoenix." Dane realized that he was shouting, and her face had gone pale. "Why?"

"Why what?"

"Why are you still a virgin?"

"I've been saving myself for the right man." Lyssa sounded absolutely certain of herself. "For marriage."

Dane forced his hands into fists at his side to keep from reaching out and grabbing her. "How will you know?" His voice was hoarse.

She understood what he was asking; he could tell that by the way her stubborn chin lifted another notch.

"I will love him more than anything in the world, and he will love me just the same," she vowed.

He pictured her as a wife to someone else, bearing another man's children, fading into domesticity. That wasn't what she was meant for. He had always envisioned Lyssa as a modern-day Athena, a warrior-goddess all passion and fire, larger than life. One of those magnificent females captured in classical Greek sculpture that had fired his artistic passions as a younger man. "You need a ring on your finger before you'll come through with the whole package?"

"That is such a repulsive way of putting it." Bristling with hostility, Lyssa tossed her wind-tangled curls and placed her hands on her hips. "It's not the ring that's important, it's the relationship. The emotions. I want a man whose life would be empty without me."

He shook his head in disbelief. He could never love a woman that much. Even Gail's defection had been upsetting more because of its unexpectedness and the betrayal of his trust than because she left a hole in his life with her absence. *Of course, she isn't really absent, is she?* he thought. *You still see her whenever you need to.*

"I want a man who would go to the ends of the earth for me, who would give up everything he owned for me, who would make my happiness his mission in life," she vowed. Her voice shook with intensity.

Dane folded his arms. "And what would you give him?"

"The same things." Lyssa took a step that brought her toe to toe with him. She stabbed her finger toward his chest. This time he was the one to retreat. "I would go to the ends of the earth for him. I would give up everything. I would set his happiness before my own."

"You'll have a hell of a long wait in your virginal state if you insist on those conditions. What you're looking for doesn't exist, except in storybook ever-afters."

She lifted her chin pugnaciously. "It does. My parents have it."

"If you've got two fathers, they must have gone wrong somewhere. You little idiot, your naive innocence makes you fair game for some guy—a whole lot less honest than I am—who's willing to say anything, do anything, to hop into bed with you and take your precious virginity." He took a perverse pleasure in seeing her flinch. "No man is going to marry a woman without trying her on for size first."

"Like a pair of slacks, you mean?"

"If she doesn't please him in bed, what's the point?"

"Is that what you want in a wife? A woman with experience? One who's been in and out of more beds than you have? That's not a wife. That's a playmate."

Her scornful tone infuriated him. "I'm not looking for a wife. But if I was, I'd want someone who wasn't holding out for a ring and a name and half my worldly property before giving of herself."

"I suppose it's an improvement that now you just sound paranoid instead of like a jerk. Is it so hard for you to imagine that a woman could love you and still 'hold out' on you because she has some respect for herself?"

"Respect? Is that what you call it? Or is it that you're afraid of letting go of your childhood and growing up? Because a grown woman isn't afraid of sex, Lyssa. She doesn't faint away when a man puts his hands on her front."

"I didn't faint! And you didn't just have your hands"—she gestured at the area in question—"there, you were all over me!"

"News flash. If you ever do find this mythical perfect man and convince him to marry you, he'll want more than I just asked for."

Her lovely, wide mouth tightened. "I know that. But you didn't ask. You moved in and took."

"Point to you. See, Lyssa, we can talk about this like adults." He watched the passion of battle begin to subside in her. Although he regretted seeing it go, knowing that such fire and intensity lurked in the depths of her soul made him all the more determined to rouse it in bed. Another time, he promised himself.

"All right, let's do." She crossed her arms, mirroring his posture. "You didn't answer my question earlier. What do you want in a wife?"

He tried to think about it, but he was still distracted. "Callicott women need to be able to entertain clients, socialize with the right people, be the perfect hostess."

"You're kidding me. Right?"

"You asked."

"Yeah, but I expected an honest answer. That's not the way you see your mother, is it? That's not why your father married her, to be an asset to the company."

He eyed her, wondering why she was so sure. "Wives are assets."

"A wife can give you something that no one else can."

Dane told himself not to ask. Just leave it. "What's that?"

"A sheltering place to come home to at the end of a long day, where you're welcomed and warmed no matter what's happened. A place to restore your body, heart, and spirit."

"Like this dump? A cramped little space with secondhand furniture? You call this a home?"

"Get out."

Dane didn't move.

"Get out of here now. You come into my house, abuse my hospitality, and then insult me and what I've chosen for my life!"

He'd blown it, he realized. He'd struck at her pride where it hurt this time.

"You're going to wake up some morning and realize that your corporate profits are worth nothing, that the money and things and people you surround yourself with leave you empty and cold and lonely. Now get out!"

He was suddenly so tense, every muscle shook with the effort of not grabbing for her again. "But if you're right, you know, you're dooming me to more of the same. You're different from everyone else I've ever known. You could fill up all those empty, cold spaces inside me, if you'd be willing to try. I can feel it."

Her eyes narrowed in suspicion, but she was listening.

"We could strike a bargain, you and I," he murmured. "I could set you up in your own place, a nice one. Buy you all the dresses—"

Lyssa came after him, raining surprisingly sharp blows upon his chest that made him stagger back against the door. "Get out of here!"

He twisted the doorknob with one hand. The other he placed on her shoulder and moved her far enough away that he could pull the door open. She knocked his arm down. Her cheeks were flushed, her hair springing out around her face, her breasts heaving with gasping breaths. She was stunning. With one final lunge and a stiff-armed shove she forced him out the door before slamming it closed and locking the deadbolt.

He wasn't getting back in anytime soon..

The door across the hallway cracked open, and one dark eye stared at him from behind a thick glass lens.

Dane hesitated, then flashed his most charming smile. "Didn't mean to disturb you—"

The crisp click of the door told him whose side the elderly woman was on.

But from within he heard faintly, "Oldest living virgin in Phoenix. That's a good one." And then, "Try chocolate. She likes chocolate."

"Yeah, like that's helpful," he muttered. "All women like chocolate. Tell me something I don't know." There was no answer.

Dane strolled back to his car in deep thought. He had miscalculated—that much was true. He'd pushed Lyssa too far. But in the process he had learned something very valuable. She couldn't be bought.

That alone made her unique.

Dane found himself rubbing his hand across his chest as if that gesture could ease the tightness of his breathing. He stared down at the luxurious leather seat, seeing as if through Lyssa's eyes the obscene amount of money he had invested in this car. And he'd parked it here, in this neighborhood, late at night, without even thinking about putting up the top and locking out the bad guys. That's how much she'd confused him. He hadn't thought about the money.

He would be going back to a thoroughly air-conditioned and well-appointed townhouse that resembled her shabby little apartment only in having a floor and a ceiling, walls to hold them apart, and doors and windows to connect the inside world with the outside. Inside, his world was cold, empty, and lonely, just as she had said.

Damn her, he thought irrationally. Then he opened the car door and eased into the cushioned seat.

If he hadn't owed Lyssa some recompense for insulting her on Friday night, he certainly did now—after all that had been said over dinner and then . . . what had just happened in her apartment. He took a deep breath, relieved to find no twinge of an impending spasm.

Callicott Properties needed Lyssa's unique expertise, he reminded himself. He couldn't allow his male instincts to jeopardize what had been a perfectly good working relationship. His mouth curved into a wry smile as he realized how easy it was to rationalize seeing Lyssa again. On any terms.

Eight

VIVIAN WATCHED as Alex Garcia's hard eyes scanned her office furnishings, from the linear desk to the sinuous lamps. She gave him time to take in the sophisticated feminine décor. It was not a place where a man of his background would feel comfortable. She planned on having him off-balance in this encounter. That was the only reason she had broken her rule against ever inviting him—or any other like him —into her sanctuary. She had long known she would need every possible advantage in this inevitable showdown.

He thrived on confrontation. It took a secure man to don a blush-pink shirt and cowboy boots, but he wore both with aplomb as he prowled across her carpet in a gray, closely fitted western-cut jacket. And his black jeans, though a deplorable fashion choice, gave the woman in her a hum of pleasure both coming and going. Smart and well educated and diamond hard, Alex Garcia was a challenge worthy of her talents. A small part of her that she had thought long dead thrilled at the notion.

She'd spent the better part of a week developing this course of action, which was designed to trap her son's friend and right-hand man into a choice that would benefit her no matter how he decided. Once she set him the task of persuading Dane against yet another risky project, Garcia would find himself in an untenable position. He would have to either pit his will against hers or accede to her wishes and work on Dane. If he succeeded in swaying Dane, she would have established her authority over him. If he failed, she would have undercut his influence on Dane.

The prospect imbued her smile with genuine warmth. "Ah, Mr. Garcia. So good of you to join me."

"Forget the pleasantries. You summoned me. I came."

But he played the game too well to ask what she wanted. Disconcertingly he reminded her of Stewart—far more than her own son did sometimes.

She ran her tongue across the inside surface of her teeth, letting the deliberate movement, invisible to her opponent, soothe her nerves. "Then I will come straight to the point. Dane seems compelled to take Callicott Properties in the wrong direction. I wish for you to put it back on course. Put a stop to all this nonsense about a New York speculator and Tucson redevelopment. We have no business embarking on such things."

"That was pretty up-front for you, Mrs. Callicott," he said with what sounded like admiration. He sat in the lavender-and-gold chair that she had placed at an angle to her desk.

No, he did not sit, she corrected herself. He lounged, making himself at home on the curves of the chair, which was undersized for his large frame but seemed to accommodate him well enough. Or perhaps it was that he had a greater ability to accommodate himself to it than she'd expected.

Vivian eyed him warily.

He studied his boots. "What is it you object to in Gaspar Adams?"

Resisting the impulse to shudder at the cosmopolitan sound of the moneyman's name, she wondered why he had picked that, of all possible questions, as his opening move. She waved a hand negligently, brushing away his question. "We both understand that redevelopment poses risks to the stability and reputation of Callicott Properties. You were there last week." Her mouth twisted with the memory of the curious whispers and stares at the reception. "You saw how hesitant people were—are—over the Highline."

"People like Turnbull."

She refused to be baited. "For one, yes. But it was a universal response at the reception."

"By locals who have a vested interest." He quirked a black eyebrow at her and murmured, "As I recall, that attitude was not quite universal. Some people wholeheartedly approve of the Highline."

Meaning Lyssa Smith, Vivian supposed. Claudia's ally at Clearview reported a snag in the progress of that project but promised it was only temporary.

Calmly she responded, "Locals with whom Callicott has enjoyed a working relationship for many years. In some cases, decades. I might also remind you that Callicott Properties has no need to go outside the Phoenix area for projects."

"Need?" Again that irritating black brow crawled upward. He laced his fingers across his midsection, causing the topstitched lapels to gape over the pink shirt. "But that's the fundamental issue here, isn't it? Whether the company can survive if it continues to hold to traditions established during Dane's grandfather's days, and the last Great Depression. I would say 'need' is debatable." He smirked. "So is the idea that the Phoenix area these days is local. There are parts of the valley that take longer to drive to than Tucson."

She reached out and toyed with the sleek pen that lay at the edge of her desk blotter. "And just who will be the troubleshooter when things go wrong down in Tucson?" She let the implication hang between them: it would fall to Dane, like everything else.

His reply was soft but intent, as was his dark gaze upon her. "Why, I suppose I will. Unless you have any objections? I seem to have plenty of time for it."

Vivian's hands stilled. "Drive the mind-numbing interstate between here and there a few times, and you'll soon change your mind," she said tartly.

His heavy-lidded gaze remained steady on her.

"There is the little matter of Gail O'Neill. You know she's not to be trusted."

He shrugged. "And you know she'll do anything if there's enough money in it."

"Do you want to see Dane tangled up with her again?"

His amusement intensified. "I don't think it'll come to that. If nothing else, she's married, and Dane won't mess with a married woman. Besides, I think Mike would have something to say if the project threatens to be anything other than a money-making proposition."

Vivian took a steadying breath. She'd saved the most compelling point for last. "Straying from our pool of trusted investors may prove hazardous to Callicott's financial position. And the stability of the company directly concerns you. If the makeup of the executive hierarchy seems shaky to the board . . ."

"Meaning I'm expendable? Oh, I know that very well, Mrs. Callicott. But I think you're blowing this out of proportion. Just what do you think is likely to happen if Dane goes east for money and south for adventure?"

She ignored the mockery in his choice of words. "This Adams may decide to pull his support, and capital, from the project at a tenuous time, leaving us scrambling to replace the funds. He may want to exert a level of control in return for his investment that takes the end result out of our hands and leads to some monstrosity that drains Callicott financially for years until it can be unloaded." Relying on long experience with far more dangerous men, she assumed an air of calmness she did not feel, given all that was at stake. "Or he may simply be toying with Dane, drawing him into investing the company's time and money on a project that falls through the moment Adams loses interest and moves on to some new amusement."

"Well," Alex drawled after a moment's consideration, "I would say money is as green in New York as in the Southwest. Right now, land is pretty cheap around here compared to what it was a few years back. It's a time to buy. And if your faithful investors don't like what Dane did with the Highline, they sure as hell won't care for the Spirit Ranch. No, I think bringing some new blood into the financial end is the right decision."

"Are you refusing to talk to him?" Vivian's hands clenched on the pen. "Are you refusing me?"

"Tell me, Mrs. Callicott. What are you most afraid of? That Dane won't come back if he goes to New York, or that he will, bringing new ideas with him? That you'll lose control over him if he finally steps out of his father's shadow?"

She tossed the pen onto the desk with a clatter. "I am not afraid of that at all!"

"Well, I have a job to do, and it doesn't entail cutting my own throat by going along with a bad idea. I could remind you that Dane is in charge."

"That could change."

"Really. Well, then, I don't know what you brought me in for."

Vivian felt the heat of battle rise in her cheeks, but her answer was cool and even. "You know perfectly well that Dane listens to your opinion on business."

"I'm surprised you would admit that, considering . . ."

Considering what? Considering how dispensable she worked to make him, with Claudia's assistance? She narrowed her gaze on him but answered truthfully, "Dane is not entirely unjustified in doing so." Alex Garcia was an asset to the company. But he was not a Callicott.

"And if I don't agree that this is the best course for either Dane or Callicott? What then?"

"Then I shall have to tell him that you have been going behind his back and seeing Julia Nolin."

Comprehension dawned on the harsh planes of Garcia's hawklike face. He smiled faintly. "What makes you think he would mind?"

Vivian saw that he had selected his words with great care. She felt a twinge of unease. "Everyone in both families knows he and Julia will eventually marry."

"Right." His blatant sarcasm made her itch to box his ears. But he wasn't finished. "It's to be a dynastic marriage, then? I think that tradition went out of fashion after the Victorian era."

"Don't try to tell me you have no concern about what he will have to say. You've been very careful to keep this fling with Julia a secret. Why else, if not to keep him from finding out?"

A muscle worked beneath the dark skin of his jaw. "Do I need a reason beyond the fact that this is between Julia and me? It's a private matter. How did you find out about it?"

"One of my acquaintances saw you together."

"I can't imagine you know anyone in the places we've been," he muttered.

Vivian wondered just how low those places had been. Claudia had not said.

"If you plan to wield this as a weapon over my head, think again. Julia and I are both grown-ups. Even if Dane didn't approve of our relationship, there's nothing he can do to stop it."

"He could get rid of you."

"He could. But why would he bother?"

"If someone he trusted convinced him that his close friend was planning to take his place. Not only with his future wife—again—but also with the company that he gave up everything for, once upon a time. Those things would weigh heavily with Dane, given his past. Do you understand me?"

"You know, I believe I do." His mocking smile returned. "Rather more than you intend, I'm sure, but there's no help for that. What I understand is that you don't know your son as well as you think you do, Mrs. Callicott." He was devastatingly polite, almost sympathetic. "And you don't know me at all." With that, he left.

"TELL ME, DANE, is it you or your mother who's the real power at Callicott Properties?" Alex leaned against the doorjamb. A two-tone gray jacket held by one finger was slung over the right shoulder of a rose-colored tailored shirt.

Holy shit, Dane thought, he's wearing pink. Then the words and Alex's tense stance hit him. He groaned inwardly. He wished his mother would ease up on Alex. She'd resented his friend ever since Dane brought him into the company. Sometimes he wondered whether her attitude stemmed from racism, classism, or just plain resentment that Alex was a better businessman than the third generation of Callicott men. He put down his pen. "Last time I checked, it was me."

"Do me a favor and let her know that, all right?" Alex pushed himself away from the door and moved a few steps forward, leaving it open behind him.

Claudia must not be at her desk, Dane gathered. When she was in the outer office, Alex made a point of pulling the door closed.

Leaning back in his chair and clasping his hands behind his head, Dane said, "Mother is just upset over things changing too fast. I'll talk to her." He supposed his mother had sent Alex another memo about some reorganization measure instituted a while ago that she was only now finding out about. That was what usually set her off.

Alex shrugged his free shoulder in a gesture that was not quite agreement. When he spoke, it was to broach a subject Dane would as soon have left untouched for at least a few more days. "Are you going to New York?"

"I'm not sure yet." He'd been putting off the decision. Not because he had any reason not to go, but because the whole setup sounded too good to be true. A piece was missing from the puzzle. He wasn't sure he wanted to commit—not just himself, but the future of Callicott Properties—until he had put his finger on it.

"Well, when you do, for God's sake don't let your mother think I had anything to do with your decision, all right?"

Dane sat up straighter at the frustration in his friend's voice. "What's going on, Alex?"

"She called me into her office."

Dane tried not to let his surprise show. To his knowledge, this was the first time Alex had been invited into his mother's lair.

Alex dropped into the chair on the other side of Dane's massive desk. Dane propped his feet on the polished top of the desk and looked over at his friend, whose posture now mirrored his own. Alex's custom-made kangaroo-skin boots, although scuffed from numerous construction sites, probably cost three times as much as Dane's Italian loafers, he mused. And would last ten times as long. "All right, out with it."

"A reminder to call the florist?" Alex's dark eyes went to the pad of paper at Dane's elbow.

Doodling helped Dane concentrate, but he wasn't always aware of what he had drawn. He cast a quick look at the uppermost page and was startled to see that it was covered with flowers, all kinds of flowers —in bouquets, for godsake. Even as he ripped off the betraying sheet and crumpled it up, he noted that the quick, unconscious sketches were pretty good. There was something compelling about the lines, the way the eye flowed from one part of the composition to another.

He halted that train of thought. It wasn't a composition. It wasn't art. It was doodling.

"Julia told me I needed to come clean with you," Alex said without waiting for an answer. "I guess she was right."

Dane pulled his feet off the desk and sat up. The odd note in Alex's voice when he'd said Julia's name registered. She had sounded the same way when she'd mentioned Alex a few days earlier. "Something going on between the two of you? You and Julia?"

"We're thinking about it," he muttered. "You don't mind, do you?"

"Mind? Why would I mind?" Dane frowned, though, wondering what thinking about it meant, exactly.

"I always expected you to wake up and see that Julia's been in love with you forever," Alex said defiantly. He lifted his head and glared at Dane. "You dumb bastard."

Dane felt himself gaping like a fish. "Julia?"

She'd always been around, practically a member of the family. She was his best friend in junior high, a holding-hands sort of friend, a fumbling-first-kiss sort of friend. She commiserated with him when his first crush landed on a girl who didn't know he was alive. She saw him through his soul-torturing over Gail. But she had always dated other men, just as he dated other women. He supposed he should have wondered just what, besides misplaced love, would have kept such a lovely, witty, intelligent, truly nice woman from getting married.

It occurred to him that Alex might be mistaken. Men in love, in his experience, sometimes overreacted. "Did she say she loves me?"

"No, not straight-out."

"Have you ever asked?"

"Hell, Dane, a man doesn't ask a woman he wants to . . . a woman he . . ." Alex finished lamely. "If she's in love with another man!"

"I suppose not." Dane thought it probably wasn't his place to ask if they slept together. Not that he was jealous. Just concerned. For both of them, his best friend and right-hand man, and a woman who was practically his sister.

"You didn't answer my question," Alex said.

"What question?"

"Do you mind? About Julia and me?"

"No." Julia and Alex. Well, well, well. "Congratulations. I'm not sure any man really deserves her, but I guess you come as close as any."

Alex grimaced. "Better hold off on your congratulations until we figure out where we're going with this."

"Where you're going?" Dane felt a brotherly sort of protectiveness rise in him. "I assume you'll be planning a trip to the altar." Alex was from a good Catholic family. Honorable intentions, for him, would mean a long engagement and a blowout church wedding, followed by a forever-after sort of marriage.

"Is that how you see it working out?" Alex looked uncomfortable. "Her family might have something to say about that."

"Her family!" Dane bit back his urge to protest that they could have nothing to criticize in Alex.

The Nolins had always treated Dane well, but he was of a wealthy family and white besides. He didn't know what they would think of Alex, who'd grown up sharing a three-room apartment with seven other people, who had been the first in his family to go to college, whose education, experience, and innate talent could never carry him to a CEO position as long as he stuck with Callicott Properties.

No, Dane realized unhappily; he knew exactly what the Nolins would think if they found out a Mexican, no matter how many generations removed, was sniffing around their daughter. "Damn."

He rubbed his temple with one long forefinger, feeling the headache start. Dane glanced up at his father's and grandfather's portraits, which stared accusingly at him from the wall.

Alex's laugh was bitter. "Edward Nolin would only invite a Garcia into his house to scrub the toilets. I can't ask Julia to turn her back on her family, even if they are bigots."

Dane didn't know what to say to that.

"I've been thinking about looking for another position," Alex finally said, stirring uncomfortably. "It's not like you need me at Callicott. The company practically runs itself."

"You're wrong about that," Dane said, wondering where Alex had gotten such a lame-brained notion. "We can't afford to lose you. I need you. Don't do anything hasty. And it's a bad time for job-hunting."

Dane might be a Callicott and have the social contacts to line up investors, might even have an intuitive sense of which proposals would work and which wouldn't, might have the patience to pore over reports and sell the ideas with his own enthusiasm, but Alex was the one who took care of the details that made every project a success. In fact, it was Alex's efficiency at everything from perusing job cost data to analyzing financial statements that permitted him to think the work would get done without him.

Dane found himself holding his breath as a new scenario flashed into his mind. Alex should be the CEO of Callicott Properties. To win over the Nolins, Alex needed the job title, which Dane didn't. What Dane needed was to keep his friend's sharp business sense.

But there had always been a Callicott at the helm of Callicott Properties. His grandfather had established a closely held corporation specifically to retain control in the family. It was an archaic way of doing things in this day and age. There might be a way of restructuring the family business to more evenly distribute the responsibilities, but any proposal to change that corporate hierarchy would meet with significant resistance, particularly from his mother. He had to find a handle, he decided, something that would put her solidly in his camp. Too bad this was a rotten time to suggest such a move, while matters between them were so strained.

He repeated, "Don't do anything or say anything to anybody just yet." He reached over the desk and grasped Alex's arm. "Please. I'm asking you as a friend and as—" when Alex's dark, somber eyes met his "—as your boss. Give me time to come up with a plan. I need you here with me, Alex. I can't do it alone."

"I'd better be going." Alex unfolded himself from the chair. His jacket, held in one dark-skinned hand, slid over black jeans that draped in rodeo-cowboy folds to the instep of his boots. The style suited him but emphasized his south-of-the-border heritage.

There was no chance that Vivian Callicott would willingly accept Alex Garcia as CEO of Callicott Properties. No more than Edward Nolin would accept him as a son-in-law. They would both have to be forced to it. It was just a matter of finding the right leverage. Dane cursed under his breath as Alex strode to the door.

At least dealing with his mother ought to take his mind off his half-assed campaign to rebuild his burned bridges with Lyssa. Alex had been wrong about one thing: the flower sketches weren't a reminder to call the florist, they were a lingering question of how the orchid he'd picked out and sent to Lyssa had been received.

Because she certainly wasn't saying.

Nine

LYSSA LOOKED OUT at the deepness of night. The air carried the familiar scents of compost and goats, of damp earth and fallen leaves and hedge roses and the dense foliage of growing plants. The birds and insects that filled the days with background sounds had mostly become still. Even Dammit, the huge mastiff-type mutt she'd rescued and brought home to the farm years ago, had disappeared a few minutes earlier. She sat on the lower steps in front of the screened porch and wondered what on earth had brought her to this pass.

She had endured two solid days of thinking about that kiss and all that went with it. "TGIF" had never had more meaning or taken so long to arrive. She'd driven up to the farm at quitting time—another phrase that suddenly had taken on more relevance—hoping for some peace and quiet in which to recharge, but her thoughts refused to be left behind.

Miserable and confused, Lyssa felt the dark solitude of the night weighing heavily on her.

It had not been enough for Romeo to act on his basest impulses and kiss her. He had to grope her, insult her, yell at her, and then follow up his transgressions with flowers and chocolates left at her door. Or, rather, Paulina's, which was far more effective.

The man was a sneak. What did he need her for, when he had women coming out of the woodwork? She grimaced at the thought. Julia, Claudia, Gail . . . Well, maybe not Julia; she seemed to have something going with Alex Garcia. And not Gail, for pete's sake; she was married! And really, if Gail thought Mrs. Callicott would bust Dane's chops over starting something with Lyssa, what would his mother think of Claudia, who was nothing more than a secretary?

Although Lyssa had to admit that Claudia was not the one who had precipitated a scene at the grand opening-reception-whatever for the Highline.

With a moan she dropped her head to touch her knees, pulled up under her, with her feet resting on the cement slab at the bottom of the steps. She had to get past that set of embarrassing memories. But every time she did, her thoughts got stuck on Wednesday night.

She blamed the disaster on her neighbor. If Paulina had only kept her mouth shut, Lyssa would not have started giving off pheromones whenever she looked at Dane's streaky blond hair or his broad shoulders or his long, graceful hands or his intent, lived-in blue eyes or the crease that appeared in his cheek when he grinned for real. In all the years she'd known Dane, no "kiss-me-you-fool" invitation had ever sparked between them until Paulina started meddling.

On the drive up to the farm she spent a lot of time figuring it out. He kissed her because she was acting differently around him, aware of him in a new way, as a sexy and sexual man. No wonder Gail O'Neill had seen fit to warn her off.

As for his dissatisfaction with the Highline, his reluctance to jump at the chance of New York investment money, his easily roused frustration and headaches and stomach cramps and muscle spasms—several possible explanations occurred to her.

One was that he'd finally achieved everything he set out to do when he took his father's place, but he was coming to realize that he'd given up something important along the way. She hoped she wouldn't likewise find herself at the other end of her mission looking back on what she had missed out on.

A more comfortable possibility was that he was a man and it was a guy thing, and she would never, ever find any reason for his behavior that made sense to her. Not that she could afford even the briefest of detours into Dane's head. He was not destined to become another of her rescues.

Nor could she, even in her fantasies, consider what it might be like to have him for a lover, much less a husband. She had that from his own lips, regardless of his conciliatory behavior since.

He was a client of her employer's. They had a professional relationship. That was all. And it was a good thing, too. She couldn't handle anything else.

Clearview was almost more than she could deal with at the moment. She still had her job. And careful consideration had led her to believe that Simon couldn't have known what Barb was up to. If there was any tacit acceptance of unethical behavior at Clearview, it was on Lyssa's part, not Simon's.

She felt lousy about that, but even principles could not stand up against practicality. Not when her family's future was at stake.

Lyssa listened for the clink and chime of Helen and Ari doing the dishes as Paris cleared the table. She caught the slow murmur of voices through the screen door. There was no glare of electric lights in the house, only the flicker of candles. Later, when everyone retired to the living room, the steady glow of gas lights would provide illumination to read by. For now, the windows were dimly lit, allowing the stars to shimmer all the brighter against the depthless arch of the sky.

Only the tracks of headlights, belonging to the cars speeding along the highway to Prescott, across the creek, proved that she hadn't been transported back in time to the nineteenth century. And that wasn't right. There should be house lights visible to the left of her parents' farm, not quite due west of where she was sitting. The folds and gullies of these foothills of the Bradshaw Mountains hid all the other neighbors from view, but not the Jacobsons.

Lyssa stood up and dusted off the seat of her threadbare jeans. Dammit came galloping up, dragging a half-chewed log off the woodpile. She patted him absently before tossing the damp, tooth-splintered log toward the tree where the guinea fowl rested, startling the hens into a cacophony of gravelly chattering.

His lips peeled back to bare large white teeth. A thread of drool hanging from one side of his mouth jerked and shook as a deep rumble started up like a chainsaw in his throat.

"No," she said. She was not in the mood for this tonight.

He stiffened on his huge paws, leaning toward her.

"Oh, fine, you're not going to go away until I do, are you?"

His chesty grumble grew louder.

She sighed. "Kill!" she told him.

His ears flattened back along the sides of his head, the hair on his withers bristled up like a pine forest, and he snarled and growled and snapped at the air.

She wondered how long he would keep it up if she walked away without feeding him the punchline. As a doggy joke went, it was pretty clever. He had invented it himself. "Good boy."

It was like shutting off a switch. His ears perked forward and his face relaxed, tongue lolling in satisfaction. "Good boy," she said again, rubbing the top of his head the way he liked. "That is the dumbest thing I have ever seen. Anybody who would take that posing seriously would have to be an idiot. Away with you, now. I've got things to do and people to see." She pushed him away when he would have sat on her feet. "Go!"

He went, lumbering out into the dark, cool night.

She climbed the steps and opened the door. The squeak of hinges ended the low-voiced conversation within, the chuckles over Paris's outrage at seeing the Nubian doe prancing through the laundry enclosure earlier that evening with a pair of lilac panties draped around her neck, the other goats nibbling at the fabric as though it were the tastiest forage imaginable.

Lyssa knew what she would observe if the sun were streaming in through the mullioned windows: handmade plywood cabinets with tile countertops, a painted cement floor, a triple sink with a hand pump for water, an ancient gas range and oven, a small camper-style refrigerator that was cooled through some kind of high-tech propane conversion, and a determinedly plain trestle table with five slatted-back wooden chairs. It was the world she had grown up in.

Tonight it appeared both familiar and strange. She wondered if that was because of her suspicion that she had just run out of time.

The inanimate objects seemed to be shifting in the flickering shadows of homemade candles. The figures that should have been moving and talking were stiff. They had whipped around at the sound of her footsteps and eyed her with the air of prisoners facing a firing squad.

These were three of the four people who had made the primitive surroundings a home for her. The fourth, her father Cal, was off to Australia, overseeing the construction of a ranch headquarters he had designed. Lyssa looked at them and felt for a moment as if she were seeing them through the eyes of a stranger.

Paris's cornsilk-fine blond hair and blue eyes had faded over the years. Whatever edges she might once have borne in her face or form had been rounded and softened by age, but right now she stood taut-muscled and awkward. Next to her was Helen—normally as queenly and poised as her ancient namesake but tonight allowing her inner disturbance to show in an uncharacteristic nervousness to her gestures. And finally, there was Ari, Lyssa's dear Papa Ari, a most distinguished gentleman despite the tattered and stained farmer's overalls he'd favored for as long as she could remember. His white, well-barbered hair (kept neat by Paris, who had appointed herself responsible for all the others) waved above his beloved square, lived-in face, naturally dark but baked even browner by the sun—and now bearing a worried frown.

"There aren't any lights on at the Jacobsons'," Lyssa told them.

Ari looked at Helen. Helen looked at Paris. Paris looked back at Helen. Lyssa noticed that none of them looked at her.

"They've decided to go into an assisted care center," Paris finally said, brushing a stray lock of hair over one amply padded shoulder.

"Assisted living?" Lyssa couldn't imagine Donald Jacobson agreeing to such a thing. Or paying for it.

"It was nothing, really," Ari rushed to add. "Ruth fell and broke her hip, and Donald couldn't take care of her once she was sent home. They couldn't think of being separated, you know that—after sixty years together."

Lyssa stifled a disbelieving snort. More likely Jacobson had figured out he wouldn't have anybody to wait on him. Ruth was lucky the miserable old codger had decided not to have her put down like he would a horse.

"Besides, they wanted to be closer to the hospitals," Paris added. "Just in case."

It was Helen's turn. "They have some great-grandkids now, and it was starting to get inconvenient for everybody to come up here to visit. So they found a nice little place on the northern edge of Phoenix, just off Bell Road. The family moved them down a few weeks ago."

Lyssa folded her arms. Her right forefinger found a stray curl and wrapped it around and around while she thought. What they were saying explained why the Jacobson place was dark but not why no one had told her about it earlier. Last weekend, say, when she'd come home to lick her wounds after the reception, and Paris chided her for not paying attention to the chores. She sighed. All right, maybe last weekend wouldn't have been the best time.

"What about—" She broke off, feeling her throat go tight as she made a few quick calculations. *"I'm not ready!"* she could have cried out, but that would have led to questions she wasn't prepared to answer. "What about the land? They agreed years ago to sell it to me." This might not be a bad time to buy it, with land values down. She had a good chunk of what it would take.

Ari looked at Helen again.

She glared at him. Then she moved to stand by Lyssa and placed one hand on her daughter's shoulder. "Oh, sweetheart, do you still want that land?"

"Of course I want it! How could I not want it?" Was the property already sold? she wondered. No. It couldn't be. No one else had enough of a stake in the neighboring parcel to pay what was certain to be an outrageous price still, given Donald Jacobson's infamous greed.

She squeezed her eyes closed and took a breath, letting it out in a measured, slow, cleansing stream of air. "I thought you'd be more excited for me, that's all."

Paris came near and wrapped one plump hand around Lyssa's. "We are glad the opportunity has finally come up."

Lyssa heard the "but" that her mother left unsaid. "You know I've been planning to buy the Jacobsons' place as soon as they were ready to sell. I have plans for that land."

Ari cleared his throat. "Actually—"

"Actually, what?" she demanded.

He cast the women a helpless look, but Helen and Paris didn't respond.

Ruefully Lyssa considered the fact that her father's mind was acclaimed by those who thought about such things as one of the finest in the world, honed by logic and metaphysical reasoning, sharpened through years of living by philosophical rules of his own creation, and broadened by exposure to every great truth that had ever been written. And yet he was unable to stand against her mothers, who obviously had selected him as their sacrificial goat. As usual.

"The thing is—" He glanced past her again, but after what Lyssa assumed was some signal from her mothers, he continued, "We don't think you should get too wedded to the idea of buying Jacobson's land and going into business for yourself."

Lyssa pulled her hand free of Paris's comforting grasp and moved her shoulder out from under Helen's hand. She groped for the back of one of the chairs.

No surprise that Donald Jacobson had let her down. All along she'd known she might lose the opportunity because the land was too valuable, because she couldn't afford it, because one of the Jacobsons' many children or grandchildren had inexplicably decided they couldn't part with it. She could never have imagined that her parents might lose faith in her.

"Cal and I have been over the figures a thousand times." She stared at her fingers as they quivered against the scarred top brace. "Between Phoenix restaurants and specialty grocers and the Internet, there's enough of a market to keep me busy."

Paris looked startled. "But dear, don't you see? That's the problem."

Lyssa blinked in confusion.

"Don't look like that, Lyssa, dearest. We love you. We only want what's best for you."

"Do you know," she said to the kitchen in general, "I have never heard that particular set of clichés from my parents. They always encouraged me to follow my heart, even if it meant making mistakes along the way."

Ari and Helen had fallen out of the tableau, retreating to the sink where the last of the dishes waited. It was only Lyssa and Paris, the woman who had indulged her interest in herbs and spices by adding a "Lyssa corner" to every garden plot, where together they tended whatever Lyssa chose to plant, no matter how odd or exotic.

"I'm going to be brutally honest," Paris said.

Lyssa found the words absurd. She could have used the warning a few minutes earlier.

"You don't really *like* plants."

Staring back at her, Lyssa wondered where that had come from. She loved plants. She loved the way they spoke to her senses: the texture of their leaves, the smell of them as they dried, the endless variety of shapes they came in. She had a degree in botany, for pete's sake. "I like plants."

"Yes, dear, you like them when they're picked and ready to do something with. But as for growing them—the planting and transplanting and weeding and watering . . ." Paris trailed off. She laid one work-worn hand on top of Lyssa's. "It's just not you, baby," she said earnestly.

"I can do it. I've done it before."

"Of course you can. But you're not driven by it. You haven't rooted yourself deep in the heart of the earth and yearned toward the clouds. You've never remade yourself in the image of Yggdrasil."

A tree. A mythological tree at that, even if it was the one that in Paris's way of thinking kept the world whole. "You want me to become a tree?" Lyssa finally responded. Paris was speaking metaphorically, she knew, but the knowing didn't help. She pulled her hand away, feeling it rasp against the calluses on Paris's palm.

"No, of course not. I was just explaining to you that you don't want to spend all your time growing herbs and flowers."

"I don't?"

Impatiently Paris said, "Lyssa, dear, don't be obtuse."

As though she had a choice in the matter. Perhaps if she were a great thinker—as all her parents were, each in their own way—she would be able to follow Paris when she went off on one of her tangents. Paris had no unified philosophy like Ari's. Sometimes trying to follow her reasoning was like picking one's way through a cluttered, unfamiliar room in the dark. This appeared to be one of those times.

"If I don't like growing them," she tried, "what was it I was doing in college? I paid my tuition with these herbs you say I shouldn't waste my time with. Now I want to make a living with them."

Paris bent a rather pitying look on her. "Lyssa, dear, it wasn't the plants."

"It wasn't?"

"It was what you did with them. Your teas and spice mixes and aromatic essences. Potpourris and spring salad blends and herbal remedies. Chili ristras and braided garlic chains. When are you going to have time to play with your creative side if you're busy all the time grubbing in the dirt?"

"I'd already thought of that. I was planning to buy a good portion of the raw materials. I'm not stupid!"

Helen came to her partner's defense. "Lyssa, you're being unfair. Of course you can put together all those wonderful blends, and you can sell them under the aegis of Elysian Fields. But there's no need to buy your own land and put so much pressure on yourself. Sometimes you have such high expectations."

While her parents had none, she thought uncharitably. But then, they didn't know they needed any. She'd kept that nasty little secret from them, to protect them.

"You could keep it as a sideline income," Helen suggested.

"A sideline. And what would my main income be?"

"The Land Trust is looking for someone." Helen gave an encouraging, hopeful smile.

"We know it wasn't what you wanted when you graduated," Paris broke in, "but you seem so unhappy at Clearview. You can always give the Land Trust a try, and if you don't like it, no harm done. At least it will get you home."

Ari asked, "It's not only a question of money, is it?" He seemed to have difficulty even saying the word. "Because you shouldn't build your life around anything so mundane."

The precarious hold Lyssa was maintaining on her equanimity slipped as Helen stated, "If you leave Clearview and take the position at the Land Trust, you'll be doing wonderful things. Instead of helping developers destroy the land, you'll have a hand in taking care of it. Instead of being surrounded by Darwinian dictators who think they can improve on nature, you'll find a whole community of people who care about making their world better. And you'll be home. You can live here, in your own room. It'll be just like before."

Lyssa scrubbed a hand over her face. "I don't think I want it to be just like before."

"You spend every weekend here, and vacations too," Helen reminded her. "Surely it wouldn't be so hard to come home for good."

"It's my choice to visit. Just as it was your choice to set up EF along the lines of some twenty-five-hundred-year-old farmstead."

Helen was not done having her say. "I don't see why you're so resistant to this idea. But I suppose I shouldn't be surprised. You've always had a tendency toward fatalism, accepting what life throws at you instead of actively shaping your destiny."

The unfairness of that particular accusation startled Lyssa into a helpless chuckle. If she didn't laugh, she would surely have to cry.

Her stomach roiled. "I'm going to bed," she told everyone. "I'm exhausted. Long week at work." She flapped a hand in their direction as she walked away. "We'll talk about all of this again, after I've spoken with Jacobson. Maybe Cal will be home by then." He had always been on her side.

Once in her room, Lyssa tumbled into her small, narrow bed and stared up at the ceiling, wondering whether she could pull everything together without having to knock her parents' world off its axis. Jacobson was bound to ask more than the property would appraise for, but Julia might be able to help Lyssa figure out a way past that.

The thought of Julia brought Dane to mind. She wondered whether his mother's lack of support for the Highline had made him as sick at heart as her family's doubts made her. At least now they had one thing in common.

She never would have considered the possibility even half an hour earlier, but all of a sudden she was looking forward to Monday. At least she knew what to expect at work.

ON MONDAY Lyssa thought back on that easy confidence. She wondered exactly what it meant that Simon and Barb were at Valley Archaeology talking to the soon-to-be-Clearview employees while she sat in her cubicle and lined up her pens just so.

She reflected that with Barb out of the office, it would be a good time to call Jacobson, as she wouldn't need to worry about getting in trouble for making a personal phone call. But she didn't move. For one thing, she would have to track down his new telephone number.

Her parents either had not thought to or had deliberately failed to do so. For another thing, though the Jacobsons' property had come available sooner than she'd expected, it was not really a surprise.

The prospect of becoming a landowner could be manageable. Once she got her employment situation under control.

Being cut out of the loop during Clearview's acquisition of Valley Archaeology was not a good sign. At the moment, there was only one strike against her—the episode with Tank Turnbull—but with Barb having declared open war, she was no longer sure she had two strikes left before she was out of a job, if not quite out on the street.

All she needed was a little more time. Was that too much to ask? she wondered. A few months was all it should take to strike a bargain with Jacobson, arrange a mortgage with Julia, manage a closing, tender her notice, and start her new life. That sounded simple enough.

The telephone rang, startling her. *I might have known,* she thought immediately upon hearing Dane's voice. He wasn't done with her yet. That shouldn't have been a relief, she told herself. And indeed, relief morphed into annoyance with the first words out of his mouth after hello.

"Where have you been?" he demanded.

Lyssa counted to five before she spoke. "I went away for the weekend."

"All weekend?"

"That's right."

"With anyone in particular?"

"I don't believe I owe you an explanation." Nor did he have the right to demand one. Not after his comments about the likelihood of her finding The One. Her perfect man. A man to spend all her weekends with.

As if he sensed how close she was to hanging up on him, Dane shifted tactics. "I suppose you're wondering why I called."

Lyssa did not bother to be polite. Politeness had not gotten her very far recently. "I'm wondering why you're still bothering me." She ignored his expostulation of "Bothering you!" and continued, "I thought we said all there was to say last week."

"Wednesday night, you mean. You haven't talked to me since. I reacted badly, I'll admit."

"You reacted like a spoiled little boy. Is it just the challenge of winning over someone who turned you down? Is that why you've been sending the cards and flowers and chocolates?" And excellent chocolates they were—rich and impossible to turn away from. As for the flowers, they were all exotics, exquisitely scented gardenias and living sprays of orchids. To add insult to injury, he'd sent her scented candles that, along with the flowers, were turning her apartment into a tropical paradise.

"I promise, Lyssa," he said, sounding as if he spoke through clenched teeth, "my reason for calling has nothing to do with anything that passed between us last week."

"Oh." She'd asked for that, she supposed, bleakly.

"It occurred to me that you might still be in Simon's black books over that episode with Tank Turnbull."

"And if I was?"

"I thought of something that could help."

"Oh?"

"If I set up an occasion for you to apologize to Tank—"

"Apologize? I have nothing to apologize for. I didn't accuse him of anything. *I* wasn't the one who lost my temper and made a scene."

With studied reasonableness Dane replied, "No, but sometimes it isn't the person in the wrong who needs to be the first to extend an apology."

Lyssa gritted her teeth but let the comment pass. "What do you stand to get from this? I can't believe you're offering to set up this lovely opportunity out of the goodness of your heart."

"I'm going to level with you, Lyssa."

"There has to be a first time for everything, I suppose."

"Damn it!"

After a moment his smooth voice came over the line again. "To tell you the truth, I want to make my mother feel better."

Lyssa closed her eyes. She hated it when people knew exactly what to say to take the wind out of her sails.

"Tank is an old friend of hers," Dane went on. "She takes things that happen to him . . . personally, I guess you could say."

"So you want me to grovel in front of your mother. And in return you'll—what, plead with Simon to forgive me for my transgressions?"

"I guess that's the gist of it."

She would have loved to refuse. But she couldn't work for Dane— even if he should ever offer a job again, after all that had passed between them—and that meant she wasn't done with Clearview. Pacifying Simon was a good idea. She could even try to be grateful for the opportunity. If Dane got something out of it, fine. She understood doing whatever was necessary to keep one's parents happy. "Okay."

"Okay? You mean, you'll do it? Show up, make nice, apologize, everything?"

Lyssa grimaced into the phone. Did he want to rub it in? "I assume you intend for this to be another business dinner. In public." She knew that he heard the sarcasm in her voice; she could practically see him wince. "The more public the better, I suppose, for a bit of groveling," she finished. "Sure, Dane, let's do it."

AFTER PROMISING to call back with the details, Dane hung up the phone, unsatisfied with Lyssa's agreement. Again. He felt some guilt over the way he was using her, but irritation and, yes, he had to admit, a twinge of hurt pride at her suspicion and her "spoiled little boy" comment overshadowed any shame he might have felt if he dwelled on what she was probably feeling right now. Ultimately it would be to her benefit anyway.

And his—as one small, preliminary step in getting his mother's defensiveness of Tank off the board. It was a peace offering. He was pretty sure Vivian would take it as that. She understood how the game was played. Besides, he owed her the gesture just as he owed Lyssa the flowers and chocolates. A "spoiled little boy" wouldn't see that, he told himself.

He'd put away his boyhood long ago, along with his boyhood dreams. A few lines from an old song came into his mind then, almost as if to taunt him—something about childish things, painted wings and . . . fairy rings? No, that wasn't quite right, but he couldn't remember anything more than a boy named Little Jackie Paper and his dragon Puff. He wouldn't have known that much if his babysitter—he wouldn't glorify her with the title of nanny, although in retrospect he suspected that's what she was—hadn't exposed him to just the kind of fanciful kid stuff his mother detested.

Dane couldn't get past that ridiculous accusation. If Lyssa really saw him as a spoiled boy and if Vivian couldn't trust him to make reasoned, mature decisions, they didn't know him as well as they obviously thought. He no longer allowed himself to be led by his passions.

Then he remembered the things he'd said to both of them and knew he was lying to himself, at least where they were concerned. They both had a way of getting under his skin.

Still, Lyssa had no call to take the moral high ground with him. She might have defended the Highline against Tank's criticism as well as his mother's—according to what Julia had told him later—but she'd been quick enough to believe he had betrayed her to Gail and Mike. And no matter what she claimed afterward, she had responded to his kisses. He still felt that lightning-bolt of sensation whenever he thought about the way she had quivered hotly under his hands.

As for his mother, she would see that Tank had overreacted to the situation once Lyssa made a nice, calm, reasonable apology. *And since the company is so damned important to her, more important than me, evidently*—he cut off that thought, irritated to find himself rubbing the cheek she'd slapped. Dane was resolved to prove that he was thinking only of what was best for Callicott, whether that meant broadening the geographical base of the company or expanding the pool of investors or shifting the type of development the company was known for.

He would go more slowly with her, give her time to adjust. She would be more amenable to accepting changes if she saw it as her own choice to let go of the past. Vivian Callicott was both intelligent and practical, a good businesswoman. She could be made to recognize that Callicott needed people like Lyssa Smith and Alex Garcia, and not just men named Callicott.

Now all he had to do was arrange for one simple dinner. He wondered if he had to tell his mother in advance that Lyssa would be attending. That would be a better justification for having Tank there, but then Vivian might decide not to show, out of spite. He considered that he might focus on the apology owed to Tank—and leave the source of said apology unnamed.

Lyssa had a promotion on the line. She might be grateful that he was offering her an opportunity for kissing up.

Dane looked down at his doodle pad to find that he had very clearly outlined a pair of women's lips, shaped around the word *sorry*. "Damn it!" He wadded up the sheet and tossed it at the wastebasket.

He and Lyssa still had to work together. And that meant he had to get his mind back on business.

Ten

AS SHE LISTENED to the telephone ringing on the other end of the line, Lyssa propped herself against the wall and wondered why she hadn't paid attention to what the universe had been trying to tell her. Any kind of relationship between her and Dane was obviously doomed.

She should have known better than to consent to see him again, despite the lure he had held out. But returning home night after night to find Paulina presiding over the continuing deliveries of fruit baskets and chocolate roses and wine actually made her look forward to putting on her new teal dress and proving that she could be an adult about everything.

After the way he'd ripped up at her the last time they were together, she shouldn't have agreed to so much as talk to him, let alone let him coax her into something that was entirely against her better judgment. Another business dinner, for crying out loud—and this time allowing herself to be skewered by his mother and Tank Turnbull instead of his ex-fiancée and a beleaguered husband. Lyssa was not looking forward to the evening. Still, she could have just refused.

She wouldn't have had to go to these lengths to get out of it.

"Callicott Properties. Mr. Callicott's office."

It was Claudia's husky voice, of course, although this was supposed to be Dane's direct line. Lyssa covered her ear against the background noise of the emergency room. She'd been hoping for his voice-mail, if she couldn't reach the man himself. "This is Lyssa Smith," she said. "Is Mr. Callicott available?"

"Hold, please, while I check."

Lyssa supposed she was in shock. Why else would she be concerned about what Dane would say when she told him she was running late?

Any normal person would be worrying about whether the police would be able to catch the guy who'd stolen her laptop, pushing her down so roughly that she'd fallen wrong and twisted her arm. She was walking across the parking lot from the campus library when someone approached from behind and seized her computer case. Fortunately, she carried her wallet and keys on her instead of in the case, or she would have lost them, too, along with her cell phone. Unfortunately, she instinctively resisted when she felt the shoulder strap slipping, and so what might have been a simple grab and run had turned into an assault. The police had informed her she was lucky to come away from the incident with no more than minor injuries for trying to hang on to her laptop, which had all her data files and the flash drive backup for a week's worth of work.

To make her feel even more the idiot, when she found a phone to use at the hospital, did she call the office right away to explain why she wouldn't be checking in before leaving for the day? No, she called Dane.

She shook her head in disgust and resolved to dial Barb the minute she finished with Dane. Though the robbery was not Lyssa's fault, Barb would be unhappy about the lost work time and the insurance claims. With all the other things going on, this incident would undoubtedly have repercussions. *Strike two*, she thought, wishing the emergency room staff had given her the painkillers they promised as soon as the doctor had seen the X-rays. *One more strike—*

Claudia came back on the line and said, "I'm sorry, he's in a very important conference and doesn't have the time to take your call right now. This is a very busy week."

"I see." And when wasn't he busy? "It's just that . . ." Lyssa trailed off. The thought of explaining her situation to his assistant was repellent. She cleared her throat. "Would you interrupt him, please? I do need to speak with him on an urgent matter, and I'm not at a number where he can call me back."

"We seem to have a bad connection. I can barely hear you." Claudia's voice was calm at the other end of the crystal-clear line. "Did you just ask me to interrupt his meeting for you?"

"Just see if he'll take my call."

"He left very strict instructions that he was not to be disturbed. You should certainly understand that personal matters can't be allowed to interfere with business."

What a bitch, Lyssa thought. *What is it with Dane and these women?* "You're not going to ask him to take my call, are you?"

"I really would like to help you out. But you're putting me in a very awkward position. He left strict—"

"I heard you the first time." Awkward position, in a rat's ass. As though Dane would reprimand his precious assistant for anything that she did. Lyssa closed her eyes and leaned her head against the wall, feeling the screaming pain in her arm intensify.

"If you'll tell me what's so urgent, I can slip him the message during a break."

"A break." Lyssa giggled. Or sobbed; she wasn't sure. "I guess that will have to do."

She was having more than a little difficulty thinking clearly. "Tell him . . . just tell him I may be late for dinner tonight. If he could push back the reservations to eight. And I'll have to meet him there."

She might have time to drive home and change before dinner, but only if it could be rescheduled. Otherwise, she would have to stay in the clothes she had on, which were decent—dark green slacks and a long-sleeved brown knit shirt—but stained from her encounter in the parking lot and, like her, rather the worse for wear.

Claudia's voice went cool. "Let me check his calendar."

Lyssa heard the click of computer keys.

To top it off, driving her stick-shift was out of the question. Not to mention the fact that her truck was a couple miles away, since the police, after taking her statement, drove her to the hospital when she refused ambulance transport. And then there was her hope that she would soon be under the influence of some heavy-duty painkillers. She would have to call for a cab.

If this deal with Mrs. Callicott and Turnbull weren't so important, she would have just cancelled the whole thing. Maybe she still should, she reflected.

"The reservations are at seven," the velvety voice informed her.

"I know that."

"It's Anton's, which is a very busy restaurant. I doubt if they'll have a later slot."

Lyssa burned at the evident pleasure Claudia was taking in torturing her. "Could you call, please, and arrange it? Anytime after eight should be fine." She glanced at the clock and wondered if that would be enough time. "Make that eight-thirty."

"Maybe it would be better if you just cancelled. Mrs. Callicott and Mr. Turnbull are not going to wish to reschedule."

A brief silence fell at both ends of the conversation. Lyssa was searching for a nice way of telling Claudia to go piss up a rope when she heard her name being called. An X-ray technician wearing a wildly patterned set of scrubs and frowning down at a clipboard stood in the doorway to the waiting room.

"I have to go." Using her back, Lyssa arched away from the wall. She winced at the renewed explosion of pain that went through her arm at the sudden movement. "Just tell him I'll be late."

"What reason should I give him?"

"It's personal. I don't want to go into it." She left unstated the two ending phrases that begged to be said: *over the phone* and *with you*. The satisfaction she would derive from the latter was less important than trying to convince Claudia to give Dane the message without putting a nasty spin on it.

The technician called her name again, more impatiently. Lyssa tucked the phone between her shoulder and her ear and gestured with the hand she had freed, asking for just a moment longer.

"Give me a number where Dane can reach you."

The speaker high up on the wall of the waiting room crackled into life, specifying a code blue somewhere in the hospital.

"I already said I wasn't at a—" She knew there was no point in talking to Claudia any longer. "Listen, I have to go now. Just tell him I'll be late. And help him out by shifting the reservations, would you?" She hung up without waiting for a response. Holding her arm carefully against her side in the sling the paramedics had fitted for her, she thanked the woman at the check-in station for the use of the telephone. Then she followed the bright scrubs through the heavy doors and into the bowels of the hospital.

This was her first time inside a hospital—not having been born in one and having been completely healthy for three decades. She hoped it would be her last. She had never been so terrified in her life.

DANE NOTICED that the light was on for the telephone line that was supposed to ring directly through to his office. He supposed Claudia had transferred all calls to her phone. He wondered if she always had done that, and he was just now noticing. It would prevent interruptions when he was genuinely preoccupied and didn't want to be disturbed. But it was his private line, damn it. There was no telling who might be calling.

The light went off just as he was about to excuse himself and pick it up, so he made a mental note to talk to Claudia about the matter sometime. Maybe they could work out a code so that she knew when he really was busy.

"I'd better be going." Alex unfolded himself from the chair.

"You didn't say what you thought of my proposal."

"Give me a day or two to get accustomed to the notion first, all right? Jesus, Dane, you can't hit a man with such a drastic change all at once and expect him to jump all over it."

"And yet," Dane reminded him, "we've been asking my mother to do something of the sort, haven't we?"

"If you somehow get your mother to agree to this—and I would say that is one hell of a big 'if'—where does that leave New York?"

"Let me worry about that. You have enough to think about." Dane still was not convinced that Gaspar Adams and the New York connection was the way to go. There was still something missing. For one thing, how had Adams learned about the Highline in the first place?

Dane ushered his friend to the door. After watching Alex stroll down the hall toward his own office, he turned back to Claudia's desk. She was in fine form today, wearing a cerulean blue blouse that draped stylishly across her breasts. She did know how to dress herself to draw a man's attention. "Any messages?" Dane made sure to keep his gaze above her neck.

"Lyssa called. She can't make it to dinner tonight."

"Run that by me again?"

"I guess something more important came up." Claudia's smile didn't warm her crystal-sharp eyes. "I'm sorry. I would have put her on hold until you were done with Alex, but she said she didn't have time."

"I don't believe it." He scrubbed a hand through his hair. "Did she give any reason?" But he thought he knew: Lyssa was having her revenge. Damn it. He should have known her capitulation had come too easily.

Claudia shook her head. "She wouldn't say. Just that it was personal. She doesn't have particularly good people skills. She was very hostile toward me. Of course, it wasn't the best connection."

Dane barely heard his assistant's plaint. "I don't know why I ever thought this was a good idea. What woman has to be pushed into getting dressed up and being wined and dined?"

Claudia watched him with a cool, elegant stillness that reminded him of his mother.

Who, he thought a little desperately, would make hay of this if she knew. Thank God he had gone with his gut feeling and hadn't told her to expect Lyssa. Maybe he should call and postpone the dinner, at least until after he'd talked to Lyssa. There was an idea.

To Claudia he said, "I'll have to call her back. Was she at work?"

"I don't think so. It was someplace noisy. A lot of people in the background." She took a deep breath that made Dane's eyes wander involuntarily lower. "If it's really a problem, though, I'm free tonight," she declared with a Mona Lisa smile. "I'd be happy to get dressed up and be wined and dined."

Dane frowned and pulled his gaze back to safer territory. "Don't you have a class tonight?" Part of the deal when he'd hired Claudia was that the company would pay for her education. Idly he realized that that had been a few years ago. He wondered how close she was to attaining her bachelor's degree. When she graduated, would she still be content to work for him, or would she, like Alex, feel compelled to move on to bigger and better things?

"Class?" Claudia looked blank for a moment. "Oh. Yes, I have a . . . a marketing class. It won't hurt me to miss it just this once. I can get the notes from somebody later."

Belatedly he realized that she had taken his inquiry as acceptance of her suggestion. Considering the idea for just a moment, he ran a quick glance over Claudia's well-showcased body, right down to the shapely legs that really should be covered a little farther by her skirt. His mother wouldn't be any more pleased to see Claudia than she would Lyssa. Particularly if she caught Tank admiring those legs. Lord, what a tangle, he thought.

"I don't think that would be a good idea." He tried to infuse genuine regret into his voice.

"Oh." She bit her pale pink, lush bottom lip, and her eyes fell away. "Of course." She essayed a little laugh.

Dane didn't relax until he was safe behind his desk and distracted with paperwork. Lyssa had always been reliable during the years they'd been associated professionally. But he had tried to shift that relationship to something more personal, and ever since, she'd become as unpredictable as one of the brushfires that periodically swept through the high desert ranges.

Maybe he should have asked Gail exactly what she had heard about Lyssa that made them decide to suggest a Tucson company. Maybe there was more than the episode with Tank underlying their concern. He remembered the discongruity between Lyssa's likely income and the student-type housing she lived in. The fact that she'd worn the same dress to both the events he'd seen her at. Her unreasonable behavior and occasional bizarre statements. Did she have a drinking problem, or drugs? he wondered. Gambling? Some kind of secret life? And where did she go on the weekends?

LYSSA SMILED at the parking valet who left his station to open the door for her. She could have managed it with her free arm, but the little bit of pampering felt wonderful after the stressful afternoon.

As if the hospital experience wasn't trying enough, she had to call twice for the cab, and that delay made her even later than she'd expected to be. Because of the off-the-shoulder bodice of her dress, she managed to get into it without help, but the color clashed with the blue of the cast material. And also with the purple of her arm, the puffy parts that showed around the temporary cast. She'd done her best to hurry, dressing hastily without taking the time to put on makeup. Not that she could have applied it wrong-handed without looking like a circus clown.

She was surprised to see Anton at the seating station, muttering to himself. The chef seldom entrusted his kitchen to anyone else, although now that he had two locations to deal with, she supposed he was forced to delegate more of his responsibilities at both.

"Lyssa, dear child!" His sky-bright eyes fell to the cast and widened in horror. "What has happened to you? Ari never said a word about this."

His Austrian accent seemed thicker than usual to Lyssa. She had trouble comprehending what he was saying. Or maybe it was that her mind, the painkillers finally having kicked in, was thicker than usual. "The parents don't know yet."

Anton looked briefly uncertain but then nodded. "That telephone thing."

"Yes." She smiled wryly. Like all of her father's restaurant contacts, Anton had been known to curse the lack of a telephone at the farm. It was one of the hazards of doing business with Elysian Fields. If the produce Ari brought in every week weren't so flavorful and distinctive, her parents would have lost their clientele long ago because of the inconvenience of being virtually unreachable. They did own a cell phone but had to climb to the top of the ridge to get a signal.

Thinking about those inconveniences at the farm made her more determined to get her hands on Jacobson's property. She couldn't do business that way. And she was not going to go back to being nothing more than her parents' daughter, living at home and dependent on them for everything.

Anton shrugged. "You are feeling . . ." He waved an elegant hand, well manicured and shapely but for the loss of one fingertip to a grinder years before.

"I'm fine," Lyssa lied. But she'd committed to this dinner, even if it killed her. Which she was afraid it just might, if she wasn't seated pretty soon so that she could get some food in her empty stomach.

"Are you come to join us with dinner to-night?"

"I'm here to meet some people. Dane Callicott."

Anton frowned. "Callicott—? I think this is not right."

"I don't understand. Aren't they here yet?" Lyssa knew it was well after eight thirty, because she hadn't even left her apartment by then.

"They were here." He enunciated very carefully and dropped his head away, looking up through long white-blond lashes at her.

"Were." Lyssa hoped he was simply having trouble with English verb tenses.

"It is the Callicott party? They had a seven o'clock reservation. They left a few minutes ago. They were not happy that one of their . . . dining companions . . . was missing. That was you?"

"I called and told Dane's secretary to change the reservation to eight thirty. Are you telling me—" She broke off. Either Claudia hadn't given Dane the right message or he deliberately stuck to his original timeframe to cut Lyssa out. Although she could not imagine how that would play to his advantage, given what he hoped to achieve. Assuming he had told her the truth about that.

"Come sit in kitchen until you do better," Anton told her, grasping her shoulder lightly in his warm hand and steering her away.

The kitchen would be a nightmare, even with Anton out in the front instead of terrorizing the sous-chef and assistants. Lyssa needed to go home where she could collapse. "Just call me a cab. Please."

It was a good thing her wallet hadn't been stolen. At least she had money enough for cab fare.

Lyssa was on the verge of weeping when Anton encouraged her to take a seat in the foyer. The walls were closing in on her. With a murmur of apology she walked out into the balmy evening.

If only she'd gone home, crawled into bed, and never come to Anton's at all, she thought. Then she wouldn't be faced with having to figure out whether it was Claudia's duplicity or Dane's inflexibility that had brought about this latest mess.

Lyssa shook her head. It was the coward's way out, she knew, but she had no strength left to do anything but pull a Scarlett O'Hara. She would worry about it tomorrow.

Maybe she would even be quick enough to sneak in past Paulina tonight, so she wouldn't have to explain why she came home in a cast and showered and changed into a new dress before leaving, only to slink back into her apartment less than an hour later. Lyssa groaned, recognizing the wishful thinking on her part. Paulina would never allow her curiosity to go unsatisfied.

The cab pulled up, and Lyssa forced herself to get in.

She wished she had somewhere else she could go, besides her barren apartment. If she could even call her parents, cry on their shoulders, explain that she was tied up in knots over some man. But what would she say?

Lyssa would have liked to blame the medication for her inability to answer that question. She was afraid the problem went deeper than that, though. She wasn't the calm, steady, nice person she'd always imagined herself to be. She was nasty and mean-spirited and wracked with anxieties that she should have grown out of a decade ago. She absolutely hated Claudia Montgomery at this moment, and she was none too sure about what she thought of Dane Callicott.

Lyssa looked out the window without seeing the familiar mountain views. She sat stiffly on the edge of the seat, eventually realizing she'd forgotten to buckle herself in. She felt as though her head would burst with the thoughts and emotions churning around and around like a dog chasing its tail. Even her hands were shaking, making her cast vibrate against her tight chest.

She, Lyssa Smith, was on the verge of being out of control, she realized incredulously. Just as she had been when she had chased Dane out of her apartment with her fists and her rage. And she wondered why he hadn't changed his dinner plans to accommodate her?

She forced herself to take a deep breath. Then she slid back and awkwardly fastened the seat belt. The way her day was going, she better not tempt fate.

Eleven

DANE FOUND HIS OFFICE DOOR AJAR and wondered if the cleaning staff had left it that way. He'd come in an hour earlier than usual to catch Lyssa at Clearview. She made a point to be at her desk by eight to check for messages before heading for the library or whatever archives she might be working in on a given day. She would find several messages from him, but he was thinking now that it might be advisable to talk to her in person before she heard his earliest comments.

They'd been made in the heat of the moment, while he was still bristling after crossing swords with his mother under Tank's oblivious plug-ugly nose, still fantasizing about taking Lyssa's slim neck between his hands and throttling her. All those flowers, fruit baskets, chocolates, candles, even the orchid he'd picked out for her on a whim —evidently none of it meant anything to her. Or worse, the fact that he sent her placating gifts meant she could take the opportunity to make a fool of him.

It might be a very good thing after all that she didn't have an answering machine on her home phone, he thought with an inward snarl. A man could be arrested for some of the things he'd felt like saying to her.

Dane pushed open the heavy door and was only mildly surprised to find Claudia sitting in his chair, computer on, e-mail up, phone in hand with message pad in front of her. She was apparently concentrating so hard that she hadn't heard him come in.

Leaning against the doorframe, Dane folded his arms over his chest. He drew in a few deep breaths to relax the tension that gripped the base of his skull. He wanted his office to himself this morning.

She looked up with a start. She smiled, nodded and lifted one finger to show that she was nearly done, then jotted down a few more numbers and placed the handset back on the base.

Dane supposed she always reviewed his e-mail and his personal calendar. He tried not to let that bother him. "Anything from Lyssa this morning?"

"No, she hasn't called." Claudia met his gaze directly. Her irises were like chips of ice, almost colorless. "But everyone else has. You're not likely to have any time for yourself today. Seems everybody wants a piece of you."

Dane lifted one hand to his chin and ran it across the freshly shaved skin.

"Dane?" Claudia had left his chair and was watching him from less than an arm's length away.

He caught himself staring at the silky sunshine-yellow blouse she was wearing, the top two buttons undone.

"Are you planning to stand there all morning, or are you going to get on some of these calls? I've prioritized them for you." She held out a neatly printed list. "The first thing is to drive out to the Red Mountain project. There's a crew standing idle up there. Something about trusses not being delivered."

He looked at the sheet but made no move to take it. "I'm not driving to the other side of the Valley during rush hour. Danny's in charge out there, right? Doesn't he have a cell phone?"

Her eyes went wide in surprise. Was it so unexpected, he wondered, to have him act like the one who gave the orders in this office?

"Well, yes," she admitted. "That's how he called in to let you know—"

"Get him on the phone for me. But before you do, bring me the job file. I want to know who was supposed to deliver the trusses and when."

Claudia drew herself up, looking wounded. "Don't you think it would be better to take care of this face to face?"

"You'd be amazed at what a phone call can accomplish."

"Yes, I suppose," she allowed doubtfully.

Dane straightened from his slouch against the door. When that placed him too close to her and a cloud of perfume that made his nose twitch, he took the paper and moved around behind his desk to scan the list.

"Call Alex," he instructed without lifting his eyes. "I want to see him at—" A quick glance at his watch showed him it was already past eight. "At nine." He sat and reached for the phone.

"Alex never comes in before ten," she informed him tightly. "I really don't think these emergencies can wait until he sees fit to show up. Besides, these people don't want to have him handling matters. They want you."

"Claudia."

"Yes?"

"I know you don't like referring matters of any importance to Alex. But for once, would you please not argue with me?" He left his hand on the phone. "I need you to make reservations for a flight to New York."

There was a moment of dead silence. Then she asked, "For you?"

"And book me a hotel while you're at it."

She gaped at him, her mouth hanging open in what was the first unattractive expression he could recall seeing on her face. Perhaps it was the first genuine one.

Dane thought longingly of the aspirin in his desk drawer. He had to get her out of his office before his headache worsened. "Not a fancy hotel, just a chain. Marriott, Hilton, whatever. Find me something geared toward business travelers. I want a week in New York."

"I don't understand."

He removed his hand from the phone. "It's like this, Claudia." She looked expectant. "I am the employer, and you are the employee. That means you're supposed to do what I tell you, not the other way 'round. Make the call."

"You're going to meet with Gaspar Adams after all? Your mother won't like it."

"She and I have come to an understanding." He linked his hands behind his head and leaned back in the chair, returning her assessing stare with a bland look of his own.

"Oh." Claudia sucked in her lower lip. She blinked, released her lip, and smiled as if genuinely pleased. "Well, that's good."

"I'd like a flight out this afternoon. Early evening at the latest."

"Today?" she squeaked. "But what about the list—"

"I'll take care of what I can. Alex will do the rest."

"Who's going to be in charge while you're gone?" Her normally pale face had gone rather pink, including the tip of her nose.

"Alex, of course." A subtle tightening of her expression goaded him into adding, "I'll expect you to support him all the way.

Anything you would do for me, you do for him while I'm gone. All your prioritized lists and information and organizing and making life two hundred percent easier. You understand?"

"Of course."

"I mean it. I want you to make him look good. I know you do that for me all the time. It's for the good of the company," he reminded her, for extra measure. "And—" The next words caught in his throat. "It's just for a week," he finished lamely.

"Umm. Okay." Claudia appeared to relax. She smiled at him. "Well. We never said good morning, did we?"

"Good morning. Get on those reservations, would you? And bring me the file for Red Mountain."

Her smile faded. She turned on her heel and undulated away on what he had to admire as truly world-class legs.

Dane dialed Lyssa's number. The sooner he reached her, the sooner he could switch his mind over to trusses. But when her recorded voice came on, he hung up the phone in disgust. He'd already left enough requests for her to call him. It was eight thirty in the morning. Where the hell was she?

He rested his head in his hands and waited for Claudia to put through the first of his phone calls. He was in desperate need of some decompression time, away from Claudia, from Alex, his mother, Lyssa, the company, and Red Mountain. Talking a complete stranger out of his money sounded perfect. And if this was the nearest he could come to a vacation, so be it.

Like Julia said, it was New York. Maybe he could visit an art gallery and take in a few ball games.

LYSSA LEANED INTO THE CORNER of her cubicle and kept her voice low. "Leave another message with you? I don't think so. The one I left yesterday didn't work out too well, did it?"

"Was there a problem?" Claudia's chuckle sounded throaty and very pleased.

Lyssa wondered if the woman had ever considered making her fortune with phone sex.

"It's too bad there was so much background noise," Claudia said. "I must not have heard you clearly." Then the tone of her voice sharpened. "I'm sorry, he doesn't have time to take your call."

"Is that him speaking, or you?"

A masculine voice rumbled in the background.

"Excuse me a moment." Claudia's voice came faintly across the line saying, "Nothing important." Then a pause.

It was Dane, Lyssa realized; when she strained her ears, she heard him asking Claudia if she'd reached Alex.

To which his snake-in-the-grass assistant replied, "Not yet. I'll try again right now."

Then she was back with Lyssa. "I'm sorry I can't accommodate you."

Obviously, Dane was standing nearby. Lyssa felt like screaming in Claudia's ear in an attempt to let him know that it was *her* on the phone. She decided, after momentarily enjoying the fantasy, that she would not stoop to that level. "Well, when would be a good—" The line clicked and went dead.

She'd assumed that Dane would have gotten past his initial upset by now and would be willing to hear her explanation. What was more, she was pretty certain Claudia was the one to blame for the mix-up last night, not Dane. She could make a simple apology by e-mail, but she would have trouble typing with only one hand. He needed to know that she hadn't just blown him off. Besides, Lyssa admitted, she felt compelled to talk to him.

When the telephone rang, she jumped and smacked her cast on the edge of her computer table. She bit back a curse at the resulting stab of pain. Gingerly she reached for the phone. "Clearview Engineering. This is Lyssa," she said after settling the handset against her ear.

"Lyssa? I just heard." It was Simon Levitt, the boss-man himself. "How are you?"

It took a few moments for his question to register, and a little longer to work out what he was asking. He was talking about her arm. "I'm all right."

"I think you should come down to my office."

"Oh. Okay." She looked at the telephone for a while after he hung up.

If Simon had heard about Lyssa's accident from Barb, there was no telling whether he was calling her in to express his sympathy, put her on sick leave until she could work again, or fire her for being so stupid. She pushed back her chair slowly, ready to run the gantlet of all the suited-up pencil-straighteners who would stare at her as she walked down the hall to Simon's office and would then whisper about her likely fate among themselves.

But instead of hopping up like a good little employee for her meeting with Simon, Lyssa pulled herself close to the workstation and pressed redial. When Claudia answered, she didn't identify herself. "Is Mr. Callicott available?"

"Lyssa Smith. Don't you ever give up?"

So much for anonymity, Lyssa mused. She wouldn't have thought that she had talked with Dane's assistant often enough for her voice to be recognized. "Let me talk to Dane."

"He isn't in."

"He was a minute ago."

"Well, he isn't now."

"When do you expect him?" Lyssa knew there was no use in asking to have him return her call. If the message got through at all, it would be garbled.

"Let me give you a piece of advice, woman to woman."

If that didn't sound just like Gail, Lyssa thought, taking the phone away from her ear in disbelief while she sighed. *Were these women issued some kind of handbook on intragender confrontation?* "I'm eventually going to catch up with him. You know that, don't you?"

Claudia only laughed. "You may not have enough experience to see what's happening here. Dane is like any other man; he wants to do the pursuing."

"Yes, well, thank you very much for the advice. If I were actually pursuing him, I'm sure it would be useful."

"Do you think I'm the one keeping him from you? You're wrong. If he really wanted you to be able to reach him whenever you pleased, he would have given you his home number."

"What makes you think he didn't?"

Claudia sounded sly. "You're having to call him here, aren't you? Not that you trust him any further, evidently. Your number isn't in his address book."

Thank goodness for that, Lyssa thought. The notion that Claudia would have access to anything personal about her gave her the creeps.

"But I can't see why you would want to take a call from him at work," Claudia went on. "Barbara Pearce wouldn't like that at all. She has quite a thing about letting personal affairs invade the work environment, doesn't she? Would you like me to tell her that you've spent the whole morning harassing Dane Callicott? Because I will, you know, if you keep calling."

This time it was Lyssa who hung up, shaken.

DANE STARED ACROSS THE DESK at Alex. "What do you mean, you don't want Claudia for your assistant? You don't have any choice. In—" He cast a quick glance at his watch. "In two hours I'm going to be on my way to New York. She's the only one around here who knows what needs to be done while I'm gone."

"I'd say that's sufficient reason in itself," his best friend said darkly. "That woman is dangerous."

"Look, as long as Claudia doesn't know that your role in the company is going to change permanently, she won't do anything to undercut you."

"Are you sure about that?"

"Pretty sure."

"You better know what you're doing." Alex stabbed a forefinger at him. "And you're the one calling Julia to tell her what you've done. I'm not having her think I asked to work with Claudia." He affected a shudder. "Man. That woman is a barracuda."

Dane laughed. "Yeah, I'll do that. Call Julia, I mean."

"You'd better."

"Don't worry about Claudia." Dane figured she would behave as long as she didn't suspect that the balance of power was shifting permanently.

A few minutes after Alex had left, Dane tapped on the office door that bore a nameplate imprinted "Vivian Callicott." He didn't wait for her permission to enter. When he opened the door and stepped through, he caught her midsentence on the telephone.

She glanced up. Her lips thinned. "Excuse me, I have to go. I will call you later." She hung up without taking her eyes off him.

"Hello, Mother. You've recovered from last night's outing, I see. You look fresh, as always." He crossed the lavender-and-gold carpeting, sparing a glance around the expansive room. Unlike the rest of the Callicott offices, this was in Art Deco style, with graceful vases and lamps and statuettes poised atop side-tables and stands. One part of the room, dominated by the black lacquered desk behind which his mother sat, looked almost functional, but it was balanced by a conversation area where she did her real work, with upholstered chairs and a small settee placed just so around an oval table, creating an atmosphere of welcome and concern.

It was one of the most elegant office designs Dane had ever seen. For his entire life he'd marveled at the sense of ease and comfort that the various shades of muted purples and yellows and golds created in him. He sometimes wondered whether the effect had led him toward his interest in art.

Considering how that notion would appall her if he ever brought it up, he smiled. Dane sidestepped the desk and stooped to kiss her cheek, which bore the merest hint of perfumed powder.

She flushed slightly at the attention but said sharply, "Don't think you can charm your way past me, Dane."

"I wouldn't dream of it."

"Oh, come and sit down." She rose from behind the desk and led the way to her staging area. She motioned for Dane to be seated beside her on the loveseat-sized sofa.

"You were very sneaky last night." She shook her head in reproof.

Dane observed that not a hair dared to shift from its proper place. He wanted her more off-balance than that. "Talking in front of Turnbull, you mean? But he's such a dear friend of yours," he teased. "I thought it only fair to let him in on the ground floor. So to speak."

"I meant your plan to leave Alex in charge while you go off to play white knight and savior," she corrected.

"Is that all?" He shook his head. In mock sorrow he said, "Mother, Mother, Mother. It's not like you to be so slow to pick up on the implications." He sighed. "Oh, well, if you want to be saddled with misplaced trusses and budgeting for computer networks and modifications to corporate structure . . ." He made as if to rise.

"Sit down."

He settled, amused to see her fingers tapping on the flowing arm of the settee. "I always assumed your talents lay elsewhere," he observed idly. "Influence, connections, charm, and an agile mind. I'd say those are all qualities that would be extremely useful for a corporate executive. Unless you prefer to remain the power behind the throne."

She aimed a carefully manicured finger at him. "Stop wasting our time. I agreed to go along with this farce for a week, because Thomas was right there and we needed a show of solidarity. But I have known you for more than thirty years, and I know all your tricks. I see what you have up your sleeve. I am telling you right now that no amount of idle flattery will convince me to promote Alex Garcia to CEO in your stead."

Dane nodded. "Of course idle flattery wouldn't," he agreed equably. "But the real thing? I'm hoping that's another matter."

She glared. "The point is, there must be a Callicott at the head of Callicott Properties, just as there always has been. It is a part of our reputation that people can count on."

"The point is, the business is changing around us," he told her, able to talk more freely now that Tank wasn't around to haul her back into the dark ages. "Callicott has become a large corporation. There are people who can be trusted in several key positions, heading up the legal, finance, property management, and personnel departments. The one who makes them all work smoothly together is Alex. I can see the potential for new projects, but taking care of the details to get them from start to finish? I depend on Alex for that."

"He is just an employee."

"Most CEOs are." He pretended to study his fingernails, knowing his refusal to look at her would irk her. "Employed at the behest of a board of directors. Which you have more influence over, Mother, than I do. If you really wanted to be rid of Alex Garcia, after a trial period, you could make it happen."

She didn't move a muscle. "What sort of trial period?"

"There's one more aspect to consider before we talk about that. If you promise to stand behind Alex and me—support him for CEO—I'll step down entirely and take a backseat role. Maybe a vice-presidency of some sort." He waved off the details, privately considering them unimportant. He didn't care what he was called.

"Hardly a tempting prospect. You know my stance on having a Callicott running the company."

He reached out for her delicate hand and grasped it gently, watching the way the rings picked up the light as he settled it in his own. "I'm not the only Callicott involved in the business." He watched as she turned that over in her head. He could tell the moment she comprehended his ultimate goal.

"Ridiculous." She pulled her hand away from his and clasped both of hers together in her lap, so tightly that her knuckles turned white. "A woman cannot head a company like Callicott Properties, not after three generations of Callicott men. What would people think?"

"There's no sense in letting the past dictate the future. Think about it. 'President, Vivian Callicott.'" He moved his hand as though marking the words on an imaginary nameplate. "It would look good on your stationery. Certainly would impress your friends."

Her cheeks flushed. "Besides the fact that I'm a woman, you have to consider my age. This is a young man's business."

Dane grinned. "That's not what you've been saying about Tank Turnbull. Hasn't he forgotten more about development than I'll ever know?"

"Tell that to your Lyssa Smith," she flashed back, as hard and cold as the diamonds in her rings. "Would you have felt so free to talk about this idea if she'd joined us last night, as you had so obviously planned? Oh, yes," she said, "I saw through your transparent invitation to Thomas." She sniffed in disdain and lifted her chin. "An apology, indeed. You were never the one who owed him an apology."

But thankfully she didn't ask why his plans had changed. Dane didn't know what he would have said if she had.

Then she leaned forward and searched his face intently. "How much do you want this?" she demanded at last. "Enough to give up New York—and that resort in Tucson?"

Dane shook his head. He rose, judging that he had given her plenty to think about for now. And needing to get away from her sharp, too-perceptive gaze. "No, not that much. Let's see how you and Alex do as a pair—" He felt as though the air was being sucked from the room. Bracing one hand on the arm of the couch, he managed to stay on his feet, but a sudden stab of pain in his sternum caused him to grab at his chest. In a moment the pain let up enough that he could get air into his lungs through shallow pants in his diaphragm, but his stomach threatened to rebel. "God!"

He became aware of his mother shrieking at him.

"Dane! Are you all right? Lie down, lie down! I'm calling an ambulance."

She rushed toward the phone on her desk. As she passed, he grabbed her with one hand. "No, don't," he ordered, tugging her around to face him.

"Dane!" She yanked at his grasp, so frantic to make that call that she didn't feel the strength in his hold.

He gathered from the wild panic on her face that she was seeing his father's final heart attack all over again. "It'll go away in a minute," he told her, pretty sure he was right. Dane took several deeper breaths, testing the intensity of the resulting twinges. He forced a reassuring smile, although that was rushing matters. "Muscle spasm."

She paled but stopped pulling. Wordlessly she took his arm and helped him to the settee. He didn't protest. Sitting beside him, she rested her hand on his chest, as though she needed to satisfy herself that his heart was still beating. "Have you consulted a doctor?" she asked, a pucker between her eyebrows.

Dane reconsidered the explanation he'd been set to offer. He could let her know there was nothing to worry about, as he had done with Lyssa, or he could play on her sympathies. "Not for a while." He leaned back as though overcome by weakness. "But they say it's just muscle spasms."

"Your heart is a muscle, too," she reminded him tartly. She pulled her hand away. As it dropped to her lap, she twisted her long, slender fingers together. "Your father had a perfectly normal stress test just before—"

Dane wondered at the irony of it. For ages he'd been suffering from signs of tension and stress without his mother noticing—and then a little muscle spasm that could be fixed in five minutes through a chiropractic-type manipulation had her going nuts. "All I need is a vacation," he told her.

Sympathy, bewilderment, and doubt were written on her haggard face. Her age showed clearly through the artful makeup. "A vacation?"

"Call it a change of scene, then," he said, a little impatiently. "I need this break. I need New York." Though it was cruel to take advantage of her fears, he went on, "I need to know that Alex will be capable of running the company and that you can take over if anything happens to me." When she stiffened, he hastily added, "Not that I expect anything to."

He wondered if he had overplayed his hand when she continued to stare at him.

"There's nothing I can say to change your mind about this trip?"

"Not a thing. Just . . . try not to worry while I'm gone. Everything will be fine."

"You'll go to a doctor." It wasn't a question.

"As soon as I get back. I promise." He considered telling her that they had doctors in New York, too—ones who wouldn't report his condition to his mother. But even he wasn't that insensitive.

Dane rose and walked toward the door, keeping any sign of weakness out of his steps. As he reached for the gracefully curved door latch, his mother's hand came out and rested on his. "I mean it, Dane. You will see a doctor about those . . . muscle spasms. You are more important to me than Callicott is."

Good to know, he thought. "Will you consider what I've said about reorganizing Callicott?"

She sighed. "One week. Then we reassess the situation."

"You sound like a corporate executive already."

"Get out of here, you foolish boy." But her face was drawn and tired, and the words had no sting.

LYSSA CALLED DANE again around two o'clock.

She'd spent most of the day struggling with office-bound tasks that she had been putting off for weeks. That was all Simon would let her do for the time being. Until the merger was complete and she had researchers to train and oversee, he announced, Barb would be responsible for the more physical aspects of Lyssa's job. Which included typing, apparently. Lyssa was not looking forward to working closely with Barb. It was one more snag in her already tangled intentions of just hanging on.

"Is Dane in?" she asked politely of Claudia.

"He's on his way out the door, but I'll see if he can take your call." Muffled, as though she had put her hand over the mouthpiece, Dane's assistant said, "It's Lyssa Smith. Do you want to talk to her?"

After a moment he came on to say, without so much as a greeting, "Lyssa, this isn't a good time."

"I just wanted to explain—"

"I'm going out of town."

"To New York?"

"—running late." His voice faded, and she heard faintly, "Take care of this for me, would you?"

Then it was Claudia again. "He really is on his way out the door. So sorry it didn't work out for you."

Lyssa settled the handset in the cradle before Claudia could say *I told you so.*

Dane hadn't given her anything. No "I'll call you when I get back." No "Did something happen last night?" Not even "You still owe Tank an apology" or "I'm not finished with you."

So. At least she knew it was Dane who really didn't want to talk to her, not just Claudia standing in the way. She tried to convince herself it was ultimately his loss, not hers.

The jerk. She was not going to cry over him. She was not—*aw, crud*, she thought. Lyssa reached for her box of tissues and was perversely glad when she smacked her cast against the edge of the computer table again, for about the fiftieth time. The thump of the cast and her resounding yelp provided a good excuse for the tears in her eyes when Barb appeared without warning in the narrow gap that served as the entrance to her cubicle.

Twelve

LYSSA BLINKED RAPIDLY to dispel the shimmer that obscured her view of Barb's expression. She wondered how long she had before Barb managed to convince Simon that Clearview didn't need her. At least he hadn't made her take sick leave. Then again, he hadn't hired a temp for her to oversee; she was supposed to borrow some of her own boss's free time. Didn't Barb have enough to do in falsifying reports, threatening employees, and generally causing trouble for Lyssa?

The mantra *a few more months, a few more months* was wearing thin already, she concluded grimly.

Over her lunch hour, Lyssa had placed a phone call to Donald Jacobson. His smug satisfaction upon quoting a price to her had driven her to that abortive final attempt to make amends with Dane despite Claudia's threat. Any hope that Jacobson would prove reasonable had been dashed. She didn't think her existing salary would be enough to qualify her for a mortgage at that level, although she hadn't yet called Julia to check. The promotion now seemed increasingly vital—at the very time when she couldn't even perform her own job duties and would have Barb hanging over her shoulder, ready to swoop down on any mistake like a vulture to roadkill.

The knowledge that so much rested on her ability to play nice with Barb sent a shiver through Lyssa. "So, I guess you're ready to see what it is I do."

Barb's smile was more a baring of teeth. The strong red lipstick wrapped around her mouth reminded Lyssa of blood. "Sure. Let's get started." She glanced at her watch and moved forward, crowding Lyssa's chair.

Lyssa rose, for once appreciative of her advantage in height. "Why don't you sit. I can show you how I organize my files. I design the research path for each project in advance. Anything that arises along the way gets incorporated, but at the beginning—"

"Now, Lyssa, you don't have to justify your work to me," Barb murmured with evident amusement.

Lyssa supposed she *had* sounded defensive. She bent to point at the computer screen. "There," she instructed. "Click there, then pull down the menu."

"I think I can manage to figure it out."

As Lyssa pulled back, she brushed against Barb's shoulder. She flinched when Barb turned her head and they were eye to eye. Straightening abruptly, for a moment Lyssa felt self-conscious, as though she had part of her breakfast caught in her teeth or egg yolk on her chin. "What?"

"That was . . . interesting."

Lyssa stiffened. "What do you mean?"

"I just found it interesting. That's all." Barb turned her attention back to the screen, but a secretive smile played on her red lips. Her hands made a few more exploratory efforts with the mouse and menus. Then she checked her watch again.

"Do you have somewhere else you need to be?" Lyssa held her breath, hoping for an affirmative answer that would get Barb out of this space, entirely too cramped with both of them in it.

Barb looked at her, that disturbing smile still in place. "Tell me, Lyssa, do you find me attractive?"

"Attractive?"

"Yes, that's what I said." She waited for an answer.

Lyssa took a deep breath. "Well, you're always nicely dressed, and I guess you shower regularly—"

"How coy." Barb swiveled around and pinned Lyssa with a direct stare. "And how clever. I meant sexually attractive. Are you attracted to me, Lyssa?"

"No!"

"Are you positive? You've never felt the slightest temptation to kiss me, or feel how I would feel against you?"

Lyssa shuddered. "I'm not interested in women, Barb, and I certainly haven't had any of those kinds of urges where you're concerned."

Barb didn't seem to take the answer personally. "I just thought that because of your parents, you might be. Tempted, that is."

"My parents?" Lyssa whispered. *How could Barb know?* She had done everything within her power to keep her family's exact makeup a secret, even from Paulina, who had known her for all these years.

"I mean about them being gay."

"I'm not—" Lyssa found her voice rising, so she took a deep breath and started over again. "I'm not oriented that way." She refused to either verify or deny what her parents were.

"So you say." Barb sounded almost amused.

Feeling her hands beginning to shake, Lyssa focused on the open dialogue box. "Select 'Options' here."

"Are you ashamed of them?"

Lyssa glared at her. "In the first place, I don't talk about my parents. It's nobody's business how they choose to live their lives. In the second place, I am not ashamed of them. They've given me no reason to be. I love them dearly." Although at the moment she didn't like them very much, for she hadn't forgiven them for their withdrawal of support for her plans. And if their sexual preferences were going to get her in trouble with Barb—

Lyssa fisted her left hand at her side.

"If you do find yourself attracted to me, maybe you should act on that urge. Just once. What would it hurt?"

Speechless, Lyssa was glad for her sling and cast, which placed a barrier—fragile though it might be—between her and this very strange woman, who seemed very much like a praying mantis at the moment. Capable of mating and then biting the head off of her partner.

"This is inappropriate conversation for the workplace," she said.

Barb's eyes glinted dully under the fluorescent lights. Again she glanced at her watch. "You know we scientist types are naturally curious." Her evident self-satisfaction made Lyssa's skin crawl. A few prowling steps took her across the space that separated them. She let her fingers trail up Lyssa's uncasted arm. Goosebumps rose along the path of her touch.

"What do you think you're doing?" Lyssa pulled her arm away and backed toward the opening.

"Just checking you out."

"You're supposed to be checking out my work."

"Am I? Maybe later." Barb caught her arm and leaned her body against Lyssa's, whispering, "Have you ever done it with a woman?"

Lyssa tried to squirm away. "Get out of here before I report you for sexual harassment." She sucked in a breath. It was weird to even think about that.

Barb didn't back off. Instead, she stepped even closer, trapping Lyssa against the cubicle wall. "I don't think so," she murmured. "No one will believe you. Once everybody finds out your parents are gay, anything you say will be discredited. As for me, I'm married. They'll think you're lying, a lesbian, you couldn't control yourself around me any longer. Whatever. The painkillers you're taking have released your inhibitions. Everyone knows you're not interested in men."

"Everyone does not know that, because it's not true!" Lyssa tried to slide past, but her breast brushed against Barb's as she moved. The sensation was creepy, certainly not arousing. She froze in place. "Get out of here. These cubicles aren't at all private."

"I'm counting on that fact." Barb's eyes flickered past Lyssa's shoulder.

Then the other woman's hands were clamped tightly on the front of Lyssa's shirt. Noxious perfume filled her nose, and eerily soft lips played over hers. She brought up her arms between them, but the pain that shot through her broken arm had her flinching instead of breaking Barb's hold.

A man's voice off to her left side said, "Hey! What's this? Lyssa caught in a lip-lock with the boss. That's one way of getting your promotion."

Lyssa finally managed to shove Barb away. She looked up to see three avid faces surveying her and Barb, curiosity and fascination plain in the trio's expressions. "I don't believe this!"

"I don't either," said one of the men, but he looked intrigued rather than horrified, as Lyssa was.

She pressed her sleeve to her mouth trying to wipe off the taste of lipstick. Lipstick—in garish red—came off on the cloth. She glared at the other woman only to find Barb doing exactly the same thing. Not using her sleeve, of course, but a convenient handkerchief. How dare Barb pretend to be disgusted at the kiss *she had instigated!*

"This is not what it looks like," Lyssa exclaimed.

But Barb burst into noisy crocodile tears. "Don't try to deny it! How could you do such a thing to me? Just because you're gay, don't think Simon won't fire your ass when he finds out." She pushed past the crowd gathered outside the cubicle, all of them goggling like rubber-neckers at a fatal accident.

THE NEXT MORNING, Lyssa stood back from the booth as her mother Helen weighed brilliant red tomatoes on the scale and laughed at whatever the customer had just said. The tomato purchaser was a craggy-faced man, flirting for all he was worth. Too bad he was wasting his time. Not only had Helen been faithful to her partner for well over thirty years, but she—unlike her daughter—wasn't interested in men.

"Lyssa! Sweetheart!" she called out with evident delight. "Were we expecting you?"

Lyssa caught the moment in which her mother spotted the cast and sling.

"Oh. My. Word." Helen's luminous face went blank. She hurried around the table, shoving past people as though they were invisible to her. She started to hug her daughter close but reconsidered and placed an arm around Lyssa's waist instead, carefully drawing her close. "What happened? This is incredible. Are you all right?"

"I'm fine. Really. I knew you'd worry, so I figured I'd better come down and show you I'm okay."

"Of course we would worry—once we found out you'd been hurt!" Helen set Lyssa back from her and stared pointedly at her, giving her a gentle shake.

Lyssa shrugged. "It wasn't that big a deal. But Anton will tell Ari, and—"

"What on earth does Anton have to do with this?" Helen's hands fell away.

"He saw me after it happened. I was supposed to meet some people at the Highline."

Helen put up a hand impatiently. "But what happened?"

Lyssa decided to stick with the simplest part of her recent disaster. "I was mugged."

Her mother drew her over to one of the chairs at the back of the booth and pressed her down into it. "Mugged! Where? Were you at home? I've always said that neighborhood of yours was too rough."

"Mother," Lyssa said, laughing for the first time in more hours than she cared to remember. So Dane and her mother were in agreement on one issue, at least. "I was crossing a parking lot at the university in broad daylight. A guy wanted my laptop, and he took it. The arm was an accident."

"Is it broken?" Helen seemed torn between outrage and vicarious interest.

No one in their family had ever broken anything before. Lyssa grinned. How perverse to feel a thrill of pride over such a thing. "It is. A greenstick fracture, they said at the hospital."

"Hospital! You had to go to the hospital for it? Why didn't you leave a message on the phone? This was an emergency!"

"No, no." Lyssa caught her mother's hand, which was fluttering distractingly in front of her face. "You wouldn't have been able to do anything to fix it even if you'd known."

"We could have been there at the hospital for you."

She shrugged again. "I was okay." Indeed, the hospital had proved the least of her problems.

"The city is too dangerous. You ought to come home for good."

Lyssa evidently hadn't been sufficiently reassuring. Worse, she was almost tempted to take her mother up on the offer. The city was turning snake-mean. It made the confines of her parents' farm look pretty good.

"Excuse me!" someone called.

Helen glanced up, evidently planning to tell them they would have to wait.

"Go on," Lyssa assured her. "I'll be fine." She shooed her mother away. Then she stretched out her legs, leaning back against the nylon webbing of the chair and closing her eyes, letting exhaustion and numbness take her.

Despite the surprise her parents had leveled her with last week, they were the only family she had. She knew she could count on their concern, their good intentions toward her. They only wanted what they thought was best for her.

For a moment she gave herself up to the tempting notion of going home and letting herself be pampered and putting all distressing things —and people—out of her mind for a few days. *Is that too much to ask?* wondered a small voice deep inside. Evidently so, she concluded, as memories of the previous day overtook her.

Simon had placed her on leave. Looking back, she supposed his circumspection was due to one miscalculation on Barb's part. If Lyssa had actually been gay and Simon fired her, she could bring a discrimination suit against Clearview. And so she'd told him, when she tired of his yammering about her disgraceful conduct and her poor judgment and the position she had put him in, because she certainly couldn't be given charge of a whole department.

"Barb is my supervisor," she had reminded him. "Sexual harassment is applied from the top, not from the bottom." The connotation of those positions hadn't struck her until he paled and began to flap his mouth like a landed fish.

Technically she was still employed; she supposed that was a point in her favor. Of course, how long that would last was anybody's guess. By her count, this was the third strike against her. She hoped Simon wasn't a baseball fan.

She would really like to run home to the farm to lick her wounds and put everything that had happened during the past few weeks into perspective. Too bad she had to lock in this deal with Jacobson before time ran out. That meant staying near a telephone—and that meant she couldn't retreat to Elysian Fields.

The crowd thickened at the farmers' market as the morning wore on. Lyssa found herself helping customers, just as she had done in her younger days. She enjoyed the contact, although she was shaken once when she glanced away from a youngish man with a sheriff-of-Nottingham beard who was asking her about a salad combination; her eyes momentarily passed over a woman who looked like Barb staring at her. When she looked back, the woman was gone.

She wondered whether that was how Barb had found out her secret. Could it have been something as simple and accidental as seeing Helen and Paris together, with her, at one of these farmers' markets?

Although Paris normally stayed on the farm—agonizing over her heirloom varieties and tending them like her own children while Ari accompanied Helen to the market and made deliveries to the restaurants and health-food stores and caterers who wouldn't settle for anything less than the best and freshest in organic produce—sometimes Ari went with Cal to job sites and Helen and Paris worked the markets. Lyssa often joined them. She wondered whether the universe could have served her such an ill turn.

"So I should buy some carrots, too, and add a few carrot leaves to the salad?" asked the guy with the sculpted beard as he leaned toward her across the basket-covered tabletop. She supposed he thought the dark line of hair against his jaw gave him a chin. He already held two bags of different lettuce varieties and a spring mix she had talked Helen into stocking regularly.

"If you'd like," she said agreeably. "Next week you could come earlier and try a bit of an herb mix that I like to add in. I'm afraid it's sold out for today."

"Do you make up these mixes with your own hands?"

"No, she doesn't," Helen said, evidently finished with her own rush of customers. "Why don't you go and sit down, honey? You must be exhausted."

Lyssa didn't argue, because when she glanced toward the chairs at the back of the booth she saw Ari working his way toward them. Besides, she didn't mind having Helen discourage the young man's flirtation. After being burned—and then frozen out—by Dane, she could use a break from men. And women, too. She sighed.

Disappointed, the weak-chinned wonder paid for what he had and left, shooting Lyssa several glances as though hoping she would change her mind.

Ari's sun-dried face brightened when he spotted Lyssa. "Your arm—how is it?" he demanded as soon as he ducked under the back overhang of the booth. He reached out and stroked the blue cast material, careful not to brush against the swollen skin exposed at each end.

"It's fine. At least, it will be in a few weeks."

He beetled his heavy white brows at her. "Anton told me."

"I knew he would." She hadn't been thinking clearly enough to ask Anton to keep news of her disaster to himself. Nor was she certain he would have, even had she attempted to extract a promise of silence from him.

His loyalty to Ari ran deep. Ari had said once that Anton was a part of his inner soul-circle, a satellite body that had orbited his own for hundreds of lifetimes. And how could Lyssa, or anyone else, she mused, argue with a statement like that?

"How did you get here? He said you took a cab home the other night."

"I rode the bus."

"Do you need a ride home?"

"That would be nice. And maybe one of you could pick up my truck? I left it in a parking lot down by the university."

Ari cocked his head to one side. "You parked on campus? You've always said there was no point—you were better off leaving your vehicle at home rather than trying to find an open parking spot."

"Well," Lyssa hedged, wondering exactly how much Anton had told him. "I had a lot of stuff going on that night."

"So I hear."

Helen joined them then, positioning herself where she could see the front tables without craning her neck. "She was attacked!" she exclaimed accusingly. "I told her she should come home. City living is not right for our daughter."

Ari eyed Lyssa with a considering gaze that made her nervous. "I'm no longer sure about that. She's not likely to meet her soul's mate if she hunkers down on the farm. The larger the population center, the better the prospects."

"Years in the city haven't accomplished anything," Helen scoffed.

"Anton said she was meeting a man."

Lyssa swallowed. She did not like the way this conversation was going. "Um, it wasn't quite like that."

Helen interrupted, snapping out, "A man! She doesn't need a man. What she needs is to dedicate her life to something worthwhile."

"Are you saying, now, that you don't think getting together to engender and raise a fine child is worthwhile?" Ari's voice was whisper-soft, but his words stopped Helen cold.

Her eyes met his, then fell away. "If she were going to meet her partner in the city, the universe would already have put *her* in Lyssa's way."

Lyssa didn't miss the emphasis on the pronoun. That was one of the essential differences between Helen and Ari. Helen still had hope that her daughter would turn away from "the dark side" and find a same-sex partner. Ari didn't care about her sexual orientation—as long as she had a child who would bear his genes one generation further into the future. "Excuse me," she said dryly, interrupting the tiresome argument. "Could we get back to making plans for picking up my truck?"

"I still think you should come home with us, at least for the weekend," Helen said.

"I can't. I have to stay near the telephone. I found Jacobson and made an offer. I'm hoping he'll counter with something more reasonable over the weekend."

"Oh, Lyssa."

Ari gave her a speaking look, and she subsided. "Now, Helen, we've talked about this," he said warningly. "The notion of her buying a neighboring property isn't so bad. It would give her a place to come to—not quite under our roof, but close enough that we would see her often."

Helen glared at him. "It would be better to have her with us."

"Ah," he murmured, "but eventually her situation might change. She might need more room. For a family."

"We're her family."

Ari turned his head away from the woman he had gotten pregnant almost thirty years ago and stared at the child they had produced. "Things change."

Lyssa's instincts went on the alert.

"This Dane Callicott sounds like a promising young man. Economically productive, good looking, genetically sound."

"You know better than to believe Anton!" Lyssa had hoped he would confine his news to the important thing: her broken arm.

"Dane Callicott is not interested in marriage," she declared. "At least, not to me! It was a business meeting, that's all. I doubt I'll be seeing him again."

"Who," stated Ari with fatal calm, "said anything about marriage?"

Thirteen

RESTLESS AND STRANGELY AT ODDS with himself, Dane paced through his hotel room.

His meeting with Gaspar Adams earlier that day had gone well. To his surprise, he'd enjoyed talking with the older man, whose eccentric unwillingness to come to Phoenix was explained by his elaborate mouth-controlled wheelchair and communication devices. Adams may have been unable to use his arms and legs, but his mind worked just fine.

Dane's curiosity about how Adams had found out about the Highline and Callicott Properties, though, remained largely unsatisfied. Adams had murmured something about six degrees of separation: he knew someone who knew someone who had spoken well of the Highline.

Partly in retaliation, and partly because he was not yet certain of the project's feasibility, Dane hadn't shown Adams the photographs of the Spirit Ranch in its current condition; he'd only sketched an overview of its history and laid out some of the possibilities for its future.

Adams had accepted that limited presentation without demur and graciously thanked Dane for accommodating an old man's wishes. "Call me when you've decided what you want to do," he'd said at the end.

The words kept coming back to Dane. With the meeting over, he was free to do what he wanted. For a whole week.

He could tour art galleries and studios. Catch a few games of the World Series in Yankee Stadium. Turn back the clock to a time when he should have been doing the stupid things that every young man was entitled to do and getting them out of his system. He was anonymous here. No one recognized or cared about the Callicott name.

Coming to a halt in the middle of the room, Dane let the absence of expectations wash over him. He really could do whatever he wanted. He laughed, absurdly pleased by the idea.

First thing was to call the Yankees box office, he decided. He found the number and arranged for tickets later in the week. That done, he headed downstairs and asked at the front desk for a recommendation to a jazz club.

The club was within walking distance, so he sauntered along the sidewalk, taking in the sounds and scents and sights of New York. The streets were narrower than he'd expected, and the smells of stale air and blacktop drifted by. The buildings, worn and gray, hulked over him, seemingly monolithic until he looked closer and saw the frequent sculptural details at lintel and cornerstone. The cacophony of blowing horns and cell phones ringing was ever-present but not unpleasant.

When he reached the club he stood just within the door for a few minutes, sizing up the place. It seemed a good choice. The room was poorly lit, the conversations were low, and the music was slick. The people grouped around small tables seemed to be more interested in listening than scoping out the newcomer. He seated himself at the bar and ordered a heady ale that was on tap. The bartender, a scrawny acne-marked kid who looked barely old enough to drink, didn't respond to his thanks but pocketed the tip.

After a while Dane became aware of a woman a few seats down. When he caught her eye, she lifted her glass to him and smiled an invitation. He moved to the high stool beside her. "Enjoying the music?"

She crossed her legs, easing her skirt a little higher on shapely thighs. "Very much. How about yourself?"

"It's good. Seems like it would be better with company, though."

"Depends on the company."

"Yes, it does."

They chatted a little back and forth. Neither asked the other one's name. Dane suspected, as her skirt crept higher and she repeatedly moistened her lips and appeared to have trouble dragging her attention from his mouth, that he could take her back to the hotel with him if he put forth a little effort.

Her breasts might not be real, but they were outstanding, in both size and shape, and showcased in an open-weave shirt that made a man wonder what she wore underneath. She was pretty in a hard-edged way, although he suspected her face was painted on, like stage makeup, to give definition to her features in the dim light. Best of all, she was obviously receptive.

Yet every time he tipped his mug, her eyes turned calculating and slipped down his body, as though ringing up exactly how much money he'd spent on his clothes. He'd left Phoenix without packing, so before his meeting with Adams he had stopped at one of the nearby stores and bought some casual clothes, khakis and pullovers. She lingered especially on his watch and his shoes—the things he hadn't purchased for this trip.

His smile felt as artificial as her headlamps, but he kept talking in a friendly, casual matter. He was vaguely interested in finding out how far she would go before she gave up on him. If she was a high-class hooker, she couldn't afford to reel in a guy who wasn't willing to pay for her services. If she was just hot for a man, any man, he might let himself be persuaded to play her game. But he wasn't even sure of that.

His vague sense of unease around her sparked into outright suspicion when she jerked her hand as she was putting down her drink and dumped the last of his ale onto the floor.

"Oh! Sorry!" she exclaimed. "Let me buy you another. My treat, my choice."

In the confusion that ensued as the bartender brought him a rum and Coke and mopped up the spill, Dane glanced at her hand fumbling over the plastic glass, as though she was adding something to it. One long-nailed finger pumped an ice cube up and down, subtly mixing the drink.

He grabbed her wrist, holding her finger in the glass. "What are you doing?"

"Nothing." She struggled against his hold. "What's your problem?"

The bartender came and stood glaring at them. "What's going on here?"

"She put something in my drink."

"I didn't! He's lying," she swore, twisting herself loose of Dane. To the bartender she said, "C'mon, Andy, you know I wouldn't do anything like that."

The kid looked back and forth between them.

Dane kept his expression even. What was it she'd planned to drug him with? Something to make him sleep for a while once she got him off to herself, figuring any man who wore a thousand-dollar watch would be carrying a healthy amount of cash? "Call the police," he urged, glancing at the telephone behind the bar.

She tore out of the club as fast as a woman in heels could move.

Very deliberately, the pockmarked Andy took the untouched drink and dumped it, tossing the glass into the trash with a hundred others. "No harm done," he muttered. "She won't be back."

Dane wondered how many guys she'd succeeded with. From the look of surprise on her face when he grabbed her wrist, she hadn't expected to be caught. Andy's closed expression made him wonder, too, whether the skinny guy was in on her scam. Dane walked out without paying for the drink. Suddenly club-hopping had lost its appeal. Maybe he hadn't missed out on as much as he'd thought by assuming his family responsibilities right out of college.

He lay on his bed in shorts and an FDNY T-shirt bought from the sundries store in the lobby and watched television for a few hours. When he finally fell asleep, he dreamed of the nameless woman, naked, rising over him like the moon. *You've taken my virginity,* she told him. *Now you'll have to marry me, or I'll tell your mother.* With horror he watched her face change to Lyssa's.

He woke up sweating. The gray light of morning seeped through a crack in the curtains. Seven o'clock, and barely dawn. He yawned, then stretched, his body still chilled from the effects of the dream.

He reached for the remote and shut off the television. After stumbling into the bathroom, he splashed his face with cool water.

He told the bleary-eyed stranger in the mirror that his life had to change. More, even, than he had thought only a few days earlier. It was no longer enough to ensure a diminishment of Callicott Properties' reliance on him, to see Alex as the company's CEO and his mother as its president. Dane needed something more.

He thought Lyssa might understand. She told him, that night at the Highline, how she desired to have a purpose, to leave the world a better place. He'd been in no mood to listen to anything then. Criticism and flattery alike had blended in his mind to a bitter stew of contempt. He winced as he recalled his defensive, mocking reply, which had reduced all of Lyssa's idealism to a naïve wish to be useful.

But now Dane had a glimmer of what she had meant. He could stop with the Highline and not leave any other monuments behind him. He could explore a partnership with Adams and try to regain a bit of his own idealism. He could throw Callicott back to his mother and do something entirely different. He could—Dane stopped himself before his thoughts became any wilder.

The problem at hand was to figure out how to balance what he owed to the Callicott name and what he owed to himself, he decided.

Grabbing a couple of aspirins from his earlier trip to the hotel store, Dane washed them down with a swirl of chemical-tasting water. It had been foolish of him to expect that his various aches and twinges would stay back in Phoenix with his troubles.

Still, a man could hope.

VIVIAN PLACED THE ELONGATED BLACK HANDSET of her telephone back in its gold cradle. Fretfully she rubbed her forehead, wishing she could smooth out the tension lodged there. Having to defend Alex Garcia irritated her.

As she'd expected—and warned Dane—people did not accept Garcia as a substitute for her son. It had taken her a full fifteen minutes to soothe a long-time subcontractor who took Dane's departure for New York as a personal affront. To his vow that he would not deal with a Mexican she had said, "I understand. If you really cannot work with Callicott any longer, I will have the legal department look into what it will cost to release you from the obligation. Onyx Flooring also put in a bid on that project, if I recall." His immediate denial of any intention to abrogate the contract might have been more satisfying if his had not been the fourth call of the morning.

She hadn't wanted to be proved right. Not this way.

Afraid for Dane, afraid for the future of Callicott Properties, and afraid of the decision that awaited her, Vivian wished he had not put her in this position. Then again, part of the blame could be laid at her own feet. She and Claudia had done too good a job of convincing suppliers, subcontractors, and investors that Alex was not the man to be dealt with.

Vivian pulled off her glasses and began twirling them by one temple piece. The only problem with Alex, really, she mused, was that he was not a Callicott. Given half a chance he would probably make a fine CEO. But could she—and Callicott Properties—afford to give him that chance?

Beyond the week that she had promised Dane, of course.

A week was not so very long, but surrender of even that much to her wily son was a slippery slope. Where would it end? she wondered. Even as the thought came into her head she smiled wryly, knowing the answer. It would end with Dane getting his way, of course. He always did. The only time Vivian had ever managed to achieve her own goal in opposition to his was when she had convinced Gail that a financial stake to establish a real estate business was less risky than an engagement to a man whose mother would see it ended.

Vivian would not count his giving up art: his notion of himself as a sculptor had been no more than a phase, a young man's fantasy. She hadn't even had to suggest it.

Her smile faded as she remembered the reason for that. Stewart's final illness and his all-too-quick passing had transferred the mantle of power over to his son.

What she had told Dane was the simple truth. He was more important to her than the company could ever be. He was all she had left of his father.

Although that was not all of it, not really, she mused. Stewart had left her a share of Callicott Properties, too. She had influence and connections, just as Dane had said.

The question was, what use should she put them to?

Should she stand behind him regardless of whether she understood what he was about? Or rid him of those—namely, Lyssa Smith, Gail O'Neill, even Alex Garcia if necessary—who would influence him to take the company in a direction she could not approve of?

But what if she was wrong and Dane was right? That made her think of the Garcia boy's parting shot several days earlier. How well did she understand Dane? She twirled her glasses faster.

Then she sighed and put them down, staring morosely at her dark, uncommunicative computer screen. She had not yet had time to turn it on this morning. She'd been too busy handling telephone calls from people complaining about Alex Garcia.

She supposed Dane had to waste his time with that sort of thing fairly often, particularly with Claudia doing her best to convince callers that they should deal with Dane and not Alex.

Would Dane even come back to that state of affairs? she asked herself, furrowing her brow in thought. Would he return after the week was up, or would New York seduce him away? Would he absorb the rarefied air of the East Coast and decide that eastern money was greener, eastern culture superior, eastern women more interesting? What did he have to come back for?

Reining in her rising sense of anxiety, she assured herself that of course Dane would come home. She took a deep breath and smoothed the lines in her forehead with her fingers as she reminded herself she was no longer a gauche college girl trying to cope with her one semester at Radcliffe. The East did not frighten her anymore.

Nor would it corrupt her son. Dane loved his life here. Of course, a sadistic little voice whispered in her head, he might appreciate it more if she went along with what he was asking of her.

Vivian turned on her computer and scanned her e-mail. One subject heading caught her eye. She opened the message and read it. Then she read it again, intrigued but suspicious over what certainly sounded too good to be true.

She lifted the telephone receiver and dialed a number that was becoming all too familiar. "Miss Montgomery," she said to the whiskey-smooth voice that answered. "My office."

While waiting, Vivian considered how irked she'd been by Simon Levitt's inaction on the Lyssa Smith problem and how many times over the past week or so she'd wondered whether Dane had undercut her carefully couched threats. This time Levitt would have no excuse. Vivian smiled at the serendipity of having this perfect opportunity fall into her lap while Dane was away and could do nothing on the Smith woman's behalf until it was too late.

Upon hearing the tapping of nails on her office door, she wiped away the smile and instructed her son's assistant to enter. "Tell me, Miss Montgomery, how did you discover this about Lyssa Smith?"

LYSSA PICKED UP the phone, hoping to hear Mr. Jacobson's crackling tenor returning the message she'd left earlier. She had made an offer on the property, and through some judicious faxing back and forth with Julia, she'd completed a preliminary application for a mortgage that would just about stretch to cover a reasonable counteroffer.

Or maybe, just maybe, whispered a traitorous voice within her, it was Dane, calling to tell her that he'd missed her so much, he couldn't wait until he returned from New York to talk to her. She could have smacked both Paulina and Ari upside the head for planting that invidious notion in her head. Wasn't her life complicated enough right now?

She shook her head and put the phone to her ear. "Clearview—I mean, hello?"

"Lyssa?"

"Yes, Simon?" She realized she was gripping the phone too tightly, and she loosened her fist. She stared out the freshly washed window of her apartment, watching a mile-long finned Cadillac cruise through the parking lot.

"Lyssa, this is Simon Levitt."

Her stomach rolled over. "Hello, Simon. How are things going?"

"Why don't you come in to the office today? Give us a chance to talk." He fell silent as though waiting for her agreement.

"What time?"

"Oh." The rustling of paper. "Let's say ten thirty. Does that work for you?"

"Sure." She should make it with time to spare if she called a cab as soon as she hung up with him. Anyway, what would he do if she was late: fire her? The joke rang false in her ears. "Mind telling me what we're going to be talking about?"

"Let's not get into details on the phone."

She chose not to argue, just said goodbye as though her heart wasn't pounding its way through her ribs.

The cab arrived early to pick her up, and traffic was light. Lyssa spent the extra time gathering herself together in the coffee shop down the street from the office. At ten twenty-five, she decided she was as collected as she was going to get and rose from the booth, where she'd been nursing a cup of lukewarm bitter liquid that some might charitably call tea. It was definitely not one of her blends. She thought wistfully of her soothing valerian-linden infusions.

When she pushed open the heavy front door of Clearview, the cubicles were quiet and the open space that divided the engineers from the support staff was deserted. Even the receptionist wasn't at her desk. Lyssa would have preferred the building to seem less tomblike on this particular morning.

She walked through the emptiness until she reached the waiting area outside of Simon's office. His assistant looked up from the monitor as Lyssa approached.

Moon-round face politely inexpressive, she brushed back a lock of graying brown hair and set her hands in her lap. "Lyssa." Her eyes ranged over Lyssa's gypsy skirt and oversized red T-shirt. "Not quite your usual style."

"It was all I could find in my closet that pulled on." She lifted her casted arm up where the woman could see it. "Buttons and zippers are still a bit of a problem, I'm afraid."

"He's waiting for you. Go on in."

He wasn't alone. Barbara Pearce was there, too, dressed in a dark pantsuit so conservatively cut as to seem almost funereal.

"Is it necessary for her to be here?" Lyssa asked.

Simon motioned for her to take a seat next to Barb. The chairs were angled so they could all see each other. "After what happened earlier in the week you might feel awkward about this, but what I called you in for has nothing to do with that other situation."

"'That other situation' is a crock, and you know it."

He colored a bit. After clearing his throat, he said, "Barb is your supervisor. She has a right to be here, as this problem reflects on her, too." He handed Lyssa a file folder that contained a stapled packet of papers and some loose fax sheets. "I'd like you to look these over and tell me what you see."

She set the folder on the desk so she didn't have to try to balance it. After glancing at the title page of the stapled material she told him, "It's one of my reports for Callicott Properties. From about six months ago."

"You remember the Berkshire project, then?"

"Yes, of course. Callicott was interested in buying an old shopping center and some other businesses and converting the entire area into —" She stopped talking when she took a close look at the summary page. "Oh, no. No, no, no." Quickly she flipped through to the middle of the report. She found the section she was looking for and felt as though someone had punched her in the gut.

"Looks like you've found the problem," Barb commented.

"This . . . this isn't what I turned in!" It couldn't be. Feeling the pages slip through her trembling fingers, she turned to the last page. There was her signature, certifying that the information in the preceding pages was both accurate and complete.

Unfortunately, it was neither.

In the summary, where the report format called for a listing of potential hazards, the single word "none" appeared where she had typed in the site identification number. And later, in the detailed histories, the paragraph that should have described the former gas station with fuel tanks still underground, possibly leaking their hydrocarbon poisons into the surrounding soil for the past forty years, was missing the most important part: the "not" before "removed."

Such minor discrepancies. Such a huge impact. Lyssa closed the folder and stared at it as if it were a cobra. She could never have made such a mistake: this project was still fresh in her mind after six months. She couldn't have been that careless. She'd been justifiably proud of what her research had yielded after some creative digging into reverse directories and microfiche records. This was not the report she had prepared.

"I'm very disappointed." Simon steepled his fingers and studied her regretfully. "This puts me in an awkward position."

Lyssa was only half listening as she tried to figure out what had happened. "The computer records. They'll have to be correct."

She rose, oddly surprised that her knees would bear her weight, and led the way out of the office, down the hall, and past the line of depressing gray cubicles to her own. After waiting impatiently for her computer to cycle on, Lyssa needed only a minute to access the file.

The date was correct, matching both her memory and the signature sheet; but when she opened the file, it was identical to the pages that Simon had shown her. The report had come from her computer, bore her signature, and was in every other aspect exactly what she had written. Yet it had somehow been falsified.

One look at Barb showed her where the fabrication must have originated. Eyes glittering, Barb seethed with excitement.

"I want to see the Callicott copy," Lyssa demanded, rising from the chair with such force that it would have rammed into Barb's knees if the other woman had not shot out her arm and stayed it.

"Now, Lyssa, I understand that you might be upset," Simon began.

Barb interrupted him. "Callicott brought it to our attention. Theirs is the same as ours."

"That's impossible," Lyssa snapped.

"Why don't you come back to my office?" Simon offered nervously.

Lyssa considered having the confrontation right here, right now, but she didn't want the audience any more than he did. She still remembered the wall of faces that had witnessed Barb's forcible kiss.

Back within the security of his four walls and with the door closed, Simon relaxed. He sank into the maroon upholstered executive chair behind the desk and sighed gravely when she asked to see what Callicott had provided for documentation.

He handed over several pages from the report, bearing the fax number and name of the originating machine: Callicott Properties. These copies had the same incorrect data, word for word. Lyssa read them twice, just to make sure. She wondered if Simon would recommend that she be locked up in a mental institution if she suggested that she was the victim of a conspiracy.

Like all the Clearview employees, Barb had a key to the front door. The filing cabinets in which copies of reports and correspondence resided were kept locked, but all the research staff had their own keys for after-hours access. Barb could have accessed her computer, taken it offline, changed the date and time, modified the report and sent it over to Callicott Properties, and restored the calendar to cover her tracks. With Dane gone, Claudia would have had the office to herself, and abundant opportunity to replace the original report with this one and to fax back the changed pages.

Before she could think beyond the "how" of it to the "why," Simon placed a single sheet of paper in the middle of the desk between them, facing her. Lyssa looked past the Callicott logo, past the two short paragraphs of text, to the name at the bottom. *Vivian Callicott.*

Only then did Lyssa read the body of the letter. The first paragraph outlined the seriousness of her error. The second demanded that she be fired for incompetence.

"This is not the first time Mrs. Callicott has contacted me about you. The first time, after your little episode with Thomas Turnbull, she only asked that you not be involved with any more Callicott business." His nose twitched as though he smelled something foul. "I accommodated her on that, of course, but subtly. I didn't think it necessary to make a big deal out of it. But this! This is too much to ignore."

Vivian Callicott. *Well, blast,* Lyssa thought. *She* would *have to get in the last word.*

"This is not the report I drafted." Lyssa tapped her finger on the folder. Her voice wobbled only a little. "I remember how the original text read, even if you don't."

But her options were limited. She had no proof to confront Barb with. Ordinarily her notes would have been kept on her laptop—but that was gone. The page of working points for the draft report wasn't in the folder where it ought to be.

A paranoid person might have made sure she kept copies of all her notes and lines of research. Lyssa had never had reason to be paranoid. Not until now.

She opened the file and turned pages, hoping that logic and reasonableness would make headway where truth and loyalty evidently could not. "Here, I put the site identification number." She marked the place with a green sticky note from a nearby pad. "Here, in conjunction with the underground fuel tanks, I specifically said they had not been removed." She marked that one, too. "If I hadn't been the one to identify these problems, how were they discovered after all this time? And why? Callicott must have given up interest in the property long ago."

Barb leaned forward. "Mr. Callicott's assistant was going through some old material on the project," she explained to Simon. "Ms. Montgomery told me she came across a reference to the fuel tanks that made her suspicious. She went through the report and discovered that even though Lyssa had claimed that the tanks had been removed, there was no record of the date or agent of removal."

"That's because they hadn't ever been removed! I never claimed they had been!"

Simon looked at her, then at Barb, then back at Lyssa before dropping his eyes to the top of his desk. "You're making this very difficult. I think we can all see what's laid out in front of us, in black and white."

Lyssa snapped, "You don't care whether it's true or not, do you?"

"Mrs. Callicott has left us no choice," Barb said. "Surely even you can see that, Lyssa."

"What do you mean, 'no choice'?" Of course there was a choice, Lyssa thought, feeling the blood rise in her cheeks. Someone could believe *her* instead of the faked documents.

"Now, Lyssa," Simon started, "I'm sure you can understand that we can't just ignore the wishes of one of our biggest clients. I can't keep you on the payroll after this."

Her voice rose. "You're firing me? On the basis of allegations you know must be false? All my years of loyal service count for nothing?"

"I'm sorry." He even sounded as if he might be.

She turned on her heel and left his office before she did something to disgrace herself, like fall on her knees and beg, or get into a fistfight with Barb, or throw up all over her shoes.

No coworkers—former coworkers, she reminded herself—came by as she was packing her few personal possessions into bags and a box she'd used to store notes for old files. She'd never brought in family photos or plants, but she had a drawer full of her experimental tea blends and a pot for boiling water, some reference books brought from home, and a few little things like a toothbrush, toothpaste, and a comb. The bags were difficult to manage with one arm, but she persevered.

When the workstation was almost clear, Barb came by. "Too bad you didn't back off from Turnbull when you had the chance."

Lyssa crossed her arms to keep from throttling her tormentor.

Barb tapped a thin file folder against her navy-clad thigh. "I guess some people just never learn the ins and the outs of their job. And you, Lyssa Smith, have been outed." She chuckled. "Literally." Her voice was amused, gloating. "I saw you, with your 'mothers,' at the farmers' market. Now, that's a strange and twisted situation. Makes me almost sorry this is all over. I could have learned some interesting ins and outs about how that all works."

Every muscle in Lyssa's body tensed, but she hid her white knuckles under her elbows and dug her fingernails into her sides. "Did you have a reason for coming by?"

Thrusting the file at her, Barb said, "Take this paperwork down to personnel. Then get your stuff—and yourself—out of here. I want you gone by noon."

"No problem."

Lyssa kept the tears out of her eyes until certain that her tormentor was gone. No problem, she thought in despair, rubbing her free hand across the trails of hot, salty tears dribbling down her cheeks. She had no job, and with her broken arm she wasn't likely to get another one anytime soon, and she had just applied for a mortgage on a piece of property that her parents needed if they were to keep their farm afloat.

The only thing that kept her from thinking that things couldn't possibly get any worse was the unreasoning fear that they could—and she just didn't have enough imagination to figure out how.

Fourteen

LYSSA SAT NEXT TO PAULINA on her neighbor's musty-smelling couch. They were demolishing a half gallon of chocolate brownie fudge ice cream, dipping long-handled spoons into the carton as Paulina generously held it midway between them. The old woman's hand might be shaky, but it was still strong enough to grasp the carton securely.

The second game of the World Series was about to start, with the Yankees prepared to take it in a sweep—or so the announcers reported. Of course, they always droned on with garbage like that. Lyssa didn't know why she even bothered to listen. She knew better than to believe what important people said.

She'd tried to convince herself that her position at Clearview was just a means to an end. Someone had to save her parents from the mistake they'd made all those years ago, and she had long ago determined that that someone would be her. Clearview had been just a job. A way of putting funds aside for the future. She might have started with grandiose notions of working within the system to change it, but that was foolish; Simon's complete turnaround had shown it to be a delusion.

Well, the future was now upon her. And she was very much afraid that she was going to fail, utterly and completely. She felt like one last lonely dandelion seed clinging to the withered head that bore it, too stubborn or afraid to release a lost cause and fly forth on the wind.

Still, she hadn't completely given up hope. The doors between her apartment and Paulina's stood wide so she could hear her telephone ring when Jacobson called back. Although she hadn't told her neighbor exactly what was so important about this telephone call.

With her eyes glued to the screen, the elderly woman grumbled, "Still don't understand why they'd believe you're gay. What do they think Dane is, some kind of sex-change experiment?"

Without reminding Paulina—again—that the trumped-up kiss was the least important detail in the events that had led up to her firing, Lyssa replied, "They don't know about him."

Paulina snorted. "Why is it he hasn't told the big boss you're not a lesbian?"

"He's gone."

"Gone? Well, isn't that convenient."

"It's a business trip." Lyssa found her interest in the broadcast waning. Glumly she wondered if she would ever again be able to lose herself in the joy of watching grown-up men getting paid exorbitant salaries to run around on the field and play a little boy's game. Her eyes glazed over with the effort of quelling the tears that threatened to rise again.

"Business? I don't think so," Paulina said. She pointed her spoon at the image of Dane in the stands of Yankee Stadium, taking up half the screen.

The camera was focused on someone beside him, whom Lyssa half recognized and so assumed was famous.

"That's him, isn't it?"

Then the broadcast image cut back to the camera behind the pitcher.

"How did you recognize him?" Lyssa demanded in disbelief. "You didn't even see him last time."

"Sure I did. He had postseason tickets!"

Lyssa tossed her spoon into the ice cream carton. "I guess I know why he took off. This way he doesn't have to come right out and lie about the Berkshire project. He found a way to get rid of me and left his mother to take the credit. After that disaster at the reception, Vivian Callicott must have jumped at the chance to be rid of me." She folded her arms across her chest but winced at the twinge. Her arm bothered her less now that the swelling was starting to diminish, but there were still occasional reminders.

"I think you're the one jumping. To conclusions. Nasty bit of paranoia you're showing. I didn't know you had it in you."

"What does that mean?"

"You didn't like that job anyway. You're well rid of it, that's what I say. Baseball-boy there is a much better prospect!" Paulina's eyes glinted behind her Coke-bottle lenses. "Go for it, Lyssa. It just makes things easier if you're not tied down with a job."

"Has it occurred to you that if I married Dane Callicott, I would have to move out of this apartment?"

Paulina cogitated on that. "Huh." She waggled a finger at Lyssa. "You already said you didn't want to marry him. Just tempt him with sex and get him primed for next season. It's about time you stopped being the last living virgin in Phoenix, anyway."

"You heard that?"

"Well." Taking another mouthful of ice cream, Paulina said around it, "I could hardly miss it, could I? The way you both were shouting."

"It was you! You were the one who told him I like chocolate and flowers. You told him how to get to me."

"Now, see, there's that paranoia again. Every woman likes to be courted with chocolate and flowers. It's universal."

Rising, Lyssa said, "I thought I could trust you. I thought you were on my side."

Paulina fidgeted on the couch. "Now, Lyssa," she mumbled, "there aren't any sides here."

Lyssa remembered her parents advising her to give up her intention of starting her own business, Dane sneering at her desire to make a difference in the world and then calling her greedy, Barb telling her that she was stupid to set herself up in opposition to the Tank Turnbulls of the world, Simon lying to her about what Clearview was all about and then buying into the lies about who she was. And now Paulina criticizing anything that would take Lyssa away from her dumpy little apartment and a crappy job in a city life that she hated.

"Sides?" Lyssa went on. "Oh, yes, there are."

She looked down at Paulina, sitting in a threadbare chenille robe on a lumpy couch, rheumy eyes blinking out from behind heavy glasses. "You can keep the ice cream," she said. "I have a telephone call to make." With that, she left, closing both doors behind her, one after the other, with a soft, echoing finality that made her heart ache.

As she strode into the apartment that she would soon put behind her—for good—she decided that she was done with waiting. It was a whole new inning, and Jacobson was going to play ball whether he knew it or not. Lyssa would go down swinging, or not at all.

DANE FOUND HIMSELF wandering near Central Park, restless again, as if he would find the answers he needed written on the damp gray sidewalks. Instead of focusing on the pros and cons of pursuing Adams' investment money or the Spirit Ranch project or whether he was doing the right thing in dragging his mother back into the business or even what to do about Lyssa when he got home, his mind refused to settle on any one thing.

The previous day's ball game had made his ambivalence worse, not better. He had wanted to go, but once there, he discovered that the game wasn't the same when he was alone. After the third inning, when the Yanks' loss became both obvious and inevitable, he went back to the hotel and downed a couple of aspirin and an antacid. He'd resolved to make sure the Highline—and any other resort he involved himself with—treated needy travelers equally well.

Unfortunately, he thought now, stuffing his hands into the pockets of his casual slacks, he was in need of something that couldn't be bought and sold.

The men on the field were doing exactly what they wanted to do with their lives. Dane could, too. If only he could figure out what it was.

Eyes drawn to an interior invitingly filled with color, Dane stood in the drizzle a moment longer. Then he entered the small gallery and gazed around.

The room was bright and airy despite the weather outside. Slowly he made his way along the wall, studying each painting as he came to it. The swirls and crashes of intense hues were not quite representative art, but they were challenging and evocative, rousing a complex response. He couldn't say that he liked them.

While he was standing before one particularly dynamic canvas, filled with crimson and gold streaks that reminded him of sex—of a particularly emotionless variety—a woman paused at his elbow. Most of the people strolling through the gallery were dressed in business suits, as though killing time on their lunch hour. She was something entirely different.

Petite, she had black hair that tumbled down her back and framed a thin, delicate face dominated by lips of an indescribable shade, which intrigued Dane, who, although he had little interest in painting, prided himself on his ability to label colors using a painter's palette. She was young, probably in her mid twenties, but her striking dark eyes bore into his with an intensity that declared she was ageless—and had seen everything. Her long, carmine-red wispy skirt was half covered by a shapeless sweater in a rich amaranth purple.

"Like what you see?"

Dane nodded. "Very much."

"Good," she replied, slanting a flirtatious look at him. "I'm the artist."

He enjoyed the way she kept hold of him after their handshake should have ended. No sparks, but an interesting heat in her touch. "If you're the artist, that would make you Sophy Mannheim," he said, having taken glancing notice of the display cards. "I'm Dane Callicott."

"So, Dane Callicott, are you here on business? Or pleasure?"

"A little of both, if I can manage it."

She arched one brow. "I imagine a man like you can handle just about anything," she purred in a voice that put Claudia's to shame. "What do you see in my work, Dane?"

He paused over his answer. Her heavy gaze demanded the truth. "Sex," he finally said.

"Sex."

"Yes."

"Are you a connoisseur or a collector?"

"Is there a difference?"

"Do you just look, or do you like to acquire?" she teased.

Dane grinned. He wasn't going to admit that he hadn't done either for a while. He was pretty sure she wasn't talking about paintings. "I used to dabble in art myself."

"You're a painter?"

"No. I did some sculpting."

She put her hand on his upper arm and said, "Nice biceps. You still have the muscles for it. Such a physical art form. Any reason you don't do it anymore?"

He shrugged. "Not really."

"I make it a point not to get involved with other artists." She slid her hand down very slowly to wrap around his. "But since you aren't one anymore . . ."

He could feel every one of her finger bones, he realized. Her skin was hot. Not damp, not uncomfortable, just abnormally warm.

Darting glances at the others in the small gallery, she whispered, "It's getting a little crowded in here. Why don't we find somewhere more private for a detailed critique?"

Okay, Dane thought. A man couldn't miss an open invitation like that. He might not have been looking for a woman, but it seemed he'd found one. Or she had found him. "I'd like that." Dane smiled at her.

He figured this woman wasn't after him for his money. He had left off his watch and Italian shoes this time. He sported olive-green slacks and an off-white pullover sweater with a black mock turtleneck underneath, and he had bought a pair of comfortable loafers.

Sophy pulled him out of the gallery door and had him halfway down the block, chattering the whole way. She wanted him to see where she worked. A man couldn't really comprehend her, couldn't know what she was about, until he saw all of her. And she wanted Dane to see everything.

Her intensity was as inescapable as her talk. He didn't want to hear that her art was so much a part of her, she couldn't imagine cutting herself off from it. How could he have done it, she asked. But she didn't probe that particular sore spot or give him an opportunity to refuse to talk about it. She was on to something else, flitting from one topic to another.

As soon as they entered a brick building that looked like one of the converted warehouses that tended to be chosen as the setting for serial-killer murder scenes, she pressed him against the wire-mesh wall of the elevator and was kissing him avidly.

Then they were in her place, and he still hadn't seen all of her, because she had peeled off her clothes and his so quickly that they could have been in a brothel instead of an artist's studio. She rolled him over and over on the wide bed, centered in the curtainless room. He should have been aroused by the huge black pupils of her dark eyes and the flare of her nostrils as she breathed in the musky scent of the sheets.

"Wait!" he managed to croak. "Protection. Do you have—"

"I'm safe," she gasped. "Don't worry about pregnancy or anything."

"Condoms." He was a desperate man. It was way too long since he'd had sex. And he had suffered through too many nights of sweaty dreams and frustration over Lyssa in the past week or so. But he knew nothing about this woman, nothing about her health history. He wasn't about to go sticking himself without protection into a place where who knew how many men had bravely gone before.

She picked up strangers in art galleries, for godsake. He looked down at himself to find that his fine erection was gone.

"What do you need a rubber for?" she exploded, rolling off the bed. "You think I've got AIDS or something?" She grabbed up his slacks and threw them at him. "Get out of here, you stupid bastard." His briefs followed, and then in quick succession his sweater and turtleneck. He had to duck to avoid getting a shoe in the face.

He'd had a narrow escape, he realized as he stood outside her steel-reinforced door and heard her throwing the locks. At least, he thought the metallic rattling and clanking was from locks. The way she'd come unglued, she might have been throwing just about anything.

As quickly as possible, embarrassed to be standing naked outside the elevator, he got dressed. Then again, he considered it more than likely that Sophy's neighbors were used to seeing strange men in compromising positions. This was a far cry from the last time he'd been kicked out of a woman's apartment.

So maybe Lyssa had made a good point when he'd yelled at her about being a virgin, he reflected. He didn't want a wife who'd had more sexual partners than he had. Not that he was thinking about getting married. He had enough headaches without that.

It occurred to him, as he stepped out onto the sidewalk and made his way back toward the hotel, that getting picked up in an art gallery by a woman who preferred indiscriminate sex wasn't much of a compliment to his masculinity. Or his intelligence.

But the women he dated—and slept with—in Phoenix, did they know him any better than Sophy and the sociopath in the bar? Maybe they saw only the Callicott name, just as the barfly had seen his money, the way the artist had seen a good-looking man. Or maybe, he considered with a wry twist of his lips, that was giving himself too much credit. Maybe Sophy had seen nothing more than a man who was breathing and looking at her with an interest she knew she could fan into desire.

Then a question that had been lodged at the back of his mind for a long time rose up to haunt him. What of Gail?

What had *she* wanted of him: the money, the name, or the man? Why had she decided, after they'd been together for years, after she had promised to be his, after she had attached his heart, that she wanted none of him?

He hadn't been able bring himself to think of taking another woman that deeply into his life after her betrayal. Through all these years, there had been only the image of Gail in his mind, at his side, wearing his ring, having his children. Boys to play catch with—his imagination stopped there, confounded.

The kids in the image were no longer the tough little boys who looked like him and followed him around like puppies. Instead he saw in his mind's eye a mix of boys and girls all gangly and loud and doing whatever they wanted. Worse, the woman in his dream was no longer the same. Where Gail was everything that was feminine, this woman was larger than life, bold and outspoken, unwilling to conform to any man's vision of her.

Oh, God, it was Lyssa. Smiling at him like he was the center of her universe.

He came back to reality then, oddly furious. He discovered that he had stopped in front of an art supply shop. Hesitating, uncertain about whether to take this adjustment to his fantasy as a sign or his subconscious overtaking his rational mind, he absently rubbed at his temple with one hand.

When a burly guy with straggly long hair and chains draped across his large belly opened the door and pushed past him, the smell of paint and thinners and musty raw clay followed. Dane breathed it in like a drowning man might gasp for air. Could it be ten years, he asked himself, since he'd last been in a store like this?

Sophy's studio hadn't produced this rush of nostalgia. Of course, there his mind had been fixated on something else. Dane cautiously stepped over the threshold.

"Can I help you?" The salesclerk had a shaved head and an earring through his—her?—left eyebrow.

The shapeless T-shirt and baggy jeans didn't help Dane identify the clerk's gender. "Just looking."

"Yeah, fine. Whatever. Take your time."

When he walked out half an hour later, relieved that the spitting rain had subsided, he was carrying two bags: one heavy, the other significantly lighter but awkward, catching the luffing breeze like a sail. The prices had astounded him. How anyone who wasn't independently wealthy could afford to be an artist, he didn't know. It would be tough to be a college student with an art major these days, that was for sure.

When he got back to the hotel room, he emptied the bags and laid out what he'd bought on the table and the bed. He considered that maybe he'd gone a little overboard with his shopping spree.

Nonhardening modeling clay to start with, to shape and reshape until he felt comfortable thinking in three dimensions again. Knives and wires to carve the clay with. They weren't the tools he preferred, his muscle memory being more accustomed to chisels and saws and rasps, but he didn't expect to have any problem getting the feel of them again. Sketchbooks of various sizes, and pencils and charcoal in a variety of weights and hardnesses, plus blending sticks and erasers—lots of erasers. He had a feeling he'd be needing them.

Doubtful all of a sudden, he looked at the array of stuff. Surely he didn't think he could go back and undo one of the weightiest decisions he'd ever made. He'd told everyone for years that he wasn't an artist, didn't have the temperament for it, never felt driven to do it, had no interest in the art world.

And yet he'd been compelled to check out the galleries. Not just the tourist attractions, either, but the small, avant-garde, hungry-artist places. He'd been drawn into the art supply store and had been unable to leave empty-handed.

Dane asked himself what the hell he thought he was doing. He had no inspiration. His creative well had run dry long ago. The chunk of modeling clay was blank; he saw nothing in it. The sketchpads were plain white paper, and likely to stay that way. He stood there for a while, tight-lipped, staring at the materials waiting for an artist's touch.

Then he scrubbed his hands over his face. Turning on his heel, he slammed out of the room and headed for the bar downstairs. Some kinds of mistakes, a man shouldn't have to face sober.

Fifteen

"GO AWAY!"

The pounding on her door didn't stop. "Lyssa, honey, open up!"

She dragged in a deep breath. "Give me a minute," she yelled. She stumbled into the bathroom. "Whoa," she said to the wild-eyed, pale-faced, ratty-looking creature who looked back at her. "You've seen better days." She ran a brush through her hair and bathed her face with some cool water, then went to the door to let Papa Ari in.

To her surprise, Helen and Cal followed him.

"Cal! You're home!" Forgetting her broken arm until she tried to throw her arms around the father she hadn't seen for a month, she settled for giving him a one-armed hug and a kiss on the cheek before doing the same, if more restrained, to Ari and Helen.

Then she stepped back. "What are you all doing here?" she demanded. "It's not farmers' market day." Was it? she wondered.

"I called you at work to check on you," Cal said.

"Oh."

Before Lyssa could think of a response, Helen declared, "This time there's no excuse for staying here. You're coming home with us."

"No. I can't leave."

The parents exchanged troubled glances. Helen said, "You don't have a job keeping you in town any longer. And with that broken arm you obviously need someone to take care of you for a while." She waved an arm to encompass the messy apartment. "Look at this place, dear. It's a pigsty. Come home and let us pamper you. It'll be like old times."

Taking a deep breath and letting it out slowly, Lyssa mustered the strength to turn down the offer. "Really, I can't. I'm waiting for Jacobson to call back with a counteroffer."

Helen and Ari turned to Cal. They all looked unhappy.

"She's waiting on Jacobson," Helen told Cal pointedly.

"I told you we shouldn't have handled it that way."

"Well, you were gone, weren't you? Not that there's anything to be done now."

Lyssa felt like a spectator at a tennis match. "What is going on?"

Cal said, "Jacobson won't be calling, Lyssa."

"What?" She stared at him and wondered if she looked as stupid as she felt. She would have liked to blame her lack of comprehension on the pain medication, but since she hadn't taken any recently, she supposed that wasn't sufficient excuse. Closing her eyes, she scrubbed her hand over her face. Maybe she should have splashed herself with more cold water, she thought.

"He won't call. He won't make a counteroffer. He won't accept your money."

Stubbornly she lifted her chin. "How can you be so certain? I made him a good offer." A respectable one, anyway.

They looked uneasily between each other again. Cal cleared his throat. "He'd already turned us down. Before I left for Australia. He won't sell that land to us, Lyssa, any of us. Including you." Cal's voice held apology. "You know he's never approved of our lifestyle."

"No, of course not," she responded tartly. "But he does approve of money. You probably didn't offer enough."

He named a figure that made her jaw drop.

"How could you possibly come up with that much?" Her head whirled. "You'd have to mortgage the farm!" She couldn't imagine any other way for them to pull together a veritable fortune.

"We can talk about all that later," Ari said gruffly. He stepped forward and hugged her close in his great bearlike manner. "Right now we need to get you packed up to come home."

Lyssa looked up at him as his heart beat reassuringly against her shoulder. An automatic refusal rose to her lips, but she couldn't bring herself to say the words.

Knowing how much she wanted it, her parents had tried to get the Jacobson property for her. They had known, when she thought they were being discouraging, that her plan was impossible. No matter how much money she managed to salt away, no matter whether she worked for Clearview for another six years or got that promotion and salary increase, Jacobson wouldn't have gone for it. Her attempts to make him cooperate with her had been in vain; he'd been stringing her along.

"Okay," she said. Then she burst into tears.

Helen sat her down on the couch and put a comforting arm around her. "It's all right, baby girl. Cry it out." Lyssa sobbed into her mother's shoulder and felt the vibrations as Helen told Ari to make up some chamomile tea to settle her.

Ari came to sit on her other side. "We are your family," he said firmly. "Your innermost soul-circle. You're not going through this alone."

Lyssa felt the sobs well up from the deepest core of her, violent enough, it seemed, to break her in two.

Cal, always more practical, assured her, "We'll help you break your lease, disconnect the phone and utilities, if they're not included. You'll have a severance check coming from work, of course . . ." He kept talking.

She couldn't tell him—any of them—that what made her feel the worst was realizing she would never see Dane again. Lyssa forced herself to think about that. *Really* think. One way or another, she would have ultimately said goodbye to Dane. It should have been within the glow of triumph rather than the shadow of defeat, but that was how things happened sometimes. Completely out of her control.

She remembered what Helen had said about her tendency to accept what the universe threw at her. And why the heck not? she asked herself. What's the point of fighting the inevitable?

The teakettle began to whistle. Ari rose, the broken-down couch cushion lifting Lyssa as his weight was taken away. She pulled back from Helen, sniffling to keep her nose from dripping. "I'm all right," she said.

Her mother took out a handkerchief, grasped Lyssa's chin in a strong, callused hand, and looked her over carefully. "Not yet. But you will be. We'll make certain of it." She wiped Lyssa's cheeks and pressed the hanky to her nose, letting Lyssa reach for it and blot away the wetness.

Helen's eyes went past her to the floor, where the stuff from Clearview lay in a heap. "What happened, Lyssa?" she asked in a soft voice. "I know you're a hard worker. And too valuable for any employer to fire. Last we heard, you were going to be promoted."

Lyssa's eyes burned. "I was let go at the request of a major client, who showed Simon some documentation. It supposedly proved I was careless on a project and missed a big environmental problem." The explanation sounded so simple. Almost reasonable, from Simon's perspective. Her stomach knotted up. "A *big* environmental problem."

"That's ridiculous!" Ari, returning with a cup of tea, removed the damp handkerchief from her hand. He replaced it with the teacup, then motioned for her to take a sip. "You make a single error, and they think that's reason enough to fire you? That Simon of yours is an idiot!"

Cal knelt in front of her. "She didn't say she made a mistake, Ari. She said there was some documentation. What really happened, Lyssa?"

"Barb—" She wondered how many times she had complained about her boss over the past half-dozen years. Never again, she resolved. After this one last explanation, she could put that woman out of her mind for good. "Barb saw an opportunity to get rid of me. With the help of . . . this client's personal assistant, she replaced the actual reports with ones she'd falsified."

"But why would she do such a thing?" Helen asked.

Wearily Lyssa said, "With the Valley Archaeology buyout pending, I guess she decided it would keep me from getting promoted to her level."

"It seems like an awful risk for them to take."

"Not so much, actually. Da— Her boss is out of town, and besides, he— Well, it wasn't him, but his— He—" Lyssa ground to a halt in her explanation, staring helplessly at her loving inquisitors. She was determined not to be paranoid. And even more determined not to mention Dane's name in Ari's hearing.

"He . . . ?" Cal prompted.

"It's not important." Lyssa felt the heat rise in her cheeks.

Helen laid a hand on the one Lyssa had locked around her teacup. "Who was the client, dearest?"

"It doesn't really matter."

But Helen persisted. "Of course it does, if he can fix this."

"She said he was out of town," Ari reminded Helen.

Lyssa nodded earnestly, hoping to convince them so that they would just drop it. "That's right."

Cal cocked his head. "What will this assistant do when he gets back? If she's lied about something like this, surely it will all come out somehow."

"Oh, I don't think it will be a problem for her. Claudia is very good at manipulating the situation to suit herself. And besides, Mrs. Callicott is the one who actually contacted Simon." Lyssa stopped when she saw Ari's tufted eyebrows lift.

"*Mrs.* Callicott?" he asked. "I thought you said Dane Callicott wasn't interested in marriage."

"I said he wasn't interested in marrying *me*," Lyssa retorted without correcting the misapprehension that Vivian was Dane's wife.

Helen glared at Ari. "No. Oh, no. You're not going to steer her that direction."

"Helen, it's been obvious since day one that she—"

Lyssa tried to stop their squabbling before it got out of hand. "Is there a particular reason why you two are talking about me as though I'm not here?"

"He wants to push a *man* on you." The disgust in her mother's voice was heartfelt.

Lyssa found small satisfaction in realizing that one thing, at least, would never change in her parents' world.

"Not just any man." Ari's eyes were sharp under his bushy white eyebrows. "Seems like this one's soul-circle keeps bumping up against our Lyssa's. Pity he's already taken."

"Ari!" Helen snapped.

"What!"

Helen's eyes narrowed. "You know what. Leave it alone." She turned to Lyssa. "I don't see why three women would take it upon themselves to get another fired. Is it possible that you misunderstood the situation? There are only so many ways for female employees to exist within a patriarchal system. It is Simon, after all, who controls the seat of power in your office. And evidently this Dane Callicott in his. Power and dominance are male weapons, not female."

"Oh, please, Helen," Ari sighed. "Let's not get into the male-bashing again."

"And why not? Men have wielded their arsenal without consideration for women—"

"Stop it!" Lyssa watched as her cup, airborne before she even realized she'd flung up her hands, vanished over her shoulder. It thudded to the carpet behind her. She jumped up, unable to sit still. "Just stop it! In this case, Mother, there's no man to blame."

She walked around the couch to retrieve her cup and ignored the splotches of tea, which couldn't stain the ancient carpeting any worse than it already was. "Let's just pack up my stuff and get out of here," she told them flatly. "I don't want to talk about this anymore."

There was no point in waiting. She could see that now. Jacobson wasn't going to call.

Lyssa spent about an hour convincing Paulina that the world was not coming to an end with her departure. She fed her parents as much as she could from the refrigerator and gave her elderly neighbor the rest of the perishables.

"That's it?" Cal asked at last, when the boxes they had gotten from the liquor store down the street were full and ready to be hauled down to the Elysian Fields delivery truck and her own pickup, which Helen would be driving back to the farm.

Biting her lip, Lyssa nodded. If a person could be measured by possessions, she was pathetic. She had never been a collector of things. Besides her stuff from work, she owned a few dishes and pans, a microwave that would be useless to her at the farm, some canned goods, clothing, books, dumbbells and hand weights, her collection of rescued plants. And an orchid she was sorely tempted to leave behind.

The realization of how tenuously she was connected to the real world was depressing. She'd been so focused on her plans for the Jacobson property for so long that now she felt as if she were cast adrift on some dark, iceberg-laden sea, with no rudder or sail or paddle to steer her and no destination to set off toward.

Her parents were intelligent, capable adults. Capable enough that if she stopped trying to protect them from the knowledge of what they had done in signing that contract with Jacobson all those years ago, they might very well figure out a way of solving their own problem.

And then nobody would need her at all. It was a very lowering thought.

THE PHONE RANG ONCE, and again. Dane fumbled for it without thinking. He hadn't realized night had fallen. The room was dark except for lights he must have turned on around the table where the lumpy block of clay sat mockingly. Where he sat, slumped, staring at it.

"Hello? Are you there? Dane?"

Dane shook his head, striving for alertness. His mouth was dry. "What time is it?" At least, that's what he'd intended to say. It had come out more like "Dime'zit?"

"Dane?"

He ran a hand through his hair and looked around him. The hotel room looked like a tornado had touched down. Rejected sketches lay in crumpled heaps across the floor and upon the bed. Broken-off stubs of pencils and charcoal sticks, almost invisible against the dark patterned carpeting, made walking hazardous. He'd put out a "Do Not

Disturb" sign and wondered how long it would be before the manager came to roust him out.

"Dane?"

He blinked, trying to get rid of the grittiness in his eyes. Then a measure of alertness returned. "Alex?"

"Yes, it's me."

Alex sounded entirely too fresh. Dane pictured him, high cheekbones and a thin-bladed nose, deep-set eyes below arched eyebrows and a bold, square brow, mouth sensitive and rather wide-lipped. He could draw his friend's face, trace the lines in his sleep. But it wouldn't do any good. He'd given up on the two-dimensional stuff a while ago—hours? days?

"How did you get this number?" he asked, sitting up straight and feeling his back protest. He rubbed his hand against his eyelids to get rid of the gravel that seemed lodged within them.

"I took it off your computer."

Dane shrugged, forgetting that Alex couldn't see him. "Help yourself, then. Everybody else seems to." He remembered walking into his office and finding Claudia at his desk, listening to his voice-mail with the confidence of long practice. What was a little computer hacking between friends?

"I'm surprised you answered. According to Claudia and your mother, you're either dead or you've run away and are never coming back."

"I'm on vacation."

"Yeah, and if Claudia thought you were actually enjoying yourself, she wouldn't give you any peace. You don't have to explain." Alex's voice had turned grim.

Dane wished he hadn't answered the phone. He'd picked up automatically. Or because, he admitted with brutal honesty, in some muddled, sleep-deprived corner of his mind he had expected to hear Lyssa's voice.

"Your wonderfully efficient assistant told me you wouldn't answer. But I thought if I called you late at night, I'd wake you up and maybe catch you off guard."

"I wasn't asleep."

"I'm not disturbing anything, am I?"

"No. Not really."

"Is someone there with you?"

Alex didn't have to sound so surprised, Dane reflected. Dane could have had the hottest sex of his life if he'd allowed Sophy her own way. Of course, he wouldn't have brought her back to his hotel. And he wouldn't have kept her with him the whole night. An error of that magnitude would likely have killed him on the spot. The universe was looking out for him that much, at least. "No. Look, I assume you called for a reason. Why don't you spit it out so I can get back to"—he hesitated, considering telling his friend what was really going on, but decided to make a pretense of normalcy—"sleep."

"You have a problem," Alex stated.

Dane laughed, thinking about what a massive understatement that was. "Just the one?"

"Soon as you get home, I'm heading for Tahiti."

"No."

"No?"

"Sorry, Alex, but you're going to be the CEO. Head of operations. Meaning that from here on out, you can't drop everything and take off for a vacation when you get bored." God, it felt good to imagine being the one who could do that for a change.

There was a short silence. Then Alex said, "I notice you're in New York as you say that."

"I'm entitled." Dane grinned. "I am now dispensable."

"How long do you think this pleasant situation will hold? Mrs. Callicott allowed it, for this week, because she's worried about you."

"She told you about . . . ?" Dane waved a hand through the clay-scented air, unwilling to finish, just in case Alex didn't really know what was wrong.

"Ve haff our vays." Then Alex dropped the fake accent. "Come on, Dane. You can't hide health problems under a rock. If nothing else, the over-the-counter medicines you've been taking look to me like an ulcer and a heart attack waiting to happen." He paused. "Have you gone to see a doctor?"

"Not yet."

"Dane—"

Dane knew how to shut up his friend. "You sound like my mother."

"Heaven forbid" was snapped in his ear.

Dane laughed. "What did you call about, Alex? It sure wasn't my health. What is this problem you think I have? Keeping in mind, of course, that now my problems are your problems." He felt great saying that. Really great. Relieved of a heavy burden, in fact.

"Not all of them," Alex said slowly, as if measuring his words.

"All right, give me a clue."

"What do you remember about the Berkshire project?"

"That little strip mall? We were still in the investigative stages when I decided to let the option lapse. But that was six months ago, at least. Why bring it up now?"

"You remember why you decided not to go ahead with it?"

Dane closed his eyes and delved into his mental files. "Clearview did a Phase One assessment." He deliberately refrained from mentioning Lyssa's name in connection with the report. Until he figured out what he wanted to do about her, he didn't care to talk about her, even to his old friend. "Underground storage tanks, hydrocarbon burden not removed, no amelioration efforts. It would've cost a fortune to clean up."

"Yeah, that's how I remember it, too." Alex fell silent.

Finally, when Dane couldn't stand the suspense, he demanded, "So, what's the problem?"

"Lyssa Smith got fired over it."

"What the hell are you talking about?" The relief was gone, just like that, as he felt the millstone drop back around his neck. The veins in his temples began to throb. "I haven't been gone for even a week."

"The project got pulled up out of the dead files and reexamined. Dane, the report doesn't say anything about underground gas tanks."

"That's—" Dane broke off, fumbling for words.

"Ridiculous? Impossible?"

"Something like that. I'll take a look at it when I get back. But Simon wouldn't fire her over that."

"He's apparently making her the scapegoat for missing that detail. Fired her for incompetence."

Dane snorted. "Now, that's ridiculous. I'll talk to him when I get back."

"And Claudia?"

"What about her?"

"Well, she's the one who apparently was going through the files and found the discrepancies."

"Discrepancies?" Dane rubbed his head, wishing he had a bottle of something about a hundred-proof in front of him instead of a chunk of clay. "If the bit about the storage tanks is missing from the report—which I don't get, but we'll leave it for now—where's the discrepancy?"

"Lyssa's supervisor, Barbara Pearce, apparently found something in the Clearview files while working on another project and got suspicious. She put everything together, took it to Claudia, and—"

Dane shook his head. "None of this makes any sense. I'll have to talk to Claudia and straighten everything out when I get back."

"There's more."

"Of course there is." The millstone grew heavier. "Okay, hit me with it."

"Your mother told Simon to fire Lyssa."

"Damn it!" Dane tried to throw off the stifling sensation that had wrapped around his chest. "All right. I'll get a flight out in the morning."

"Dane. It is morning."

He stood up and walked around the table, as far as the telephone cord would stretch. "Okay." He found a hint of something in the clay, a shape. A dragon's snout? He hung up, only vaguely aware that Alex was still talking. He ignored the phone when it rang a few minutes later.

His earlier exhaustion vanished as the excitement of creating took over. He recalled, after some time had passed, that his best memories of college were of moments just like these.

Almost done, just a few more touches, he thought, even as he brought them into existence. He stood back and looked at what he had done.

The piece was crude, certainly not up to what he'd once produced. It was the goofiest dragon he'd ever seen—charmingly hideous. Beady eyes protruded from lumpy eye sockets stuck on the long-nosed face, and its jaw hung unevenly agape. It was a fat-bodied, bat-winged dragon with a long pointed tail, right out of a Tolkien story. Or a little kid's song. Not the sort of thing for a serious artist, but damn! Making it had been almost fun.

And then he remembered the telephone call from Alex.

LYSSA SAT AT THE KITCHEN TABLE, resting her broken arm on the scarred wood in front of her. Under the cast, her skin itched. "Cal, what's the deal? How could you offer to buy out Jacobson? Were you planning to borrow against Callicrates?"

Cal, his yellowish gray hair sticking out, inhaled his sweet-smelling pipe tobacco mixture. He leaned back in the chair and lifted its front legs off the floor. The leaves in the bowl of his pipe flared red. A tendril of spicy smoke wafted past her. "Not exactly."

"I don't know how much you've managed to put aside over the years. I guess I never asked. I always figured it couldn't be anything more than a . . . I don't know, a comfortable retirement for the four of you."

"We have a little more than that. It's in bonds and stocks, so it would take some time to liquidate, but it can be done. If you need a place of your own to be happy, all you have to do is ask."

She squared her shoulders. "Look, if you have so much money that you can afford to spend it on me, why don't you use it on the farm instead? Bring in a telephone and electricity." Taking a deep breath, she hurried on. "Dig your own well, maybe."

"You know the rest of them will never go for that. They figure a phone and electricity will ruin their utopia." He puffed. "They may be right. This is a peaceful place to come home to when the world becomes too much. Isn't it, Lyssa?"

Ignoring his steady regard, she pressed the point. "With a landline, I could have called home about my broken arm." True enough; in her pain and confusion that day, she would have appreciated the comfort of talking to her mothers, even if only by phone.

"You could have texted with the emergency code."

"But I couldn't have told everyone I was all right," she replied stubbornly. "And with a real phone, you could have called to find that out instead of driving all the way down to the apartment."

He reminded her, "We called Clearview first. That conversation was less than satisfying." He lowered his chair so that all four feet were on the ground and pointed at her with the bowl of his pipe. "All we found out was you'd been fired."

"Well, you could have called me at home."

"Would you have told us to come and get you and bring you home where you belonged?"

Lyssa didn't miss his emphasis on the word *home*. He, and the other three, had never liked to hear her refer to her apartment as her home. But darn it, she had lived there for more than a decade. She sighed. "Look, we're getting off the subject. I just think that instead of spending your savings on me, you should do something for you, for the farm. Like, drill a well." Before dropping her bombshell, she wanted to plant the suggestion that there were other alternatives.

He took a few more draws on his pipe before lowering it. "Helen doesn't like wells, you know that. Says they're like leeches, sucking groundwater out of the aquifer."

"Yes, but sometimes they're necessary," she persisted.

"Not when you've got a perfectly good spring just up the hill." He rapped his pipe on the edge of the table.

"And somebody else's well to draw from when the spring dries up."

Cal looked uncomfortable. "Now, you know Helen doesn't much care for that. But Jacobson was going to put in a well anyway, and when he offered to sell us that strip of land in exchange for half the capital to drill the well, even Helen came around to it. One well is better than two, in her mind. It's worked out just fine for all these years."

It's now or never, Lyssa thought. "Well, you see," she told him, "there's a bit of a problem with that. You don't own the land or the water rights. Jacobson cheated you." She leaned forward. "That contract was nothing but a lease. When Jacobson sells his property, the new owner doesn't have to provide you with any water."

"Is that why you wanted his land? To keep us from losing our water rights?" He scowled. "You were worried about us? Trying to protect us?"

She didn't understand why he should be focusing on her. "Ye-es," she said slowly. "Partly."

"That's why you wouldn't leave that job down in Tempe, too, isn't it!" Cal crossed his arms over his stout chest and leaned against the back of his chair. "It paid better than the Land Trust, and you figured you had to put aside funds to buy out Jacobson. To rescue us!"

"That wasn't the only reason," she returned. "The Land Trust just isn't my thing."

"I knew we made a mistake in not telling you about our financial situation." Cal tapped his fingers on his arms. "We tried to raise you to be independent. Made you pay your own way through college, then grad school. Let you pick your own job and then stay with it no matter how wrong for you it was."

"*Let* me! And just how would you have stopped me?"

"By telling you the truth." Cal's ruddy face was grim.

Jeez-Louise, she thought; how many secrets did her parents have? "What truth?"

"Ari wrote a book."

"Right. *Soul-Circles.*" Ari had meant for the book to be his farewell to academia, a way of thumbing his nose at the ivory tower. A few copies still lay around the house. Lyssa had read it, of course. She'd found it heavy going, but she never told Ari that.

"It became a cult classic, you know."

Lyssa's smile froze. "Oh-kay."

"It made a lot of money. Buying the farm barely made a dent in the fortune."

"The fortune," she said hesitantly, not sure how much of this to believe. Cal didn't look like he was joking.

"And EF has never paid for itself anyway. If we have to cut back production because of an unreliable water source, that's fine. Paris won't like it, but—" He shrugged. "She'll get used to it."

"You never told me," Lyssa breathed. "Why didn't any of you ever tell me?"

Gruffly he said, "Mostly, we didn't want you to wind up as a spoiled trust-fund baby. Once you got a little older, though, I thought you deserved to know. I wanted to at least help with college expenses so you didn't have to worry. But I was overruled. As it turned out, that may have been for the best. We were so proud of the way you put yourself through school."

Lyssa didn't listen after that. She wasn't angry or resentful. Just . . . numb.

Her parents were rich. Wealthy enough to buy Elysian Fields and have money left over. Wealthy enough to make a solid offer on Jacobson's property without blinking an eye. Wealthy enough, evidently, to have sent her to college and grad school and to have spoiled her rotten with material things, had they chosen to do so.

Lyssa pushed away from the table and rose.

"Lyssa? Where are you going?"

She ignored the question and kept on walking out the door and around to the driveway, just to be moving, to see a road stretching out ahead of her, to *get away*.

Her arm was broken, she was homeless and out of a job, the only man even marginally interested in playing a personal role in her life had run off to New York so that his mother could destroy her, and her own loving family had just blasted her entire world to smithereens.

All those years of struggle, all that time she had assumed her existence had meaning and purpose—they had taken all of that away from her.

Lyssa had nothing left.

Sixteen

DANE TOOK THE STEPS to Lyssa's apartment two at a time. It was too late in the day to find Simon or Claudia, Alex wasn't answering his cell, and Dane didn't want to beard his mother in her den until he knew what the hell was going on. So it would have to be Lyssa.

He denied that the inexplicable heating of his blood had anything to do with seeing her again. It was being back in the warmth of the Valley of the Sun after being bit by the Big Apple.

He banged on the flimsy door.

"Lyssa! Lyssa, you open up this door right now or I'm coming through it!" He rubbed a fist over his cheek, felt the stubble there, and supposed he should have taken the time to shave and clean up after his art binge. But he'd fussed so long over that dragon that he hadn't left New York until after noon. Three cities and one plane-change later, he picked up his car from the long-term parking lot at Sky Harbor and drove straight here.

The door across the hallway opened a crack. "Back again, baseball-boy?"

"Where is she? I know she's in there." Dane crossed the hall with two long, impatient steps and braced himself against the doorframe with one hand, ready to shove the door open if necessary.

The door swung wide. The liver-spotted hands of the elderly woman within were clenched in the folds of a floral housedress, and she shifted from one foot to another like a boxer. "The hell she is!

Lyssa's gone. And I'll be calling the police on you in a minute if you don't haul your skinny rich-boy ass right back down those steps."

"What do you mean, gone?" he demanded and then winced at the hammering in his head, which he was trying to blame on jetlag. "Gone where? When will she be back?"

With a snort of disgust she went to close the door, but Dane stuck his foot between the flimsy door and the frame. "Where is she?" he repeated.

"She loaded up her stuff and took off. She's gone, you idiot."

Dane pressed the heel of one hand to his face, lodging it between his eye and his temple, where the throbbing was the worst. "Where'd she go?" he managed to say.

"Back to her folks' place, I assume."

"Where do they live?"

"Don't know that she ever said."

Dane refrained from taking her shoulders and shaking the truth out of her. "Damn it—"

"Uh-uh." Lyssa's neighbor shook her finger at him. "Don't you curse at me. This is all your fault!"

"The hell it is," Dane muttered, shoving his hands in his back pockets. "I haven't even been here."

"Exactly." The weather-beaten face puckered into a glare. "You haven't been here. Not since the night everything started to go wrong. I expected her to fall down and break her neck in them skyscraper shoes, she was crying so hard, and off balance besides, with the cast and all."

Dane let the words rattle in his brain for a moment. "What cast?"

"The one on her arm, that got broke when she was mugged."

"Mugged!" He straightened with a jerk, pulling useless, suddenly shaky hands out of his pockets.

"That's right. She would've told you herself, if you'd given her the chance instead of running off to New York."

"Oh, God." When she'd called, he had purposely given her the impression that he was too busy to talk. "How badly was she hurt?"

"Not bad enough to keep her from thinking about how she was inconveniencing you by showing up late for dinner. But when she tried to explain, you set that bimbo on her and wouldn't give her a chance."

"She was mugged that night? On her way to dinner?" he demanded in horror.

"No, stupid, she wouldn't have had time to call to postpone, then, would she?" the elderly woman sneered. "It was in one of the campus parking lots. Some screwed-up druggie came out in broad daylight and grabbed her laptop away from her. The creep shoved her down, and as she fell, she got her arm twisted under her. Guess it snapped just like a matchstick."

Dane felt the blood drain from his face. "A matchstick?" He closed his eyes, but that didn't quell his vivid imagination.

"Yeah. Snap!"

He flinched. "Jesus." This neighbor of Lyssa's might look like an old-fashioned wrinkled-apple doll, but she had the heart of a demon. He swallowed hard.

The whiskey he'd drunk on the plane churned in his stomach. He retreated along the scarred linoleum toward the stairs, seeking fresh air to pump into his tightening chest.

He went home and wandered from room to room, trying to rid himself of the overpowering guilt and frustration he felt.

It wasn't his fault Lyssa had been attacked. Or that because of it she apparently had shown up late for dinner, sometime after he and his mother left; the message from her had been garbled. It wasn't even his fault she'd been fired. And he had come home from New York the minute he'd found out. Within a few hours, anyway.

Then there was the knowledge that he had come all too close to sowing some dangerous wild oats in New York.

Dane poured himself another drink. It was bourbon, which he didn't care much for but had been his father's favorite. His mother bought him a bottle every Christmas.

He squinted at the caramel-colored liquid in the glass. Then he shuddered and put it down, untasted.

Dane walked to the spare bedroom, where he had dumped his art supplies. The dragon was no more, as he had squashed it back into a rough, shapeless lump to fit it into his luggage. As he started to open the plastic bag containing the clay, the musty odor of it turned his stomach, and he backed away.

He went into the bathroom to wash his hands to get rid of the smell. On the tiny beaten-copper stand beside the sink, a bar of handmade soap placed there by the designer his mother had hired to decorate the condo caught his eye. He picked up the soap and shifted it from hand to hand, feeling the heft of it, looking at the play of color on its translucent surface, and sensing a shape deep within.

Dane carried it into the kitchen. He rummaged through the drawers and found a paring knife. Too impatient to worry about the mess, he made one careful cut. He followed that first slide of the knife with another, and another.

He managed to rough out a face and then a body.

It wasn't a dragon, he saw with a distinct lack of relief. No, this time he had come up with a miniature gargoyle. Its faintly simian features, reminiscent of the flying monkeys of the *Wizard of Oz*, were rendered harmless with a flirtatious wink.

Dane didn't bother trying to sleep that night. He did clean himself up in the morning, shaving and putting on fresh clothes. He couldn't do much about his bloodshot eyes. If his prey thought he looked half insane and not to be trifled with, so much the better. He wanted them as off-balance as possible.

He suspected that was the only way he would find out what the hell was going on.

LYSSA, DRESSED FOR THE MORNING in an oversized sweatshirt and jeans, stared up at the ceiling. She was aware of the stale mustiness of the handmade quilt on which she lay. Her nose felt stuffy, as it had been ever since she'd collapsed on her bed the night before. She supposed the bedding had always smelled that way and she was only now noticing, now that she was facing an indeterminate number of nights sleeping in her childhood bed and waking to her childhood life all over again.

The previous day had been a long one, she reflected. She wondered how many more she could take before she went completely bonkers.

After dinner, her parents had sat down to figure out what to do about the threat to their water supply. "But Lyssa," Paris had said over and over. "We've always used that water. It's ours!"

Lyssa had explained over and over that if the land was sold, her parents would have to negotiate a new contract for the water rights. Or try to buy the parcel of land with the well and the pump from the new owner. Or either cut back on irrigation or dig their own well. She had suggested several possibilities.

Looking at the water stains above her, she now remembered the optimistic notion that her parents could solve their own problem. That had been in the old days—yesterday—back when she had assumed that they would worry about their problem and let Lyssa handle hers.

She put that thought on the back burner, rose, and went to breakfast.

DANE CLOSED THE FILE DRAWER with a bang and ran his fingers through his hair, ruffling it more than the sleepless night had done. The Berkshire file showed exactly what Alex had told him over the phone. But it wasn't the original report.

At eight, he was waiting in Claudia's chair, legs propped up on her desk and crossed at the ankles.

She came into the office looking well rested. She wore a celadon-green jacketed dress that hugged her curves and revealed about six inches of thigh.

Her cool gaze dropped to the open folder but then met his. "Good morning. I wasn't expecting you back just yet."

"I bet." Dane shifted his legs off the desk and rose slowly. "You're fired. Collect your things and get out."

Her cheeks paled beneath the subtle shadings of makeup. "Dane."

"That's Mr. Callicott to you."

"Dane!"

He arched one brow.

"Mr. Callicott. This is a joke, right?"

"No joke. You're through here."

Claudia threw him a thousand-watt smile, although her nose looked pinched and her eyes were hard. She practically oozed sensuality. But after the crazed Sophy, Dane thought, he was immune.

"You don't want to do that. You've told me I'm the most efficient administrative assistant you've ever had. You said you'd be lost without me."

"That was before you took to forgery."

"Forgery?" She toyed with her lower lip. "I don't understand."

"The Berkshire report," he said, stabbing a finger at the file.

"The Berkshire report? What about it?"

Dane stared at her until her gaze fell. "There's no use playing dumb. Ms. Pearce has already told us everything. Implicating you in the process."

She lifted startled eyes to his, confirming his bluff. When he figured out that someone in Simon's office had to be involved, Barbara Pearce had come to mind right off. Her contempt for Lyssa had always been thinly disguised.

"Did you think your co-conspirator wouldn't turn on you?"

"I don't believe you!" But she had the glassy stare of a deer in the headlights.

"It seemed simple, didn't it?" he persisted. "Change a few words on a few pages, make some copies, send some faxes. No one would ever know the difference."

Claudia's shuttered face relaxed infinitesimally. Giving a gracefully feminine shrug, she said, "I did everything on your mother's instructions."

"My mother is no fool, and she would never do anything illegal."

"Are you so sure of that?" she asked slyly.

He refused to dignify that with a reply. "Let me make something clear to you. You're finished at Callicott Properties."

"I'll take you to court—"

"If you so much as talk to a lawyer about suing for wrongful termination," Dane vowed, "I'll make sure you never get another job in Arizona besides flipping hamburgers. I'll call everyone in the business and let them know your propensity for forging documents. If you persist, I'll bring countersuit against you for fraud and theft."

"I haven't stolen anything." Despite her confident words, she had gone stiff and wary.

"Keep arguing, and I may file charges against you right now, just for the satisfaction of seeing you in jail. There are some advantages to having money and power, I find. Now, pack up and get out. There's a box for your personal things." He pointed to it.

Then he left her alone, retreating to his office and pulling the door partway shut. He moved to his chair and leaned on it so that it squeaked.

With jerky, uneven movements Claudia cleaned out her desk. Dane watched through the crack at the hinges.

She glanced toward his office, caught her lip between her teeth, and then interposed her hips between his door and her desk. The top drawer slid open with but a whisper of sound.

If Dane hadn't checked through her desk carefully, she could have gotten away with it, he mused. Silently he rose and walked up behind her just as she slipped a thumb drive into her purse.

"It's blank."

Claudia let out a stifled shriek and whipped around.

Dane showed her an identical one. "This is the one you're looking for, with the client list and the bid and planning information. I'll be keeping it as insurance. I think you'd better be on your way now." He handed her an envelope. "You'll find your last check in here. I've paid you through the end of the week. Don't come back here again, don't ask for a recommendation, and don't talk to a lawyer. If you do, I'll ruin you as surely as you did Lyssa."

She searched his face with glittering eyes. Whatever she was hoping to see, she apparently didn't find it. She snatched the envelope and tossed it into the box. "This is it, then? You're really prepared to end it this way?" She faced him defiantly, crossing her arms and pressing her breasts nearly out of the jacket. For not having expected him in the office, she was suitably dressed for an attempt at seduction. Maybe she had plans for Alex, too.

"There is no 'it.' There never was. You were an employee. You were never going to be anything but an employee." He knew of a few men in his position who had been caught by ambitious secretaries and assistants. He'd decided on her first day on the job that he wouldn't become one of them. "Goodbye, Miss Montgomery. You'll excuse me if I don't wish you good luck. Oh. And the keys. Hand them over."

Her eyes brimmed with what he supposed were genuine tears as she dug into her purse and extracted the ring of keys that fit various doors in the Callicott Properties offices. She dropped them on her desk, ignoring his outstretched hand. Without another word she picked up the box and walked out of the office.

One down, one to go.

Dane had some time to prepare his strategy for the next stage, since Simon never showed up in his office before nine. He doubted that Claudia felt enough loyalty to Barb Pearce, particularly after the tidbits of misinformation he'd dropped, to warn her partner in crime that they had been found out.

It was quarter past nine when he pushed open the glass door of Clearview Engineering, strolled through a poorly defined space that he assumed was supposed to function as a reception area, and positioned himself in front of the cluttered desk of Simon Levitt's secretary. The woman pushed her graying hair behind her ear and looked up at him. Her mouth shaped into an "o" and she produced a wobbly smile. She seemed more flustered than the occasion warranted. "Mr. Callicott. Was Mr. Levitt expecting you?"

"Probably not. He'll see me anyway."

She blinked up at him. "He's preparing for a meeting with some of the Valley Archaeology people. This isn't a good time—"

Leaning toward her so that she caught the full effect of his red-rimmed eyes, he said very softly, "I'll show myself in." He stood up and walked past her, ignoring her yelp of distress.

Simon was halfway out of his chair. When he spotted Dane, he eased back with a look of resignation.

Dane didn't bother with the pleasantries. He picked the more comfortable of the two chairs in front of the desk and seated himself without waiting for an invitation. "Let's talk about the Berkshire project."

"I have the situation under control," Simon assured him. "Lyssa isn't here anymore. I've taken care of it."

"Yes, well, we'll talk about where she is later. Right now you have a more urgent problem. I want you to get her back."

Simon blinked. "I can't do that."

"If it's my mother you're worried about, I'll bring her around to my way of thinking." Dane didn't feel friendly enough toward Simon Levitt to reassure him that he had already straightened out his mother. She hadn't been happy to learn how ably Claudia had played her. "I know my mother told you to fire Lyssa. But she wasn't in possession of all the details." Dane leaned forward, rested his forearms on his thighs, and clasped his hands loosely together. "Lyssa was set up, Simon. I've taken care of it, to use your own words, at my end. What I can't prove is who was responsible here at Clearview."

"At Clearview?" Simon ran a finger under the knot of the tie and tugged at it. "I don't understand."

"Someone at Clearview had to have inserted those falsified pages into the report."

"Falsified pages? What are you talking about?"

Dane's hands tightened on each other. "The report in my files isn't the one Lyssa originally presented. I assumed yours had been changed as well."

Hesitantly Simon responded, "I don't know about any change. She missed the underground tanks. That was a major oversight, Dane. When Mrs. Callicott pointed it out and asked for some response from me, what else could I have done?"

Dane shook his head. "Lyssa informed Callicott—me—about the underground tanks. That is why I didn't proceed with the project."

"All these months . . . You can't be certain. I don't remember any of this."

Dane commented, "Alex and I do. Environmental hazards are not something we're likely to forget. Any more than Lyssa was likely to overlook them. She's too good at what she does."

Rallying quickly, Simon blustered, "Even the archived materials say she missed those tanks. And it's not just the hard copy. It was on her computer, too."

"Then someone was playing around with her computer."

Simon's face grew red, and the tip of his nose quivered. "That's ridiculous. You make it sound like a conspiracy."

"It is. I'm just trying to find out how high up it goes."

"I can't believe this." Simon's eyes rounded, and he snapped, "You can't possibly think I had anything to do with it."

Dane straightened, unable to maintain his casual pose any longer. "I'm willing to assume you didn't. As long as you give Lyssa her job back. That's the first thing."

Simon muttered, "I thought things were complicated enough around here, what with bringing in Valley Archaeology and getting that new division set up. Lyssa was expendable. And after that thing with Barb . . ."

"Barb. That would be Barbara Pearce?" Dane had hoped Simon would bring up her name without needing to be prompted. "Lyssa's supervisor? With access to her computer?" He read the truth in Simon's horrified glance. "Just what was this thing with Barb?"

"It has nothing to do with what we're talking about," Simon huffed. "I had to put Lyssa Smith on probation for unprofessional conduct, that's all."

Dane wondered how many of these details of Lyssa's downfall he'd been blissfully unaware of while locked in his hotel room in New York playing with paper and clay. "What sort of unprofessional conduct?"

"I can't discuss the specifics of it—"

"You'd better, Simon."

"—because it affects other people!"

"Remember who you're talking to. I've sent a lot of business your way. Imagine my surprise, upon returning home from my first vacation in years, to find my company the target of what appears to be industrial espionage, traceable to Clearview Engineering." Dane wasn't above stretching the truth, particularly when doing so elicited the response he wanted. "I have a stake in getting to the bottom of this, and a little matter of employee privacy isn't going to stop me."

"You can't be serious. Industrial espionage?" Simon's voice cracked.

Dane nodded. "Trust me, you don't want to know. Now, what was Lyssa accused of?"

Simon shuddered. "Do you have any idea how much trouble I could get into for telling you this?"

"Consider the alternative," Dane went on ruthlessly.

"Lyssa Smith covered up information of a personal nature that would have made it impossible for her to be employed here."

"Spill it, Simon."

"All right, then. She's a lesbian."

Whatever Dane had expected, it wasn't that. He laughed.

"It is not funny!"

Dane figured Simon would have stamped his foot if he'd been standing; the man was red faced and puffed up like a child about to throw a tantrum. "Oh, it is," he said. "You have no idea."

Primly Simon informed him, "She was caught making sexual advances to Barb Pearce. Barb was very upset. Of course I put Lyssa on probation. We can't have that kind of behavior around here. And Barb could have come back with sexual harassment charges. When I learned that Lyssa Smith had been careless in her work and jeopardized a project for a major client, I saw no problem when said client requested that she be fired."

"Stop talking like a lawyer. It doesn't suit you. You have a problem, Simon. Lyssa isn't gay." That, he was positive of. "Even if she was, firing her so soon after you found out would be grounds for a wrongful termination suit. The ACLU would be all over you. Besides, to the best of my knowledge, sexual harassment in the workplace goes the other way. The superior is the harasser and the subordinate is the harassee." Exasperated now, Dane asked, "What made you buy into that ridiculous idea in the first place?"

Simon muttered, "Her parents are homosexuals."

"What?"

"Her parents are gay, all right? They all live together, two men and two women, on some farm up north of town. I couldn't have a woman like that working for Clearview. What if somebody found out?"

Dane held up one hand. "Wait a minute. You actually did fire Lyssa because she was—because you thought she was gay?" He shook his head, wondering when everybody around him had gone nuts. "Get her back, Simon. Offer Lyssa her job back. And fire Barbara Pearce."

Simon ventured to say, "I can't do that."

"Which part?"

"Either part." Gaining confidence, Simon leaned toward Dane as though to share a secret. "I can't run this place without Barb. And you don't have any proof she was involved. As for Lyssa, I can't keep someone like that here. Besides, Lyssa would never come back now that everyone knows about her perversions."

Through his teeth Dane said, "You would be served right if she did choose to leave this place for good, and sued you right into bankruptcy." He watched as the other man's jaw dropped. "We've been friends a long time. We've helped each other prosper in business. Are you willing to turn your back on all that?"

Blinking, Simon finally asked, "Is that a threat? Are you actually telling me you won't do business with me anymore if I don't do this?"

"Yes."

"But you ought to be thanking me for doing you a favor," Simon looked flustered. "That spectacle Lyssa made of herself with Turnbull was at *your* reception, and then there was that error she made on the Berkshire report, which I still don't see . . ." He trailed off miserably at Dane's murderous glare. "All I'm saying is, you have no proof . . . Well, anyway, that was on *your* project, and your mother was the one who told me to get rid of Lyssa!"

"Don't—" Dane caught himself and went on more reasonably. "Don't worry about my mother. Worry about yourself, Simon. I've told you what I expect you to do."

"You would never fire Claudia if you were in the same—"

"I already did. She cleared out her desk this morning. Who else in my office do you think could have pulled off such a stunt? Falsifying documents, Simon!" Dane reminded him. "You see," he said with a commiserating smile, "I do know what I'm asking of you, at least in dismissing the indispensable Ms. Pearce."

"Claudia? You fired Claudia?" Simon sagged back into his chair again and buried his head in his hands.

"Call Lyssa right now," Dane ordered, picking up the handset and holding it out to Simon. "I don't want to hear any more of that crap about homosexuals. She isn't one, and even if she were, you would have no right to can her."

The other man, shaken, opened a drawer and took out a sheet of paper. After looking up the number with a painstaking slowness that made Dane grit his teeth, Simon dialed and then listened to the tones and brief recorded message.

"Her phone's disconnected." He looked relieved as he set the receiver back in its cradle.

Dane folded his arms and sat back. "Then call your human resources people and get some other numbers. Emergency contacts, alternative phone numbers, whatever it takes. Try the . . . the farm, whatever it is, up north, where her parents live." Dane hoped she had been more forthcoming with her employer than with him. "She's not likely to hang around town when she has family to go to."

But Simon drew a blank with her personnel file.

"What do you mean, there's no other number?" Dane demanded. "Where's her severance check supposed to be sent?"

"To her apartment." Simon's mouth tightened at Dane's persistence.

"She's not there. She's moved out."

"Then it'll be forwarded to wherever she is," Simon told him impatiently. "Dane, you can't be serious about having me fire Barb."

Dane stood up and leaned over the desk. "I have never been more serious about anything in my life. Get rid of Barbara Pearce, or kiss the Callicott account goodbye." He turned on his heel and strode out.

DANE GROWLED HIS FRUSTRATION. He stared up at his father's and grandfather's portraits and vowed that the first thing he would do upon turning over the presidency to his mother was give her those smug faces for her own office. Then he looked over at the clock and sighed. It was nearly ten o'clock at night, midnight by New York time. He had spent twelve hours trying to track down Lyssa.

And had nothing to show for it except a headache that wouldn't go away.

Her last name *would* have to be Smith, he thought bitterly. He didn't know if her given name was Lyssa, or if that was a nickname, so he'd had the investigator check under Lyssa and Melissa and Melisande and every other similar name they could think of, in every county from Maricopa north, in every records system that could be legally accessed. And maybe even some that couldn't.

Nothing had panned out. The damned woman seemed to have no identity apart from her abandoned apartment in Tempe and her former job at Clearview. No vehicle title, no property in her name, no former address in the past ten years.

He'd even driven over to Anton's after remembering her familiarity with the restaurant. Anton had brusquely denied knowing her. But a white-haired, distinguished gentleman-farmer, burly in his bib overalls and carrying boxes of produce like they weighed nothing, had suggested that if her parents had a farm up north, maybe he should try the farmers' market downtown.

He would do that, Dane thought, if he couldn't find her sooner. Thinking about Lyssa at the reception gave him an idea.

Dane called Alex.

"What?"

The rasp of the masculine voice that answered owed more to irritation than to sleepiness. He hoped he was interrupting Alex at an inopportune moment. Dane already knew Julia wasn't at her house, since he had just gotten her answering machine. "Is Julia there?"

"Of all the . . ." His oldest and most loyal friend muttered a creative curse under his breath. "You better have a good reason for asking."

A feminine voice in the background validated Dane's suspicion that Alex had company. Dane heard them both breathing, could picture the dark head and the blond one angled intimately over the phone. They were an "us" now, the woman his mother wanted him to marry and the man his mother was afraid would steal both his prospective wife and his company.

"Ask Julia," he said. "I need to know where Lyssa might have gone. The name of her family's farm. The town they live near. Hell, I'd settle for the county."

Alex was silent for a few seconds. His breathing sounded heavy. "I assume Lyssa has gone off to lick her wounds, but can't this wait until morning?"

"Alex!" Julia's exclamation was audible this time. So was the sound of a slap—to a bare shoulder, Dane assumed.

"Ouch, woman. Damn it," Alex muttered.

There was a rustle of cloth and a giggle. Then Dane heard a faint, "Give me the phone." More distinctly, Julia asked, "So, Lyssa decided to cut her losses and get out, did she?"

Dane hesitated. "You knew she was going to leave Clearview?"

"Well, at some point. I didn't think it would be quite so soon. Last I heard, she was still waiting for her offer to be accepted."

"What offer?"

Julia fell silent. After a moment she said, "At the reception I assumed . . . I figured she would have let you, in particular, know what she was doing."

Dane's hand went to the back of his neck. He rubbed at the tension as he said, "Julia. My friend. If you don't tell me what you know, right this minute, I will—" He realized he had raised his voice and finished in a more reasonable tone that wouldn't cause Julia to hang up on him. "I swear I will turn my mother loose on Alex."

"I don't know . . ."

Dane closed his eyes. "Whatever Lyssa had planned, I don't think it was this. Simon fired her while I was gone. I'm going to get her job back, but to do that, I have to know where she is."

"I doubt she wants her job back. She had me handle the mortgage application for some property up by Mayer. From the sounds of it she plans to live there. If she's left her apartment, Dane"—Julia's voice was gentle—"I think she's gone. And if she didn't let you know about it, I don't think she wants you to find her."

He ran a hand through his hair and confessed, "We didn't part well before the New York trip. Figured I'd smooth things over with her when I got back, but, well . . ."

"She isn't a woman you can play with and then set aside."

"I know that. But she's her own person. Would she thank you for not giving her a chance to tell me to go to hell on her own?"

Julia chuckled. She didn't have the legal description of the property in front of her, but she promised to call him with it as soon as she got into the office the next morning. It was a lead, he assured himself. That was all he needed.

Then Alex took the phone again and thanked him for getting rid of Claudia. "That woman made my life hell while you were gone, Dane."

"Yeah, I know I had to get rid of her, but she was the best assistant I'd ever had. She knew everything about Callicott. Even how to cover her tracks."

"You didn't find the originals, I take it? Too bad. Lyssa would probably be glad to have her reputation cleared."

Alex didn't know the half of it, Dane thought wryly.

Julia was obviously listening in. "What originals?" she asked.

Dane explained the problem of the falsified pages and admitted that he had searched through every file he could think of, hoping to find the originals to convince his mother, if not Simon, that he hadn't lost his mind. "Claudia probably shredded them," he concluded. "Or threw them out, and the cleaning staff dumped the trash already."

Julia gave a little hum. "But she wasn't expecting you back for several days. And, really, she wasn't all that bright. I bet she figured she could get away with this. Because of her big . . . assets, you know."

Silence fell. Dane was about to say thanks and goodbye when Julia suggested, "Did you try Claudia's secret files?"

"Secret files?" He rubbed the back of his neck again, wondering if he would have any skin left if he didn't find Lyssa soon. What was it Julia had said that night at the reception about him always getting his own way? What a crock, he thought.

"Claudia files things she wants to hide under 'F' for Ferragamo."

"Why?" The two men spoke together.

"Beats me," Julia said. "Some kind of foot fetish?"

Dane asked Alex, "Do you know what she's talking about?"

"Not a clue."

Julia informed them that Ferragamos were shoes.

Dane didn't care what shoes had to do with hiding files. What was important was finding the proof that Lyssa had not, in fact, made a blunder of gargantuan proportions. He would need that as leverage. If not on Simon, then on his mother. "I'll give it a try," he said.

"Goodnight, Julia. Alex."

He hung up and went to the mahogany filing cabinets again.

There, in the drawer marked "De" through "Fi," he found the original Berkshire report, under "Ferragamo," just as Julia had suggested. He wondered how Julia had learned about that little quirk of Claudia's, and how many other secrets he would eventually discover that Claudia had kept from him.

She had made it damned hard for him to turn over control of Callicott Properties to his mother and Alex as he had planned. This business with Lyssa had complicated everything. He could hardly delegate any of it away.

Seventeen

THE GUINEA HENS sent up the alarm first, cackling and chortling like small-town gossips. Their racket drew Lyssa out of the stillroom cut into the side of the hill. The beach-ball bodies of the hens, covered with white-speckled sage-gray feathers, were pointed toward the sports car sending up cascades of dust along the gravel drive. Then Dammit figured out they had a visitor and added his deep bark to the mix.

The sun overhead glinted off Dane's blond hair and caught the face of his watch as he lounged comfortably behind the wheel. Lyssa stopped where she was and considered slipping back into the dim coolness. She wore a pair of ancient jeans, more hole than material. The most revealing areas were covered by one of Ari's old sweatshirts.

A voice that had been singing a seductive aria inside her for the past few weeks woke up and belted out a full-blown chorus. A tingle slid through her belly. If he put his hands on her again, she would be a goner, she concluded unhappily. So much for moral principles.

She walked around the house and headed for where he had ground to a halt. Dammit galloped over to stand beside the Boxster. He reared up and placed his front paws just below the window before Lyssa could stop him. Then he shook his head and left a long slimy deposit on the driver's-side door.

Lyssa told herself to act reserved but not unfriendly. She would not run to Dane and fling herself into his arms like some silent-movie heroine rescued from a fate worse than death.

"Hi," Dane said, without taking his eyes off Dammit's amber-brown stare.

"Hi."

"That's some dog. Is he . . . okay?"

"You mean, will he bite? Probably not. Dammit." The dog spared her a glance. She waggled her fingers at him and murmured, "Come away. Leave him alone." Dammit reluctantly padded over to her and pressed his nose into her crotch in rebuke. She shoved his head away but scratched him behind the ears until he sighed.

Dane pushed the door open and unfolded himself from the car, which was still sexy despite being covered with dust and drool. Just like its owner, Lyssa supposed. No amount of dirt could make Dane anything less than what he was. Even in khakis and dress shoes, he didn't look out of place on her parents' farm.

She recalled that he had worked construction in his younger days. Much as she would like to pigeonhole him as a spoiled rich boy, he was undeniably more than that. Come to think of it, she mused, he probably had no more family wealth than she did. Of course, *he* had a job.

"What breed is it?" Dane hesitantly extended a hand but pulled back when the massive black head swung his way. "I'm assuming it's a dog rather than a pony." He grinned at her. Then he spotted the cast, and his face went still.

Lyssa kept her voice even. "*He* is a dog. Breedwise, we're talking Heinz fifty-seven. Probably rottweiler and mastiff, at least."

"What's his name?" Allowing Dammit to sniff his hand, Dane laughed at the demanding nudge for attention, then scratched behind the dog's ears the same way she had.

"Dammit," she said.

"What?"

She could tell that Dane had just found out how silky smooth and soft those short black hairs were. His blue eyes were nearly as blissful as the dog's. "Dammit. That's his name."

Dane lifted one eyebrow skeptically.

"We figure he got into a lot of mischief as a pup. That was probably the word he heard most. One of our seasonal workers saw that he answered to it, so we went with it. Someone dumped him off on campus when he was a few months old."

"So you rescued him, brought him home, and loved him."

"Just what are you doing here, Dane?"

"I got your job back for you."

"Gee, thanks," she said politely. The last thing she needed was another job. Cal had one lined up with Gaspar Adams, in New York. Helen was pushing the Land Trust at her. Paris thought she should open a store in Prescott. Ari just watched her with secrets in his eyes. "I don't want it. Now go away."

His head snapped back. He looked nonplussed, then determined. "I drove all the way up here to talk to you. At least hear me out."

Dammit bounded off, unconcerned by the man who was making Lyssa's muscles wind as tight as the tendrils on a pea-vine. "I don't think so. I don't have anything to say to you."

"Then you can listen, while I apologize. I'm sorry, Lyssa."

Darned if she was going to make it easy on him this time. "Sorry for what?"

"Mostly, I'm sorry I wasn't here when you needed me."

"I didn't need you." She turned and started walking. Toward the Jacobson property, she realized in a moment, although she hadn't intended to head that direction.

Dane fell into step beside her. "I suppose I deserved that. In case you wondered, I didn't know what was going on. Any of it."

Lyssa shrugged as though it didn't matter. She kept her eyes on the narrow trail she'd worn through the weeds in the past few days. "I never really believed you did."

"Then why did you run off without letting me know where to find you?" Dane grasped her shoulder and swung her around to look at him. "Without even calling me to say goodbye?"

She faced him, calling on reserves of strength as his ungentle touch electrified her. She would not let that chorus of hormones dance her into his arms again. "Let me think. Oh, right. You were in New York, and you were pissed at me. And wasn't your mother the one that got me fired? In my book, any one of those would be reason enough." Tugging away, she started walking again.

"I wasn't nice to you before I left."

"No. You weren't."

"I'm sorry for that, too—going to New York without straightening things out between us." Dane caught his toe in a tangle of drying weeds and nearly fell. He cursed under his breath but caught up with her again, struggling his way through the undergrowth, which became thicker the closer they got to the Jacobsons' property.

It was his own fault, she figured, for wearing slick shoes and trying to blaze a trail beside her instead of falling in behind.

"How many times do I have to say I'm sorry?"

"I guess until I believe it," she told him dryly.

"Let me make it up to you. Let me put everything right again."

"'Right' being the way things were last week?" Lyssa shook her head. "That isn't right for me anymore. I can't go back to Clearview. I won't."

"I can see where you might have hard feelings, but don't you think throwing away a job you've held for all these years is a little shortsighted? Besides, I've already talked to Simon about it."

"Listen, Dane, blackmailing him into taking me back might make you feel better, but it doesn't do anything for me. The only thing that would make me feel better would be hearing that Claudia is out on the street along with me. I figure she's the one who deserves most of the blame." She strode along faster as her blood began to boil.

"I fired Claudia. And told Simon to get rid of Barbara Pearce."

"Barb!" She hadn't said anything about that fiasco. Lyssa stopped, suspicion rising in her like a tsunami. "What do you know about that?"

"I know enough." His evident discomfort showed that he did.

Lyssa whipped around and began walking again, inwardly cursing Simon. She couldn't look at Dane.

"Lyssa—" Persistently he came after her. "Okay. I can see you're still upset."

"Oh, so now you're Mr. Perceptive?" she tossed over her shoulder.

"Actually, what I want to be is Mr. Perfect. Isn't that what women call him? That man who would go to the ends of the earth for them, who would make their happiness his mission in life. My life is empty without you, Lyssa, just as you said. Empty and cold and lonely."

Lyssa halted. "*You* do not fight *fair*," she whispered in a shaky voice.

"I don't want to fight at all. I want you to let me in."

"No, you don't. I remember what you said you wanted in a wife, even if you've forgotten." She recalled what Gail had said, too, when they were in the bathroom. "I am not for you, Dane. The universe did not put me here to be a pawn in your little game of life."

He opened his mouth and closed it again. Then he told her, "When I was in New York, I did a lot of thinking."

"In between ball games, you mean?" She took refuge in sarcasm.

He blinked at her. "What?"

"I saw you. In the stands. At the World Series!"

Dane heaved out a breath. "I took in *one* baseball game, that's all. The rest of the time, I was working. So, is that all you do, watch baseball?"

"That sounds like a great way for me to spend my time now that I don't have a job!" she snarled. "Why didn't I think of that? What do you want me to do? Play golf? With one arm! That would be fun."

Dane scrubbed his hands over his face. "I arranged to get your job back," he pointed out. She continued to glare at him, and he sighed. "Let's start over here," he suggested reasonably. "I did a lot of thinking this past week. About what I want out of life, and who I want in my life."

"Who you want in your life." Lyssa whirled on her heel and said over her shoulder, "I'm supposed to imagine that you mean me? That all of a sudden you've decided I'm not such a naïve, stupid little prude, you're no longer in love with Gail O'Neill, you're going to defy your mother and run off with a farmgirl from the boonies who would be laughed out of the country club if I showed up there, after that fiasco with Tank? I don't think so."

"It's not like that."

His resonant voice, so close to her ear, sent a shiver down her spine. In self-defense she said, "Tell me, Dane, did you really expect that you would come up here and show me how much more powerful and influential you are than I, and I would fall at your feet in gratitude?"

"It wasn't like that." He sounded annoyed. "I don't want your gratitude."

"What do you want, then?" she responded.

He made no answer, just frowned lightly as though puzzled by the question. Maybe, she thought, he didn't know.

Folding her arms, Lyssa quelled the urge to cry. "I'll make it easy for you. You don't have to feel guilty. You don't have to feel anything. You don't have to do anything for me. In fact, I don't want you to do me any favors. I'm fine. Better than fine." She flung her arm out, wishing she had the use of both arms so that she could be suitably dramatic. "For the first time in my life, I can—" Her teeth clenched. Then she inhaled. "Never mind. It's not like you care."

"I do care," he said with every show of sincerity. "I care about you, Lyssa. I want to know what you're thinking, what you're feeling, who you are down deep in your heart."

"Right. That's why you tore into me in my apartment when I wouldn't put out. That's why you threw me to your mother and Tank like chum to the sharks, using the excuse of keeping my job! Well, I don't need that job anymore. And I don't need you!"

His frown deepened into a scowl. "What about the land?"

"What land?" she asked tightly. She supposed Julia had told him. That was undoubtedly how he had located her—through that aggravating, pointless little strip of land she had built her whole life around for so long.

"Without your salary from Clearview, without money coming in, how are you going to buy your neighbor's land?"

"There's a very simple answer to that." Lyssa stood straighter, gathering the shreds of her dignity around her. "I'm not. Donald Jacobson wouldn't sell to me if I were the last buyer left on this earth."

"What?" Dane reached out and touched her arm, then let his hand fall. "But Julia said it was a cinch you'd get the mortgage." He angled his head slyly. "As long as you had a job, that is."

Glad to have one suspicion confirmed, Lyssa nodded at his mention of Julia. "You can stop dangling employment in front of me like a carrot. I could throw a million bucks at Jacobson and not be any further ahead." She didn't tell him why. Some things were private.

"You're giving up, then?"

She felt like kicking him.

"You're going to just accept all this crap that people have dumped on you in the past few weeks?" He put up a hand to stop the words trembling on her tongue. "And, yes, I'm including myself in that. You deserve better. Much better. That dream of a home and a family and a husband who would do anything for you—you deserve all of it, Lyssa."

But he didn't offer to give it to her. Feeling her eyes fill with tears, Lyssa turned her back to him before she gave herself away. That left her facing the Jacobson house.

She swallowed to clear her throat, then swung her arm to encompass the scene before them. "*This* is my dream home. Still want me to have it? The roof is in desperate shape, and the siding is more like air-conditioning, and the additions tacked on are so awful—" She choked to a halt.

He was staring at the house through the trees. "It has good bones," he finally said.

"No. The Highline has good bones. This place is like one of those skeletons they used to make up out of various animals to create an imaginary monster."

"Like a dragon?"

She stared at him, uncomprehending.

Lyssa shook her head, weary of the argument. No matter what he said, she was not going to wind up with the land and the glow of knowing she had accomplished something truly worthwhile. And he thought she just wanted someplace to live and settle down with her Mr. Perfect. "Look, Dane, I'm sorry you wasted your time coming all this way to find me and let me know about Simon changing his mind. It was very nice of you, particularly since your mother can't be very happy about it."

"She'll come around."

Yeah, right, Lyssa thought. "So, you've done what you came for, and now you can go."

"Just like that?"

"What else do you want?" *What else do you want from me?* She willed him to go before she lost her resolution to be calm and adult. Her hand crept up into her hair.

He reached for it and drew it down gently, lacing his fingers with hers. "I guess I want you to forgive me." He looked unhappy and frighteningly sincere.

"Okay." Anything to get him out of here.

"Just like that, 'Okay'?"

"Sure, why not?" She tugged on her hand, but he wouldn't release her. "It wasn't your fault I got fired. Any more than it was your fault that I had to talk to Tank Turnbull that night, or that I—" She stopped before saying anything about Barb leaving that file out for her to find. He was not the one for her to confide in.

"I suppose it wasn't my fault everybody at your office thinks you're gay? Believed you made unwelcome advances to your boss?"

Lyssa smiled weakly. "Sometimes, Dane, you give yourself too much credit."

"Christ, Lyssa, if only I had forced the issue, called you at work, sent you flowers there, something to show that you did have a man in your life!" His heavy-lidded eyes were intent on hers, and he drew closer. "I can't believe they bought into that nonsense."

"Dane."

"I could have done something about it. Just like, if I had known, I could have kept my mother from sending that letter to Simon . . ."

Which letter? she asked herself, perversely relieved that there appeared to be one small fact about this episode that he didn't know.

"I could have stopped Claudia before she went too far."

"Yes, and if you could see into the future you'd be really scary instead of just a little. *Will* you let go of me!" She tried to twist her hand free.

An unfamiliar expression shadowed his face. "You think I'm scary?"

Lyssa hadn't realized he could be vulnerable. She wondered if it was genuine. "No, not really—Oh, Dane, I don't know!" she exclaimed. "You confuse me all to pieces!"

"Well, then, that makes us even." He lifted their joined hands between them and stepped closer, resting his free hand on her hip.

The little voice that had awakened when Lyssa saw him drive up was now clamoring, *This* is what I want! as he bent his head and softly, gently, affectionately touched his mouth to hers. There was none of the groping and hot eruption of passion that had terrified her the last time he had kissed her. This time warmth flowed over her, through her, lulling her senses.

Dane touched his forehead to hers and let their hands—and their bodies—slide apart. "God, Lyssa, what you do to me."

Ditto, she might have said. She speared her left forefinger into her hair, wound a curl around it, and tugged hard enough to bring tears to her eyes. She pushed Dane away, putting some distance between them; her own knees were too weak to permit her to move.

Dammit nosed her hand, which she had let fall helplessly to her side. He stared fixedly at her. *Of all the times*—she broke off her unspoken plaint and looked into the brown eyes of her rescuer. "Dammit, kill."

When the huge black-and-tan body started to rumble like a mudslide, the ears and tail perked, the massive jaws dripped with drool, and the dark lips drew back to show a set of teeth that would be the envy of a wolf—when her four-footed friend, descended from war-dog ancestors, placed all of his considerable attention on Dane—evidently it was just too much for her would-be lover.

She had never seen the man move so fast. Obviously that kiss hadn't turned *his* legs into spaghetti.

From the safety of his car, Dane assured her that he would be back.

At least this time, she thought, he left the possibility open.

VIVIAN STOOD BESIDE her formerly pearl-white Cadillac, begrimed with dust from the long drive, and stared in disbelief at the small house that had obviously been cobbled together out of recycled materials found at hand. It was not country chic, did not even reach the level of genteel poverty she'd expected. Bemused, she decided it looked like a farmhouse from an era she'd thought long past. The stench of untreated manure offended her nose, and she wondered if the odor would seep into the fabric of her peach linen suit. Round, fat birds ran loose, making strange chattering noises. And . . . were those goats in the grassy area beyond the house?

She felt her heart clench in an unwilling wave of pity for Lyssa Smith. The girl had obviously wanted to make something of herself, had achieved a college education, had been employed as a professional woman. However, Vivian was not fool enough to let her son delve into his portfolio or mortgage his condominium to buy some neighboring farm out of some misguided combination of lust and benevolence.

Then the screen door on the porch banged open, and a black monster charged toward her. Vivian barely registered the two-legged figure behind. "Eep," she squeaked involuntarily.

She had heard that dogs zeroed in on any sign of weakness. *You've faced down more fearsome opponents before, in the boardroom*, she told herself, and she stood her ground.

"No," she said sternly when she thought the beast was close enough. *Could you see the whites of a dog's eyes?* Infusing her voice with all the authority she possessed, she commanded, "Sit."

Wonderfully, it obeyed. That big black body skidded to a halt, the rear end tipped downward, and a long tail slid back and forth, sending up puffs of dust as it moved, like making snow angels in the dirt.

Vivian looked up, beyond the dog, to the porch, where a stunningly beautiful woman—about her own age, she concluded upon registering the striking salt-and-pepper hair—lounged against one of the posts. With a face like that, Vivian decided, one could afford to age gracefully, without the participation of any stylist or surgeon. "I'm Vivian Callicott."

"Are you."

A long silence fell. "Might I have your name, please?" Vivian asked.

"Just call me Helen."

"You're Lyssa Smith's mother?"

"One of them."

"From Boston originally, I take it?"

"Thereabouts."

"I thought so. I picked up on the accent."

"I'm surprised you did. I rather imagined I'd lost it, after all these years in the wilds of Arizona."

"I do not believe that sort of thing ever goes away entirely."

"I think," said Mrs. Smith slowly, "I was wrong about something I told Lyssa. You enjoy flexing your muscles, don't you?"

"Your daughter would know more about muscle-flexing than I. She seems particularly . . . blessed with them." Vivian regretted the cattiness of that almost before it was out.

Helen Smith responded, "I was speaking metaphorically." She paused momentarily, as if uncertain whether to explain the multisyllabic word. "You've come to see Lyssa, I gather. I'll get her for you." She turned to go back into the house. Then she glanced back over her shoulder. "Dammit, come."

Vivian, stunned by the insult, opened her mouth to refuse but saw that the black dog had risen and was trotting toward the porch. The nervy Helen vanished inside, paying no further attention to Vivian. Confused, she ran through the woman's statement a few times. Only belatedly did she understand. These people had named their dog Dammit. Unbelievable.

In a few minutes Lyssa came around the side of the house. She wore ragged jeans, an oversized stained sweatshirt, and boots with stuff clinging to them that Vivian was afraid to identify. Not that Vivian spent a lot of time looking at the clothing. Her eyes were on the blue cast that covered the girl's forearm and extended all the way back to the pushed-up arms of the gray sweatshirt. Dane hadn't warned her about that.

Vivian climbed the stairs but still lacked several inches of her quarry's height. "Miss Smith, I hope this is not an inconvenient time for you. I owe you an explanation and thought it would be best delivered in person."

"What, exactly, do you think needs to be explained?" Lyssa leaned against the porch railing.

Vivian wondered if the girl knew she'd given away her height advantage and a significant amount of intimidation value. "I am not often fooled," she replied. "And when I am presented with what seems like incontrovertible proof, I act upon it. It was an unfortunate happenstance that you bore the brunt of my hasty decision."

"A happenstance? Purely accidental? How dumb do you think I am? You had me fired because you were looking for an excuse. I know all about *both* your letters to Simon, Mrs. Callicott."

Taken aback, Vivian blinked. She had actually forgotten about that first letter. If the girl had only gotten the idea then . . . She raised a hand to stop Lyssa and discuss that issue but was ignored.

"You couldn't be content with having me taken off of your own company's projects, could you? You had to make sure you put the final nail in my coffin."

Vivian's eyes drifted to the cast again. She wished Lyssa hadn't used that phrase. "How very morbid. I never wanted anything bad to happen to you. I have great respect for you—" and she realized with some astonishment that it was true.

"Since when?" the smart-mouthed creature responded. "You were certainly eager enough to have me lick Tank Turnbull's boots."

Vivian let the nickname and the truth underlying that bald statement pass. "Since seeing where you came from." She gestured first toward the primitive little house and then toward the bucolic view of gardens and orchards below. "It must have taken a deal of courage and determination to go to college and become a professional—" Grudgingly she added, "A well-respected professional, as I hear it—after being raised in this."

The girl's dark hazel eyes rounded in what looked like amusement. "Not so much as you might think."

Vivian let silence speak for her.

But instead of glancing around in embarrassment, Lyssa Smith smirked. "Too bad that pretty little speech was wasted on me. I don't need your pity." She rubbed at her cheek, leaving behind a smudge of dirt. "Or guilt, or remorse, or whatever brought you here."

"I have nothing to feel guilty for. Responsibility for the actions of one's employees is not the same as personal culpability."

"Okay."

Vivian glared at Lyssa. "I merely wanted to make amends for the part Claudia Montgomery had played in . . . in interrupting your career."

"Listen, Mrs. Callicott, I don't have the time or the inclination to deal with this power-play right now. Go back to your own plane of existence and tell Dane that Callicott doesn't owe me a thing." She shifted her weight and her attention.

Vivian realized that the girl was about to walk away. "Let me get to the point then."

Lyssa shook her head. "I really wish you wouldn't." She twisted against the railing so that it was at her back, crossed her ankles, and then placed her unbroken arm protectively over the cast. All hint of amusement was gone.

"You'll need some funds to tide you over until you can reestablish yourself. Particularly given that unfortunate circumstance." Vivian stared significantly at the cast, which stood out against the gray of the ancient sweatshirt like a neon bar light.

"Excuse me, Mrs. Callicott, but I think you have the wrong idea."

Vivian gave up on indirectness. "I am not planning to stand by while you drag Dane down to your level, Miss Smith. He does not belong here, in this world of . . . of manure and livestock."

"Dane is old enough to make up his own mind, I'd say. Or are you going to force him into this, too?"

"Just what do you mean by that?" Vivian snapped.

"You could have named someone else to head the company at the time of your husband's death. Or jumped into the role yourself. There was no need to force Dane into it."

"He chose to do it."

"Sometimes expectations are just as coercive as force."

"Miss Smith. I will attempt to put this into the simplest of terms. You are not the right woman for my son. You have no understanding of his needs. For his own sake, I would ask you to give him up. And for yours."

Lyssa straightened. "Are you threatening me, Mrs. Callicott?"

"No, not at all." Not yet, she thought. "I'm offering you a choice. I have gotten rid of more than one woman on my son's behalf."

"I am not Gail." The girl's voice was quiet, but every word fell hard as a rock.

"You know about her?" Vivian would not have expected Dane to let Lyssa see that side of him—a defeated lover, another woman's cast-off.

"She told me everything. And let me point out that all your money didn't break Gail's hold on your son."

"I beg your pardon?"

"You take my meaning, I'm sure. He's still gone on her. Why do you suppose he's never married?"

"I'm not sure what Gail O'Neill told you." Vivian felt a stab of apprehension at the thought of what Dane would have to say if he ever learned what she had done. "She had a mountain of debt. I paid her student loans to take the pressure off, and funded the start-up expenses for her real estate business. It was an arrangement that benefited us both."

"I'm not after your son," the tall young woman declared, tossing her wild mop of auburn curls. "If I were, though, you wouldn't be able to buy me off. You don't have that much money." The cursed amusement was back, a wry curve of her mouth and no more.

Switching tactics, Vivian said, "Nothing so crass as money needs to change hands between us. How about a job? I have something lined up for you in San Diego. A position in your field, doing just what you were hired to do at Clearview, at half again the salary, and with an excellent chance for advancement. What do you say?"

"I say no. That's a load of bullshit, and believe me, a shit-kickin' farmgirl like me recognizes manure when she sees it."

"There's no need to be crude." Vivian's blood started to heat.

"Maybe not, but being nice hasn't gotten me very far with you. Strangely enough, I have job offers coming out of my ears at the moment."

"If you plan on holding out for employment at Callicott to put yourself in Dane's way," Vivian hissed, "you had better not hold your breath."

Closing her eyes as if pained, Lyssa Smith said, "I told you, you have the wrong idea about Dane and me. I'm not pursuing him. And if you're worried about his feelings about me, let me set your mind at ease. He feels guilty, and maybe he wants to get me in the sack, but that's all. There's nothing permanent in his mind."

Although Vivian had been telling herself the same thing, it sounded wrong coming from Lyssa. Maybe it was just the difference in how young people thought.

Lyssa shrugged, the movement of her broad shoulders barely visible beneath the sweatshirt that enveloped her. "Anyway, there's no use throwing money or a job at me. You've wasted your time coming up here this morning, Mrs. Callicott."

"I said I was not threatening you." She let her voice trail off ominously. "But that might change. How would it feel, Miss Smith, to know that you are the one responsible for their ruin? I could slap a lien on this farm so fast it would make your head swim. Go after their customers, destroy their business. Make it impossible for them to ever earn another dollar."

Lyssa Smith laughed.

Vivian itched to slap her.

"I'm sorry, I shouldn't have done that," the girl apologized. "I think you'd better meet the rest of my parents."

ONLY LATER, after Vivian had a chance to reflect on the encounter, did she realize the full extent of what she faced. The Smith family was wealthy. Money enough that they could be considered eccentric rather than weird. Enough that even the Callicott wealth and influence could not touch them.

How had the one bearlike man put it? "Our lifestyle is a conscious rejection of the modern consumer existence." He had a doctorate. They all did, all the parents. And he had written a book. A book Vivian had heard of.

She'd thought that Lyssa Smith had crawled out of poverty and ignorance? What a joke. Vivian's hand clenched on the steering wheel as she dealt with the traffic around her. What a pitiful, tragic joke.

She wondered if Dane knew.

But of course he did. He was a practical man, her son. He made it a point to find out those sorts of things. He simply had not seen fit to let his mother in on his little secret.

Eighteen

"You have got to be kidding me." Lyssa stared at Dane. Her ears rang, and she thought she might be sick on his beautiful, expensive shoes. "No. I could *not* have heard you right." But she knew she had.

He thought she was for sale. Of course, in his frame of reference, everything was for sale, so why not her?

She had even told him the price.

His mother's visit, a few days before, was nothing compared to this. That had been a slap in the face. A momentary sting. This was . . . this was a betrayal of everything she stood for.

"Now, wait." He looked confused, the idiot. "Give me a chance to explain. I wanted you to have your dream."

"My dream." Her jaw was clenched so tightly, she was amazed she could speak at all. "A Frankenstein's monster of a shack and a little dollop of land. That's what you think my dream is?"

Now he looked offended. "All I did was buy the Jacobson place," he said. "I want you to accept it as a gift. No strings attached."

"A gift?" she snapped, reeling from his evident expectation that she could accept.

"No written contract between us," he went on determinedly. "No terms, no loans, no talk of repayment." He caught at her hand, but she stepped back.

Lyssa shook her head, trying to clear it. "How much?"

"How much what?" The lines of puzzlement between his blue eyes deepened.

"How much did you pay for that . . ." She ran out of words and could only gesture in the direction of the house that had almost been hers. "For *that!*"

The amount he named, with evident reluctance, made her go cold.

"In *this* market?" She wrapped her arms around herself and hugged. The situation had gone from bad to impossibly worse. Now that the first shock had worn off, her mind was functioning again. Barely, but enough.

He had the nerve to look unhappy and confused and . . . angry? She wanted to think it was that rather than hurt. "Take it back," she told him. "Retract your offer."

"I can't do that. It's signed, sealed, delivered, accepted. I have a contract, Lyssa. What the hell is wrong with you?"

"Do you have any idea what you've done?" Her voice was no more than a whisper. She willed herself not to break down now. Not in front of him. She still had some pride left.

"I'm getting the idea that what I thought I was doing isn't what you think I've done," he replied self-righteously.

"Oh, that's brilliant." Her arms loosened from around her, and she flung them out. Her good one, anyway. The twinge in the broken one when she moved it too fast made her flinch, and then she had to twist away from Dane's extended hands. "You are Dane Callicott, of Callicott Properties, one of the best-known developers in Phoenix. What do you think people are going to believe when they hear that you've paid practically three times too much for a piece of land out here in the middle of nowhere?"

"It'll make your parents' land worth more," he informed her, glaring down at her.

"It'll make their property taxes go through the roof!" she cried. "The county assessor's office is going to look at this as a sign of things to come. Highest and best use—any of that sound familiar? Everyone for a hundred miles around is going to think you're planning to build some kind of fancy housing development. Or a resort, now that you've gotten into that end of the business."

"Oh." Then he said offhandedly, "It's just one small parcel. Not enough to do anything with. Surely when I give it to you, when the deed changes hands with no exchange of money—"

"I wouldn't accept it if I were starving in the gutter!" she vowed.

"—everyone will see that I have no personal interest . . . What? You can't refuse."

"Watch me. Didn't your daddy ever teach you not to buy anything you don't want to be stuck with? You're stuck with it, Dane, because . . . now, pay close attention here because I'm only saying this once. I. Don't. Want. It." As she said the words, something deep inside felt as if it broke, hard and sharp and fast.

"The hell you don't."

Lyssa thought she would explode from the effort of holding herself together under his searching gaze. "Go away."

"Uh-uh." Dane shook his head. "You're not getting rid of me until we settle this."

"You mean, until I give in and do it your way," she said bitterly. "That's not happening this time. Go away." Her voice rose at the end until she was shrieking at him, and still he stood as immovable as a mountain, dense as Dammit at his worst.

"I mean, until you accept what I'm offering. I said no strings, and I meant it, Lyssa!" He speared a hand through his hair.

"I've gotten rid of you before, and I can do it again," she threatened.

"Don't try to sic that animal on me again," he warned, narrowing his eyes. "I brought him a big, meaty bone."

Lyssa could have screamed. She felt lightheaded and wondered if she was hyperventilating. "Well," she said in a low, nasty voice that sounded so far away, she thought it might just as well have belonged to someone else, "you know all about bribery, don't you?"

She only barely stopped herself from saying, *You and your mother are two of a kind.* No matter what happened, she would not tell him about that.

Lyssa turned on her heel and headed for the house. If he would not leave, she would. She would accept what fate had to give her, just as Helen had accused her of doing. That seemed so long ago, but it wasn't. So much had happened in those intervening weeks. She'd been buffeted left and right by the vagaries of the universe, until she lost her footing and was drowning in the sea of confusion her life had become.

Just let it go, she told herself. There was nothing else to do.

DANE ROCKED BACK ON HIS HEELS, jamming his hands into his pockets. She'd spent years preparing to acquire that property. It was important to her, damn it all, and he had gone to considerable effort and expense to make it happen.

Enough was enough, he told himself. No woman was worth this. He would do as she said. He would go back to Jacobson and the lawyers and break the contract. It wasn't as much of a done deal as he'd implied in the heat of the moment; Lyssa had enough experience in the business to know that as well as he did. He could afford any penalty that was imposed as a result. It would certainly be less depressing than allowing that old bastard to cheat him, as Dane had been willing to do for Lyssa's sake.

He would do as she said in one other thing, too. He would go away and leave her alone. Leave her the hell alone.

The last time he'd come up here with a gesture of kindness, she had tried to force his hand, to push him into baring his soul.

And had come damn close to it. He had told her that he couldn't get her out of his mind. That he wanted her in his life. At the time, he had meant they could explore what they could be to each other someday—someday far in the future.

Dane squirmed inwardly, uncomfortable with the notion that she might have read too much into his words. They had only had one date! And at the end of it, he recalled, he'd offered to set her up with an apartment and clothes and jewelry. A mistake, that. He hadn't really meant it.

And hadn't he done all he could to make up for it? He sneered. If she thought she could punish Dane Callicott by walking away, she had another think coming.

Dane strode up the steps and across the narrow porch. The screen door still quivered from Lyssa's sharp slam. He opened it and walked in. His eyes took a minute to adjust. He stood in a small room with three exits and no Lyssa. That was all he could take in at first. Then he noticed the four strangers who sat around a table in the adjoining kitchen. After an instant's surprise, he corrected himself. Three strangers besides the man he'd met at Anton's, the one who had steered him toward the farmers' market when he was trying to track down Lyssa.

That man rose to his not-inconsiderable size and approached Dane with a smile and an outstretched hand. Welcome was not a part of the expressions worn by the two women close at his heels. The fourth of the family quartet remained at the table, watchful and smoking a pipe.

"Dane Callicott. What a pleasant surprise. I'm Aristotle Smith," said Lyssa's father—the large one—as he reached out and took Dane's unresisting hand in a firm shake. "Just call me Ari. We didn't have a chance to exchange names when last we met."

Dane was impatient to make Lyssa hear what he had to say, but he was not about to brush off her parents. "Ah." It took everything he possessed to focus on them; he couldn't think of anything to say. He retrieved his hand and for lack of anything better to do with it, rubbed it across his solar plexus, which was not feeling any too steady.

"This is Paris." Ari indicated a plump, matronly woman with ruler-straight hair that once had evidently been blond but had faded over the years to the almost colorless translucency of fishing line. "And Helen."

If not for the grim set of this woman's jaw, Dane would have said she was the most beautiful—certainly the most striking—he had ever met in person, with centerfold proportions, a face that was classically perfect, and eye-catching iron gray-and-black-streaked hair.

Ari went on, "The one with the pipe"—who raised it in a salute as soon as all eyes turned to him—"is Cal."

"Nice to meet you all," Dane said warily. He did not offer his hand to either of the women. He might pull back no more than a stub if he did.

He glanced around the living room, prepared to utter some pleasantry about their home before he demanded to know where the hell Lyssa had run off to this time. The furniture was obviously handmade, primitive but sturdy. The couch was little more than a plank on legs, supporting a thick cushion. The chairs looked marginally more comfortable. Although the furnishings seemed spartan, the artwork didn't.

The walls were covered with architectural drawings, professionally framed and matted. Dane walked close enough to read the draftsman's label. It bore only one word: Callicrates. Dane recognized the name—how could he not? It belonged to an internationally famed architectural design firm that was said to be today's answer to Frank Lloyd Wright. Callicrates. Cal. Oh, hell.

He turned toward the kitchen. "These are yours?"

"Yes," Ari replied on Cal's behalf.

Dane had underestimated Lyssa's family background. That was the first realization. The second was a wild leap. Ignoring Lyssa's more voluble father, Dane addressed his next question to the man in the kitchen. "I suppose you're the one who told Gaspar Adams about the Highline?"

Cal—Callicrates, Dane corrected himself—made a production of tapping out his pipe on a plate beside his elbow. "Guilty." Cal's voice sounded rusty. He nodded at the mug in front of him. "Sore throat. One of Lyssa's brews, fix me right up." His voice faded to a whisper on the last few words. He smiled apologetically and lifted the mug to take a sip of whenever herbs steamed within.

Dane also steamed. He would have liked to demand to know why Cal had taken an interest in the Highline—as a favor to Lyssa, or because in his professional judgment it had merit? But with the man unable to talk . . . Dane forced himself back to his original purpose in coming here.

Lyssa's mothers arrayed protectively in front of an archway into a narrow hall gave him a good idea of his target. Still, he could hardly just push past the two women, no matter how strongly the urge to do so rode him. "Lyssa and I have had a small misunderstanding." He could see no softening of their stance as he moved forward, keeping his eyes on theirs and wearing an easy, practiced, reassuring grin that seldom failed with older females.

Paris's eyes were a pale ice-blue. Dane could see, despite the relative dimness of the light, that Helen had Lyssa's changeable hazel eyes. He decided from the fierce glint in them that Helen was the stronger willed of the duo.

His smile wavered briefly when he barked his shin on a piece of very hard and solid furniture that had escaped his notice earlier. As he stifled a curse, his gaze dropped to the low table beside the couch that had so painfully gotten in his way.

It was then that he saw the book. The room held no bookshelves, no other books or even knickknacks. Just this one. *Soul-Circles*, by Aristotle Smith. He didn't have to try to read the title in its sweeping curlicues of stylized text from this distance, because he recognized the jacket. He turned accusingly to his large, bluff, genial host in flannel shirt and overalls. "You're Aristotle Smith."

"Yes, I am. You're familiar with my little book, then?"

"I've read it. Who hasn't?" Dane felt sick. He'd been feeling sorry for Lyssa, imagining himself as the only one who could help make her dreams come true. Inwardly he wondered if she had gotten a good laugh out of that: her family could have bought and sold him three times over, and the adjoining property along with him. He didn't know how much money a cult classic like *Soul-Circles* produced, but considering how many millions of copies it must have sold in the thirty years since it had erupted into the American consciousness—

Dane gritted his teeth. "Why the hell didn't you just buy Lyssa that blasted land?"

Paris snapped, "Mind your language!" even as Ari shook his head sadly and lifted his hands in an apologetic shrug. "Jacobson hates us," he explained, as if this said it all.

"That's it?" Dane said in disbelief.

"It's enough," Helen growled. She advanced on him as though his show of frustration was enough to ignite her own temper. "You got what you came for. You've poked and pried about the family and learned all of our dirty little secrets." Her voice was richly modulated and heavily ironic. "Now—"

Dane ignored the last part of her statement. "Not hardly," he informed her stiffly. "I came for Lyssa, and I'm not leaving without her. Lyssa!" he shouted, this time shoving past her mothers. Manners be damned. "Lyssa!"

She did open the door to him. When he saw her standing within, looking apprehensive, his mood shifted. She seemed more vulnerable than he'd ever seen her before. Anything he uttered right now was likely to rebound on him. Worse, he was pretty sure it would be like kicking a puppy. He said only, "There you are," as casually as if picking her up for a date.

The words had popped out unplanned, but as an idea it had merit, he decided. He grabbed her hand. "Come on."

Dane started back toward the living room, preparing himself to run the gantlet of her incredible family. She didn't follow him but dug in her heels. He stopped rather than break her in half or suffer the humiliation of being outwrestled by a woman, and one with a broken arm at that.

"What are you really doing here? Why can't you just leave me be?"

Dane matched her honest confusion with his own. "I don't know." But he was beginning, finally, to suspect. "I need to tell you—" He broke off, uncertain what to say now that she was listening. That was what he had wanted, wasn't it? "I just want to talk."

Lyssa sighed. "I—" She glanced at him and then surprised him by acquiescing, no matter how grudging her tone. "Okay. I know how important it is to have someone to talk to."

Dane felt a pressure in his midsection. It wasn't the twinge of muscle or the churning of an acid stomach, but a heavy, almost warm, weighty significance. "I would be that someone for you, Lyssa." He paused, aware that her parents were too near for him to say anything more.

"You said you had something to tell me. So. Talk," she prompted.

"Not here." Dane struggled to put his thoughts together. "I saw in Prescott they're having a craft fair. Let's go walk around there."

"What's wrong with here?"

Her wariness stabbed at him, but he knew he deserved it. "I don't need your parents listening in." Mustering a faint smile, he confided,

"Your mother is—hell, they all are—a little intimidating."

Lyssa's face brightened a little. "Let me change my clothes."

While waiting for her, Dane returned to the frigid silence in the living room. "Helen and Paris. That's interesting," he said, deciding to start with the difficult pair first. Ari and Cal seemed to like him well enough.

"It's an allusion," Helen snapped.

"More of a literary conceit," Ari put in. His comment earned him a sidelong look from her that bore an unspoken promise of more to come later.

Politely Dane offered, "Helen's name seems particularly apt."

She swelled with outrage. "This is not the face that launched a thousand ships!"

"She's touchy about being beautiful," Cal offered hoarsely from his place in the kitchen. "Hard to have your brain taken seriously when it's behind such a face." His voice broke a few times, but nothing detracted from the perfect seriousness with which he had his say.

Helen fell silent.

Clearing his throat, Ari said, "Paris changed her name from Kristen Amundsen. And it fit better with the rest of us."

"The rest of you had Greek names, then?" Dane asked, willing to keep this casual.

Cal chuckled. "You think I was born Callic—" A spate of coughing cut off the rest of his name.

Ari smoothly picked up the thread of conversation. "Cal was born Calvin Bancroft the Third. He adopted 'Callicrates' as his legal name, after one of the more famous Greek architects."

"Mostly I hated 'Calvin,'" the man observed before taking another sip from his mug. "And being a number."

Dane knew there had to be more to the story than that. "What brought you all to *this*?" He took in the surroundings with one brief, comprehensive glance.

With a noise that might have been intended as discouragement or disgust, Helen walked to the couch and instead of sitting on it as a normal person would do, lay down on her side, propped herself up on an elbow, and stared with resignation at Ari. "You may as well tell him the whole story. He's obviously not going to give up until you do."

"Good, good," Ari said, beaming at Dane. "He'll understand our Lyssa much better for it."

"Let that be on *your* head." Helen spoke the words like a curse.

Ari began by casting her a fond look. "Helen was my graduate student, long ago."

"That really was where everything started," Paris interrupted. "Ari took her seriously. It was hard for a woman in those days, of course, and when he supported her dissertation on the equating of women outside the household with monsters and tragedy, she would have done anything for him."

"Within reason," Helen added sourly.

"Some might say—" but Paris subsided at a look from her partner.

"In any case," Ari went on, "my book proved no little success. Financially, that is. But the situation at the university was . . ." He paused, visibly casting about for the right words. "Becoming untenable," he finished.

"People had a hard time accepting our sexual choices," Helen put in. "Apparently, some still do." She stared at Dane.

He remembered his conversation with Simon and winced. "I don't have a problem with it," he assured her.

Ari hushed Helen when she would have responded. "Anyway, we decided to look for a place where we could create a homestead with fewer of the distractions of modern life. Re-create the time of the ancient Greek philosophers, as it were. Their intellectual prowess—"

This time Cal was the one to interrupt. "Ari. Keep to the point."

"Right. Back to the story," Ari said easily. "We came to take a look at Arcosanti, up the road. The place spoke to us, Spring Valley generally, I mean, and we found this spot, with its own spring and the creek below and enough isolation to have quiet when we wanted and a market for our produce near enough. Once we were settled, we decided that a child was the next step."

"*You* wanted a child." Paris went over to Helen and took her hand.

Ari shrugged. "It was time. What do you think about children, Dane?"

No answer came to mind. "So you had Lyssa," Dane prompted. He didn't care to pry into the mechanics, but he guessed from Ari's build and something in the way the big man carried himself that Lyssa bore his genes. It had been Ari and Helen, he concluded, who had gone through the physical act. He couldn't help but wonder how that affected the obviously complex relationships among the four of them.

"So we had Lyssa," Helen replied, without giving Ari a chance to do anything but open his mouth. "And we take care of her. She doesn't need a man in her life. Not for sex or anything else."

Ari made a sound of protest.

Quickly Paris added, "Her name comes from Lysistrata. So you see —" She spread her hands wide.

It took Dane a few moments to make the connection. "Do you think that somehow foreordains her to . . . to . . ." *To withhold sex* was what he wished he could say. But it was too weird to be talking to her parents that way.

Certain that Helen was prepared to detest him on principle, no matter what he said, he decided to go on the offensive. "What the hell is wrong with her having a man in her life? Lyssa ought to have the opportunity to explore her emotional and passionate sides, not just the intellectual."

Helen's face paled, and Ari chuckled. "Got you there," he said.

But Dane wasn't finished. "She deserves to have people around her who see her as an adult, not a child."

"Your way will damage her," Helen bit out.

"You don't think your way has inflicted scars?" Dane could have throttled Lyssa's mothers. Both of them. And maybe her fathers, too, for although they were staying out of this argument, they'd allowed Lyssa to be stifled for her entire life. "You're so afraid that people will only respond to the surface of her that you've taught her to wall herself off. She's a butterfly and you have her convinced she's a caterpillar! Good God, can't you see that? She's so beautiful it makes my chest hurt."

Helen told him, "Looks are not everything. We never wanted Lyssa to rely on outward appearance."

Dane felt his anger ebb. He let it go. With a rueful half smile he said softly, "I wasn't talking about her face, or her body, either, if it comes to that."

Helen sneered. "We want Lyssa to choose a nice woman to build a relationship with. Women aren't as fixated on physical appeal."

Dane didn't know where to start refuting that sexist comment. Ari and Cal looked as unhappy to be lumped in with the rest of their gender as he was. He settled for asking, "Are you aware that Lyssa isn't gay?"

"She's too young to know what she is yet. She hasn't met her soulmate."

"What will you do if that soulmate turns out to be a man?"

"She won't. Lyssa has simply lived in the dominant culture for too long. As soon as she progresses past this brief experimental phase—"

Ari interrupted her. "Now, Helen, we've talked about this. It may not be all that brief."

"Regardless," she snapped, "Once Lyssa discovers her true self, she'll be capable of assessing where everyone else in the world fits into her soul-circles."

With strained patience Dane said, "Lyssa is attracted to me. I am attracted to her. We are a man and a woman who have the right to experience a normal man-woman relationship that isn't screwed up by other people's expectations."

"For crying out loud." Lyssa's voice came from behind him.

He spun around to see her. She had dressed up—for him, he realized with pleasure—in a pair of cobalt slacks and a zinc-white turtleneck, topped by a black leather jacket.

She went on, "I leave you alone for five minutes, and you start raking him over the coals." But she looked more exasperated than angry as she chided her parents.

She kissed her fathers on the cheek and hugged her mothers, promising that she would be back in a few hours. Dane wondered how much she'd heard. And whose side of the argument she was on. Despite his claims to both Simon and Lyssa's parents, did he really know her well enough to be certain of her sexual orientation?

Then he remembered her response to his kisses. Oh, yes.

Nineteen

SITTING BESIDE DANE in the car, Lyssa missed the feel of the wind in her hair. Still, it wouldn't have been practical to put the top down, she told the thrill-seeking part of herself, given that her parents' driveway was dusty and the day was blustery.

She wasn't quite sure why she had agreed to go to Prescott with him. She had been safe in her room with both a door and her anger between them. What had changed both her mood and her mind?

Lyssa glanced at him. His eyes were steady on the road. His left hand wrapped competently around the steering wheel while the right one cradled the shift knob. The long muscles of his thighs bunched and relaxed as he downshifted and upshifted with each turn, every dip and rise of the narrow road. He was calm now.

But that wasn't what had changed her mind. No, that was the image of his hurt face when she lashed out at him. She had the power to make Dane *feel*.

She glanced at him again. Now that he had her here, in private, he evidently didn't feel like talking. Of course, she wasn't saying anything, either.

How do you tell a man that you want to sleep with him?

Lyssa was not entirely sure when that had come about, exactly. Maybe the night in her apartment, when fear and pride had prevented her from giving in. Every encounter with him since, every last kiss and touch, inflamed a yearning she'd never felt before.

But even her recently awakened brushes with desire hadn't been enough to overcome caution and good sense. Not until today, when she had decided to take advantage of the situation before he changed his mind.

She could be misreading his signals, of course, since she had no experience with this sort of thing. But they seemed pretty definite. Even Gail O'Neill had recognized what was going on. *"He'll take you as a lover but not a wife,"* Gail had said.

That was all right. Lyssa didn't want to be Dane Callicott's wife. He needed someone far more socially adept than she could ever be.

But for someone to help her explore her passion and open herself up to her sensual side, he was perfect. And given Dane's hot kisses and even his attempts to fix things for her, to romance her, she didn't think she was misreading anything. He was interested.

So was she. And that had been perhaps the greatest surprise.

It hadn't been difficult for her to remain a virgin. She had sailed through her days oblivious to any man's offer to change her condition—if anyone before Dane had thought to make such an offer. She'd felt no urge to become physically intimate.

Lyssa did want, eventually, to find a man who completed her innermost soul-circle. She did want to build—with him—a normal life, complete with children and a warm, loving home. But Dane had convinced her of one thing. She did not need to save herself for her mythical man.

Nobody expected that these days. How had Dane put it: any prospective husband would want to try her on for size?

She had every right to try on one or two men who appealed to her. Just because Dane was the first who did, didn't mean he would be the last.

That was a weak justification, she knew, but for once she gloried in her weakness. Reason, common sense, and pride were cold comfort in an empty, lonely bed. Reason was no match for rationalization, sensibility topped common sense, and as for pride . . . Lyssa had no more use for it. Dane now knew that she had no need of his money.

All she needed was an introduction to sex.

The thought made her shiver.

"Cold?" he asked.

"No, I'm all right." She might not know what was keeping Dane mute, but darned if she had to wait for him to start the conversation. "The craft fair is a good idea. You might enjoy seeing what some of the local and regional artisans do. It's usually pretty well attended. I might pick up some ideas for my herb business, too."

He looked at her out of eyes as sharp and color-drenched as a pair of new jeans. "Herb business?"

"That's right."

"Is this something else your parents are pressing on you?"

"No!" But his voice held concern, not criticism, she realized belatedly, and she explained, "It's not a new venture. I put myself through college with it. Partly. Paris agreed to put in some herbs and I made up blends for them to sell along with their own produce."

"You worked your way through school."

"That's right. I didn't know my parents had money," she told him, feeling as if some explanation was called for. "Not until a few days ago. And if you think I'm stupid for never thinking about it, you're right. My only excuse is that . . . well, you've seen what the farm looks like. I always figured we were living on the edge by necessity."

Dane did it for her. "Instead, it was a choice. But your parents' choice, not yours. I don't think you're stupid, Lyssa. Remember, I was taken in, too."

"Yes, but you figured it out on your own."

There was a long pause. Then he asked, "Are you thinking about operating out of your parents' house?"

"Not exactly. This situation is just temporary." She hoped he was interested in the subject of where she might be living in a month or two. "I thought about setting up a website."

He shot her an unreadable look again. "You have a guaranteed source for the herbs?"

"Paris will grow them for me. And some of the rare stuff I can buy."

"But you're not planning to stay at the farm?"

"No electricity," she said.

"Excuse me?"

"My parents wanted to avoid the dictates of centralized utility systems. Electricity belongs to 'the man.'" She managed to get the words out before giving in to the laughter that bubbled up when she thought about their fixation on "the man."

Dane joined her, so that they were both roaring with it. Lyssa subsided first. Her ribs ached, and she wiped away moisture that had trickled onto her cheeks without her noticing. "Oh," she sighed. "That sounds really foolish, doesn't it?"

"Whatever floats their boat."

"Do you think there's a chance this business will work?"

He glanced over. "You haven't told me much about it. But you have a good idea, the will and the experience to carry through, and the organizational skills to take care of nitpicky details. I don't see why it wouldn't."

While she was still smiling from the praise, he continued, "I'll assume your parents will stand behind you with financial support until you're ready to fly on your own. It's obvious that they care about you very much. But if you have concerns, I'll help you write up a business plan, and we can run it past Alex. He has a better eye for that sort of conceptualizing than I do."

"Dane—" But she stopped herself. Protesting every time he wanted to do something nice seemed like a stupid way of seducing him.

"Does this business have a name?" he asked.

She accepted the change of subject with relief. "Actually," she offered with a sidelong glance at his profile, which to her eyes was badly in need of relaxing again, "I was thinking of 'Wisewoman Herbs.'" That had been one of Paris's suggestions.

"Wisewoman—" He looked suitably horrified. Turning his head to stare at her, he said, "You might as well call it 'Eye of Newt' and be done. For God's sake, Lyssa, tell me you're kidding."

"I'm kidding." She smirked. "Do you like 'Plants by Proserpina' better?" That one came from Ari.

"Lyssa!"

"Would you believe 'Pungent Thoughts'? Or 'The HerbaList'? Though I bet that one's already taken."

"In other words, you don't have a name."

"Nope."

"Thank God." Dane laughed.

As the tension in the car eased, Lyssa grinned and patted the hand that was resting on the gearshift. Humor. Dane liked humor. She would remember that.

They caught a quick breakfast at a pastry shop just off the courthouse square and then strolled through the rows of booths. The weather might have been more cooperative for the vendors, but Lyssa didn't mind. The chilly breeze meant that Dane kept his fingers wrapped around hers as they walked, and he would frequently put his large body between her and the wind when they stopped to take a look at something in particular.

They were passing a wall of black-and-white photographs when Lyssa spotted a lighthouse standing adamantly against a storm-driven surf. She stopped short, struck by what it said to her. Dane was looking at her, not the artwork, so she pointed at the print, unable to describe what she saw.

"You like that?"

She couldn't tell if he agreed or was humoring her. "Yes, though I can't explain why," she admitted.

"I used to do good stuff like that."

"Used to? Not anymore?"

His laugh was polite, not genuine. "Hardly. And I was a sculptor. I was never much for the two-dimensional stuff."

Lyssa thought about the Highline, the way every surface there had shape and depth and texture. She turned their hands, which were laced together. With her thumb she traced a couple of the thin cuts, pink healing streaks on his calloused skin. "Is that what are these from?"

"I've taken up carving again," he admitted. "But it's not the same. I can't do what I used to. I was an art major. A long time ago."

She shrugged. "I'm sure you've changed since college. Shouldn't you expect that your art would, too?"

Shaking his head and compressing his lips, he looked as if he would refuse to talk about this. Then he said, "Yeah, well, I figured I'd lose some of my dexterity. What bothers me is the kinds of subjects that come to me. They're . . . weird."

"Weird?" Lyssa was unable to visualize Dane Callicott doing anything truly weird. "What are we talking about here? UFOs and crop circles, or ghosties and ghoulies and things that go bump in the night?"

The charming crease in his cheek reappeared as the shadow in his eyes was replaced by a spark of humor. "Halloween must be a big deal for you."

"Generally speaking, this is so." With her tongue metaphorically wedged in her cheek she went on, "I have a deep appreciation for several of the pagan holidays: Halloween, Easter, Christmas, and, of course, Fourth of July. So what do you mean by weird?"

"Maybe that's not the right word. Mythical might be a better description. Dragons and gargoyles and fairies and the like."

"Really?" She was charmed by the notion of Dane with a fanciful side.

"You don't need to sound so pleased." He dropped her hand but hugged her close against his side, careful of her outer arm. "They look ridiculous. Silly. They're not serious art."

Lyssa studied the small part of his face that was visible to her as he looked away. "Is 'serious' art the only kind worth doing?"

"Think about your own reaction, Lyssa. That lighthouse reached out and grabbed you, made you stop, made you feel. Made you want to share the experience with me. Lopsided ugly dragons and leering gremlins just don't do the same thing."

"Okay," she said slowly, considering the leer. "But if dragons and gremlins are on your mind, why not go with them?"

"Come on, Lyssa. Who would take me seriously with subjects like that? What would you think of a man who makes a reputation for himself out of imaginary beings?"

"You mean like Spenser?"

"Spenser?" he repeated, as if he had never heard the name.

"*The Faerie Queene.* Then there's *Midsummer Night's Dream,* from the Bard. Both are classics of English literature."

Dane's smile was thin. "Literature is not sculpture."

"I'll admit that, but I don't know much about sculpture." Not that he seemed to know much about literature. Did that make them even? "Those were the first examples that came to mind."

"And we're not living in the sixteenth century anymore."

"That's true. But Dane, if you're inspired to create dragons and fairy queens—"

"I don't think that's the politically correct term these days."

"—then that's what you should do," she went on, ignoring his interruption. "And never mind what anyone else has to say about it. If these mythical creatures are well done, people will appreciate them."

"And if not?"

"Well, then, you'll still have the satisfaction of knowing you were true to yourself, won't you." She left it at that, as a statement rather than a question, knowing he would think about it even if he didn't want to. She felt as if one more word would pitch her off a cliff into dark, treacherous, unknown territory. She wanted to build a physical connection with Dane, not an emotional one.

And it seemed as if he agreed. Without saying anything more on the subject, he turned her and started walking again. Through the remainder of the booths, he kept his touch on her: his arm on her shoulders or across her waist, his hand at the small of her back or covering her hand, his thigh or hip sometimes bumping hers. Lyssa felt every one like a static shock.

She supposed that was part of the reason she wasn't expecting what came next. Dane drew her off the sidewalk and over to one of the benches near the old-fashioned gazebo. "You were worried that taxes might go up if people got the impression that Callicott Properties was developing out here."

Her heart felt like a rock in her chest. "Not *might.* They will. It's a guarantee, Dane. You know how it works." Not that it was likely to affect her parents. They could afford it.

"We don't have to tell the truth about why I bought the land. A well-placed rumor or two might be useful."

She didn't trust the glint in his eye. "Like what?"

"We could convince everyone that Jacobson cheated a dumb city-slicker."

"Oh, please." Lyssa sat back on the bench and felt the slats dig into her spine. When Dane placed his arm across her shoulder, she relaxed. "No one would believe that. You're Dane Callicott. The golden boy of Phoenix development."

"Even Midas made some mistakes," he informed her loftily.

"Maybe. It still won't work."

"All right. How about suggesting that there's a gold mine on the property, and I've taken it in my head to dig it out?"

"In the first place, there's no gold in these limestone hills, and in the second place, you didn't buy the mineral rights. Did you?"

"Sadly, no." He cocked his head to one side and watched her pensively. "How about buried Spanish treasure?"

She chuckled. "You think the conquistadors hauled Aztec gold all the way up to Prescott? That's only a myth. Try again."

"A myth. But powerful for all of that." He drummed the fingers of his left hand on the back of the bench, beside Lyssa's ear. "That's what I need for the Spirit Ranch."

"What is?"

"Well," he confided, "I'm having trouble getting a handle on that project. Adams is pushing me for ideas, and I'm drawing a blank. I think, Lyssa, that you have become my muse."

"Your what?" Maybe she'd fallen asleep and his strange comment was in a dream. She closed her eyes and opened them again. Nope, Dane was still there at her side, the bench was still beneath them, the fading green lawn, studded with tall, mature, November-bare trees, still spread out before them.

"You gave me the essential theme for the Highline. I need the same thing for the Spirit Ranch. The photos Gail sent just don't have the right impact. Maybe you would drive down to Tucson with me and take a look at the property. Just the two of us." He drew a finger along Lyssa's arm, then brought his face a hair's-breadth closer.

She could feel his warmth against her skin. It made her shiver. He was putting the moves on her, she realized. He intended to kiss her. She turned her mouth to his with an encouraging hum of pleasure, relieved beyond measure that she wouldn't have to make the first move.

DANE EYED LYSSA SURREPTITIOUSLY as he drove with her beside him, jostling over the rough country road toward Elysian Fields. She had been quiet ever since—well, ever since he had drawn back from that deliciously soft and tender kiss.

Had he offended her by bringing up the Spirit Ranch? He'd intended the offer of involving her with the restoration plans as an olive branch, a way of letting her know that his trust in her skills and expertise hadn't lessened.

His lips curled in a self-deprecating smile. The Spirit Ranch project was little more than an excuse to get Lyssa to go away with him. He wanted her, wanted her in his arms, in his bed, in his life. For as long as he could have her. But he was determined that her first time would be romantic, well planned, in a quiet bed-and-breakfast after some private time together. She deserved no less.

It had nearly killed him to draw back in Prescott and take her home rather than haul her off to the nearest hotel room and bury himself in her, wrap himself in her scent and draw her into every cell of his being, but he knew it was necessary. Lyssa had told him she needed more than the frenzied promise of passion. It seemed he did, too.

"Who's running Callicott while you're here with me?" she asked idly, as if she had just realized that it was a weekday and he might be expected to be in the office.

Dane was relieved at her reasonable tone, and on a safer subject than the image of Lyssa, naked and glowing under his hands. "My mother, and Alex."

Lyssa looked startled. "Your mother?"

Grinning, Dane said, "She's taking to the business like a born executive. She handles the money end—and the social connections—better than I ever could."

"I have no doubt." Lyssa chewed on her lower lip. "But I got the impression that you were . . . indispensable to the company."

"My mother decided some things were more important than making sure the company operated as it always has."

"Oh?" Lyssa's eyebrows lifted in mock doubt. "Like what?"

"I had one of my attacks in front of her. She thinks it's from the stress." Studying Lyssa's expression as he said this, he was satisfied by the quick change from mockery to concern.

"And is it?"

"It's nothing to worry about. Really." He took his hand off the gearshift and held it up to stop whatever she was about to say. "That's not just a guess. I went to see a doctor when I got back from New York." After he found Lyssa. "She made the same diagnosis as the last time I had these symptoms. Muscle spasms caused by poor posture and too much office work, compounded by stress. She prescribed a vacation."

Dane laughed, recalling his succinct response to that suggestion. "I don't think I could take the pressure of any more time off—not after everything that went wrong while I was out of town. But the fact that Callicott Properties survived my absence did prove to my mother that I am not indispensable."

He gazed at her, wishing he could touch her, bury his face in her hair and breathe in the apple-pie scent of her. "And then there's you. I didn't like being so far away from you."

Her hazel eyes went wide. "I don't know what to say when you flirt with me like that," she said haltingly.

"Do you think you could get accustomed to it? I have a lot of powerful feelings inside me for you, Lyssa."

She didn't answer. He wasn't sure whether he was more disappointed or relieved. Something was stirring in his mind. He felt like a Rube Goldberg device, with one out-of-kilter piece after another slipping into place, making connections and setting other things in motion, everything shifting and changing with no clear purpose or end in sight.

"I was angry with you," she told him.

He simply looked at her, not sure which of his many mistakes she was referring to.

"For buying the Jacobson land. That was for me to do. Not you."

"It was for your parents to do," he corrected gently. "But it seems I was the only one who could make it happen. Would you really rather I hadn't?"

"No." She sighed. "No. I wouldn't take back anything that's been done."

"I would." He thought of all that had happened to Lyssa, all that he had been unable to protect her from.

"You can't change it, can't go back and make it not happen," she told him softly. "You have to go on, Dane, and forgive yourself. I have."

He threw her a disbelieving look, but she appeared perfectly serious. "That only makes it harder," he said. "These past few weeks—"

Only weeks, he thought, rubbing a hand over his forehead. Had it only been that long since the reception at the Highline? "My life was turning into a disaster. I put everything I had into the Highline, and nobody understood. Then you came along—"

"And insulted you by calling it beautiful?"

He had to smile. "Something like that. I didn't think, at first, that you understood. Did you know Adams was going to seek me out and offer to finance another project like the Highline?"

"I knew Cal had talked to him about it. I didn't know he would do it right there at the reception, through intermediaries, without any lead-in or preparation. That wasn't fair to you, Dane. But he's used to getting his own way—" She broke off.

"Well, then, that's two of us," he said with easy self-mockery. "It should be interesting to work with him."

She drew a deep breath. "I take it, from what you said earlier, that you're going forward on the Spirit Ranch project?"

"That depends." Dane waited for her to ask *On what?* so he could say *On you.*

But she fell silent again, and all too soon he pulled into the driveway at the farm. He had to slow down to a crawl as he approached the house. Several of the noisy speckled birds erupted from the shrubbery near the porch. He hoped they had sense enough to get out of the way.

"What are those things?" he asked, unwilling to let this time together come to an end. He turned off the engine and unbuckled his seat belt.

She didn't seem to be in any particular hurry to get out, but sat there and looked at him. At his mouth. Just that long, wistful stare was enough to half arouse him.

"Guinea hens," she finally said, shaking her head as if to clear it. "They do a good job of keeping down the insect population."

Dane opened his car door. "And announcing strangers," he said as the flock went into frantic carioles at his movement.

"That, too."

Dane decided to ask for a tour of the property—Elysian Fields, to start with, and then the land he had just bought. Anything to keep from having to go.

"Would you be interested in seeing the stillroom?" she asked. A bit of extra color brightened her cheeks. "It's nothing much. Just a small cave, with a seasonal seep running through it. That was the original water supply for the farm."

"I'd like that." As they walked along, Dane slipped his hand around hers, noting the absence of a ring. Lyssa seldom wore jewelry of any kind. She didn't really need adornment, he thought. But would she wear something if he bought it for her, or would that violate too many feminist principles?

They took a well-beaten path past a small orchard. Some of the trees had apples hanging heavily enough to bend the lower branches nearly to the ground. "Cherry, apricot, pear, peach," Lyssa said, pointing to various trees in turn. "Nut trees are in the lower orchard." Halfway up the hillside, she turned and indicated the farm spread out below them. "That glassed-in greenhouse has some miniature grapefruit and orange and kumquat trees, plus some of my herbs that are more sensitive to frost. The greenhouses are Cal's design."

"Of course." He wouldn't have expected anything else. When they turned back to the hillside and he glanced up, he realized that he owned a part of what he saw. Or would, as soon as the final paperwork went through. He didn't know quite what he thought of that.

He hadn't owned anything other than investment property before. Even his condo had been purchased with an eye toward its escalating resale value. Of course, that was before the market crash. Now he'd be stuck with it for a while, unless he wanted to take a loss. Would she like his condo? Somehow he thought not.

"The cave's temperature and humidity buffering are perfect for storing produce," Lyssa said. The breeze carried her voice away, and he had to lean close to hear her. "My parents can harvest crops a few days to several weeks before transporting them to market. It's good for herbs, too."

She halted in front of a wide hole in the rock of the hill, shored up with heavy supports, like a mine. A pair of propane lanterns hung beside the opening. She lit them both, then handed him one and entered the darkness.

He waited a beat, observing the sway of her hips, and then plunged in behind her. After a quick look around the uneven stone walls he admitted, "This is really something." The stillroom was larger than he'd expected. Marks in the dust on the cement floor showed where crates and boxes of produce had been stacked several deep.

Lyssa's work area was surrounded with hanging bunches of dried plants. Her bench had a thick top that looked like marble. A knife block stood at one corner, and a wide shelf about eye-height held mortars and pestles of various sizes; a squared-off wooden contraption with a screw rested on the right-hand edge of the bench. "This is incredible," he breathed.

"You think so?"

Except for the lanterns, it was like stepping back into ancient days. "It's magic."

She ducked her head as though embarrassed by his choice of words. "I don't know. I wonder, sometimes, what the health inspectors would have to say about it. I'm not sure what the regulations are going to be, if I expand into packaged foods like herb blends and teas." She hung her lantern upon an iron ring suspended from the ceiling and motioned for him to hang his on a matching one. The paired circular beams cancelled out each other's shadows and made a pool of light over the center of the workbench.

Dane thought about that. "I could have someone from my legal department make inquiries, if you're concerned."

"Really? You would do that?"

I would do anything for you, he felt like saying, but he was pretty sure that would be a tactical error.

"Dane, I don't want to be a bother—"

He placed a finger on her lips and marveled at the feeling that washed over him at the sensation of their softness moving against his skin. He replaced his finger with his mouth, in a quick kiss. Best to get out of the close quarters before he did something irretrievably stupid. "So, where are you taking me next?"

Twenty

ARI'S VOICE came from the cave's entrance. "Why don't you show Dane the greenhouse, Lyssa? It's nice and warm and out of the wind. Lots of handy benches."

"Good thinking," she called, missing the feel of Dane's mouth on hers but hoping Ari hadn't seen the kiss.

As they walked down to the greenhouse, Dane laced his fingers through hers. She wasn't sure exactly how to seduce him, but she rather thought she should be more subtle than setting him down on a bench, taking off her clothes, and yelling, *"Take me, I'm yours!"*

The door had barely swung closed behind them when he stopped and pulled her to a halt, too. His gaze was fixed on the large purplish orchid spray that hung prominently over the nearest bench. "That's my flower," he breathed.

"*You* picked it out?"

"Well, yeah. What else would I have done?"

"Call a florist?" *Or send Claudia for it.*

"No!" He seemed appalled by the idea.

"And the other flowers? The gardenias?"

"Gardenias?" he asked blankly.

"White ones, like roses, with waxy petals," she explained. "They smell delicious."

"Like vanilla?"

"Yep. Those are the ones."

"I saw them, and thought of you. Beautiful. Mysterious. Intriguing."

The compliments, the flirtation, the mood were exactly what Lyssa thought she wanted. But somehow they were unsatisfying. "The chocolate roses, too?"

"There's a chocolatier around the corner from the office."

"And the candles?"

Dane hesitated. "Those I sent Claudia for." Lyssa must have involuntarily made some sound, because Dane rushed on. "I'm sorry! I didn't know, then, what she was doing. But I got busy, and I . . ." Dane shook his head. "I'm just digging my hole deeper, aren't I?"

"Maybe." But he wasn't. Knowing how much of his own time and attention Dane had lavished on his guilt gifts made her feel warm all over.

She smiled and touched his cheek. As he leaned into her palm, the sandpapery roughness of his five o'clock shadow made her blood sizzle.

"I'm sorry," he repeated. Gently he opened his arms and drew her flush against him. He nuzzled her hair.

Her heart leaped at the sweetness of the gesture.

"I keep saying that, I know. But I need you to understand that I mean it. I didn't expect Claudia to do anything to you."

"It wasn't your fault," she managed to say. "She's gone now."

"I count myself well rid of her."

Pushing back far enough that she could lean up to see his face, Lyssa asked, "Is that the truth? I always thought she did a good job for you. It must be hard to replace someone that capable."

Dane shook his head, smiling at her. The crease winked in his cheek. "She can be replaced. So can Barb. You can't."

Lyssa felt a long-closed gate deep in her heart begin to swing open, but she couldn't tell whether it was to let some rare emotion in, or out. She let out her breath on a long, shuddering sigh. "Dane."

He urged her to lean her back against one of the trays, but it shifted when their weight came to bear on it.

"Oh!" she exclaimed.

He laughed. "Not such a good idea."

"The bench." She glanced down the aisle and saw the reason that Ari had suggested the greenhouse. "Not this one," she told Dane when he looked at the one closest to the door. "There. Over there." She nodded toward the one that had a thick pad on it.

Kissing her as if he couldn't get enough—pausing only to run his hands along her back, up her sides, just brushing the outer curves of her breast, and down the hollow of her spine to the indentation where it ended—Dane gasped, "I didn't want to do this. Not yet," he added, taking the sting out of his words before Lyssa had even absorbed it. "That's what Tucson was for. I wanted to give you romance, soft music, privacy. Was planning to do this slow and easy. Damn it all, Lyssa, I wanted to make love to you with room service!"

He couldn't have said anything more romantic, she thought. She loved knowing she had upset his plans. "Do it here instead."

SHE WASN'T SURE which of them was the first to gasp out "I love you" after his eyes rolled back and she collapsed on him. She thought it might have been her.

"Don't move," he said when she would eased away on the narrow bench.

She sat up anyway, a little sore and with her thigh muscles protesting the unusual position.

"We didn't consider protection, Lyssa."

"Um." She didn't know what to say.

"You don't need to worry about my sexual health," he explained. "I've never gone without protection before."

"I wasn't worried." At least, not about disease. She wouldn't catch anything from him; if he said so, it was the truth.

Even getting pregnant wouldn't be the end of the world, she told herself. Pregnant and unmarried wasn't the same level of disaster as when she was a child. Taunts of being a bastard had only made her tougher, more determined to prove herself, to succeed.

What did worry her was the question of whether she would want to do this again. The first time was supposed to be uncomfortable, and it should get better after that. It might not be exactly her dream of being with one man forever, of a real marriage and a normal family. But she had at least found her one man.

He lay curled around Lyssa with her head on his chest, listening to his heart beat. His arms held her on top of him, crossed over her hips and thighs.

What have I done? she wondered in sudden panic.

But the answer was obvious. She had said it herself. She'd gone and fallen in love with Dane Callicott. "Aw, shoot," she muttered under her breath.

"What?"

"Nothing." She forced a light laugh. "I guess this has ruined my reputation for being the last virgin in Phoenix."

He received that in silence. Then he said, "Oldest living virgin, I think it was."

"I stand corrected." At least he didn't seem to suspect that she had just fallen in love with him. Oh, she said the words, but that was just sex talk, right?

"I want you to marry me. We can go to Las Vegas. Do it now. Tonight."

She went perfectly still. "Is this your idea of a joke?"

"No! It's no joke!" His voice was raw.

Lyssa pressed her hands into his chest, forgetting about her broken arm. He grunted as she connected with his ribs. Levering herself off him, she struggled to gain her feet, uncaring about where her knees and elbows landed.

He sat upright and watched her almost angrily. "I didn't mean it. I mean, I did, but—" He shut up, looking wild around the eyes. "I do. I want you to marry me," he declared. He ran his hands through his hair. "We'll fly to Vegas. No long engagement, Lyssa." He reached for her, but she stepped back, bumping into one of the long succession-tables. "We might have made a baby."

"You don't want me, Dane. Not as your wife. I would not be a good Mrs. Callicott." Miserably she thought of what his mother would have to say about that. And Gail O'Neill—*Now, wouldn't that be a fun dinner party?*

Except for rubbing his hands over his face, he sat perfectly still on the padded bench. She remembered the feel of those hands on her body, remembered admiring his body unclothed, remembered reveling in their mutual nakedness, which now made her feel queasy in the pit of her stomach. He seemed oblivious to the fact that neither of them had any clothes on.

"No. That was stupid," he said, looking up suddenly to catch her staring at him. "I should never have said what I did about you, about myself, about what I wanted in a wife."

"Why not? Have you changed your mind?"

"No." He reached out and locked his fingers around her wrist. "I didn't have to change my mind, because I never really believed those things I said. They were notions I'd been force-fed since— Well, for as long as I can remember. They're other people's ideas, not mine. I want a wife who makes me feel as though no matter where I am, no matter what is happening around me, as long as I am with her, I'm home. I want you, Lyssa. Only you."

She stared at him, desperately wanting to believe. "You don't."

Forcing herself to be sensible and practical, she shook her head in denial and jerked her hand away. "You don't want to be saddled with a woman like me. I'm not the wife you need. I'm not good around people. I can't stand small talk, you know that yourself. I don't approve of developers. I don't like to get dressed up and flash tacky jewelry all around." Seeing that she wasn't getting through to him, she tried for anger. There was strength in that. "I can't be the 'little woman' who stands behind the 'great man.' I can't be Mrs. Dane Callicott! Don't you see? That's not me!"

Dane was off the bench in a heartbeat. He grabbed her by the shoulders and shook her lightly. "Don't be an idiot. I don't care about any of that. You know me too well to think I do. You were right that night, when you told me what was really important."

"You told me it was impossible, that I was fooling myself."

"I was scared to death, okay?" He pulled her close. "Won't you please let me in?" he whispered.

He leaned over, giving her time to move away, and kissed her sweetly, lightly, tenderly, lingering over it until her mouth softened.

"I can't. I'm sorry, Dane, but I just . . . can't." She ended with a heavy voice and a heavier heart.

"You said you loved me."

She shook her head, unable to claim that she didn't mean it.

He looked at her, his face pale and his mouth drawn. "Give it some time," he said, finally.

They dressed in silence, neither having much to say to the other.

Lyssa walked him out to his car. She pressed a finger against the dust and grimaced. "This dirt isn't going to do your paint job any good."

"It doesn't matter. It's just a car." He reached down and scratched Dammit's ears. The big dog had come over to sit on his feet.

"*Just* a car?" Lyssa felt as though she would burst into tears at any moment. She needed to lighten the moment.

It seemed he did, too. "All right, it's a fast car," he allowed. "And with the top down, it makes your curls go wild. I like that." But he stayed a few steps away and didn't touch her.

Lyssa wondered if she had hurt him with her refusal. Of course it had been a blow to his pride, but he couldn't really love her, even though he'd said the words too. Could he?

"I'm sorry. I do have to go."

"I know."

He embraced her, then, a gentle hug.

She shook her head against his chest, not even knowing what she was saying no to.

"The closing won't be for a while," he said over her head. "Maybe by then you'll be able to accept the land as a wedding gift."

"Dane." Lyssa raised her hand and stroked his cheek, feeling the rasp of stubble. "I don't want this to end." She took a deep breath. "But I can't marry you. It wouldn't be right for either of us."

"I have no intention of letting this end," he said with fierce determination. Then he moderated his voice. "Your parents can purchase the land on time from me for what you should have paid for it—with no interest."

"That's not fair to you. You're in the business."

Dane shrugged. He placed his hands on her face, caressing her cheekbones with his thumbs and cradling her jaw in the curve of his fingers. "It's just money. I want you to be my wife, Lyssa. Doesn't that make your family, my family?"

Her eyes flew open.

He brought his lips to hers. "Think about it." Then he pulled away, slowly, as if it pained him to let her go. He took half a step back, and then another.

Without taking his eyes off hers he moved to the back of his Boxster and popped the trunk. He pulled out a box with the picture of a cell phone angled temptingly on it. "I want you to have this. I'm tired of not being able to talk to you when the notion strikes me."

"I have to go up on the ridge to get reception."

"Do text messages come through?"

"Maybe."

"Well, we'll try it anyway."

She accepted the phone.

"There's a reception on Friday, celebrating Julia and Alex's engagement. Will you come?" When she nodded, he looked relieved. "It's at the Highline. I'll call you with details later in the week."

The Highline, she thought as he climbed into his car. Of course.

He started the engine. She waved. He turned the car around and drove off. Only the faint hint of dust billowing up over the hill marked his departure.

Lyssa looked at the box in her hand and wondered how she was going to keep the phone charged. Maybe she could plug it in at the well house; Jacobson owed her that much.

"Think about it," the man said. Like she needed another impossible situation to puzzle through.

DANE WANDERED into what had once been his spare bedroom and now appeared to be well on its way to becoming a studio. The art supplies he'd bought in New York were piled on the bed. Several boxes of materials and books, long packed away, filled one side of the closet. He picked up a sketch pad and a charcoal stick and took them out to the dining area, where he had the best light, a table, and a relatively comfortable chair.

A shape was itching to come out; he could feel it under his skin, as had sometimes happened in college when his subconscious was assimilating an idea that it wasn't yet ready to share with his controlling, organized mind. Some of his most creative work had been born that way. He hoped it was a sign that he was finished with overfriendly dragons and gargoyles. The legitimacy of medieval bestiaries aside, he wanted to produce something important and meaningful.

In sketching out the basic form of the sculpture, he discovered that it appeared to be a tree with a woman's upper body peeking around the trunk. He added a few details here and there, toying with what it might look like from several angles. But it seemed incomplete. He was missing a fundamental part of the concept.

Setting aside the sketch, he considered materials. He rejected the possibility of rendering his vision in stone. It required wood. It needed to feel smooth to the touch and, like living skin, to give back heat from intimate contact.

Immediately he remembered the sensation of Lyssa's fragrant skin under his caress. Apple pie and cinnamon. He growled under his breath. Forcing his mind toward memories that predated his association with her, Dane returned to the spare room. He pulled out a couple of boxes that were heavy enough to contain various-sized blocks of wood along with a set of chisels and gouges that had been a Christmas gift from his father.

That year had marked the beginning of Stewart Callicott's final illness. The tools and wood might have been a hint—and if so, they would have been the first—that Dane shouldn't give up on art entirely. Or they might have been a peace offering. Dane hadn't accepted the necessity of stepping into his father's shoes graciously.

In retrospect, he'd been moody and irritable. He supposed he had wanted to punish his parents for pulling him away from his dream of being an artist. All that he had truly accomplished was making his father's final days miserable.

Dane found the box he was looking for. When he lifted out a block of rosewood, he lingered over it for some time, turning it this way and that, as though to absorb its essential nature through his fingertips. Even rough sawn and unpolished it was beautiful, very nearly the color of Lyssa's riotous curls, with darker streaks playing through it. He wished he knew what his father had had in mind; had Stewart picked it out himself?

Not that Dane would ever know. His father had taken that secret with him, to the grave or to heaven or to the next life, whichever applied. Dane wished he had enough confidence in Aristotle Smith's philosophy to be certain that there would be another life, and another, and another, in which his father's life would be entwined with his own, until at last they got it right.

They'd bungled it this time around. There had been a distance between them, which Dane had once blamed entirely on his father but was beginning to attribute at least in part to his own self-centeredness.

He didn't want to make the same error with Lyssa. Bad enough that he had wasted so many years without her, when all he'd had to do was open his eyes and see who the universe had provided to fill his innermost soul-circle, the core at the heart of his existence that for so long had ached with emptiness.

She had said she loved him, damn it; didn't that count for anything? As he pulled a hand through his hair and tried to banish the pain caused by Lyssa's refusal of him, old scars on his fingers caught in the thick layers.

He was reminded of what he was about. Taking the mahogany and the box with the woodcarving tools into the dining room, he set them on the table beside the sketches.

In three more days he would see her again. He started plotting how he would ensure that this separation was their last.

She was more than a shining example of a whole person. More even than the woman he loved. She was his muse, grown in the mystical gardens of Elysian Fields by a family of philosophers. No wonder he was unable to turn his mind to serious art. He had tapped into the secrets of the universe.

He was not going to give that up.

Twenty-One

"HOW DARE HE?" Vivian had glanced toward the double doors of the Highline's Grand Ballroom and now stood poised in predatory alertness.

Lyssa wondered who Vivian had found to target, now that Dane had laid down the rules. She wasn't sure how she felt about this new relationship his mother seemed intent on establishing between them.

Through an exchange of text messages and a few tricky-to-schedule phone calls, she had let Dane convince her to come to this event, more because she truly liked Julia than because she thought it was a good idea. But as soon as she got to Phoenix, both the Callicotts took her under their wing, daring anyone else to object. And here was Vivian out in public treating her like an ally, part of an Us rather than Other.

She followed the older woman's sharp gaze.

Near the entrance, the guests of honor held court. Julia was flushed and beautiful in a pale green, fluttery dress. The men clustered around her were young, good looking, and as well dressed as she was. Still, they might have been invisible for all the attention she paid them as she laughed up at Alex. A waiter in a penguin suit with a bronzy cummerbund almost the color of Lyssa's new dress offered around a tray with some kind of finger treats.

But Vivian seemed unconcerned with that happy scene. She was watching Thomas Turnbull stroll along with Claudia Montgomery.

The rosy-silver gown Claudia wore emphasized her sensuous elegance, but she reminded Lyssa of the villainous Snow Queen of fairytale.

Vivian said, "I told everyone not to have anything to do with her. Socially or professionally."

"I'm guessing Tank didn't get the memo," Dane commented.

Lyssa elbowed him. This was not the time to alienate his mother. He only chuckled.

"Don't worry." Vivian patted Lyssa's hand. "I'll settle this." She inclined her head in a polite, if cool, farewell before heading toward the door and the hapless couple.

Before she reached them, though, Claudia separated herself from Tank. *Probably saw Vivian snaking through the crowd*, Lyssa thought. Then she realized the Snow Queen's destination. "Oh, shoot, here she comes."

"I'll get rid of her," Dane assured her.

"No! What *is* it with you Callicotts?" She wondered why they both assumed that they should step in and take over from her. "I don't need rescuing. We can have a conversation just like civilized people."

"I don't trust her."

"Smart man."

Then the blonde was upon them. "Why, Dane! I thought I might run into you here."

"What do you think you're doing?" Dane demanded.

"I came to give poor Thomas some moral support."

"Why?"

"For one thing, right now he's telling your mother he was the one behind this whole mess with Clearview."

And indeed, flushed and flustered, Turnbull appeared to be telling Vivian something upsetting. A wall might have come up between them for all the do-not-touch signals Dane's mother gave off.

Lyssa asked, "*Was* he?" Falsifying documents seemed too subtle and manipulative for Turnbull, and the sexual harassment nonsense was certainly only Barb's. She didn't see how Tank fit into the scheme.

"His conscience was bothering him. Apparently he hired someone to steal your laptop."

"What?" Lyssa and Dane burst out at the same time.

Claudia slid an index finger down Dane's arm. "I convinced him to tell your mother. It seemed the right thing to do." She smiled disarmingly at him, the witch.

"But why?" Lyssa asked. "And how did you come to know about it?"

"Apparently your friend Barbara convinced him you had information on it about that development site. But he isn't very familiar with computers. He asked me to help him find what he was looking for. You really should use a password," she advised.

"That makes you an accomplice," Lyssa pointed out.

Claudia looked at her. "Not really. I turned him down. And then I convinced him to confess."

"To my mother," said Dane. "Not the police."

"Oh, but Lyssa, do you really want to file charges against Mrs. Callicott's dear, dear friend?"

Lyssa thought about Vivian's change in attitude toward her. Should she force the woman to choose between Dane and a long-time friendship?

"I didn't think so." Claudia nodded in satisfaction.

Vivian leaned very close to Thomas, their heads together as she spoke into his ear. Then his shoulders slumped and she turned away.

"Looks like my mother wasn't as sympathetic as he expected," Dane observed.

Claudia's colorless eyes glittered. "The Callicotts aren't known for letting loyalty get in the way of getting what they want. Keep that in mind, Lyssa. It doesn't look like Dane has told you he's tired of you yet, but he will."

Dane took her hand and gave it a warning squeeze. "You know better than to believe her. Trust me."

She tried, really she did, but doubt assailed her and tightened her chest.

"Didn't you guess he's seeing someone?" Claudia asked. "Don't you wonder where he disappears to, when he's not with you? He doesn't go home. Or to the office, either."

Lyssa pulled her hand free and turned to search his face. She'd expected it eventually, she reminded herself. Still, it hurt so much. Spots drifted in front of her eyes, and even breathing was an effort.

"There's no other woman. You have to trust me." His words sounded sincere, but then, he was good at convincing people he meant what he said.

Trust. He wanted her to trust him. To place herself in his hands. To prove she'd actually forgiven him, in her heart. Could she? The answer was simple: *Of course.* She already had.

There were no guarantees in life. She might eventually lose him to another woman, or just to boredom. But listening to vicious rumors was what people like Simon did. Not Lyssa. Breathing came a little easier then, and she saw no deceit in his expression.

"You put a nasty spin on things," she said to Claudia. "That doesn't make it true."

Dane pulled her close, tucking her to his side with an arm around her waist and his hand flat against her thigh.

"Such a charming display," Claudia said. "Too bad it won't get you very far in these elevated social circles. Your problem, Lyssa, is that you don't fight for what you want. You turn your back and run, just as you did with your career. You think Mother Callicott will respect you for it?"

Vivian, coming up behind Claudia, paused.

"The difference is, I didn't want my job." Lyssa could see that if she did not take care of this situation soon, Mother Callicott would. No scenes, she reminded herself, struggling to tamp down her anger. "It was just a means to an end. You know all about that."

Claudia shrugged one shoulder. "As if being practical is a bad thing. I'm no different from Vivian or Dane."

Taking a step forward into the blonde's line of sight, Vivian declared, "You and I are nothing alike."

"Tell me you admire Lyssa," Claudia shot back. "She's so very good at playing the victim. Go on. Let's see if you can make it sound like the truth."

Crossing her arms, Vivian directed her words at Lyssa. "This is not the time or place, but you know I owe you a real apology. We'll talk later."

"See what you're getting yourself into, Lyssa? There's no place in their world for the weak."

Lyssa leaned in toward Claudia, ruthlessly using her height and intensity against the more delicate woman. "Don't mistake principles for weakness. I've learned to choose my battles."

"I don't think so. Against these people, you're an amateur. Are you so sure you want to go through with this little game of yours? Think about what you've lost already."

"But look at what I've won." Lyssa smiled at Dane, hoping he could see that she had opened her heart to him, torn down that wall around it.

"That's not love you hear in her voice," Claudia taunted him. "It's ambition. Don't you hear it? She really has you fooled. It'll be interesting to see how the story changes once she's got a wedding band and the same last name."

Shaking his head, Dane said, "You're wrong. I've already asked her to marry me. She turned me down."

"She's after your money, you idiot! Can't you see through her act? She's taken your guilt and twisted it to her advantage."

"Like you did with Turnbull?" Lyssa demanded.

"I've done nothing wrong!" But her voice rose, shrill and cutting.

Vivian snapped, "Thomas told me the truth. There's no hiding behind him now. You hired that thug to steal the laptop, and then you convinced him to be chivalrous and take the blame."

"No! He's lying!"

"I told him he could either have you in bed, or keep a business relationship with Callicott. Evidently you don't have as much talent as you thought."

Chalk-white and with nostrils flaring, Claudia raged, "Don't condemn me for doing the same thing you did!"

"You think my mother married for money?" Dane laughed.

Vivian cast him a grateful smile. Lyssa guessed that wasn't the first time she'd heard that accusation, but maybe it was the first time he had defended it. So the Callicott family had its own secrets? That was an interesting turn of events.

"And you see, *I* didn't do anything illegal," Vivian said to Claudia.

A waiter, apparently not paying attention to the mood of their little group, approached with a tray of chocolate-covered strawberries.

Claudia shouted, "You're not going to take this away from me! I'll have Thomas and see you—" Her right hand swept out toward Lyssa and smacked the tray, sending the berries cascading down the front of Lyssa's new dress.

"Hey!" exclaimed the young man. He would have stooped to pick up the errant fruit except that Lyssa stopped him.

"I'll take care of it," she said.

"That's not—"

"Go!"

He took a quick look at her face. Pale and appearing close to tears, he backed away.

Lyssa looked down at the greasy streaks, like snail trails all down the front of the lovely dress Vivian had picked out for her. Broken fruit lay scattered around her feet. *Okay,* she thought, *this is definitely a scene.* She knelt and gathered a couple of berries.

If her right arm weren't broken, she mused, she could just backhand the delectables into Claudia's chest, like picking off a runner at home plate. But she was limited to what she could do with her left. Still, the distance was short, and that meant her aim didn't have to be great. Almost idly she flicked the berries, with chocolate still clinging to them, onto the bodice of that icy pink dress.

"Oh!" The outraged little blonde charged Lyssa, who turned her left side toward the attack and braced herself. Claudia ricocheted off her opponent's mass—*Never mess with a ballplayer,* Lyssa sent as a belated mental message—and went down in a tangle with the young waiter.

Julia and Alex hurried up while Claudia was still on the carpet, screaming invective at the woman who had humiliated her in front of a few hundred dazzled observers. "What happened?" Julia asked, while Alex helped the mortified waiter regain his feet and somehow made Claudia settle down.

Lyssa didn't know where to start. She just shrugged.

Oblivious to the greasy smears on her dress, Dane wrapped her against him and smoothed back her mop of hair. "Are you all right?"

With a sigh, Vivian murmured something about a solution and departed, leaving Lyssa to stare sadly after her. "She hates me," she murmured to Dane, pushing back from him.

"She doesn't hate you. She's being nice, and she doesn't do that for just anyone. Didn't she help you find that dress?"

"Did she?" Julia asked, though her voice was faint. "It's lovely."

Lyssa gazed down at herself. Then she looked at Dane. "I have to get out of here."

"What? Because of the dress?" he demanded.

"No, it's not the dress! I was such an idiot to think this would work." To Julia, she said, "I'm so sorry. I really didn't intend to make a scene."

"It's not so bad." Despite the reassurance, Julia looked concerned.

Alex gathered up the now-subdued Claudia and hurried her away, trailed by Julia. Everyone else was still watching, apparently bemused by the train wreck that had just transpired at the Highline. Again.

Lyssa rubbed a tired hand over her hot cheek, backside first and then palm. "I can't do this," she whispered.

"Just wait to see what Mother has up her sleeve."

"I can't." She couldn't meet his eyes. "I have to go."

"Dammit, you're not running away from me again!"

"Fine. Then take me home. Otherwise, I'll call a cab."

"You will not call a cab," he said through his teeth. "I brought you. I'll take you home." He grasped her arm, not gently but not tightly enough to bruise, and led her toward the doorway.

"All the way home, Dane. To the farm."

His face went pale. He stopped in the crowd's midst. "You're not staying the night?"

"I need time to think."

"Time to think? You can't think at my place?"

The doors were within reach. "No. No, I can't, as it happens," she told him as she plunged through and took a deep gulp of the night air.

He ground out, "This is a really bad idea."

Snatching her arm back and letting her anger and frustration lend her some strength to oppose him, she snapped, "But it's *my* bad idea. Is this what I can expect from being mixed up with you and your mother? Won't I get to make any decisions about my life anymore?"

VIVIAN MOVED THROUGH THE ROOM, giving the briefest of greetings and cutting off all comment about the performance of a few minutes earlier. The food fight had been entertaining, though she would never admit to it. Lyssa would have to have her rough edges polished before coming out in public again. But for now, the spectacle could be blamed on Claudia, and Vivian would have everyone's sympathy in choosing her new daughter-in-law over Thomas Turnbull.

If this business about trying to buy a favorable environmental assessment were not enough, there was his taking up with Claudia. Word of her instability would spread quickly, without any need to publicize how she had taken advantage of Callicott Properties. Everything could be blamed on her participation in this collusion between Thomas and Clearview.

With vast dignity, greeting the guests as if nothing untoward had just happened, Vivian crossed to the dais and stepped up to the microphone. "I would like to extend a welcome to all of you," she stated without preamble.

As she took a breath, letting her gaze roam to attach the interest of one person after another in the crowd, she found Dane and Lyssa halfway through the door. Love must have softened their brains. Hadn't she had assured them both that she would take care of this situation?

This was another thing Lyssa would have to stop: a hasty departure wouldn't solve anything. Only a good distraction would establish Lyssa as anything other than "that girl who ruined the Callicott receptions last fall."

Then the mass of people thickened and hid the couple from her sight. She could hardly call out to them to stop; she could only presume that good manners would make them listen to what she had to say. She would have liked to see their reactions, though.

She spoke to the people closest in, the ones she could watch and gauge. "For the sake of anyone out there who does not recognize me"—but her humorous tone implied this was unlikely—"I am Vivian Callicott.

"Recently I took my son's position as president of Callicott Properties, while he pursues other interests." She raised her hand to stop the murmurs from the crowd of listeners. "You'll all be relieved to know he isn't divorcing himself from the business, merely fine-tuning his role. As I'm sure you know, Dane was the creative force behind the Highline Resort, this lovely setting for our evening together. In time, we at Callicott Properties hope he will generate many more such landmark properties."

Appreciative applause pealed out. She let it die away. "To make sure he has the opportunity, another change that has been under consideration for some now will be implemented on a permanent basis."

She looked out and found Alex Garcia's handsome carved face, watchful and wary. "You all know our guest of honor this evening, Alex Garcia, for you were invited here to celebrate the announcement of his engagement to a dear friend of my family's, Julia Nolin. What you have not heard is that Alex is the new corporate executive officer for Callicott Properties."

She led the applause herself, enjoying his surprise at the very public announcement of what had been kept between Dane, Alex, Julia, and Julia's father until she gained the formal agreement of the board of directors earlier this afternoon.

Again she let the enthusiastic clapping fade before continuing. "But that is not the news I am most pleased to share this evening." She paused, letting the suspense build. "My son is engaged to be married. His future wife, Lyssa, is also here tonight. Many of you have been fortunate enough to meet her."

Not by a single word would she betray the fact that Lyssa had turned him down. Dane wanted the girl, and that was enough for Vivian.

As the applause rang out, she sent a silent plea winging heavenward to Stewart: *If you're listening, don't let them screw it up.*

Then someone in the crowd shifted, and she saw Lyssa's appalled expression.

Twenty-Two

EARLY THE NEXT MORNING, Lyssa's restless sleep was broken by the shrieking of birds and bracing sunshine. She staggered into the kitchen and dug to the back of a cupboard for some stale Earl Grey tea, the only caffeine to be found. She thought she would be comforted by having the farmhouse to herself while her parents did the morning chores—no questions about how her party went, no comments about either her developing attachment to Dane or the culture of conspicuous consumption.

But the tea did nothing to soothe her jitters. As the walls of the small farmhouse closed in on her, she downed her morning bracer and wandered out into the orchard.

As she leaned against a sturdy trunk and gazed at the yellowing tips of the tall cottonwoods of the Jacobson place, she found irony in having left the reception because she'd felt claustrophobic in Dane's world. Now even Spring Valley seemed circumscribed. It hadn't changed, she realized. That meant she must have.

In retrospect, she had to admit that until Claudia's arrival, she had enjoyed the reception, as well as the lead-up to it. Spending time with Dane on his turf and even shopping with Vivian had given her hope that they might find common ground. That spark was fanned into a solid, warm fire when the other guests at the reception treated her as some intriguing new part of Dane's life.

Too bad her second chance to make a good impression had been spoiled, she thought as she watched the leaves play tag with the sunshine. Now, her role in the dramatics would be all they remembered her for.

She sighed. Fidgety again, she pushed away from the apple tree. As she strolled through the orchard, ducking below limbs and shifting to avoid tangles at her feet, she remembered the drive home afterwards.

She'd tried to explain her sudden desperation to get away. But Dane had refused to listen. And his mother's parting shot had made everything even more confusing.

While Lyssa was convinced they needed to slow down, take a step back, Dane heard that as a rationale for no longer seeing each other, and he'd accused her of running away. She told him that wasn't what she intended, she only meant they should get to know one another better before taking the relationship further. His answer made clear that he thought they already knew everything that counted about each other—why else would she tell Claudia she forgave, trusted, and believed in him? "Hell, Lyssa, you gave yourself to me. What more is there to know?" he'd snapped.

She hadn't been able to summon a response last night, and they'd finished the drive in silence, marked by frustration on her side. She couldn't tell what he was feeling.

When they rolled down the driveway, his anger seemed to have eased. He hadn't argued any further, just gave her a brief kiss and left.

But it wasn't the kiss or Vivian's bombshell or even the fiasco with Claudia that had kept her awake far too long into the night. No, for that, she had to look inward, to her inability to explain to Dane what she wanted from him, from herself, from their relationship. In the dark, her brain had kept churning through the events of the past few weeks.

Now, standing under the same sun-washed limbs that had been her pretend-horsies when she'd been little, the limbs she'd climbed as a teenager to pick green apples to use for throwing practice, the limbs she'd treated as couches while reading tales of Hercules and Athena, Lyssa realized some of her uncertainty boiled down to how he felt about having kids.

Did Dane want to be a father—or not? He'd proposed a quickie Vegas wedding if she got pregnant from that first time. At least he hadn't suggested terminating the pregnancy. But such a casual approach to a weighty decision didn't bode well over the long term.

She just didn't know him that well.

The fact that they'd never discussed the issue of children suggested it wasn't as important to him as, say, the Spirit Ranch or his revitalized interest in sculpture or how she made a living—all of which they had managed to find time to share their feelings on.

Not that Lyssa had the absolute final answer even where she alone was concerned. Despite her desire for them, she might not be able to have children. Or might not be able to have them with Dane.

She'd always had this dream of a normal life with a normal family of her own. Married. A couple of kids. A career that made some money but would allow her plenty of time to spend with the people she loved.

Did Dane want the same? Or would he stand beside her and do everything he could to help her achieve her dream, even if he didn't share it?

She had learned from observing her parents that long-term success of an intimate relationship depended on an open mind, negotiation, and communication from both sides. Last night, she'd rather incoherently asked for him to consider her point of view. The next time she saw him, she would learn whether Dane had thought about what she was trying to say and was willing to talk about her concerns.

Lyssa paused in the shadow of the greenhouse and thought about what those were, other than the possibility of extending the family tree.

If she married Dane, how would they live? she wondered, absently rubbing at an ant bite on her hand. To start with, that meant *where* they would live. He would need to be close to the office, but Lyssa, after having experienced both city and country, was tired of the teeming confines of Phoenix and the whole metropolitan amoeba. What she would do for a living was still another question. She could take advantage of Dane's connections if she wanted to retain some role in the development world. But did she really want to work for Vivian and Alex?

She sighed and continued on to the kitchen door. This being practical was so frustrating sometimes. So much better to be a dreamer.

All four of her parents sat around the table, watching for her. Sensing an ambush, she halted in the doorway and folded her arms, letting the door fall against her hip.

Helen said, "I was wrong. You and Dane . . . Well, I withdraw my objections." She glanced sulkily at Paris, then glared at Ari. "I think the two of you should marry."

Lyssa didn't know what to say. She glanced at the table and saw her phone. "Did he send some kind of text message to work this miracle?"

Then she heard the rumble of a diesel-engine truck turning off the road into the driveway. Her parents turned impossibly innocent faces to her. "What in the world . . . ?"

"You go, dear," said Paris. "See who it is."

"You're expecting someone?" she asked with deep suspicion.

Seeing that she would have no answer until she investigated for herself, she walked through the house and onto the front porch.

A large black extended-cab pickup pulling an enclosed trailer crested the hill and started down the drive. The heavy tint on the windows concealed the driver of the unfamiliar vehicle. When the truck stopped and the engine shut off, Dammit charged forward with a great show of barking and growling, hackles up and ears back.

The door to the house swung open behind her. As the driver stepped out, only the guinea hens kept up their noise. Dammit trotted up to sit on the man's feet. He pressed his back against the jean-covered shins and let his tail flail in the dirt.

"Dane!" Lyssa called out to him. "I wasn't expecting you this morning." After the way they'd parted last night, she would have excused him for sulking—or at least thinking—a little longer. She certainly had needed the thinking time.

He strode over and gave her a very satisfying kiss. After a while he drew back far enough to ask, "So you did miss me?"

"Of course." She gestured at the truck. "What's all this?"

"It's a surprise. Remember what Claudia was talking about last night?"

"Which part?" She wasn't sure she was going to like this surprise, if it had anything to do with Claudia.

"The part about what I've been doing when I'm not with you, or at work." But he didn't explain. "I'm closing on the Jacobsons' property Monday. The lawyers have no problem with my taking immediate possession."

"You're moving in?"

"Well." He cleared his throat. "If you don't mind."

Lyssa could do no more than stand there and blink.

Cal came down the porch steps with an outthrust hand and said, "Congratulations. We'll be proud to have you as a neighbor. Lyssa's needed her own place for a long time."

Dane tucked her against his side before shaking hands with Cal and Ari. "Paperwork's nearly ready on the transfer of the strip." He inclined his head toward the hill.

"Anytime," Cal assured him.

Dane urged her toward the truck. "Come on, love."

"But—" she started before running out of things to say.

He opened the passenger-side door and boosted her in, then braced himself against the doorframe, blocking out most of the light. "I brought my sculpting material and what tools and equipment I had.

I'll find a welder and some metal up here easier than in Phoenix."

"A welder."

"Yeah. I've always wanted to try big metal stuff. And maybe some kind of foundry for casting."

"Foundry? Wait a minute—"

Dane closed the door. He went over to speak to Cal, and Lyssa reached for the window crank before she realized the truck was all electric. She opened the door instead, in time to hear him say, "There's a couple of outbuildings that'll serve as storage for the time being. I've dreamed up some ideas for a sculpting studio. I'd like to run them past you sometime in the next day or two. I imagine Lyssa wants everything on the place to be as environmentally sound as possible."

"Sounds good." Cal nodded thoughtfully.

Dane waved to her parents as he strode around the hood, waves of heat-vapor distorting his image. He stepped up and seated himself behind the wheel. Lyssa turned to him. The solid thud of his door closing prompted her to do the same. Once they were sealed in together, she asked, "You're moving in?"

"It's part of the surprise." He started the truck.

She took a deep breath. "You're moving in next door. To live in that wreck of a place."

"Well, we've got some things to go over, where all that is concerned." Dane concentrated on turning around in the wide part of the drive. He didn't talk again until the truck and trailer were straightened out and heading back up the hill. "Whether to tear down the house and start over, or just remodel it."

"You want to live next to my parents?"

He took his hand off the gearstick and waggled a finger at her. "Now, see, that's the kind of question that gets a son-in-law in trouble. I want to live wherever you can be happy. I figure that's here."

"About that son-in-law thing." Lyssa pressed her hand to her stomach, wishing she could blame the backflips there on the rumbling of the diesel engine. "Did you know your mother was going to announce our engagement last night?"

"She knew it was only a matter of time before I talked you around. You said yourself I always manage to get my own way."

"I also said I wouldn't marry you."

"You didn't say you wouldn't get engaged to be married. We can have a long engagement. It's sort of a family tradition for you, isn't it? Your parents must have been engaged for going on thirty years."

She stared at him in horrified silence. Then she reached across her body for the door handle.

He seized her arm. "Where are you going?"

"I think I'm going to be sick."

He let her loose and grabbed for his own door all in one movement. As he took his feet off the pedals, the truck lurched, shuddered, and died. It began to roll backward, but his hasty fumbling with the clutch and brake stopped the truck before it had gone more than a few feet. He put it in gear and pulled the emergency brake. Then he was out his door and around to her side to help her out into the sunshine, where the ringing in her ears drowned out the birdsong.

She gulped a few breaths, thankful that the dust had had time to settle and the breeze was blowing the diesel fumes away from her.

"My proposal really made you sick?" Dane asked, shaken.

"No. It's just—" She waved her hand in helpless rebuttal.

"Could you be pregnant?"

"I just need the air," she gasped out. "I'm not, I can't be." When she got herself somewhat under control, she asked, "What if I was? Would you mind? We've never talked about kids."

"You want to know if I want children with you?" His voice was nearly as ragged as hers.

She nodded.

"Cute little girls with curly red hair?" His face softened.

"But what if I can't have kids? No Callicott heirs. Your mother would hate me," she wailed.

"Look, you were right, we do need some time to get to know each other. We didn't talk about kids, so let's take care of that. If you really don't want to get married, no wedding. But we'll have to make a plan. Not just 'Let's set a date.' It's got to cover a lifetime together. Maybe more, according to Ari. Several lifetimes."

That startled her into a laugh.

"Good. That's good. Laughing is good. So we'll get you settled in your new job, and then we'll figure out the rest."

She pondered that for a second. "What new job?"

"At Callicott Properties. Just part time, so you'll be able to start your herb business or a family, whichever takes priority."

"Now, look, if this is going to work, you've got to stop arranging everything for me."

"But this will be perfect."

She placed her fists on her hips and faced him head-on. "Perfect? Perfect for who? What makes you think I want to work for your mother? Why shouldn't I just take this chance to walk away from the whole sorry mess?"

"Is that what you really want?" He looked stunned.

"Of course not!"

He swiped a shaky hand through his hair. "This way, you can finally make a difference, just as you said."

"Make a difference?"

"As a Callicott, you'll be working from the inside. You have to see the possibilities in that."

Lyssa's breath caught.

"You wanted to feel useful," he said, angling toward her and taking her hand. "Think of it. With the Callicott name and my mother backing you up, there won't be anything stopping you. You'll be able to breathe new life into the old guard."

Her heart pounded so hard, she thought she might burst. She laced her fingers through his and hung on tight.

What she'd been demanding of herself, in staying at Clearview for the sake of making money, had been all wrong. She'd been trying to fit herself into a mold of her own making, a square peg in a round hole. No wonder she'd gotten battered in the attempt.

Then Dane had come along and restored her ability to measure her worth beyond the monetary. His attempts to set everything right were clumsy but so well-meaning. He'd listened to her and really tried to understand. While she had resisted his efforts and dug in her heels.

"It's such a gift, Dane . . . but I don't deserve it. I certainly don't deserve you."

"Pop the glove compartment," he ordered, releasing her and folding his arms.

Off balance on the uneven gravel and with fingers that felt thick and clumsy, she managed to find the latch and open the compartment. She felt around in the deep blackness and found an object wrapped in folds of black velvet. As she drew it out, she discovered it was heavier than she would have expected for its size. "Should I unwrap it?"

"Yeah."

She did, bracing it on her cast, and found herself holding a statuette carved of dense black-streaked wood. After a moment, she made out the figures of a man and a woman, entwined, with the line of their bodies suggesting the shape of a heart. The woman's hand was on the man's chest; his lay on her breast in a reciprocal gesture of exquisite promise.

"I'm going to cast that," Dane told her. "Life size, or close to it."

"You made this?" She stroked the surface, marveling at his talent. "It's gorgeous!"

"I'm going to put the big sculpture out in the middle of our lawn so you see it every day. As a reminder of what you did for me. You breathed new life into my cold, empty existence. What little things I can do for you in exchange, those aren't a gift. It's just what you do for those you love. It's why my mother announced that we're engaged. Not because she was obligated, but because it's something she could do for me. The same thing that made you try so hard to get Jacobson's water rights for your parents. I wanted to make that happen for you because you made this life worthwhile for me, in a way it hasn't been for years. Am I making any sense?"

"Oh, Dane!" Crying and laughing, she threw her arm around his neck. The sculpture rested on his shoulder, a temptation beyond her imagining.

He eased away for a moment and gazed at her with glistening eyes. "You gave me my heart back," he said huskily. "I'm entrusting it to you now."

"I won't let you down. But be very sure, Dane. There won't be any going back from this, if we get married. Once I get myself a normal family, I won't give it up for anything. And you'll have to let me make at least some of the decisions. You won't get your own way in everything."

"So you're saying yes?"

"With conditions."

"You drive a hard bargain. Can we talk about this?"

A smart woman knew when she was beaten. "I have no chance against a handsome, silver-tongued charmer like you, do I?" But she smiled as she said it. And she kissed him to seal the bargain.

About the Author

SALLY BENNETT BOYINGTON has been fascinated by Arizona since she first visited as a child. She spent decades exploring the state on foot, by horseback, four-wheeling, and in a hot-air balloon.

Sally has written several novels set in Arizona, including the Tales of the Watermasters series, a fictionalized portrayal of the long-vanished Hohokam civilization. In addition, she recently published *Deep Roots in a Dry Place,* an illustrated collection of Sonoran Desert plants that contrasts her original poetry and photographs with poems and images generated by AI. As a copy editor and publishing coach, she has helped several hundred authors see their words in print.

She currently writes about Arizona in absentia, for she lives in Knoxville, Tennessee, with her husband and four-footed friends.

(Author photo by Kara Hudgens Photography Co.)

www.ingramcontent.com/pod-product-compliance
Lightning Source LLC
LaVergne TN
LVHW011932070526
838202LV00054B/4599